May 22, 2011

to Marilyn & Norm,

Hope you enjoy the journey.

PAUSING FOR A BACKWARD GLANCE

A WORK OF HISTORICAL FICTION

Jack Salem

JACK SALEM

Author's Note

The joy of writing historical fiction is that it gives the author freedom to write about real people whose lives shape, and are shaped, by recognizable events, and then, with liberal doses of embellishments, distortions and general shenanigans, even in imagining things as they might have been, it gives him vast fields to create a fantasy world woven with fact and fiction. In so doing, the author hopes to get closer to the truth.

All references, of course, to historical events and people are used fictitiously.

ISBN: 1456322710
ISBN-13: 9781456322717
Library of Congress Control Number: 2010916407

PART I

FIN-DE-SIÉCLE FRANCE

To the noble offspring of that blindfolded
Titan of Justice, Themis

CHAPTER 1

I arrived at Twentieth Century Fox at 7:30am and found the street filled with circus performers—clowns, sword-swallowers, fat women, hirsute women, skeletal men, flame breathers, acrobats, elephants, dwarfs, men on stilts, dancers in circus costumes, horses colorfully plumed, monkeys dressed like jesters, grotesque freaks—heading onto a studio set ready to shoot a film. Their forced joviality was not enough to counter my gloom. Nor could it arrest my palpitations, sweaty palms, clammy underarms, and dry mouth. Nor could the radiantly sunny morning, embellished with soft, cottony clouds seldom seen in Los Angeles. A gauzy haze hovered over the Santa Monica Mountains blurring its contours, giving the sky immediately above it an azure tint, lighter than the saturated blue of the sky above.

I wish it were raining. That's usually a mood-elevator.

At 7:45am, as I approached Mr. Lapidus's door, I thought I heard, "Yup! That's the broad." I knocked boldly and before hearing a response, opened it.

"Oh, Sally, I knew I could count on you for being early. Glad you're here. You know Noah Shalon from Personnel?"

"I've seen you around the lot, but we've never been formally introduced. Hi! I'm Sally Apple," and gave him a strong handshake. "I don't know why I used the qualifier, 'formally.' Introduced is introduced, right?"

I hate small talk so I attacked my fears head on. "So, Mr. Lapidus, what is it you wanted to talk to me about?" pretending an insouciance despite what I overheard yesterday. My revved–up heart pulsated everywhere—my mouth was Mojave–dry.

Ever mindful of tics in body language that can convey apprehension, I made a point of not playing with the pen on my clip board, running fingers through my hair, joining and un-joining hands, crossing and uncrossing legs, rubbing eyes, swallowing hard, tightening jaw muscles, or the many other ways I could signal that I'm nervous as hell.

The phone rang and without regard for Noah and me, he talked for about thirty minutes. I heard only a "Yes, but." "Well, maybe." "I don't really…" "You think so?" "Right now?" "I've got visitors." "Noah and Sally Apple." "Yeah, sure."

He looked at me and said, "Sally, Peter Nathan is coming over to discuss something, and he wants your input as well. Do you mind?" Without waiting for my response, he turned to Noah, "Noah, excuse us, please."

"Of course—talk to you later."

Well, that's it. Now the conversation I overheard yesterday makes even more sense. I'm going to get canned and the deputy studio chief is going to assist Mr. Lapidus in the unpleasant business of firing me. But why is he getting rid of the Personnel guy? There's never a good time to lose a job, but does it have to be while I'm pregnant? Damn! I'm going to throw up as soon as they start talking. Did he say 'input'?

A moment later there was a heavy knock on the door and it opened immediately. A voice said, "Hi." Mr. Lapidus got up to shake his hand, "Hi, Pete." While still holding onto his hand, turned to me and said, "Pete, remember Sally Apple?"

Dressed impeccably, he seemed the manikin for a perfect size 42, everything coming together, the shadowy gray stripes on his midnight blue suit, his azure blue tie emphasizing the white on white shirt, cuff links that had a blue stone imbedded within, wing tip black shoes, and when he sat down I saw pale blue socks—the kind you might expect Fred Astaire to be wearing during a dance number.

With an affable smile, he said, "Yes, we met in the commissary several times, and occasionally when I barged in on your story conferences. I've been an admirer of your work, Sally. You bring an impertinent," and pausing for a moment to choose the correct words, said pleasantly, "tabasco-like acerbity to your scripts making them rise above the banal."

Oh, this sweet praise and congeniality—I'm about ready
right on their precious Oriental rug. So this is the way they do it
the guillotine drops.

His strong voice conveyed an unquestioned authority that belied the smile. You knew he could cut you off at the knees so deftly that there would be a delayed reaction before you realized you were now two feet shorter.

"Glad you like them, Mr. Nathan," I lilted, making my response as brief as possible before my dry mouth issued its embarrassing click. I can act too.

"So what did you want to chat about, Pete?" Adam asked. "You did want Sally around, right?"

"Yes, I did." The smile disappeared. "You know about HUAC, the House Un-American Activities Committee and their campaign of intimidating Hollywood."

He didn't wait for a response. "After they viewed our film, *Gentlemen's Agreement,* we received this letter from them." He got a letter from his briefcase and started reading.

❈ ❈ ❈

"'May 21, 1950

"'Gentlemen:

"'The America you showed in the film, 'Gentleman's Agreement' recently seen by members of the House Un-American Activities Committee, was not the kind of country we know to exist. Your film suggests that there might be Jewish writers among your staff who are imagining hateful conditions that the communists in our midst keep inventing.

'We are a free people offering freedom to everyone regardless of race, religion or ethnicity.

'Not everyone, however, is equal, and if we treat some with less respect than others, it's because they don't command the same kind of respect that others deserve. It has nothing to do with prejudice, but everything to do with abilities and attitudes. Our country is a meritocracy. Your film suggests, quite erroneously, that there is a blanket pre-judgment about different groups resulting in prejudicial behavior. That is an utter falsehood.

'To suggest otherwise is un-American. The Committee is planning a trip to Hollywood this summer to further investigate your previous films and those you have in production to ascertain whether there has been, or if there is now in progress, any film that we consider to be un-American.

'We're planning to re-open our hearings in Hollywood sometime in June or July of this year, 1950. You will hear from us soon.

'Congressman Peter Stuyvesant Coughlin, Mississippi. (Written and signed by Horace Peoples, special assistant to Congressman Coughlin, by authority of Congressman Coughlin.)'"

"*Gentlemen's Agreement,* it seems, has rankled Congressman Coughlin," Pete said. "The implication, of course, is that they think we might have a whole bunch of communists and Jewish writers pleading the case for Jews in America."

He let us absorb the depth of the problem. Then I said, "I've read about Congressman Coughlin and his *'fellow travelers.'* Like many Americans, they believe in the false tautology of communist and Jew, don't they?"

He nodded his head in such a puzzling way that I wondered whether he agreed with what I said, or with the allegation. Clearly he had prepared something and continued, "You may know that Coughlin's House un-American Activities Committee was originally created in 1934 by a Congressional Representative from New York, Samuel Dickstein, himself a Jew, who wanted to have such a committee—not to investigate communists, but to investigate Nazi propaganda and activities in our country because several congressmen were concerned that many Americans of German descent, the largest ethnic group in our country, thought that Hitler was doing a fine job, and was not a threat at all."

"Ironic, isn't it?" I said.

"I'm reminding you of this because you should have some background before they come."

My God, I hope my face doesn't show panic. Has someone accused me of being a communist? Did one of my characters in my screenplays behave communistically? I'm not a communist, but would an innocent remark indicate political orientation? This is big time trouble. My career is over. How do I fight this crap?

I didn't write *Gentlemen's Agreement,* but wish I had. So that's it, then—I'm going to be part of the next *Hollywood Ten!* Nine writers, one director—all communists. All following the recommendations of the lead attorney, Robert W. Kenny, not to justify their beliefs in communism, nor to ask for the protection of the First and Fifth Amendments, but to 'answer in their own way' which ended up disastrously because all they managed to do was befog and obfuscate, and in so doing, irritate the committee to such an extent that they issued citations for Contempt of Congress. When the Supreme Court refused to hear their appeal, they went to jail.

On this second round of hearings were they going to begin bottom feeding—getting to the lowliest of that caste system of writers—the 'B' movie writers like me? What the hell could they accuse me of? Holy Cow! Jail? Me? With a baby coming?

Afraid of my own liberal leanings, I blurted out. "Have we fallen into the tautological trap of communist and liberal as well?"

Adam Lapidus, without answering the question, and with a face furrowed with concern, said, "I was wondering when the other shoe was going to drop. I've been anticipating this for the past several weeks..." He then went silent, which left me with the impression he had chosen to submerge the thought, 'I've got to cover my ass'. The way Adam kept changing positions must have raised some suspicion in Pete as well. Adam spoke louder than was necessary, "And, of course, HUAC people are encouraged by the likes of Robert Taylor, John Wayne, Ward Bond and that assertive, cocky, know-it-all boulevardier, Adolph Menjou," he sneered, "and Ginger Rogers's mother, Lela—the whole bunch think there's a communist under every bed—and," glancing at me, "in every screenwriter's typewriter."

"Boulevardier, he is," Pete said, "but Menjou is a very well-informed auto-didact."

"What are you driving at, Pete?" Adam asked.

"I want both of you to search what you may have said or done, or," looking at me, "written, that may have given these goons any basis for an accusation, and to be prepared to deny the implications, rationalize them, point to work that may contradict what you may be accused of. You know, develop a defense," and with a slight lift of eyebrows looked at each of us for a beat, "if, of course, a defense is necessary," raising his voice at the end as though it were an interrogative question.

"I was afraid of this," Adam said with the kind of trepidation in his voice I hadn't heard before. "Besides *Gentlemen's Agreement,* have there been other hints? Any accusations?" and pausing for a moment, continued, "Are they after us, Pete?"

Pete, with elbows on his knees and chin supported by intertwined fingers, stared at the ballpoint pen in Adam's hand, and said, "You're driving me crazy, Adam, constantly plunging the top of your ballpoint. Please stop, okay?"

"Sorry—wasn't aware of that."

The nervousness was a facet of him I've never seen—as though—I really don't know. Concerned for us? The Studio? himself?

Pete got up abruptly and said, "Gotta' see others. Tell me soon if you think of anything you might have said or written. I want to be prepared," dropping the delayed time bomb of not answering Adam's question to address the puzzled look on our faces. The door closed, and as I turned to face Mr. Lapidus, he took a firm grip of his desk hoping I had not seen the tremble in his hands. Drawing emphasis away from his own concerns, asked, "Anything come to mind, Sally?"

I haven't been accused of anything, so I answered, "Not a thing. My writing has been apolitical, very 'American Ideal,' like most of the pictures the studios make, supportive of our ethical and democratic standards."

"Though," Adam snarled, "we have demeaned Negroes and Indians, haven't we? And Asians?"

Was he testing me with that question—with that severe look? "Yes. You could argue that was subversive to those ideals. Yes, I agree."

"So much for *American Ideals,*" he said, "so long as you aren't black, red or yellow."

"Or Jewish," I added.

"Well, neither you or I qualify in any of those categories, do we?" he asked rhetorically as he turned towards the window to see

Pete walking towards building B. Pete was close enough so that we could see a furrowed brow on his face. Suddenly, I noticed a fearful look on Pete's face, like he had remembered something scary.

I let Adam's question go unanswered. The film, *Gentlemen's Agreement,* demonstrated that there's a lot of anti-Semitism in our society and I'm not going there. Although there are many Jews in Hollywood, you never know. Jews are always changing their names, so you never know who was what.

"Mr. Lapidus," I asked, "on the same note, didn't you once tell me that you wondered why Negroes fought for our country? That had you been one, you might not have?"

I saw his head rise a bit, but without missing a beat he nodded from side to side in a dismissive way, waved his hand in a throw away motion, and said, "That was idle reflection on my part. Do you suppose though that the blind chauvinist could argue that that was subversive?"

I pretended it was a rhetorical question and didn't answer. I shook my head from side to side in the same dismissive way, now sure he was testing me. Something strange was going on—his pretense at calm—the weird look in his unfocussed eyes.

"O.K. Sally, that's enough to swallow for one day. See what changes you can make after that story conference yesterday and finish up this week."

I've got to find out why this meeting was called for in the first place otherwise it's going to be another sleepless night. I made no effort to get up. Nonchalantly, I asked, "What was our original meeting going to be about—before Pete came in?"

"Sally, let me check Noah's schedule. We'll cover that question then."

"Sure. Do I have anything to worry about?"

"No—not really. Just thinking about something."

Not really?

When I came home, Josiah barraged me. "So tell me what the hell is going on at the studio? Are you safe? Was it better or worse than you expected? Did they can you? Or were you imagining everything?" he asked, certain he was right about my paranoia.

I ignored his questions and asked, "Do we have a cold beer in the fridge?"

"Sure do. I'm sure your doctor would approve if we split a bottle. Let's see if I can fit two glasses in the freezer to really chill us out." He took me in his arms and asked, "Do we need to chill out, honey?"

"I really don't know—really don't know."

"Something's going on, and you don't know what. Is that it?"

We sat down but I didn't answer him right away. I wanted to have a cold beer in my hands first, but the look on his face was compelling.

"Here's a synopsis—I'm still on the payroll—he wants me to finish the script, HUAC has popped up through its snake hole, and we may or may not be under suspicion, and in a day or so, Lapidus wants me to meet with him and Noah, the Personnel guy."

"About what?"

"Damned if I know. He's thinking about something. What about, I can't guess—but it sounds ominous."

"What's this thing about HUAC?" he asked with a look so worrisome, that in retrospect it seemed way out of proportion. I should have suspected something then.

"Mr. Nathan asked if we had done, said, or written anything that could compromise the studio."

"That doesn't apply to you," emphasizing the 'you,' which once again I should have paid more attention to, like while he was asleep, his sudden gasps and shivers, "so you have nothing to worry about."

"You know, Jo, the truth has little to do with it," I went on, "innuendo, ambiguity, hints, suggestions, casual and innocent remarks, an innocent line you inserted in a movie, someone with whom you may have had a drink, or played tennis with—they all can kill you. They have a reputation for damning people based on gossamer—on rumors alone."

"You're safe. Don't worry about it," and came to my side.

I inched away and said, "Josiah, please sit opposite me—so I can see your face when I talk to you."

"Sorry, honey," he mumbled, "I've got your number."

"Problem is, Jo, that appearances can sometimes be more important than reality. Even when false, the perception of impropriety can destroy. Why even being called before the Committee appears suspect."

"Sweetheart, don't worry about possibilities, please—you've got the baby to worry about."

"I can't help it—my career is on the line, and when I worry so does the baby."

"Sally, my dear, the mother of my first child, the love of my life—you've got to take it easy, and if you're canned, so be it."

"Jo, I was right when I told Mr. Lapidus and Mr. Nathan about the tautological trap of 'liberal and communist.' Damn it, we're in favor of the New Deal and the laws that seem to be enriching our lives, and that makes us 'liberal,' so are we now suspect before the eyes of those right-wing committee members?" I asked with a mixture of desperation, futility and anger.

"Fortunately I'm making a good living as an assistant director. If worse comes to worse, you can let your husband support you. Why just the other day I overheard my grandparents say it was unseemly that my wife should be earning more money than their grandson."

"Your grandparents died before you were born."

"So?"

I took a deep breath and asked, "Where's the beer?"

"Oops." He opened the bottle and asked, "You think Lapidus is clear?"

"I think so. He's no commie. We once talked about the Soviet purges, the Ukrainian famine, the confessions, the closed society—not for him, but he did complain about the treatment of minorities in our country."

"You guys have nothing to worry about. Drink up."

"Nothing except the Noah thing."

"Try not to lose any sleep over it, if that's possible for you."

"Yeah, but what about that diatribe I heard yesterday? He sounded so angry with me. Today, it seemed as though that had never happened."

"Maybe it didn't."

"That's all I need, Josiah—a hint that I may be losing it. You're no comfort at all," I said with a wave of my hand.

He forced a slight smile and said, "Rely on the beer then."

CHAPTER 2

"Honey, would you get the phone, please? I'm in the middle of making a sauce."

"Oh, jeez, I can't right now. I'm in the middle of something too—drawing some shots for tomorrow's shoot," came his impatient response.

"Damn. O.K. I'll get it," I said, hurriedly washing my hands and drying them on my way to the phone.

"Bonjour?"

"Bonjour? Glad to see you've already made the transition. Bonjour and hello," came the cheery voice at the other end.

"Mr. La-pi-dus?" I asked, emphasizing each syllable.

"There's a special timbre to my voice that makes me recognizable no matter where in the world I might be, despite the quality of the telephone."

"My, God. It is you. How are you? Why are you calling me from California? It's only been a few weeks. I've barely started and have nothing to report. I'm still going to Berlitz," I rattled on defensively. "Why are you calling? Is everything all right?" I sat down to catch my breath.

"The reason I'm calling, Sally, is that I'm hungry and wonder if you've mastered the art of French cooking to qualify for a Michelin rating?"

I stood up. "Mr. Lapidus, you're kidding, right? You're not in Paris, are you? This is all a joke, of course. You're not calling from Paris, right?" I asked, aware of my stupid repetition.

"Turns out I am in Paris, but only overnight. I leave early in the morning for Rome. I can tell you all about it over a nice home-cooked French meal and a bottle of French red wine which I will bring. Deal?"

"Of course, of course," I said, heart racing, "but all I can guarantee is a fusion of American, French and God knows what else. Cooking is not instinctual with me, so if you're brave enough, how about 7:30? You surely know my address since you engineered the whole thing in the first place. Do you need directions?"

"No, I know exactly where I'm going."

"As always," I said, knowing he'd take my double entendre as a compliment. "See you later."

Josiah walked in and saw my hand resting on the cradled phone. "That sounded awfully familiar. Who was that?"

"Mr. Lapidus."

"Why is he calling you from California? Is he checking up on you already? You haven't even learned the streets of the neighborhood yet. That's premature as hell. What's going on?"

"We'll soon find out."

"What do you mean 'soon'?"

"He's coming for dinner."

"Sacre bleu!"

"Honey, we have less than an hour. Can you stop what you're doing and help me, please?" I asked. "Otherwise, we'll never be ready."

"It's okay to prepare food while he's here, considering the surprise. But I've got to finish up before midnight."

"Take a break now. After dinner you can excuse yourself and go back to work. You don't have to dawdle over coffee. He's coming to see me—mostly."

"With him 'mostly' is *everything*. I can't believe this visit. Did he think he'd find us out partying?"

"Jo, please don't go there. I can't handle that now." I went back to making my sauce not remembering where I had stopped. Had I already added salt and pepper? What about the oregano? Another minute on the phone and the onions would have burned.

At the entrance to our apartment building there was a doorbell with the unmistakable guttural sound of an old hand-cranked bell, an abrasive sound reminiscent of my apartment in Harlem and an old bike ridden to school each day by an aggressive school friend who liked the authority it gave her.

I had to go down two flights of stairs to open it and when I did, I ignored his extended hand and grabbed him by both shoulders. "Welcome, but first, permit me to kiss you on each cheek to impress upon you how I've adapted to Parisian ways."

"A hand shake won't do?"

"No. Not friendly enough. And appearances must be kept up," I said with a sly smile. Why the hell did I say that?

Josiah met us at the door, shook Adam's hand with friendly enthusiasm, and said, "Welcome to our Parisian garret. You've already met, Mimi, of course."

"Yes, indeed. So for the rest of the evening, shall I call you Rudolpho?"

Everyone was smiling. A good start, I thought. "Glad you could see me on such short notice. What's to eat?"

No niceties? "What's to eat?" Is he kidding?

Josiah took the extended bottle from Adam and said, "Let me open the bottle and let it breathe."

"But don't let it hyperventilate because I haven't eaten since breakfast. When I asked about what you're cooking, I wasn't joking."

"We're ready right now, Mr. Lapidus." When am I going to be comfortable calling him Adam? Funny, he's never asked me to call him by his first name. I tried to conceal my anxiety at his presence, so I continued in a spirited way, "Actually, we haven't adapted to the French way of eating salad with the meal—too many contrasting flavors and textures for us simple folk. We'll do what we do back in the old country—salad first, main meal second. Can you live with that?"

"You bet. Besides, I'm a captive audience. And your slave. And looking for a handout," he said with a joviality I had never before witnessed.

"Well, you've come to the right place," Josiah said friendly-like, "we often feed the hungry and homeless."

I knew that all this *hail-fellow-well-met* crap was a front and it was no great leap to figure out why he was here in the first place.

We went through the salad fast. He was more interested in eating than talking, but when he dug into the entrée, he said, "This is the first meal you've ever served me, Sally, and it's a winner!" he said sincerely, I thought. "By the way," he asked, recognizing the irony in the question, "what am I eating?"

I turned to Josiah and said, "Imagine, enjoying a meal you can't define." I turned to Mr. Lapidus and asked, "Is that a compliment, Mr. Lapidus?"

"I am embarrassed," he said raising his eyebrows, "but it is a compliment indeed."

"It's hake. A fish. I bought it down the street from a Spaniard who called it, 'merlusa.' I don't know the French name yet. Anyway, for an unskilled cook, I can tell you my magic formula for masking gross errors. Sauté onions for a few minutes, add some fresh tomatoes until it gets saucy, add some spices, then add whatever you want on top of it–in this case, fish. Guaranteed to deceive the most discerning palate."

"Honestly, Sally, the deception worked its magic. It really was wonderful."

"Coffee? Tea? Milk? Anything?"

"Nothing, we'll just empty this wine bottle," he said. "I find that wine never keeps until the following day," looking at us with a wicked smile.

I wondered when his smile muscles would collapse from exhaustion.

"Adam, I've got to finish up some layouts for tomorrow's shoot," Josiah said, "so I won't be able to stick around for long. But tell us what you're doing in Rome and how long you'll be staying there."

"Let me help bring these dishes to the kitchen first."

"Don't bother, Mr. Lapidus. Our kitchen is tiny and can barely fit two people. Josiah is the live-in help and clears the deck." Josiah got up and bowed to me. The small table in the middle of the living/dining room was so small our six knees occasionally touched.

Mr. Lapidus sipped more wine and held it. I thought he was on the verge of gargling when he finally swallowed and said, "Shortly after you left, we had a conference at Charlie Chaplin's hotel in Montecito on the outskirts of Santa Barbara. We discussed changing developments in the movie business, TV's impact on it, and the need for radical departures from the successful formulas of the past."

"We're aware of the need to change, and soon," I said. Adam nodded.

"During our discussions," Adam continued, "we talked about how movies from France and Italy challenged our outlook. That's one of the reasons, Josiah, I sent you here, to see if we can learn something–if we can skew our films in a new way."

Josiah nodded.

"Anyway, Pete Nathan thought it would be a good idea if I too spent several months in Italy learning from some of their film makers. They're young and inexperienced but extremely talented and intuitive, relying more on realism and less on fantasy. We like the way they tell stories. Like what I asked you to explore, Josiah—how they insert the grit of French life. That's what I've been asked to do with Italian film."

Am I now going to have him on my back? I can't work with someone looking over my shoulders. How often are we going to have story conferences now that we're closer than half a planet away? I like to explore and do research at my own pace. Damnit!

Before the bull left its starting pen, I decided to grab it first and said, "Mr. Lapidus ...." but interrupted myself, and to my surprise, asked, "may I finally have your permission to call you Adam?" Why did I blurt that out in such an impatient way? Damn.

In a genial voice, he said, "I wondered when you were going to start doing that? I know you're not a slow learner yet it took you more than a dozen years. How come?"

What a relief, I thought, and let out a burst of air. "Because I've been taught to respect my elders, Mr. La—Adam—and address people older than I, by Mr., or Mrs., or Doctor," I said in a deferential way, hating my subordinate position. Someday—someday.

"Well, I'm glad you've gotten over that hurdle," he said.

This evening, I thought, is too high caloric for me. When is the shoe going to drop?

I then barreled on, "On the phone I mentioned that I've accomplished little. I'm frantically studying French. Jo and I practice with one another all the time. I've been to those three cemeteries you suggested: Montparnase, Montmarte, and Pere Lachaise, amazed at what an effect place has on a sense of time.

"I opened up a book about Colonel Picquart and browsed through the array of books in the library, and though my French is not good enough yet, it seems that the Dreyfus Affaire was the catalyst that caused all sorts of latent and overt prejudices to emerge, one that created a schism in French society which erupted like—like a fulminating volcano."

Almost breathlessly and talking fast, I continued, "I'm beginning to realize that the tentacles of the Dreyfus Affaire spread wide and deep, not only in France, but in Germany, Norway, Spain, the United States and other countries. It seemed that everyone had a take on the issue—and a stake in it as well.

"Did you know that the composer ... "

Adam motioned me to stop. "Please, Sally, no details. Just put it in your screenplay."

"Okay, I just want you to know that the issue is much larger than Picquart, involving people in the arts, politics and even science. I may not finish this in six months, you understand, but I'll have done most of my research and analysis, and an outline, maybe even a few pages. I can finish it after I have my baby.

"So," I asked, finally slowing down, "may I respectfully ask you to lower your expectations, Adam?"

"Respectful still," his smiling green eyes said. "Of course, Sally. But you will send me periodic progress reports, won't you? And now that I am in Europe too, maybe we can meet every so often in Switzerland or Spain for a story conference. How does that sound?"

"Perfect," I smiled, belying my true feelings.

"By the way, I discovered that during the war, those Nazi puppets, the Vichy Government of France, was made up of many anti-Dreyfusards, and that Dreyfus's granddaughter was killed in the extermination camps."

"You know you shouldn't be going there. I made that very clear to you, Sally," he said without that smiling garment he's been wearing all night long. "Your screenplay should not be about the Dreyfus Affaire, nor Zola, nor Jews—none of that. Much has already been written about them. Your focus should be only on the French Officer, Colonel Picquart. Though a vocal anti-Semite, after he discovered a conspiracy to frame this Dreyfus character, he did his best to try to exonerate him, and in the process was *jailed. Your task is to write about the factors that led to his change of heart. How and why did that happen? What did honor have to do with that change of heart?* That's the main reason I sent you here—to breathe life into that man, *to help us understand that reversal.*"

His eyes seemed to have glazed over, like he wasn't looking at me but through me. Was it the wine? Was he deep in thought? Before I could defend myself and tell him I got it, he continued, "Do you want to hear about French hypocrisy?" he went on with his monologue, "Do you know that no film about the Dreyfus case can be shown in France? That in 1938 when France's Prime Minister Daladier saw the Academy Award winning film, *The Life of Emile Zola,* even though the only reference to Jews was a passing glance at a document, he claimed that showing it would tarnish the honor of the French Army and banned it from ever being shown there?

"It appears," Adam continued, "that the French, who believe they hold the torch of liberty higher than most, subscribe to Schopenhauer's belief that 'Jews have that special Jewish stink.'"

"What?" I gasped. "I never did like that pessimistic pilosopher!"

"Well, on that note, I'd best be going. I have an early train to catch. Can we interrupt Josiah to say goodbye?"

"Of course. Jo?" I yelled into the other room. "Adam is leaving."

Adam asked, "Sally, do you kiss on both cheeks when you say goodbye as well?"

"Whether they do or not, we will," I said as I pressed one cheek against the other while pecking the air.

"By the way, Adam," Josiah asked as we walked him to the door, "The International Herald Tribune said that HUAC is coming to Hollywood this summer. Is that true?"

"Yes and no. Originally that was their intention, but a week after I got here, I was told they had changed their *Second Coming* to January or February of 1951. That took us all by surprise," he continued with a facial grimace that seemed to be written with a mixture of anger, concern, regret, disappointment and irony.

"Are the studio people going to be okay?" Jo asked.

"Why not?" he said with what seemed to me like feigned assurance, "now that Ring Lardner, Jr. is no longer with us, there are no commies left at 20th, to the best of my knowledge. We're all perfectly safe."

What's this all about? I asked myself.

"I'm glad to hear that, of course," Josiah continued, "when I read Jack Warner and Louis B. Mayer's testimonies back in 1947 or 1948, I thought they had stopped the committee cold. What the *hell* are they coming back for?" he asked with discernable anger and trepidation, emphasizing the word, *hell*. It actually frightened me a little.

"Damn if I know," Adam said echoing Jo's tone. "Senator Joe McCarthy is a growing influence. But we'll stop him cold too. There's nothing to worry about. Gotta' go," he said as he opened the door. "I'll send you a note with my phone number and address. Thanks again, my Parisian friends," and sang a few bars from the aria, 'Mi chiamo, Mimi.'"

He walked down the winding stairs that seemed never to end, and when he turned to look up at me, I thought I detected a sly grin on his face.

I plopped down on the couch, and heaved an audible sigh. "I'm glad that's over."

"What are you talking about? I thought it went very well. It's the first time we've ever socialized with him, and it couldn't have gone better. That can only improve the relationship, honey. Why are you apprehensive?"

"You'll have to forgive me, Jo. I don't know whether it's the surge of hormones, or my naturally suspicious attitude, but something isn't kosher. First I'm sent away on some nebulous project, then you're sent away, maybe for me, maybe not. Now Adam is sent away. Why?" Before he could give me his comforting rationalization, I went on, "Do you suppose HUAC has anything to do with it? You think the studio wanted to get rid of us until this crap blows over? And, Jo, you scared me a bit before, like you were worried about something yourself."

"Only about tomorrow's shoot," was his too quick response, "but Foster's Freeze ice-cream with double-dipped chocolate, your favorite, is well-known for erasing worries. Shall I go out and get some?"

"In Paris?"

"There must be something close."

"No. After that delicious fish, nothing sounds tempting."

"Massage might relax your wrinkled forehead."

"That feels good, Jo." After a few moments, I said, "But my breasts are not tense." We giggled and I continued, "You know, every question asked, even though it might sound innocent, implies a suggestion, a thrust, an arrow pointing towards something, something that might have potentially baleful implications."

"No wonder you're a successful writer. You have an unbridled imagination. Remember what Freud once said?"

"Now that I think about it," I continued, ignoring his question, "Adam did say something once—about his fear of being called a subversive."

"What?"

I wondered whether telling him might implicate him in some unimaginable way.

"Don't let me hang in mid-air. What kind of 'subversive'?"

"Oh, it was nothing, honey, just idle chatter."

"Sally, my dear, *I'm* not a subversive, *Adam* is not a subversive, *you're* not a subversive! Your writing is totally apolitical. No one can accuse you of anything. Or me. Relax, please. Tell me what he said."

"If the studio sent me away," I went on, "it might be because I might have been called before the committee. It doesn't matter if anything is true or not—being called before that committee is indictment enough."

"You should have been an FBI agent because you have an over-engineered sense of paranoia. You doubt everything. You question everything. Nothing for you is as it seems to be. C'mon, sweetheart," he said softly, "you're worrying over nothing. Don't let it get the best of you."

"I hate the unknown, Josiah."

"Lean on me, honey. I'm here to protect you from vampires, bats, black cats and witches. Tomorrow first thing, I'm going to get you a set of worry beads."

"Funny thing is that I can deal with black cats and witches—it's the vampires I'm having trouble with."

"I want to know about that subversive thing," he asked again.

When he gets dogged, he doesn't let go, so to get him off track I told him about a part of my checkered career at Fox. "Before I met you, Josiah, I had written a script called *Garden Land Road*, that was being directed by Tynan Danard, a classy lady I genuinely liked. I had heard she was butchering it, so I ignored the red light and barged in, guns ablaze. 'You're going to substitute Culver City for *Paris? Culver City? For Paris?* Are you out of your *fucking mind, Tynan?'*

"Nose to nose, I roared, 'That's blasphemy! You're going straight to *Hell*, you tasteless *bitch!'*

"I did this, Jo, in front of the crew, the actors, the camera people, everybody. I was breathing fire and shouted, 'Ty, you *stupid-ass philistine*, the last part of the film will have to be rewritten! For that pivotal skating scene in front of the *Eiffel Tower*, you're using the skating rink in *Culver City*? That mausoleum? The story makes sense *only in Paris*, love on the banks of the *River Seine*, the music of *Ravel, Debussy, Bizet*, impressionists–*Monet, Cezanne, Pissarro*. The architecture of *Old Empire Buildings*, the beauty of its grand boulevards, the trees, the parks, French accents, croissants, baguettes. Where the hell are going to find that in *Culver City*—you—you *fucking idiot?*'"

"Sounds like you totally lost it."

"Yeah, but I thought everyone knew that whatever I wrote was carved on stone tablets. Anyway, she fired off a short right to my mouth and knocked me onto a couch. She then pulled me off and shoved me towards the door shouting, 'This *bitch* is no longer allowed on my set! She is *persona-non-grata*, once and forever! Does everybody get that?'"

"That's humiliating, Sally—but you deserved it. You would have done the same."

"You're right. Later, I tried to apologize but she wouldn't answer my calls or let me anywhere near her. Maybe that's why I'm here—*'to get rid of that truculent, loud-mouthed, quick-draw writer.'* But to Paris of all places? Poetic justice."

"I'm glad you've grown up, Sally. I wouldn't have tolerated that kind of behavior, no matter how much I loved you."

I nodded and said, "I understand, Josiah. Once someone called me 'crisp' because, in a voice that could be heard down the block, I yelled at him for letting his dog poop on my lawn. In the middle of the night, I thought of how much better it would have been had I softly said I would get a plastic bag for him to pick the poop up. It was then I realized that my second thoughts are often better than my first. For a long time I had a note on my make-up mirror with a phrase,

'Be Mellow—Don't Bellow.'

"Maybe I'll learn something from Picquart—about behavior."

He lifted me off the chair and gave me a prolonged hug. It was the kind of understanding hug I needed. But I had changed the subject. "So what pearl of wisdom were you ready to quote from Freud?"

"Sometimes a cigar is only a cigar."

"Right."

"But either way, this situation stinks. Like a cigar."

CHAPTER 3

Adam had arranged for Josiah to work with a French director who preferred night shoots, freezing rain, numbing cold, ravaged buildings, gritty streets and mumbling actors, so once again, he wouldn't be home until late—or early.

I drifted off into a fitful sleep, glad to move freely, to allow my restless legs to roam the bed without disturbing Josiah. In our small bed, the slightest movement caused ripples everywhere.

The following morning right after he left I went straight to my desk in a small room alongside our bedroom. It had lots of light–light that, ever since childhood, I seemed to need to think clearly—like having a hole in my head for illumination. Learning French is not as easy as I expected. Constantly looking up words and idioms is like trudging through mud. But if kids can get it, so can I.

Only thing is, I'm not 5 anymore. Keep working at it. It'll come.

Every time I read something about Colonel Picquart, strange information about all sorts of people pops up. Why was Saint-Saens the first person Adam mentioned? And that he was buried in Montparnasse Cemetery—because Dreyfus is buried there too? There must be a connection.

And Degas at Montmarte Cemetery? Proust and Gertrude Stein at Pere Lachaise Cemetery? Yet not where Picquart is buried? Could he have been suggesting something or was it all general information from his vast storehouse of trivia? Suddenly it was dinnertime. Afterwards, Jo went to his room to work. After a while, I asked, "Jo, may I interrupt you for a moment?"

"Can it wait? Half an hour or so? I'm trying to figure out the line up of some camera angles," he said staccato-like, not welcoming the interruption.

"Yeah, I guess ... "

From his room, I heard, "I can tell from your voice that you can't." He sat beside me, and asked, "What?"

"The stuff I overheard coming from Adam's office that day sounded so much like a death knell that it continues to haunt me. Despite all his good wishes and other congenial crap, it's coloring my thoughts. So .... "

He interrupted before I could continue with my concerns. "Honey, give up the ghost already. You're here. I'm here. We're embarked on something we never could have predicted a few months ago. When we look back on our lives we're going to be delighted to have had this unexpected experience. That's what makes for an interesting life."

He realized his tone was not helpful, so he switched to a less impatient one. Snuggling up to me, he said, "So," he murmured, "enjoy the time we're here."

"Sweetheart, when I need it the most, you provide equilibrium," and kissed him on the cheek. "But let me continue, okay?" I said, lowering the anxiety in my voice.

"Before I get to Picquart, to add some balance, I think I should find out about several of those famous people—so I can figure out what Adam may have left unsaid, don't you think?" Without waiting for a response, I went on, "Nothing is casual or accidental with him, so maybe I should be researching the people who were affected by or had an affect on the Affaire—to get their perspectives—even though they may be ancillary—so that I'm not caught unawares. While I'm doing that, it'll give me a chance to improve my French before I tackle the big guy. Whadyathink?"

"Maybe—hard to tell."

"But considering the scope of what I've read so far, I've got to be sure that whatever I write is not going to end up like an academic treatise. I want to avoid didacticism and try to breathe life into the subject."

"Like our baby?" he said both as a question and an answer. I loved the safety of his smile.

I returned the smile and said, "On a different scale of course, but essentially that's what writers do, don't they? The cliché of breathing life into characters?" After a few beats, I continued with my thoughts, "Writers have no gender. Male and female alike become pregnant with their work—pregnancies with complications to be sure—but ultimately, they give birth."

"Yes," he said, "at publication time."

I nodded but wondered whether writing: *Finis,* was the actual birth, or was it the publication date?

He broke into my reflections. "Even before I met you, Sally, I had read some of your scripts and saw the films made from them. You inhabited your characters—you became them—spoke from their points of view, their individual experiences—from deep in their marrow. Like when you wrote about your parents—you *became* them in order to *understand* them."

He came close again, took my hands and looked at me, and said, "Don't lose sight of that. When you write about Picquart, and all the other characters involved, *become them—inhabit them.* That might help you avoid the academic trap."

"Thank you, my love, for letting me interrupt you," I said, kissing him on his lips, warmly, lovingly—then once again. When I allow him, he does console.

He left me alone to consider what he had said. I sat there watching the rain meander down the window, wondering where my meandering was going to take me, whether I'd ever complete my journey. And then it registered. That's it, of course. A phrase from my Latin days at William Taft High School in New York, a phrase Mrs. Mangus used to quote. How does it go? Ahh–I remember:

ESSE QUAM VIDERI
TO BE—NOT TO SEEM

Josiah and Mrs. Mangus helped me emerge from the waters of my muddy confusion, as though they had waved a rod that parted those waters. I knew now that to do justice to my characters and their struggles, I had to steep myself in the lives of prominent people who may have been involved with the colonel and to get a sense of the zeitgeist of the times. Yes, to breathe the same air. Adam mentioned that Saint-Saens is buried where Dreyfus is. Maybe I ought to start with him, to get some background, to see the connection.

CHAPTER 4

To most Americans the name Camille connotes gender, but I'm a man. Few people know that my first name is Charles. How that happens is curious, differing from family to family. No one can remember why Camille stuck. Perhaps it was a loving aunt who made up songs while she rocked me on her lap using the more euphonious name, Camille. Perhaps there were too many Charles in the family, perhaps Camille was derived from a beloved relative. Who knows? No one can remember. So Camille was how I was known—affectionately by some, less so by others.

On October 27, 1907, at the age of 72, I witnessed the unveiling of a statue located in the court foyer of the opera house in Dieppe, France, dedicated to me, Camille Saint-Saens. Statues are often dedicated to the deceased. To see mine before I died was a thrilling experience. A culmination.

I was still in good health, however, so I hoped more good things were forthcoming.

That I'm still alive, having been born in 1835, represents somewhat of an achievement. That I will live until the age of 86 is still more of an achievement. My two children weren't as lucky. They both died in infancy–one falling out of a four-story window.The other, of illness, a short time later.

Parents never recover from seeing their children die. It's the discordant rupture of an idealized cosmic order. The price of living was almost more than I could bear. I could have remained crippled all my life–immobilized–but that would have meant the loss of still another life.

I never risked having children again.

Though I was not attracted to art that did not conform to the Greco/Roman/Renaissance genre, a few days before my statue was unveiled, I had a dream that a contemporary of mine, Auguste Rodin, known to adhere to a modernist approach, had sculpted my body out of liquid alabaster that morphed from a bar of sixteenth notes to a bar of thirty-second notes, from a G clef to a Treble clef, with my face rippling, like the moon on agitated water.

My earliest memories were at the shore listening to the music of the surf as it changed melodies with every crash of the wave–how the pitch would change as the tide ebbed and flowed–how it gurgled–how the seagulls seemed to understand the musicality of the surf and would synchronize their sounds to the crashing water–and even the sunlight, glittering like gold confetti, added a complementary sound to the music I kept hearing.

I added that purling elegance to my music.

In my back yard, hummingbirds flourished. If I stayed perfectly still, they would defy gravity and investigate this intruder, come within inches of my face and make eye contact, unashamedly showing off their exquisite iridescent ruby-red throats and emerald-blue feathers. While studying their colors, I would listen to the thrumming of their wings and add their music to my repertoire of sound.

I learned how to read and write when I was three and, blessed with perfect pitch, started composing immediately. When I was ten years old, at my debut recital I dazzled my audience by playing Mozart's piano concerto #15 without a score in front of me.

As an encore, I offered to play any one of Beethoven's thirty-two piano sonatas from memory. Any one of them.

I continued as a pianist and organist, one of the best I say modestly, though Franz Liszt thought I *was indeed* the best organist in Europe. I was also a composer of five piano concerti, several symphonies, the third of which, the organ symphony, I dedicated to him. Symphonic poems, chamber music, thirteen operas, violin and cello concerti, oratorios, and countless other works. Everywhere I went, musical ideas kept coming, awake, asleep, at the shore, reading my gazette, during spirited and dull conversations, at all times of the day and night, during all seasons.

It seemed as though at the very moment I was writing notes to the music I was composing, the empty spaces in my head were being filled with the waterfalls of new music gushing forth from an endless reservoir.

Musical notes danced wildly in my head. My temples throbbed with melodies. I could taste sounds. Sweet, sour, savory, salty, peppery, silky fat–they were all there. They oozed out of my pores. I trembled with the emotions sound generated within me, anger, love, regrets, longing, vengeance, sensuousness, and disappointments—the entire spectrum. There was a direct connection between my eyes and that mysterious musical gold nugget in my brain—between my ears and the nugget—between my nose and the nugget—between my touch and the nugget, and above all, between my heart and that beneficial nugget. Even my rhythmic breathing sounded musical to me.

Without a piano or organ at hand, notes pulsated at the tips of my fingers. I wrote music as an apple tree grows apples, apples growing all year long–like in the Garden of Eden.

It all sounds pretentious, I know, and self-aggrandizing, but the proof is in its general acceptance, for my music is performed to enthusiastic audiences throughout Europe. My friends, generous in their praise, quipped that my frenzied fecundity, if directed towards women, could populate much of the world. Debussy, on the other hand, sneered at my musical prolixity, as though a large output of compositions implied mediocrity, as though wide ranging interests implied superficiality and dilettantism. He is so gifted and innovative that he doesn't have to demean me to stand tall.

My interests are eclectic. I have an over-arching, non-discriminatory interest in everything. Incapable of being a dilettante, I've become an accomplished astronomer, attending both solar and lunar eclipses throughout Europe, even calculating when the next ones would occur. I also gave a lecture at the Astronomical Society on "The Effects of Mirage." Using the proceeds from some duos for harmonium and piano, I commissioned a telescope made to my own specifications.

I avidly followed new discoveries in archeology and bored my friends with excruciating detail. To all who knew me, I was a font of knowledge—geology, botany, mathematics, history. I wrote novels and poetry. I excelled at everything. I even wrote a philosophical work, "Problemes et Mysteres" which speaks of my belief that science and art should replace religion. Convinced that reason always wins out, I am certain it will happen in my lifetime—or soon thereafter.

I wrote numerous essays on, "*Materialism and Music–Harmony and Melody,* even one on *Decoration in the Theatre of Ancient Rome,*" and on many other subjects of little interest to the casual observer.

Overall, I was a polymath. Very much aware of the many gifts I had been born with, it was impossible for me to disagree with my friends who called me a renaissance man. Above all, I tried with all my heart and will, not to squander those gifts.

My abilities awe me. It doesn't embarrass me to tell you as much. To pretend an air of humility would be disingenuous. With such formidable gifts, it would strike a false note to act otherwise, to pretend modesty. To act as though it were nothing would insult those who know better. I don't boast. I do.

Sounds like someone insufferable, I know. Accomplished at everything, I try not to be patronizing to those who have less to offer, but I know at times I am intolerant of those whose words or accomplishments are mediocre–especially if they pretend otherwise. At times, people have called me a most irritating man.

I traveled often, especially to North Africa, to places where I listened to the musicality of the language, the folk songs, the mourning and morning chants, the religious harmonies from the minarets calling the faithful to prayer, the noise of the streets, the shouts of children, the sound of wind coursing through narrow streets, rain falling on tin roofs–cultures far removed from my beloved France, so I wasn't fine tuned to the nuances of the Dreyfus Affaire. The battle was between Dreyfusards and anti-Dreyfusards.

I believed that taking sides was not in my best interests so I never let on what my views were about this incident that was tearing our nation apart, that was visiting upon us the opprobrium of much of the leaders and press of the world. What did I care about a Jew who had betrayed his country?

That must not have been the whole story because I did contribute money for his defense.

When I discovered later that it was our country that had betrayed him, a surge of ambivalence overwhelmed me–that I was right in supporting him and should have done more, yet discovering that my country was at fault.

At an early age, I knew I had been blessed with astonishing gifts given to few others. I was determined to embrace life fully, to fulfill whatever potential I had—unwilling to look back on my life to find pockets of empty yesterdays. When I was buried at Montparnasse Cemetary in 1921, resplendent in the effulgence of my achievements, I arrived devoid of anything I had neglected to do.

Everyone was bandying around the word, *honor*, as though it were a badge, a thing to be strived for, noble, exalted, worthy, ethical, even though I knew it to mean contradictory things to different people.

What then did honor mean to me? Only one thing—it meant that I had an obligation to myself, my parents, my audience, not to let this manna go to waste. To others not so amply blessed, I had an even greater responsibility. For them it would have been a double loss—not to have been given those gifts in the first place, and then for me to have ignored those rare gifts. That for me was honor.

To have done anything else would have been dishonorable.

CHAPTER 5

Unlike Saint-Saens, I, Edvard Grieg, have a moral duty to enter into the Dreyfus fray. My honor is at stake; my belief in the rights of all people; my revulsion at cruelty and prejudice; my optimistic belief that justice will win out, *but* only if we who are outraged at injustice speak out.

I am as Norwegian as cod.

It began on April 3, 1869 in Copenhagen when, at the age of 25, I premiered my piano concerto. Critics and audiences said that I had established myself as a major composer, something that both delighted and embarrassed me because I am reticent, retiring, solitary, unassuming.

Paris was the North Star of European music, and in April of 1894, my friend and advocate, Frederick Delius, that gifted but under-appreciated British composer, introduced me into the cultural circles of the Paris Salon. Once, at a large gathering Frederick announced that Modern French Music is simply Grieg, plus the third act of Tristan. Compliments don't get much better than that.

And to have that said by a composer whose first work I heard, *The Florida Suite,* a piece that overwhelmed me with its complex sonority, its sublime textures and its wondrous melodies–a piece, which, for Scandinavians who are not known for overt demonstrations of emotions, was, and no other word will do, voluptuous, so it was high praise indeed. And to my great joy, young Maurice Ravel agreed with Frederick.

Two years later, in 1896, to great accolades, my Peer Gynt Suite premiered in France. Like many of my much-heralded fellow Scandinavians, painters, composers and writers, I was pleased with its reception by the French who were among the most sophisticated in Europe.

In 1899, I received an invitation to play my piano concerto in Paris. At the same time, results were announced about Captain Dreyfus's second trial that found him guilty once again, but this time with '*extenuating circumstances*.'

That infuriated me so I wrote the concert promoters a bitter letter in which I stated,"I was so upset by the disdain for justice demonstrated in France that I don't feel the possibility to be in touch with the French public in such circumstances. I therefore refuse to play anything of mine in France. Cancel my performance!"

It was for me truly Manichean. The state wanted to protect the 'honor' of the French Army by reaffirming Dreyfus's guilt, even though they knew that letters he was alleged to have written were forgeries. So much for their concept of *'honor'*.

No, I did the *honorable* thing but blundered in the doing. I was so angry at their lies and cover-ups that I allowed The Frankfurter Zeitung to publish my letter of cancellation. The substance of my cancellation was news enough, but editorials throughout Europe emphasized my quote,"It's evident that the interest of the State cannot be more important than the innocence of a man, and that my sense of public morality and general rules of conduct were violated."

What I hadn't realized was that I was accusing the French people, publicly that is, of a denial of justice. Still smarting from their defeat in the Franco-Prussian war, the French did not take kindly to receiving from others lessons about honor and justice, principles, they believed, had originated with them. I should have known better. The self-righteous tend to be un-diplomatic, and often, uncivilized.

But I was right and the French military and much of the public were egregiously wrong!

I continued to follow Captain Dreyfus's saga. Zola's 'J'Accuse', the forgeries imputing guilt to the Captain, the polarization between Dreyfusards and anti-Dreyfusards, the rabid anti-Semitism amongst many French and Europeans, the cries of *"Death to the Jews."* The French media were perpetuating this ugly cry, but I was certain that amnesia was a function of time, equally proportional to one another. It was 1903 after all.

While I was conducting some of my works in Paris, my piano concerto, the Peer Gynt Suite #1, some elegiac melodies, my Swan and other pieces I suddenly heard angry shouts from the audience, a few of whom were making such commotion that I had to step down from the podium. Anti-Dreyfusards were in the audience. The divisiveness had not diminished. To my embarrassment, the police intervened and expelled some of the rowdies. When I began again, there were still so many shouts that it became difficult to listen. Soon, however, my quiet songs and Pugno's virtuosic performance of my piano concerto helped to decompress the swollen atmosphere. It ended as I had intended, though I had to be escorted from the concert hall between lines of policemen.

How the mighty had fallen.

Behavior like that unnerves me. I thought once again, that nothing lasts forever.

Paradoxically, many considered my concert a triumph. Despite the ruckus, I was admired for my stance in favor of liberty, truth and justice. What I did not know, however, was that Claude Debussy disliked Zola, and that any supporter of Zola was going to get skewered in his review. And I did.

Debussy wrote that my songs are " .... very sweet, very pale music to soothe convalescents in well-to-do-neighborhoods." He also disliked the trumpets and fanfares in my piano concerto which, he said, were " ... announcing the arrival of a little cantabile section at which we are meant to swoon." Mercifully, he liked the Peer Gynt suite. At a dinner party soon after, I heard that he had pronounced even more severe judgment on me.

He had, characteristically, a general enmity towards most people, charming when he liked you, but often, his mind had been made up even before engaging you in conversation. If you were one of the unlucky ones, you'd be the object of his curmudgeonness, of his nastiness.

His wit was not so much trenchant as vitriolic. He called one of my pieces " ... a pink bon-bon stuffed with snow."

About Beethoven " ... he had terrifically profound things to say but did not know how to say them because he was imprisoned in a web of incessant restatement of German aggressiveness … must we now re-define inarticulateness in music?"

Of Saint-Saens, "I have a horror of sentimentality and I cannot forget that its name is Saint-Saens."

What's wrong with "sentimentality?" For me, for Saint-Saens and many others, it connotes a connection with life, not a withdrawal from it. A bear hug of the full range of human emotions. A zest for embracing what makes us happy, for life and its possibilities, for the accompanying sadness that comes with loss or disappointment. Sentimentality implies engagement. Why should we conceal that? We don't spend all our time writing requiems and dirges.

To the extent that those of us who become artists do so out of egotism and hubris, and yes, conceit, hoping that what we have to say will resonate with strangers who are not as forgiving as family and friends, it embarrasses me to ask myself, *how could he have disliked my music?*

I tried to understand Debussy's motivation behind his bad reviews and discovered he belonged in the camp of the anti-Dreyfusards, while I remained a staunch Dreyfusard. France had become so polarized, so anti-Semitic, that most of the salons were closed to the Dreyfusards. Supporters of Dreyfus were physically attacked on the streets, and Debussy didn't want to be one of them.

One of Debussy's former friends, Alfred Bruneau, wrote an opera, Messidor with a libretto by Zola, who by this time had written, "J'Accuse." Because they were both Dreyfusards, it failed. Debussy wrote a letter to one of his friends, Pierre Louys, in which he said, "I haven't gotten much further than you with the score of Messidor, for life is short and I'd rather go to a cafe or look at pictures. How do you expect people as ugly as Zola and Bruneau to be capable of anything but the second rate, they are just a lot of dreary fatheads." He reviled Zola's realistic novels as offensive to his refined aesthetic.

We were not alone as targets. He thought Maurice Ravel "... was like a charmer/fakir having flowers to grow around a seat." Of Gabriel Faure that, " ... he was the music-stand of a group of snobs and fools." Of Cesar Franck's violin concerto, " ...its facile sentimentality."

To be in the company of such great composers as well as Zola's, to share in Debussy's vitriolic wit, was elevating and unifying, but of little comfort. Company or not, I am who I am. Ultimately, I compose to suit myself alone. Never to please the critic. No matter how famous. What would Freud say about such egotism?

After these events, I wrote to a friend,

"I am fortunate enough not only to be uninfluenced by Debussy's utterances about me, but to be able to feel in sympathy with his music. He shows a fine sense of color and is highly imaginative. I acknowledge the earnestness and genuineness of his work, and it is in this earnestness, which he denies to my musical outlook, that attracts me towards him, because it is my own ideal."

I wrote that later—much later—long after I had recovered from his review of my concert.

In 1914, seven years after Grieg's death, Debussy personally performed several of Grieg's compositions. Go figure.

This is bigger than I thought. Josiah and I lost family in the Holocaust.

But keep your focus—Adam had in mind exploring the counter-intuitive, not the intuitive.

Now's the time to walk into the darker part of the forest.

CHAPTER 6

In 1860, Emile wrote to me about a dream he had in which he had written, as he described it, 'an elegantly expressed' book that was illustrated with some of my sublime prints. On the front page of his dream book, in luminous gold letters, were our names alongside one another,

ZOLA and CEZANNE—FOREVER

Forever heralded by posterity. When I remember that dream, I tremble with emotions of longing, regret and nostalgia for what might have been if things had stayed just the way they were. Do they ever?

It's painful to realize that thirty years of intimacy can disappear as quickly as a morning fog. Where, I ask myself, in what conversation, in what painting was there an adumbration of what appeared in Emile's novel, L'Oeuvre?

Zola's abandonment in his later years of Manet and the rest of us Impressionists was painful enough, but writing about me, and it could have been only me in L'Oeuvre, as an artist condemned to mediocrity by his genes—one whose ambitions were greater than his abilities—about my artistic impotence—that my work, like the work of the rest of my contemporaries, Monet, Pissarro, Signac, was careless, unfinished, exaggerated and incoherent, that we were precursors waiting for a genius to point us in the right direction. That demonstrated the triumph of his duty to truth over friendship, as he, a journalist, perceived it, contrasted with my duty to the truth as I, Paul Cezanne, perceived it. Even my old friend, Monet, in a discussion with mutual friends, said he believed in truth over allegiance. So what the hell is friendship anyway?

For Zola, Monet's luminous paintings of La Gare Saint-Lazare, were insufficient because he failed to show the burdensome strain on the man in charge of that train.

Sacre Bleu!

In Zola's book, the artist realizes that no matter how much he strives for excellence, he can never rise above his nature—shackling him thus to un-blest insignificance—and hangs himself. Was he suggesting something to me?

He sent me that book, like he had his others, as a gift. I thanked him for it. I never wanted to speak or write to him again. Nor did I. Ever.

Pissarro, the most truthful amongst us, advised not to despair—that it was just a bad novel—not to read anything more into it than pure invention deserving only to collect dust on a shelf. That was easy to say, but the pain lingers.

When Emile, that fool, in defending Capt. Dreyfus, wrote five incendiary articles that resulted in his conviction for slander against the Army, then escaped his one year prison sentence by exiling himself to London—the coward—it seemed he had found, finally, a challenge worthy of his enormous abilities. As an art critic supporting us Impressionists in 1866, a time when we much needed support, those of us who knew him realized that his support had been merely a second-rate endeavor insufficient to tap fully into his reservoir of capabilities. A romantic idealist, he had become the public conscience—the folk hero of Europe.

We were close friends at university, and frequently, the word prodigy was thrown at both of us. It was an intoxicating time, his heart beating in time with prose, mine with the verse of Virgil, Lucretius, Baudelaire. With my prodigious memory, I could recite them hour upon hour, much to the discomfort of my bored friends, one of whom fell asleep, and upon my complaining, identified me as 'un ecorche,' *super-sensitive.* Born shy, he was right. Later when another friend wrote, 'that he was much more promising at drawing than he turned out since,' I stopped all contact with him.

Who needs friends like that?

Was L'Oeuvre the only reason for the break between Emile and me? No—not the only reason. The other was that damned Dreyfus Affaire! That insidious Affaire was also responsible for my break with Camille Pissarro, another one of my very closest friends. Goddamn that man, Dreyfus! When a painter at our gallery, Durand-Ruel, remarked that we would have been spared this commotion had they shot Dreyfus on the spot, everyone agreed—except for the doorman—but I would have been one of those joining the firing squad!

Life is a series of interruptions.

Two of my best friends, one from childhood, the other my mentor when I started painting—ended up being interruptions—inter-*eruptions*—inter-*ruptures*—inter-*disruptions*.

Merde!!

Painting is solitary, private, isolated, personal, yet for years I painted every day alongside my mentor, Camille Pissarro. We looked over each other's shoulders but never imitated. We looked at small corners of the world in similar ways—attracted to the same views—influenced by the same colors and light—shared the same artistic sensibilities. Even though he was a Jew.

Perhaps I did offend him when I said he *used* to paint better, that he should retrogress, that the new doesn't always surpass the old. Just because it's *now* doesn't make it better.

But, I think my Cezanne *now* is better than my Cezanne *then*.

He thinks I'm copying his earlier works, but his artist's eye is failing. His judgment, I'm certain, has been colored by my vocal antagonism towards Dreyfus specifically and Jews generally. Everyone knows that Jews are unworthy of the trust our Republic has put in them. That case was the polarizing topic of the day even during the quiet contemplation of painting—an inescapable presence hovering like mosquitoes, biting, stinging, irritating, inflaming at every moment, at every event, during every silence.

It began to corrode our relationship, its acid destroying its very fabric. We couldn't avoid the topic—it was intermingled with the oxygen we breathed. His relationship with Degas, another close friend, soon burst. We were next. That damn Affaire was the catalyst, the giant squid coming from its inky depths, grabbing us, drowning us, rupturing the bonds that once bound us together like brothers.

How did I let that happen? How could I not?

We should have shot that Jew! Immediately!

Now, look at the polarization—Renoir, Degas, Rodin, and I, against Monet, Pissarro, Signac, Seurat, Cassatt, Vuillard. Even Anton Chekhov and Mark Twain, as though Zola were not enough, wrote eloquently about the injustice and corruption of the military and legal system that had incarcerated an innocent man. Henry James wrote his brother, William, about France existing "en decadence." What did they know about the injustice and corruption of the Jewish Syndicate and its effort to take over our country? Our beloved Army? Our beloved France? Those Dreyfusards attempted to clear that traitor's name, by besmirching the honor of our Army and French justice system. Bastards!!

Perhaps Edgar Degas is right—there are *germs of propensity* within us that determine what we believe in and not believe in. Why otherwise, would some choose one way and some the opposite? Some people, however, have unsettling ambivalences or contradictory ambiguities, and are condemned to perpetual vacillation. I have what Degas has. Certitude! To know what one knows without doubt is empowering!

And don't compare me with that chameleon Picquart. He changed into something he had never been. His fundamental beliefs were superseded by his dubious version of the truth. How can you trust his *germs of propensity* if at first they lead you one way, and later, in the opposite direction? My germs, on the other hand, are trustworthy. I remain true to them—to my upbringing, to my class, to my country. Resolute and unbending, certain about those perfidious Jews.

Degas had many close Jewish friends once. No wonder he hated them. But I didn't hate Camille—I just couldn't stand him anymore.

What difference does it make to my art? Am I, like Toulouse, painting corpulent Jews with large drooping noses and sleazy eyes haggling with prostitutes? Even Camille, when painting Jews, did so with stereotypical characteristics. I never did that, even as I drifted towards a non-finito type of painting, of wanting my viewers to fill in the blank spaces on the canvas.

Everyone knew where I stood—in everyone's face.

Perhaps I shouldn't be so judgmental about Emile's choice of integrity and justice over friendship. After all, I too have made my choice—condemning Dreyfus for betraying his country superseding my friendship for Emile and Camille. Too late, of course, to review the matter with either of them, as though we could have ever talked through our disparate views—despite what that other self-righteous Jew, Sigmund Freud, claimed was his *talking cure*. Emile, quite unexpectedly, died from asphyxiation in 1902—Camille, of old age in 1903.

Does one ever get over the disentanglement of an entangled friendship?

In 1906, I couldn't resist attending a ceremony for the unveiling of a bust of Zola at the Bibliotheque Mejanes in Aix-en-Provence. It was as though I were drawn by some electro-magnetic force—no, that's wrong—not a scientific force, but an un-quantifiable human force that everyone generates—known to everyone except scientists who know of nothing unless it's measurable. Call it the past—call it love—call it humanity—call it conviction—call it disappointment—call it regret—call it longing—aghh, je ne sais quois!

At that ceremony, I sat in the back to hide, when suddenly I heard the speaker pointing to me and publicly alluding to my deep friendship with Zola. That was more than I could bear, and broke into tears.

The grief lingered, but I continued painting, my salvation, my anodyne, my medicine of forgetfulness, my ecstasy, my journey to the heavens, confessing to my son that I still can't do justice to the intensity unfolding before my eyes.

My wife, Hortense, thinking I was out of earshot, told Matisse that Renoir and Monet knew what they were doing, knew their craft, but that I never knew what I was doing.

So what? Who cares? Only I matter.

It comes from deep within me, from some unknown place, onto my brush, without thought or deliberation. I let it flow un-encumbered, without meddling. Once I expressed myself as living in harmony with my model, my colors, my landscapes—trying to catch passing, elusive moments. I hesitate to use the term, 'harmony.' There is no harmony involved in my art—that implies a balanced separateness, a counterpoint. There is no dichotomy, even a harmonious one. There's only one unity—my landscape, my model, the moment and I, a seamless intermingling—all of a piece—a oneness. Realize that I'm not painting these objects—they are realizing themselves.

With almond trees in full flower, distant hills a rich purple, sky a sparkling blue polka dotted with bosomy clouds, I was not apart from them—they not apart from me—we had joined hands and through some weird alchemy, had become one.

When I painted a bowl of fruit—apples, glistening and waxy—apricots, an exquisite blending of pink, yellow, orange, I didn't want someone to reach inside and take a bite of them. On the contrary, I wanted them to step back—to savor from afar. Like Baudelaire, Zola and Proust who perfumed their prose with the beauty of their words, I wanted viewers to breathe in the subtle fragrance of my fruit, to see how the embracing light imparted an alabaster translucence, to appreciate their beauty, to understand what makes an apple an apple, an apricot an apricot—not to take them for granted—not to destroy them by eating them.

If I had one wish for the world, it would be, *Notice!* Notice everything around you so that you don't miss how rain cleans, yet sometimes destroys; how sunlight warms yet sometimes scalds; how fruits, vegetables and flowers, with the opulence of their shapes and colors, enrich but soon putrefy; how the color and expression on faces can be either salutary or saturnine; how words enlighten or disturb; how nature with its sumptuous and resplendent landscapes can be breathtaking or breath-denying—nothing should escape notice.

Every time I see an apple or an apricot, it's as though it were for the first time. When I see almond trees efflorescing with new spring blossoms, it's as though I had never seen them before—as though as they are reborn, I am too. And with that re-birth comes the ineluctable specter of their brevity and ultimate demise.

In 1906 Dreyfus was exonerated, with full apologies, and restored to the good graces of a repentant Army. Why did I not buy that? Why did I think that the infamous Jewish Syndicate with their bags of gold had bought off *My Beloved Army, My Beloved Government?*

Don't bother me with value judgments. I don't give a rotten escargot for anyone's opinion about honor, truth, and integrity! There are absolutes out there—ask Moses and Jesus—why the hell did I mention that Jew? Those Jews. Are we forever condemned to having Jewish influence in our lives?

Merde!!

Aristotle and Plato, St. Thomas Aquinas, Emmanuel Kant, Jeremy Bentham—all a bunch of windy blowhards—thankfully non-Jews, except for that half-breed Marcel Proust.

What they had to say was just so much bafouillage, nothing more! What did they know of human nature? What did they know of right and wrong? What the hell did Jesus know? Preachy-treacly!

There is supposed to be an absolute truth and integrity and justice out there, but I know differently. They each change with the times, like weather, like seasons. The only truth—indeed the only *honor*–is what my old friend, William, said eloquently—"*to thine own self be true.*" And true I was to my art.

And the rest of you can go to hell—or heaven—and talk a blue streak about right and wrong. Just leave me alone with my art—that is my truth! That's how I demonstrate my integrity! My *honor*!

Even though he was lying through his teeth, what Iago said to Othello about one's good name, means only one thing to me—my art—not my political beliefs or hates or loves. My art—only. That's where my name belongs.

One day a friend brought news that The Imperial Museum in Berlin bought two of my paintings and that The Louvre was next, to be followed by our merit badge, the Legion of Honor. Baubles all! I don't want those kinds of badges so I can lead someone by his nose. Juries are swine—the Beaux-Arts and Salon—abominations all of them!

I no longer believe my paintings will last.

I would like someday to have a studio, to have pupils, but with no program or instruction in painting, to teach them nothing, to pass on my love of art, to take them to view and study masters like Tintoretto, to discuss Sophocles and Descartes, to look at life and nature—to teach them how to tap the *within* from their *own within.*

Though some accuse me of increasing misanthropy, they don't see me at some of my favorite boulevard cafes drinking coffee—or the wine that softens my strong opinions but wreaks havoc with my diabetes—or when peddlers signal one another about how irresistible I find their hungry eyes, that I buy everything thrust in front of me, incapable as I am of disappointing them. To strangers I would offer the flowers and toys and sweets I eagerly buy. I urge them to give them to children because children must be kept happy.

After spending the last six years of my life in my beloved Aix, in a small house I built with a huge studio overlooking the vast plain of Aix, rising with roosters, going to early mass, painting every day in the solitude that enables me, through my art, to explore myself through the myriad changes of the munificent nature of which I'm an integral part, reading my Baudelaire, my Stendahl, my Virgil, my Racine. At nightfall, I visit my favorite olive tree around which I had built a stone wall to protect it from damage, embrace it, speak to it lovingly, for it is indeed a loved one, and it responds silently and knowingly, for it knows all about me, always giving me good advice.

On October the 22nd 1906, I took my last breath of the oils and turpentine that every morning of my life had held such promise, that had so magnificently enriched my life, that exquisite fragrance that must surely be the very air breathed by the gods on Mount Olympus.

CHAPTER 7

Though I've tried in my fiction to understand myriad aspects of the human condition, I've never succeeded in understanding my own anamnesis—as though I had lived before, obsessing me even as a child. As though, how dare the past have gone on without me, as participant, as observer? How could it have been real without my having lived through it?

I peppered my family with obnoxious persistency, asking about what had happened in their past. Ceaseless in my quest, I couldn't blame them for running away whenever I appeared.

No wonder—few people care to remember their past.

And even when they do speak of it, memory, distorted by exaggerations, rationalizations, embellishments, omissions, co-missions, and rich helpings of fiction, is an unreliable guide to the truth, not unlike seeing oneself facing those distorting mirrors at fun houses. Haven't historians quipped that the only thing one can change is the past?

Yet, when I wrote, *Remembrance of Things Past,* it was, to be sure, fiction from which I hoped my readers would extract from that falsehood, some glimmer of truth. Readers know, of course, that they often find truth the more so in fiction than in non-fiction.

In 1902, my friend, Anatole France, wrote a book, *Monsieur Bergeret a Paris,* in which he tried, like me, to describe not the well known facts about the Dreyfus Affaire, but its adverse effect on French society. A classics professor, Monsieur Bergeret and a colleague, the only Dreyfusards in their city, he writes, watch in horror as "ordinary citizens, energized by ... a respect for the Army, to honor that venerable institution," keep breaking windows at Meyer's shoe store, shouting slogans like, "Death to Zola!"

Much of my novel takes place during those seminal years of 1895 through 1905, and despite what I told my friends in that dogmatic way of mine, that politics should be excluded from social circles and the military, everyone, myself included, ignored the advice. It found its way, socially and militarily, into the narrative of my magnum opus, *Remembrance of Things Past.* Swann, a Dreyfusard, measured everything by one's stance on the Affaire, often distressing his fictional friends. Some have called my work the most notable expression of how the Affaire polarized French society.

My book, rather than I, Marcel Proust, should be my measure. I was not writing an editorial essay—it was a novel. I described the varying perspectives of my characters, their prejudices and values, how they impacted events, and reciprocally, how those events impacted them, and what effect they had on relationships. I passed no moral judgments, no value judgments. People behave and misbehave—that's life—I wasn't a preacher or a rabbi—I told it the way it was—and is—and will be. If my characters behaved in a way that resonated or irritated the reader, let him make the value judgment. Novelists should maintain their valued place in society's hierarchy. Above all, we must entertain, but also we should encourage people to question their own pre-conceived notions.

I believe that, but I must add that anti-Semitism in the press, in pamphlets, in posters had reached pandemic proportions and mobilized the street, fueling numerous acts of violence. I was compelled, therefore, to have Swann, at the beginning of 'Remembrance,' quip that the order of reading newspapers and The Great Books should be reversed, that the former be read every few years while the latter, every day.

I was the first Dreyfusard. Though people accuse me of supporting Dreyfus because my mother was Jewish, I was raised a Catholic and that I remain. Actually, I may not have been the first because Bernard-Lazare, the avant-garde-anarchist-intellectual-writer, claims he was. Most interestingly, during the height of the Affaire, he discovered that his Jewishness, once ignored, was now paramount, even vital, wearing it like a badge of honor, wholeheartedly supporting Herzl's quest for a Jewish State—-in the hopes of banishing that blight, that plague, that black death—anti-Semitism.

In my writing, I can't nor won't deal with *honor* as an absolute—it's *relative* to the perspective of each person—relative to that time—periodic, like seasons, sunspots, eclipses, Haley's comet. Today's morality could become tomorrow's immorality. Ultimately, on the time scale of historians—like mercury slipping through our fingers, no one will remember the Dreyfus Affaire and the tumultuous role it played in our lives, except for an occasional reference to one thing or another—for example, the role it had in 1905 in getting our government to deny, *for the first time,* the Catholic Church's exclusive position as the State Church—to give us, like those early Americans beneficially decreed, a separation of church and state.

In retrospect, those events shaped me into the man I've become. But time has capriciously exacted a price for living beyond my youth—ageing eyes, weakened skeleton, wizened but no wiser. Ah, for the gods, our passions, foibles, antinomies, hubris and descent, *everything*, are played as comedy. Damn their perverse laughter!

In time, sooner than later, we're condemned to become faded ink on dried up scrolls stored in the dark, moribund shadows in a dusty mausoleum, in some obscure, undiscovered place, whispering to the uninterested uninteresting stories of people no longer around, if ever they were around. Vague, amorphous glances of people, of a time, of a place that no one cares about anymore, except for perverse patricians and plebeians like me with an uncontrollable, unquenchable anamnesis.

CHAPTER 8

Enough of this already!

I want to understand everything but it's easy to get sucked into these tangential issues. I still haven't tackled Colonel Picquart. My French, though better, is not perfect. So when? Now!

I opened my book as Josiah opened the door. "Hi, Jo," I said happy to see him, "wine and cheese before dinner or are you starved?"

"Both. Wine and cheese sound good first," giving me that treasured kiss of his, glad to feel that the shiver within me had not diminished. He poured the wine as I laid the cheese and crackers on the table.

I liked the feeling that as our glasses touched so did our knees. I didn't waste any time complaining. "Why don't we all speak the same language? It's coming slowly, but it's like I'm slogging through the mud of idioms and nuances."

"Humans are hard wired for language, Sally. It'll come. Be patient," he assured. "You're probably understanding more than you realize," trying to mollify. "But don't worry, sweetheart, Adam is not due for several weeks. Keep up your research, and in the meantime, enjoy the baby's kicks," he said laying his hand on my belly, hoping to feel a gentle kick.

I smiled. "Minor thing—I'm finding that I'm enjoying Grieg's music more and Debussy's less—that bothers me. I love Debussy's Afternoon of a Faun, La Mer, Suite Bergamasque, La Plus Que Lente, his contributions to piano literature. Why should his nastiness affect enjoyment? Art should be an end in itself—politics should find no place there, right?" I asked as though trying to convince the other half of my brain.

"Don't fight it, Sally. For years people have argued about Wagner's anti-Semitism. We can't expect exemplary behavior from anyone, so why should it be different for artists? Except for their astonishing gifts, they're just like everyone else," he said pouring himself more wine. "Geniuses are entitled to a lot of slack so enjoy their contributions."

"Some geniuses, however, might have fueled the Holocaust. I'm supposed to focus on Picquart, but French anti-Semitism has gripped me and I can't seem to satiate my curiosity. I'll get there," I said with a mouthful of cheese, "but I don't want it to color how I look at things. Gotta' remember Polonius. Problem is, I don't know which 'self' is me, so how can I know—to which self should I be true'?"

"You'll get it right soon. Like your French. Stop worrying."

"Ahh, Josiah of the spirits," I said, "aka, Mr. Pollyanna, aka, Mr. Salubrious."

He lifted me gently from the couch, and mindful of my swelling belly, gave me a gentle hug holding his face close to mine without saying a word. He breathed me in, smelling the sweetness emanating from my body, the fragrance of my pregnancy, my fullness, the new life efflorescing within me, our good fortune. Then said, "I'm so glad you fell in love with me."

With a wry smile, I said, "I got the better deal."

"Let me take you away from these musings and show you, while we still can, how we're benefiting from the deal—in equal parts."

"Before dinner?"

"Can you think of a better appetizer?"

Always dependable, Josiah's delicious soporific assured me a restful evening.

This morning, onto Picquart. My room was messy, just big enough for a desk, an oak chair with a cushion, and a bookcase piled high with books resting horizontally. It had an important ingredient—a large window to let in the abundant light I needed to contemplate and write.

On top of the pile was a book on Rodin ablaze with his magnificent Balzac. Los Angeles had some reproductions but nothing like the originals here in Paris.

Maybe just a taste.

Josiah should be home already. He didn't say anything about working late tonight. Why hasn't he called? I need him. I don't know which is more disturbing, the kicking in my belly, or the kicking in my head. With the construction going on in the next building, I can't hear the front doorbell, but no one could open my apartment door without hearing it. When it opens it sounds like doors in a dungeon. It's probably ironwood—no artillery shell could penetrate it. I should lock it before making the salad. With my hand on the latch, the door sprang open. "Oh, Josiah, you startled me! I was just going to secure the latch. Glad you're home, honey! A glass of sherry and cheese before we get started?"

"Sally, who the hell were you on the phone with all day? Adam has been trying to reach you. I was trying. Your line was constantly busy, damn it."

"No one. I haven't spoken to anyone. Let me check." My book on Rodin was open to page two hundred and thirty six.

"Oh, damn—it's off the hook."

"Never occurred to me. I thought you were telling your life's story to someone."

"It's not that long. Adam? Did you say, 'Adam'?"

"Yeah. He's coming for dinner tonight."

"*What? What?* I haven't even started my outline. I'm nowhere. For dinner? I'm nowhere with that either. What the hell!" I felt the beat of my heart everywhere.

"Not to worry. We'll serve him white spaghetti, garlic sautéed in olive oil, Greek olives and chunks of the feta. If he hates it, he won't return."

"With no advance warning? I hate this kind of pressure! He knows me better than that. How dare he?"

"But he did try to call."

"On the same day he's planning to visit?"

"That's probably what he had in mind."

"Merde!"

"You've got that word down pat."

I proceeded with dinner, fuming all the while, the pounding outside and within, unabated. It's 7:00pm and they're still working? I thought I heard something. The transmission of sound at such a low pitch barely made it through our door. With no doorbell, knuckles were needed more than once, and often the flat of a hand. Someone must have let him in downstairs.

Josiah was coming out of the bathroom, so on the way to the door, I whispered, "I'll open the door. Maybe I won't be able to mask what I think of his surprise visit. That might give him some pause about repeating this crap."

I dressed my face with an insincere smile. "Hi, Adam. What a surprise! How nice to see you."

The faux smile didn't register. He said with bonne humeur, "Hi, Sally. I'm delighted to see that your baby hasn't affected that smile of yours."

"Why should it?" I asked in a voice that reflected my attitude at his unannounced intrusion—as well as my vanity.

"Please don't scowl. It's just that women tend to get fatt... heavier, and the face doesn't quite escape that … " he said, realizing he was falling into a ditch.

"But, the doctor is very pleased with my weight! Have I gotten fatter since the last time you were here?" I turned to Josiah. "Have I gotten fatter, Jo?" Without waiting for an answer, I turned back to Adam and asked with more irritation than I should have considering he was my boss. "Does my face look distorted to you?"

He was taken aback by my reaction and said, "Sally, let me start all over. You say, 'bon soir' and I'll say, 'buono notte', or 'di buon umore' which means 'with good humor.'" He paused for a beat, "then I'll give you this bottle of wine without editorializing about your looks—though you look radiant," he said, I suppose sincerely, "we'll kiss each other's cheeks like this," and, pressing his cheeks to each side of my face, continued, "did I get my technique right?"

Even though he was smiling, I wasn't biting. I'm sure he was thinking about whether his apologetic posture had cost him his edge. Before he could continue, and to everyone's surprise—mine too, I said, "In the movies, we retake scenes until we get it right," emphasizing the word 'right.' "Since your first take didn't go well, let's do it over," I said like a director, deliberately omitting 'please.' I grabbed his arm and escorted him out the door. "Enter afresh."

Josiah said, "Sally, cut it out. You're not going to do that, ... "

"Damn right!" closing the door behind him.

Josiah pushed me aside and opened the door. He then said with a 'buon umore' smile,

"Why Adam what a pleasant surprise! And all the way from Italy. Is that Italian or French wine? Are you hungry?"

Adam went along and said, "How nice to see you," kissing us on each cheek. "We should export this greeting to the USA. It's disarming and ingratiating, right, Sally?" he asked with no hint of tremulousness or apology in his voice.

I took a deep breath and said, "Yes, it is a friendly greeting. Let's have some cheese and wine first. We're loyal to France now, so I hope your wine is French," I added with a meager smile.

"Oh, sorry, since you have so much of the French kind, I thought you'd be interested in what the ancient Romans have to offer."

I forced myself to relax and said, "Well then, we'll compare them over the cheese. Josiah, please decant the bottles while I go to the kitchen."

Jo directed Adam to the small table in the living room that had just enough room for six knees. Adam looked at the walls and saw posters of pre-war France—iconic pictures of The Riviera's beach, the Loire Valley and its vineyards, the Arc de Triomphe, the Eiffel Tower, Renoir's picnic scene, Degas's ballet dancers. They helped brighten the mood.

"This cheese is excellent," Adam said, "but I'm having difficulty deciding between the wines. You suppose because I didn't let them hyperventilate?" He didn't wait for a reply. "I'm famished and could make a meal of this cheese, this loaf of bread and wine—made all the more pleasurable with the 'thou' of both of you," he said rolling his eyes. "Do I sound like Omar Khayyam?"

"Only if you also happen to be an atheist, fatalist, *and* wino," Josiah quipped.

"Ah, but what a heart and mind!" he shot back.

Josiah responded, "Thank goodness it doesn't take all three conditions to be brilliant."

"The pasta will be ready in seven minutes," I called out, "al dente the way we like it. Stop eating and drinking. I'm serving the salad first, like we do in the old country."

"Great dressing, Sally. Where do you buy it?"

"It's not from a bottle. Simple, peasant stuff, lemon, oil and salt."

We piffled along while eating the salad. I got up and said unapologetically, "Do me a favor, mop up the dressing with bread. We're going to use the same dish for the pasta, like we do in the old country—peasant style." Oh, I'm so sweet.

From the kitchen I heard Adam, "That's the second reference to 'the old country.' Is she trying to tell me something?"

"No, not at all. She loves Paris and is testing the waters of her mind with the contradiction between what we, in our new country, refer to Europe as 'the old country,' and her allegiance to America in what now appears as her 'old country.' Convoluted enough for you? As for the 'peasant' stuff, Sally is an anti-snob snob, unabashedly proud of her 'peasant' background."

I never mastered the art of small talk and was glad they had lowered their voices. Again, I feel my growing irritation. Brittle when hungry anyway, I know he's going to ask questions as soon as I sit down. I'll change the subject and direct the conversation away from me.

I sat down and said, "The pasta will be ready in two minutes." Furrowing my brow, I asked, "So Adam, how are you finding Italy? The cultural differences? The people? Any progress in reconstruction? What do they think of their conquerors, like you, in their midst?" The word 'conquerors' should resonate with him. "Are they harboring ill will towards us? What about their film industry?" That should keep him off balance for awhile.

With his normal business-like gravitas, he answered, "The war is still fresh with them, as it is with us, but it's hard to equate Italians with Nazis, even though Mussolini was a Fascist and Hitler's ally. People seem downtrodden, but much like Italian/Americans, they're buoyant, spirited, friendly. I've made the transition from viewing them as 'the enemy' to 'partner.' It's difficult putting the past behind—must be even more difficult for them, but if appearances are any indication, they're getting over it, and they show an affection for Americans. The film people are not sophisticated, but they're not amateurs either. They don't go for cotton candy, for superficial smiles and happy endings. They're more realistic than we are as their most recent history condemns them to be."

"Ah," I replied, "but we do fantasy and dreams and aspirations like no other."

"Yes, but there's no reason we can't do it all, especially since television has rattled us, the way it's asked us to reconsider our past certainties."

"I'm finding similar sensibilities," Josiah added, "they're not afraid to film conversation that's more than two sentences long. They give the audience credit for intelligence. The same, right?"

"Yes."

"Adam, maybe at some point, we should trade places, to make this learning process more complete. Hmn?"

"Good idea."

What the hell is Josiah thinking? If that happens, I won't be able to join him. What I'm doing is French, not Italian! Besides, I don't want Adam in Paris looking over my shoulder. When Adam leaves, I'm going to kick Jo in the shins!

"The pasta should be ready, let's go into the kitchen. You'll have to forgive me, Adam, I had no idea you'd be coming tonight so I didn't prepare anything to show you what influence the French have had on my cuisine," I said with a tinge of sarcasm.

"Well, I tried calling all day. Your lengthy conversations must have taken you away from your script. Were you able to do any work today?"

I turned from the pot, stopped adding pasta to his plate and looked squarely at him. He's my boss and has a right to ask these questions, so why is he pissing me off so much tonight?

"After dinner we'll discuss what I've accomplished, if you don't mind, but I wasn't on the phone. It was off the hook. And, you'll be pleased to know I've done a lot of research. I work assiduously by myself, and I might add, without supervision," I said with a taste of vinegar on my tongue masked by a broad smile—not too broad—the taste of vinegar, not too well disguised.

I saw Josiah shifting from one leg to another. He threw me a dirty-look-telegraph with a clear message—*cap your loose wires or I'm going to kick you in the shins if you don't throw your bad manners into the Seine.*

"I know your work habits, Sally," Adam said. "I wasn't suggesting anything different."

Josiah, relaxing at Adam's tone, said, "O.K., Adam let me explain about the pasta. We had no tomato sauce and didn't have the time to make our own, so we're going to present you with one of Sally Apple's ancient Greek specialties dating back to Aristophanes, who, in addition to being a great poet and dramatist, was a fantastic cook! You know that research Sally mentioned? It was to uncover this recipe from one of his ancient scrolls."

"I can't wait to dig in."

"Well, that's a nice pun, but don't rush, we have all night," Josiah said. "Are you going to leave after dinner or stay overnight? You should stay, it's a beautiful city."

I'm going to kick this insensitive husband of mine on both shins—twice.

"I can't. There's a midnight sleeper to Rome leaving at 12:30am so I'll sleep on the train."

I took a deep breath and said, "That should give us some time then," hoping the conversation wouldn't go beyond 11:30, which would be just like him.

"White spaghetti? Seems like an oxymoron. With olives and feta? It's going to be an adventure," he said with 'good humor.'

Ah, the Italian spirit is getting to him. It's a temptation to say, 'Hope you hate it and won't return for months.'

"In those ancient scrolls," I said, "Aristophanes insisted that the feta and olives be Greek, otherwise his recipe wouldn't work. If you don't like his offerings, you can fill up with sourdough bread and cheese," I managed to say with a smile.

He picked at the spaghetti two strands at a time, so I thought I'd take the initiative before he puts me on the defensive. Before I started, he said as though he meant it, "Say, this is a winner! When I get home, I'll have to introduce this dish to my family."

With a disingenuous smile I said, "Great, Adam. I'm so happy."

Damn. My food isn't bad enough to keep him away. "There's more left," I added with a forced smile that was beginning to stretch my jaw muscles into an ache. Maybe he'll over-eat and over-drink, and with a little luck, throw up.

"More wine?" Josiah asked.

Good boy, Jo. That's the one thing you said all night I'm happy about.

"Please. Both wines pass muster. You agree?"

"Actually, they're virtually indistinguishable from one another," I said. "Wine doesn't keep well—an observation I heard from a well-known wine connoisseur whose name shall remain unspoken," giving Adam a nod, "so let's polish both bottles off," sure I'd leave that to them, and if Jo restrained himself, mostly to our guest.

"Adam, I'm going to change the subject from the stomach to the cerebral cortex, so let me bring you up to date."

"Yes, please do. That's why I'm here," he mumbled through a mouthful of pasta.

"None."

"What?"

"There is none," I said as I swallowed hard, looking at him straight in the eyes. "No progress, I mean. Not even an outline, let alone a few pages of a script. An amorphous mass of information clutters my mind. I don't know where I'm going—my compass is spinning all over the dial. With a hodge-podge of disparate voices from the many actors weighing in on the subject, I find myself looking for a piece of dry land on which to start building my framework. And if that's not difficult enough, learning the language has slowed me down. Constantly looking up words is a drag.

"You had mentioned that Captain Dreyfus was buried in Montparnasse Cemetery as well as Saint-Saens—that Proust was buried in Pere Lachaise Cemetery. I wondered why you mentioned those names so I read about them, and then about Cezanne, but not about Dreyfus because you didn't want it to be about him," I went on helter-skelter. He let me go on, a sense of satisfaction, like the wine, warming him, showing on his face.

"Of course, one thing leads to another, and Grieg was mentioned. He was affected by the Dreyfus Affaire—made some career choices because of it, but wasn't conflicted the way Picquart was—his choice was natural to him. Suddenly I'm deeply involved in the lives of people other than Colonel Picquart, my original purpose for being. I postponed tangling with him until I got a full grasp of the language." I went on, "That's a confused sentence I know, but this Affaire was such a seminal event in France and throughout much of the world, that many artists, intellectuals, politicians, and lay people got into the act. Everyone had an opinion! Everyone took sides! From Moscow to New York.

"There was such overt anti-Semitism from the French—from their media, military, government, universities, the church, and from ordinary people, that some historians argue that this was the forerunner of the Holocaust!" I continued apace, hoping he'd get the picture. "This *was* a very big deal, Adam! It *is* a very big deal!"

He kept eating and seemed like he was concentrating more on the food than on what I was saying. That was good because I felt like I was slightly incoherent.

"Monet, Vuillard, Pissarro, Galle, Henry James, Sarah Bernhardt, Marcel Proust, Oscar Wilde, were Dreyfusards. Battle lines were sharply drawn. Degas, Cezanne, Renoir, were anti-Dreyfusards. How does that affect our appreciation of their art, Adam? Does it bother you that some artists have habits and attitudes that are despicable? Dostoevsky was a compulsive gambler and Richard Wagner was rabidly anti-Semitic and cadger. Should we care? Should it influence our attitude towards their art? Should their personal lives be immune from criticism? Are they above reproach because of their major contributions? Should we let it matter? Shouldn't appreciation of their art be the only thing that matters?" I asked, not remembering if I had taken a breath. "Yet how can it not affect our attitude towards their art? Throughout all this, I'm asking myself what in the world does this have to do with betraying your class, your upbringing, your fundamental values, like Colonel Picquart did?"

The mellowing effect of the wine has gone. I find myself leaning forward, both elbows on the table, chin resting on closed fists, less than a foot away from Adam's face, a stream of consciousness streaming from my mouth. I suddenly realized that I had been speaking to him like an adversary. How long have his hands been up like a railroad stop sign waving me to stop?

"Sally, Sally, stop already—you're getting all revved up—like you're taking a personal stake. You should remain at arms-length. You're right. What does all this have to do with Picquart? Why are you bringing in all these other elements? You said something disturbing, "tangling with Picquart." Why did you say that? You're not doing battle with him. Your mind is adrift. Why are you complicating your life and delaying your screenplay that should be based on one person only, Picquart? That's all I asked you to do—I don't care about all those others and their bullshit," he said.

"Adam, for God's sake, IT'S NOT BULL...."

He interrupted, this time an octave higher, "I told you several times, damn it, that I don't want you writing about Jews or about Dreyfus. Enough has been written and said about them. I want this to be different, a story about the factors that cause someone to deny his fundamental upbringing and embrace a contrary position. Write a screenplay about the struggle and its resolution—good or bad, you understand?" he said more like a demand than a question.

Out of the corner of my eye, I saw a worried look on Josiah's face, but I remained undaunted, "Adam, this is not about one person only. Picquart was part of a piece. He was not an end in himself. It's about a culture, a country, a state of being. It's about the army, its lies, its deception, its conspiracy to imprison an innocent man. It's about the over-arching nature of justice. It goes far beyond these immediate acts of injustice.

"It was France's horribly conflicted Weltanschauung! Though you assigned me one small segment of the Affaire, I found the problem to be much bigger."

His dismissive, stolid face, spoke, "Well it's your responsibility to sort this thing out, the sooner the better. I want this project finished before your baby comes, understand? Focus!" With hardly a pause, he dropped his incendiary words, "Remember, Sally, you're not here to sight-see!"

That cocked my pistol. I tried not to lose it, but I did. "What the hell are you saying, Adam? That's insulting, Goddamnit! Do you really think I've been sight seeing, for God's sake?

"This evening hasn't gone all that well, has it? You walk through the door, insult me and make demands. I explain that this Affaire has enormous implications, that I'm trying to learn the language, that I'm trying to distill the key issues from my reading, and all I hear from you are impatient and ignorant demands. You don't know the extent of my struggles trying to understand all the tentacles stretching out from this Affaire, this giant octopus taking me every which way—what it takes to deliver a coherent, well thought out script, one the audience can understand and empathize with!"

"Decompress, Sally," he said through clenched teeth and narrowing eyes. "Remember who I am!"

"I certainly do remember! How can I forget? You're the man who gave me a challenging task because you thought I was up to it. I am! I will be! You need to understand the enormity of your request. You may not have when you first assigned it. You're smart enough to understand what I'm going through!" I said, knowing that I was breaching a wall, but Goddamn it, that's who I am, so he can lump it or dump it.

With unabated anger, I went on, "How I'm trying to grapple with the definition of *honor*, a word we take for granted, but is, in fact, elusive. Can one retain his honor by deception, or by truth? It means one thing to 'Honor Thy Mother and Father' and quite another to deceive in order to retain the '*honor*' of The State or its institutions, like the Army. What does it mean when you receive an academic '*honor*'? When you acknowledge the '*honor*' among thieves?

"It's like Einstein's special theory of relativity—different observers in different positions or hierarchy, see different realities. In my reading, the characters and ideas are struggling for supremacy and I'm trying to assert Picquart's primacy. But right now, my mind is a broken kaleidoscope with all the disparate pieces vying for cohesion.

"In my high school, lining the walls were prints of The Impressionists and I fell in love with them, never realizing that I had idealized them, made them perfect. How could they not be when they created such magnificent works? Also, some of the teachers had an amateur string quartet and my friends and I used to listen to them practice after school. I was introduced to many of these guys, and now I'm finding out they're not gods!

"You've got to get off my back," I said, "give me some time to assimilate all this information which I've hardly tapped yet."

His green eyes turned black. He swallowed his mouthful of pasta, threw his napkin on the table and got up to leave. "I'm unaccustomed to being spoken to in this manner by an underling, Sally. I demand respect from subordinates and superiors. I do have my own *honor* to uphold. There should be no ambiguity in what I mean by that word."

He grasped the door handle and asked—no, commanded, "Do—you—get it?"

I rushed over to him. "Listen, Adam, I don't mean to be disrespectful. You started me on my career and I can never forget your largesse and support. But please understand, I cannot do a half-ass job. There's a supererogatory gene in our family. My paternal grandmother in Turkey was known for always doing more than what was expected of her. I'm proud to say it's been passed down through the generations! It's an integral part of who we Aboulafias are!"

Josiah's face froze. I then realized what I had said. He uttered an audible, "Oh, merde!"

Adam managed a know-it-all smile that looked like a smirk. He sat down again.

"So the truth comes out at last, *Salty*. It's been many years since you deceived your way into our profession, and after all the subterfuge, I finally made you blow it. Your clandestine days are over. I hate people pretending to be what they're not."

I stamped my fist hard on the table knocking over two of the glasses of wine that spilled onto Adam's trousers. I yelled, "Adam, I never pretended to be what I'm not. I only changed my name, that's all, Goddamnit," and threw my napkin on his lap. When Josiah tried to wipe up the wine still running over his trousers, I grabbed his wrist and with a scowl that spoke, 'not now,' he stopped.

Adam ignored the spill, and made no attempt to dry himself off. "If I hadn't come in on you at the hospital where your boss, Frank, was fighting his amnesia and discovered your pretense, you would have foisted off your work as someone else's," he smirked.

"That's one helluva' lot better than foisting someone else's work as my own!"

"You should have told me, Salty. I don't like being lied to!"

"Adam, that was about fifteen years ago. Why the hell are you bringing that up now? Hasn't my output through these years counted? My God, isn't there a statute of limitations on errors, Goddamnit? Is there no such thing in your life as redemption? Maybe it's time to visit The Vatican and seek understanding. You're certainly close enough now!"

"As you know, my dear, I remember everything," he said imperiously, "and I don't need anyone's help in understanding, thank you. Maybe you should consider going to Notre Dame."

I ignored that comment and, unable to soften my response, went on, "Aren't there some things that are better off forgotten or repressed, Goddamnit?"

"You've used the word, 'Goddamnit' several times, Salty. You're using the Lord's name in vain. Isn't that forbidden in the Jewish Ten Commandments?" he asked in a way to get me to acknowledge my religion as well.

Josiah, unable to stop the battle between two warriors, said, "Adam, they're not Jewish anymore—they're part of civilization's patrimony, like the ethical teachings of the Greeks, Romans and Asians."

He nodded slightly. With barely masked disgust, I said, "O.K., you know everything, so what the hell difference does it make?"

"Not the slightest! Just don't ever lie to me again!"

I gave him a flat look.

"So where were we, Salty?" with special emphasis on the diminutive of my real name.

I didn't answer at first. "Let me sort this out by myself. If I become overwhelmed by the enormity of the task, I'll let you know. I've always earned my way and would never take money for doing nothing—that's also in my genes.

"I'll try to focus on the Colonel alone. For the record, I'm about to start my research on him. As I mentioned, this Affaire touched so many lives, broke so many relationships, joined together such disparate groups, was so divisive, provoked so many duels, that it's hard to wrap my head around any one thing. Please understand, Adam, that to do justice to Picquart I have to understand the zeitgeist of the times."

"Is that muddled or what?" he asked.

"Yes, I'd say that's the right word."

"Well, when you're through with Picquart, Salty, you need to start writing. *You need to start writing*."

"Adam, I told you why I wasn't ready, but now I'll give it a shot."

Everyone seemed washed out.

"Do you mind calling me Sally, please? I don't want to have to explain to everyone back home."

"Actually, a couple of people know, but you're pretty safe with the name, Sally Apple."

"Thanks," nodding my head from side to side in disbelief about how badly the evening had gone.

Josiah looked at his wristwatch and blurted out, "Oh, my gosh, Adam, you have forty minutes to catch your train! Shall I call a taxi?"

"No. I'm so energized by tonight's lively and *revealing* conversation that I'll make it. Oh, thanks for your spaghetti recipe. Ciao," he said closing the door behind him.

Josiah and I looked at one another and said simultaneously, "Thanks for your spaghetti recipe?"

"After all that," I asked, "The spaghetti is what came to mind?"

"He did say, 'revealing,' and indeed it was, you idiot!" Josiah said with a thin smile.

"And to think," I said, "he left without even kissing us goodbye."

I brought the dishes into the kitchen. The evening had been a painful ordeal for me, and until I was ready, he knew better than to review it. He knew me well, or so he thought.

After doing the dishes, I asked Jo, "How about a walk?"

"Honey, I can't. Gotta' finish this before tomorrow."

There was a cool, drizzly gloominess in the air, made all the more dreary by lamplights casting amber rays of light on old Empire buildings creating strange shadows, making them appear older and wearier, befitting the checkered history of the city and its inhabitants. I wondered whether Adam felt what I saw on his face—smugness with a hint of prescience. Wondered too, if passersby noticed wine stains on his trousers and thought he was either incontinent or a drunk who forgot to open his fly before peeing.

CHAPTER 9

When I returned, Jo had just finished so I said, "Let's sit in the living room and talk."

He put his arm around me and I pulled away. "I'd rather look at you when we talk."

"Sure," he said, and moved opposite the table.

"Was that a train wreck or what?" I asked.

"Are you projecting?"

"No, not consciously, but that would solve my immediate problems."

"Would you stop what you're doing?"

"Absolutely not! I said with a determination that surprised me. "I'm caught up in this project and had no idea of the cross-cultural damage it caused. It was a huge pustule that had ruptured, spewing its pus all over France."

"Do you wonder, Sally, when the Nazis conquered France, that if a few prominent Dreyfusards had emerged within the police they might not have cooperated so fully in rounding up their Jews?"

"Adam had raised that point, also, and you may very well be right, though I don't see how anything could have stopped the Nazis from pursuing their intended extermination."

"So what are your thoughts, my dear? What *are* you going to do?"

"How the hell do I know?"

"Don't bark at me, please! You know they don't allow dogs in this apartment."

"Oh, for God's sake, Jo, not you too."

"Remember, I'm on your side, even though during your jousting I hardly said a word. You two were going at each other so rapid-fire that I couldn't come to your defense. There was no breathing space."

"Oh, Josiah, have I become fat and ugly, and worse, a harridan?"

"No, you're not fat and ugly. Pregnancy becomes you. For me, it's very sexy, except when your short fuse exposes your sharp-tongue, but you're still my beautiful dragonfly."

"Emphasis on the dragon part, right? Don't answer that. The short fuse part though, wasn't that always my style?

"Yes. Well, not all the time. Don't confuse candor with temperament. It's gotten shorter, your fuse I mean. But tonight you were disrespectful."

"I thought I was just being candid."

"Candid with a dagger in your hand."

"That bad, huh?"

"Yup."

"But he didn't fire me. Why do you suppose?"

"I really don't know. At the studios, people were fired for less. It got pretty close, though."

"That had to be bad for our baby, Josiah. All that adrenaline, that anger—go right to the baby. That can't be good. Maybe the tension I've been under, this confusion in seeking my lodestar, is beginning to get to me. Maybe he's right. I haven't distanced myself. I've become so deeply immersed. I feel for those people. The good ones. What's so fascinating to me is that I can't stop reading about the bad, wondering if people like Cezanne, if under Nazi occupation, might have been part of their killing industry. We lost family, Josiah." I began crying.

"I *am* too close. Maybe I *should* quit the project. Maybe he *wants* me to quit." With each sentence, I could detect a rise in my voice, unsure as to whether I was asking or telling. "Maybe I'm deliberately postponing Picquart?"

"Listen, you've got to stay with the project. In addition to your supererogatory gene, you've inherited the *'never quit'* gene, the 'once you start, you don't leave until you finish' gene. Sleep will help unmuddle your brain, but before that, I've got a prescription that always works. Dr. Josiah Castelnuovo-Tedesco's special elixir ready for immediate injection," he said wickedly.

I relaxed a bit and smiled, "You know, Dr. Josiah, if you hadn't come willingly, I would have bought you."

"How much would you have paid?"

"I would have bartered, a baguette, some feta, a croissant, yeah, that's about it."

"Sold to the lady over there, the one with such low standards."

"So, refresh my memory, Josiah, why did you fall in love with me in the first place? I don't have many redeeming qualities that I present to the world, do I?"

"Sweetheart, we've had a tough day so I'm going to give you a short answer and leave the longer one for another time. Blame that lecherous old Scottish Philosopher, David Hume, who observed that *reason is slave to passion*. Time to go to the bedroom."

He has an early morning shoot and since I'm wide-awake at 5:30am I should be able to do a lot today. I know enough about Colonel Picquart to begin my outline—emphasis on the antinomy of his struggles. Before I begin though, I've got to finish this book on Rodin.

There was another 'Affaire' at the same time, you know, the 'Balzac Affaire,' an unwitting creation of mine, tied, like most everything else in France, to that divisive and polarizing 'Dreyfus Affaire.'

I'm a shy man—timid. Finely tuned to the world around me, to the architecture of living things, how they're put together, their bilateral symmetry, what it is that gives them shape, the emotions affecting those shapes, the wholeness of them, the hollows that unwillingly invade them. All those things I'm keenly aware of, and as I look at them, as I look at a face with such few features—nose, eyes, lips, cheeks, chin—I see all the permutations that make no two faces alike except in rare cases, my fingers twitch with a strange sensation, a tingling—not like they've fallen asleep, but like they're wide awake, like they have a life of their own.

Words don't come easily to me. They're not tactile, not three-dimensional. Clay, marble, plaster, stone, metal, that's where I become eloquent at communication, to satisfy me first of all, and second of all—no, last of all, others. No, there are no others. Me. First and last.

Ah, the beatific sensation of tearing chunks out of a block of clay, molding plaster or wax to conform to my wishes. Chipping at marble or stone, at first aggressively, then, with a surgeon's hand, refining the final shape. The forging of bronze, the finishing and polishing of this weighty metal, durable, impervious to age and weather. Ah, this is what God must enjoy doing the most, the crafting with his hands myriad objects He alone has designed. Look at the beauty of everything on earth—from the human form to the beasts that roam the earth and soar above us—to the shapes and colors of watery creatures—to the sensual shapes of hills deliberately rounded by glaciers to look like breasts—to sharply chiseled mountains—to flowers with outrageous colors and fragrances—to purling streams and raging rivers—to towering trees. What gifts we've been given!

Puny by comparison I know, one of His gifts is to challenge us into giving our perspective on those things He created. With what I like to think is a wholesome mixture of conceit and hubris, and aware of my irreverence and lack of humility, I became a sculptor to interpret—to create—to recreate.

Ultimately, it has become my apotheosis.

I recently finished my statue of Victor Hugo and the avant-garde press was calling me 'the man of the hour.' That's high praise indeed. Though my primary goal is to satisfy myself only, when I heard that, a tingle ran through me. It was great comfort as well, to receive a note from my friend, Claude Monet, saying how happy he was to see my triumph. Despite my assertion that I am the only judge of my work, an artist is never indifferent to the viewpoints of others, so whenever praise comes from an artist like Monet, it takes on special significance. When I now look at my unfinished work, I realize my standards must be even higher.

The Kiss, commissioned by the state in 1888, was finally finished in 1897. Other commissions got in the way, as they often do, because it's impossible for an artist to exist on praise alone. Besides, it took long periods of revisions to finally achieve what I wanted, an evocation of the numinous passion of love—the mystery of a kiss—its sublime fusion. When I finished, the marble glistened flesh-like in its translucency, soft to the touch, blood pulsing through their bodies. I wanted to make the lovers impatient to leap to the next step. I was as proud of that accomplishment as I was of my plaster rendition of 'Balzac,' a commission I had received by the Societe des Gens de Lettres five years earlier.

In 1894, at about the same time that hideous Dreyfus Affaire emerged with its Medusa-like head, I had been given the Balzac commission, and because people have a tendency to draw parallels and associations, prominent people were suddenly linking the two 'affaires.' My friend at the time, Emile Zola, President of the Societe, was undoubtedly responsible for my commission. But, we were no longer on good terms.

My Balzac, exhibited at The Salon, received some glowing critiques, but many critics were trying to outdo themselves in condemning it. 'Ordure and monstreuse,' *garbage and monstrosity,* were descriptions frequently used. Bernard Berenson, the highly regarded art critic, called it a stupid monstrosity. One of the members of the commissioning Societe recommended it be cast in bronze—to demonstrate to future generations how low, in the latter part of our century, the standards had become.

There were groups vying for the privilege of preventing Balzac from being erected as a public monument. I, Auguste Rodin, much to my chagrin, had become a polarizing figure. People were taking sides, like being *for or against Dreyfus and the Army. For or against my Balzac.* How loathsome!

In the spring of 1898, the 'Committee of the Societe des Gens de Lettres' advised me that they had a duty to inform me that they could not accept my sculpture.

Five years of my life!

The stink of Zola's famous letter, 'J'Accuse' on January 13, 1898, pervaded all of France. No one was immune from reeking of it. I was caught within its chaotic orbit. Many artists, composers and writers expressed their displeasure about the decision, hoping that this dreadful 'Dreyfus Affaire,' juxtaposed with the 'Balzac Affaire,' would not lose for France the exalted respect it had among nations. They sent letters of support, and touchingly, they began a subscription to collect money to buy the sculpture and erect it in Paris. Toulouse-Lautrec, Signac, Maillol, Monet, Bourdelle, Renoir, Cezanne, Sisley, Debussy, Anatole France, and Mallarme contributed money. Around the world it became a 'cause celebre' resulting in contributions from surprising sources, an American painter, a Russian Prince, reporters, critics, museum members, and many others.

In the press, during May of 1898, the Balzac Affaire rivaled the Dreyfus Affaire. How dreadful! With the exceptions of Renoir and Cezanne, and possibly Toulouse-Lautrec who had drawn some stereotypically ugly illustrations of Jews, most of the contributors to the 'Balzac Fund' were Dreyfusards. Being associated with one camp or another could lead to ostracism. Whichever side you were on, there was the toxic fear of being "one of those."

I worried about being associated with Dreyfusards. After all, everyone knew there was a Jewish Syndicate plotting to overthrow the government, and I couldn't dismiss the possibility of Zola being their tool. If I expressed anti-Dreyfusard beliefs, most of my supporters would desert me. One of my friends challenged me by pointing out that if I rejected the many subscriptions from those Dreyfus supporters, I would be demonstrating the triumph of genius over character. I had to think about that. Didn't he mean 'the triumph of character over genius?'

It was unthinkable to declare myself either for or against Dreyfus. After all, politics should be kept out of art. There is or should be, *the neutrality of art*, its transcendence over politics. I needed to distance myself from any indication of preference, to remain at arm's length.

By becoming a Dreyfusard, I would be taking a position against my beloved France, the Army, the Church, backbones of our society. This was all a distraction and I loathed its cancerous effect on my country. I want to be left alone. I have one consuming passion, my work. I'm immersed still in the baptismal waters of my passion, not wanting to step out and get involved in worldly matters. My world is my art. I think about it while I dine, sleep, make love, entertain, while I have coffee with friends, go to museums, to the country—while I breathe. Above all, it's in everything I see—animate and inanimate. All else is merde.

My responsibility, indeed my honor, lies in the sacredness of my independence and in my work. I have to preserve my honor. That nebulous word—what does it mean?

I have to remain true to my vision, my vision only, to my perceptions of reality unfettered by political considerations, to make a principled, not an expedient, decision, mandatory for my ethical strength, for my probity. I wanted to maintain equilibrium between genius and character, an equal footing, a balance, something sustainable. Yes, that's honor. No, that's integrity. Are they not opposite sides of the same coin?

I was aware of how art and literature reflect the zeitgeist of society, so I struggled with my conscience, like Michelangelo's slaves trying to escape their marble prisons. I decided to write each of the subscribers and return their money. When I did that, an artist friend of mine said, I was at heart an anti-Dreyfusard.

Edward Degas had become a vocal anti-Dreyfusard, and though he demonstrated in several ways that he didn't like me—when that happens it often turns into a reciprocal feeling—we exchanged some paintings for some sculptures—our tacit attempt at loose political solidarity.

In the meantime, the Societe commissioned Falguiere to do a sculpture for Balzac's centenary. It was banal, predictable and unimaginative. Pretty, and unexpressive!

I remain resolute, however. Balzac satisfied me beyond any work I've created. Yet, ironically, I consider the 'Balzac Affaire' a defeat. We carted the plaster statue back to my studio in disbelief, unable to comprehend the incongruity of it all. It was like someone had kicked me in the stomach. No, rather like a piece of my heart had died.

What a disappointment! I recovered, my integrity intact, and returned to my 'Gates of Hell.'

With welcoming wrinkles, my life continues with important commissions and unconsummated love affairs with many women whom I love and whose bodies remain exquisitely sculpted by that non-pareil Master. When new models disrobe for me, I remain in awe of their shapes, no two alike, never once taking for granted the gift their creation has been to me—to us.

A contentious figure I remain, not surprised to find some critics castigating my work as pornographic, vulgar, too naturalistic, too modern, too whatever nasty word they could conjure. That will never stop, of course, nor will it alter my vision. I satisfy only myself.

The first day Joseph Pulitzer sat for me, he had the temerity to give me instructions about how to portray him. He got my immediate and unambiguous response. *"I will not do what you think I should do, but what I think I should do. Otherwise, don't sit for me!"* You should have seen the look on his face.

In 1916, I had several strokes. At seventy-six, perhaps out of petulance, perhaps out of spite, perhaps out of regret for that missed opportunity when I was younger, when it was fresh, when I was exhilarated by my creation, my Balzac needed to be consummated, to complete the circle. Artists will recognize that. When it had not been, I was bereft. I had seen the Promised Land but couldn't enter. Or to give my detractors something else to gloat over, it was coitus interruptus. I still had not authorized a bronze fabrication for my precious creation. I remained very protective of it. Finally, for two thousand francs, I sold the rights to a retired dancer from the Folies-Bergere.

The sale too was never consummated.

I made a bequest to the state of my works. Drawings, sculptures, manuscripts and personal art collection, to be housed in a special Rodin Musee. Contention again. The *Chambre des Deputes* debated the merit of *'Offering a museum to every French artist. Where will it stop? Who will pay for upkeep?'*

The body of work was estimated at three million francs. Who could ignore such largesse? Three hundred and seventy nine deputies approved, fifty-six did not. I noticed that all the Israelite representatives in the Chambre voted in favor. Before the *Senat* debate, some worried that being unmarried was a serious problem. I was accused of being a decadent bachelor—immoral and revolutionary. On November 9th the debate began.

203 in favor—22 against.

To satisfy all those intrusive, self-righteous, puritanical busy bodies, Rose Beuret and I married on Monday morning, January 29, 1917. Two weeks later, Rose developed a bronchitis that turned into pneumonia, and died.

On November 16th, that same year, before I went into a coma, I recognized that it was not true when once I had said, *'I am like a moon that shines on an immense, unknown sea where ships never pass.'*

No, I realize now that that moon has shone on a vast, shimmering sea frequented by many ships filled with passengers who sailed with me—uncertain—hesitant—towards that inscrutable center of mine—a center I had worked so laboriously to discover and uncover. They now have a clearer sense of who Rodin is.

I wonder though, whether my work will outlive those with whom my work resonated, whether my work might ever become a part of the cultural lives of those as yet unborn.

As I tumble into the depths of my coma, I imagine being laid on a slab of Carrara marble. In my hands, the friends who never betrayed me—my chisels and mallets.

At 4 am on November 17th, as I took a feeble breath, someone kissed me on my feverish forehead. I don't remember exhaling.

CHAPTER 10

"Josiah! You startled me! What are you doing home so early?"

"I couldn't call. Let's pack, honey, we're going on a trip," he said, keeping the important information from me for a few tantalizing moments.

I tried to mask my emotions of having just witnessed a death in the family, so through a forced smile, I asked, "Are we running away from something?"

He kissed me on the forehead and said cryptically, "No, not *from something*, but *to something*."

"Oh, I was going to tackle the big guy, but funny, I'm relieved that I can set it aside for a few days."

"Doesn't sound auspicious, my dear."

"Not to worry. Going away for a few days might help. So, where are we going, or are you sworn to silence? Is it a secret mission behind enemy lines?"

He bent over and whispered in my ear, "Remember, this is only for your ears—and the baby's." Then taking furtive glances, pretending to see if anyone were within earshot, he said, "We're going to Giverny."

"Where? That's where Monet lived, isn't it? Why?"

He grabbed an apple, took a big bite and mumbled through an open mouth that showed what he was eating, something he always did, and though I've gotten used to it, I didn't want to be his second mother, again and again.

"Right. Monet's flowers are still blooming but beginning to fade. The director wants to do a shoot in his garden while he still can."

"Too bad he can't shoot in color. Flowers in black and white look funereal."

"Not enough money."

"Is there ever?"

"We'll be staying at a small house near Monet's. I'll put a chair on the Japanese bridge overlooking the famous water lilies in that pond of his, and you can ponder. That's a pun, right?"

I mirrored his grin.

"That should give you all the inspiration you need. Excited?"

When I said, "How soon can we leave?" he planted an apple-juice kiss on my forehead.

I resisted all warnings about exposing myself, and my baby, to the rain, insisting on sitting on the bridge, watching the rain fall, sometimes gently, sometimes torrentially. When Josiah came to visit and expressed his concern for the tenth time, I said, "This place is magical. It's not meant for writing. It's meant for painting."

"Changing careers?"

I threw him a wet smile and said, "Despite this raincoat, I'm getting drenched and chilled. I'm going into Monet's house. Okay?"

"Sure. We're doing interiors so ask Sid what room you can go to, one with a fireplace. See you later."

With a fire still roaring from the shoot a moment before, I wanted to sit right there, but noticed all those books on his shelves. He was a reader, that man! How can I write with so much to read?

When it got dark, I went to our temporary home carrying several books from Monet's library and waited for Josiah. Clearly spent, he walked into our teeny house that had one small bedroom big enough for a lumpy double bed pushed up against a wall that meant that Josiah had to crawl over me when he needed to pee. I, of course, with a growing baby, had to get to the bathroom frequently and easily. There was a small living room, not much bigger than the bedroom, two stuffed chairs upholstered in what must have been at one time, an elegant silk fabric decorated with a fussy pattern of multi-colored fleur-de-lis that spoke of a Napoleonic past. There was a closet-size kitchen, a two-burner stove, no oven, and small icebox that had been converted into a 'refrigerator' by a noisy motor that sounded like it was not up for even this small job.

Its water supply came from a plumbing system that groaned in pain whenever a faucet was turned on, spurting out water, wetting us in unintended places, because, as Josiah explained, there must be air imprisoned within its pipes. I wished I could grant it a pardon. With a small water heater that gurgled loudly, we had small amounts of hot water with which to bathe and wash dishes. The whole house reeked of mustiness. I realized how lucky I was to live in semi-arid Southern California. Its cracked mirror was okay. I didn't want to see my figure growing stouter by the day. Its dim lighting made it difficult to read after sundown so I was glad we weren't staying through fall and winter, especially since there was no source of heat except for the tiny fireplace.

"Honey, a glass of wine and cheese. I'm starved and need a drink to settle down. You up to it?"

"Sure. You know how rain charges me up." I should have asked him about his day, but as soon as I laid the cheese and stale baguette down and poured him a glass of wine, I started enthusiastically, "Jo, what a man this Monet was! His bookshelves are filled with a wide range of esoterica, and his diaries and letters from friends and critics reveal a complex, political animal.

"Did you know he was a Dreyfusard?"

He raised his hand. "Hold off for a moment, please. Right now I'm interested in myself only. It was a difficult shoot, the director and I were not seeing eye to eye, the actors couldn't remember their lines, there was one interruption after another, the rain never stopped and the tension was palpable, so please, give me a break.

"And to top it off, I can't fully express myself in another man's language. That's especially frustrating when things are not going right. Goddamn language barrier! Why the hell doesn't the whole world speak English?"

"Why are you whining so?" I asked planting a soft kiss on his forehead. "You're in France, mon amour. C'est ca."

He ignored me and said, "Problem is that I think I'm picking up on the rawness and grit of French cinema, so when I saw how the rain made the flowers droop, like in mourning, I thought that close ups would be better, to show that everything was not pretty and perfect, a reflection of what was happening in the story, yet the director wanted a long camera shot to avoid showing that droopiness."

"Like you guys had exchanged roles?"

"You got it," and took a deep breath. "Right now, sweetheart, the only thing I want from you is to hold my hand, and treat me like the baby you're cradling in your belly."

I squeezed his hand but was impatient to tell him everything, so I waited a minute then asked, eyes wide open, "May I now tell you about Monet?"

He looked at me disconsolately and grumbled, "Don't you get it, Sally? I just want you to hold my hand and be quiet while I take some deep breaths and decompress. Quietly. Let the wine do its thing."

"Okay, okay. Don't be impatient," I said trying to hide my disappointment. He wanted to be quiet, I wanted to talk, so I compromised, by whispering. "It's just that I wanted to share what I discovered about Monet, to tell you that now that I have a glimpse of him, how enthusiastic I am."

He looked deep within my eyes, and resigned to my persistence, asked, "So you didn't write anything today—just read?"

"Honey, I didn't bring books about Picquart. I wanted my mind to go fallow before I started the screenplay, so, yes, I read after I came in," I said with chin raised, "and stayed dry, in front of the fire, from late afternoon until now."

"And what do you think Adam will say when he next barges in and finds you've not written anything?"

"Listen, Josiah, SIR, you've had a bad day, but I don't need pressure from you as well," I said, knowing my strident tone wasn't the best way to calm him, "so lay off your questions, okay?"

"Should I try coming in again the way Adam had to?"

This was going downhill, so I got up, went behind him, wrapped my arms around his neck and pressed my cheek against his.

"Am I going to be garroted?"

"No, honey, just smothered to death."

"Either way ... " he said relaxing somewhat. I had learned early in our marriage that hugs had a salubrious effect on him. He soon asked, "Can you have at least a sip of this wine?"

"Better not. I don't want our child to grow up with a taste for alcohol."

"By the time the wine reaches the baby, it will have been converted into sugar and water."

"I know that, but I'll stick with this pecorino. Lots of calcium which we both need, and this sour dough, if not nutritious, certainly delicious, even when it's chewy-stale."

With a mouthful of cheese, I asked, "Jo, we've been in France for a few months, and despite the confrontation with Adam, I'm delighted to be here. After today, I shouldn't be asking you, but how do you feel?"

"Comme ci, comme ca. On the one hand, I could have been told in L.A. to make a film grittier. I know what that concept means, but on the other hand, seeing how the French actually do it—though certainly not today—there is a difference. It puts an empirical spin to it. So, yeah, in a sense," he said, "but I'm treated like an American intruder, not like I had expected, the *superior-American-film-maker*. I can hardly wait for this to be over, for you to finish and have our baby at home. Focus on Picquart, please, stop involving yourself so deeply with all these others."

"My love, I get it, but understand that there's a conflict between my reason and my passion, that I had no idea about the world-wide impact this Dreyfus case had at the time. Queen Victoria was shocked at the behavior of the French Army and public. The Russians were amazed. Kaiser William II, well aware of Dreyfus's innocence, wanted to defend him, but his Chancellor, Bulow, in a display of schadenfreude, persuaded him that having the French ripping themselves apart was in Germany's interest. Our government was appalled because of France's vile actions against a Jew," I went on, surprised at how much information I had gathered, some of it just today from Monet's library.

"Yet thirty five years later," I continued, "before and during World War II the world didn't give a damn about Jews. How in hell did that happen? When the Nazis took over, no country gave them refuge. Even our own country. Hitler proved his point when he said that no one cared about what happened to Jews.

"But the Dreyfusards," I said, "were not just talk—they went out and did something! So," sucked in by passion, I asked, "where the hell were the Dreyfusards in the thirties and forties? How do you explain their absence?

"Jo, I've read volumes about Picquart, but can't stay focused on him alone. It's much bigger than that. How many times have I bored you with this stuff? It's personal as well. We both lost family because of it so I need to understand the *why* behind their behavior. The only way I know how is to become them, to uncover their *germs of propensity*. Be patient, my love, please."

"What germs of propensity?"

"Not now, Jo, later. I'm irritating you, I know, but I'll try to finish before my eighth month."

"And if not?"

"I'll finish while I'm suckling our baby. It won't be the first time a script has been delayed."

"I hope Adam sees it that way."

"Do you have any doubts?"

"Well, the last time we got together, it didn't go well, remember? You were asked to write about honor—are you doing the honorable thing by studying these other guys?"

Before I could answer, he said, "Let's eat already. What's for dinner?"

"Garbanzos and rice. Plus a salad."

"Sounds like what you had as a kid. Why the throwback?"

"For one, meat is very expensive, and right now I have peculiar food habits. Suddenly that's what I was in the mood of, so you're a victim of my whims. A willing victim?" He looked at me blankly, so I added, "Besides, it's nutritious, so don't complain, okay?" making it sound like I had gotten his permission.

When we got to bed, the rain stopped for the first time that day. I went to sleep wondering how long it would take the flowers to resume their vibrant colors and erect posture. The following morning, as I stood at the railing of Monet's bridge overlooking his pond, I stopped breathing. With a barely emerging sun and a light drizzle bejeweling my face with tiny pearls of shimmering water, a wispy fog blanketed everything, me, the water, the flowers, we all were part of a piece. It cast a misty silvery gray to the colors, a moist softness, to the electric blue water lilies—the silky blue, white and gold of irises—the bright canary-yellow calendulas—the blue-purple-white-crowned lianthus trimmed with a crinkly rim of purple—the plectranthus, their tiny lavender orchid-like flowers offering their nectar to competing hummingbirds—the echinacea, purple and pink and violet—the hibiscus, dazzling yellow and bright red—the dianthus in myriad variations of purple and pink. Sunlight javelins struggled to penetrate the fog.

There was no distinct fragrance in the air, but a synergistic composite of multiple fragrances that had been sprayed on all who wandered in the garden by the magic wand of a perfumed fairy goddess. A naiad.

Oh, Claude, no wonder your paintings were so beguiling.

I breathed in the sweetened air and absorbed the sight before me, then began reading. In mid-afternoon, Josiah dropped by, planted a kiss on my forehead and asked, "How's it going?" and continued walking. He did a double take. "Honey? Are you okay?"

"What?"

"You okay?"

"Yes, fine. It's just … I'm absorbed in this man's life."

"Are you going off on yet another tangent?"

"No, Josiah, but I'm living where Monet lived, looking at the garden he so lovingly planted, breathing in the same air he did, as though, as though, I'm inhabiting him. Do you know how special that is for me?"

He walked away mumbling, "Here we go again."

CHAPTER 11

At the end of April 1883, at the age of 43, I wanted to find a permanent residence away from the center of Paris, so I went to the small, medieval village of Vernon situated in a valley abounding with cornfields and poppy fields, and in the distance, hills. I walked randomly through the fields and came upon a tiny hamlet called Giverny. It had a single street, a few houses, and one, a country house with two stories situated on about two and a half acres of wild land, facing the river, an unkempt garden and a weed-congested pond.

I went to the back, sat on a tree stump and scanned the horizon. As the sun coursed through the sky, I watched as shadows altered the landscape, bringing to mind the Greek Heraclitus, who observed that you cannot step into the same river twice. Objects bathed in sunlight never remain the same either.

Yes, I know what I'll do. I'll have six canvases with the same motif in front of me. With the sun, in its slow trajectory, altering everything it illuminates, I'll go from one canvas to another trying to capture these evanescent changes. Because I will be dealing with changing scenes, not static ones, my paintings will capture the momentary and the continuous, thereby giving my work a seamless, palpitating fluidity. Yes, this place will afford me unlimited possibilities to explore the metamorphosis of everything. I rented the house immediately.

Color is as vital to me as the breath I take. I can no sooner paint monochromatically as hold my breath for a month. Hills are sometimes violet, sometimes spinach green. Flowers change from saturated brilliant splashes of color to soft pastel. Clouds, often violet soon discolor into gray. Air itself, never transparent, is bathed in the reflected light of its surroundings. Trees, fogged with blue and pink. I see everything in color. Alice's hair, the pinkness of her children.

Through the years, I painted at different times of the day, during different seasons, thirty canvasses of haystacks and thirty of the

Cathedral of Rouen. My series of twenty three 'Poplars on the Bank of the Epte,' was rich with violet, rose, yellow, green, blue, gold, and combinations of each, mostly brazen and brilliant, while some were muted, subtle, suggestive. When I finished, it was clear to me, as I hoped it would be to others, at what time of day or season the painting had been executed. These paintings became my pagan solar dial and calendar. The process and its completion brought me great joy, and, frustrated as I was at times by trying to capture those elusive moments, when I did succeed my lungs filled with an exquisite, exhilarating, and exultant fragrance that blushed my cheeks as well as my spirit.

Irrepressibly exuberant were the colors of spring, summer and early fall, metamorphosing into the morbidity of winter. Ah, Shakespeare's The Seven Ages of Man. Living and inanimate things disrobed unashamedly before me, permitting me to see them in all their guises, their mercurial moods, their responses to snow, wind, rain and clouds, beaming with joy and innocence when looking directly at the sun, drooping gloomily under rainy skies—at their birth and at their inevitable death—witnessing their life cycles—all their caprices displayed before me in an astonishing, magnificent, awesome *Folies Bergere* extravaganza.

I saw God all around me. Not the personal, bearded gentleman of myth, but a pantheistic one. Yes, there was evidence all around me, and I tried, with the tools available to me, to reveal Him. The way my French contemporaries like Saint-Saens and Ravel and Debussy are doing now, and in their time, Mozart, Beethoven, and Bach.

I was influenced by Hume's Law that drew a sharp distinction between 'what is' and 'what ought to be,' so I remained busily engaged in exploring my vision of 'what is', as *I, Claude Monet,* and no other, saw it. My house and garden in Giverny became my refuge, my escape, my shelter, my sanctuary, and above all, my visual paradise. My art was my compulsion, a source of great satisfaction, especially when it became the 'ought to be.' Sometimes, as I stepped back and looked at a finished canvas, I couldn't help thinking proudly, 'Mon Dieu!'

I had no patron, regrettably, but after many years, I had two important dealers through whom I sold my work, to those few who shared my vision. Of course, that was the necessary ingredient enabling me to continue my profession. Beyond compulsion, to continue enthusiastically, reality demands that one has to make money. And I did, lots of it, but much later.

In the late 1880s and early 1890s, Theo van Gogh was one of my most important dealers, as he was for my friend, Camille Pissarro, so I was crushed when he wrote that his brother, Vincent, had committed suicide in July 1890. One doesn't recover from that easily. It's bad enough to die of an uncontrollable illness, but to die by one's own hand is anathema to me. Suicide is an incomprehensible act—such a permanent solution to a temporary problem.

Perhaps his problems weren't temporary, but what do I know of the irresolvable horrors that may lie within? I slowly recovered from that news and went back to work, only to be crushed again when just a few months later, I learned of Theo's breakdown in October, and death in January 1891.

Life does go on, the cliché reminds us. I've never been one to dwell on the unpleasant, nor especially on death, though it took a long time to recover from the death of my beloved first wife, Camille. Painting for me has always been an anodyne. Concentrating on what I'm doing leaves no room for extraneous thought. Immersed as I am in my art, I focus so intensely on what I'm seeing that the passage of time loses its significance—its place—its meaning—except, of course, for the influence it has on color, on shadows.

I recovered and flourished, but I was also a Frenchman with political cares for, and responsibilities to, my beloved country. The Dreyfus Affaire had become a cause celebre, and I couldn't be indifferent to that hideous travesty of justice. So unlike Saint-Saens or Rodin, I didn't object to crossing the intersection between art and politics.

For several years I had been out of touch with my old friend, Emile Zola, but as soon as I read his "J'Accuse," I wrote him congratulating him for his courage, his erudition, and for his admirable rectitude. An old anarchist friend of mine, Camille Pissarro, a Sephardic Jew, praised Zola as well for 'his nobility of character.' We, along with Signac, Vuillard and Cassatt, supported him and signed on to the *The Manifesto of Intellectuals on Behalf of Dreyfus.* After all, to save the soul of France, Zola was committing his fame and fortune to right this grievous wrong by demonstrating how his concept of justice overrode his dislike of Jews. What does that tell you about him?

Though I think Marcel Proust's mother was Jewish, he never considered himself one, yet he wholeheartedly supported Zola and Dreyfus, believing that one's racial status should not determine one's political position. The only thing that mattered was the integrity of that position. Swann, one of the principal characters in Proust's 'Remembrance of Things Past,' based his assessment of friends—esteem or disdain—by establishing a new criterion for himself—that of 'Dreyfusism.'

Renoir, on the other hand, an artist whose paintings I admired, was openly anti-Semitic. He was quoted as saying that there must be reasons for the expulsion of Jews from every country, that he was going to wash his hands of Jews, to have no further contact with them, including his Jewish patrons. In 1882, even before The Dreyfus Affaire precipitated the polarization of French society, he refused to show his work with "that Israelite, Pissarro," as he called him, because to exhibit with him 'meant revolution.'

Degas and Cezanne were anti-Semites, quite vocal—verging on the rabid. I don't believe, however, that an artist's work should be invalidated by a political litmus test. Unless one is making a political poster or caricature, or composing a rhyme with a political theme, art should be sans politics. But even Pissarro, trying to make a political point, painted some people as having Jewish faces with stereotypically large noses and fat bellies. On the other hand, there are artists, like Goya, who deliberately created art works with explicit political themes, as did the cartoonist, painter and illustrator, Daumier. With few exceptions, no one could accuse the impressionists of similar behavior.

I've resolutely believed that artists have a profound obligation and responsibility to their audiences, whether they be readers, listeners or viewers, to give them the very best vision they have, the very best aesthetic, without viewing it through the prism of their political views. But conversely, the audience has an obligation and responsibility to the artists not to measure their art by how the artist behaved personally or politically.

Between the two, a dichotomy must exist.

The audience must consider the art, *qua* art. Is it worthy of esteem and respect? Does it come from the very marrow of our souls? Does it register as a creation of un-compromising probity? And that basically should be the *definition of honor—its requisite.*

Despite that, during the Dreyfus imbroglio, I was so distressed at the way many Frenchmen were hissing their venom against Jews and their supporters, so offended at the false accusations against that honorable man, so outraged at the dishonest behavior of French Army Officers, that I left my beloved France to spend several years in England, hoping that in time, my countrymen would recognize the extent of their misdeeds and elevate themselves to those noble ideals we hold so dear.

I was no Picquart, you understand. I didn't have his struggle, and struggle vigorously he did to prioritize his values. Like Grieg, I found within me no fundamental conflict. And since all artists are egotistical anarchists at heart, it's easy for us to believe in the virtue of truth over allegiance.

While in England, and upon returning to France, I continued with my first and only passion, painting—its undisguised goal? *Does it please the eye and stir the senses?* I dreamed that my work would someday, of an unsuspecting viewer, *'elevate the soul, fortify the spirit, intoxicate the senses and paralyze the powers of the mind.'* I forgot who said that.

I continued sedulously with my painting—my métier, and though I didn't consciously strive to achieve what the author spoke of, deep within me, I hoped it would do all of that.

Early on, during the 1870s, we Impressionists were a cohesive group, more or less, strengthened, as are all groups, by rejection and ostracism, and in our case, by the French Salon Juries. Within a decade, over-arching political and social issues, and attitudes towards the French Jewish population frayed our loose bonds. When the Dreyfus Affaire raised its monstrous head, the fault lines became sharply delineated. Degas, Renoir and Cezanne, trashed Zola's letter and attacked him and his supporters. Renoir savagely fought with Berthe Morisot. Cezanne and Degas stopped speaking to their former friend Pissarro, friends for over a quarter of a century. Why from time to time they even painted alongside one another! Degas once was one of Pissarro's biggest champions, but now, he disparaged his art. When reminded that he used to be one of Pissarro's most ardent supporters, he was quoted as saying that "*that was before the Dreyfus Affaire.*" Mary Cassatt, a vocal suffragette, knowing that it might mean a rupture with her friend Degas, came to the support of Zola. He stopped talking to her as well.

It was painful to see the triumph of politics over shared aesthetics. At the close of the nineteenth century, the ties that once bound us vanished, and the Impressionist movement collapsed. That wasn't the only reason, of course. Degas, Renoir and Cezanne were anchored in tradition, whereas the rest of us were open to the new, the scientific, thus provoking derision.

During that troubled time, I judged the output of our group not by their political posture, but only by their work. Amongst some of my colleagues were vocal misogynists, but I didn't share their gender based elitist attitude. Women's points of view and their take on society fascinated me, but the loss of their unrealized potential shocked me. When I read Tolstoy's Anna Karenina I recommended it to everyone. In Scandinavia I saw many of Ibsen's plays, interested as I was in the perception that others, besides the French, had of the human condition. When I read about Maxim Gorki's arrest by Tsarist police, I immediately signed a petition of protest.

In December 1919, Renoir died. I can't begin to describe what grief that caused me. He takes a part of my life with him. For three days I've re-lived the years of struggle and hope of our youth. He once told me that the happiest days of his life were from July 1866 to December 1867, when he and I shared a studio on Rue Visconti—how we traded our paintings for bags of beans which we used to pay the rent, pay our models their fees, buy coal to keep them warm—and cook our beans.

It's difficult remaining alone. Many of my old friends have died, but some of their works, a part of their supreme contribution to France's patrimony, grace my bedroom, artists like Morisot, Renoir, Cezanne, Callebotte, Degas, Pissarro, Manet, Boudin. Among these are three paintings Renoir did of Camille, one of which was of her with her son, Jean, in the garden of Argenteuil. Before I go to bed, I visit each of these paintings, these dear old friends of mine, and when I put the blanket around me, I'm overcome with happiness, yet with much longing.

I approach the end of my days on this glorious planet with my sight, my precious sight, the sine qua non of my profession, my very life, waxing and waning. Though I thought that there was no such thing as black in nature, during periods when my eyes give out, I know for the first time that there is such a thing as black. I've painted the twilight and dawn before, yet I have never painted darkness. Despite a growing impatience with my doctors' efforts, they succeeded in restoring my sight, and so, once again, compulsively, with a sense of urgency, I continue to paint, and this time, my 'Grand Decoration' and the great cycle of 'Nymphaes.'

At eighty-four I could see out of one eye only, and that, mercifully, because of the glasses I wear. Despite that handicap, one of my friends told me what I have known all along, that my colors are as true as ever. Another old friend of mine, the statesman, Georges Clemenceau, said that I had not only retained my creativity, but in these panels, I had reached new levels. I knew though, that in the shrinking of my days, in that soft golden glow of a setting sun, I needed to tap into whatever reservoir I had remaining, to do the very best I was capable of doing.

There, at Musee de L'Orangerie, in each of the several elliptical galleries, can be found one continuous, uninterrupted spectacle of water, transparent and shimmering, islands of lilies and irises, reflections of willow trees and clouds and sky, those things of sublime beauty that have enriched my life, my world at Giverny, my Eden, my Arcadia, and for the non-believer that I am, my earthly paradise.

One of my friends described my work as a great pantheistic poem. And indeed, I do want it to be a place for contemplation of the wonders of the world, a place for personal reflection on the gift of life that has been bequeathed to us, a place where one ultimately understands that life is ephemeral, that we must protect—indeed it's a responsibility—an imperative—to preserve and cherish what we have, that nothing in life should be taken for granted. Is it too hubristic to think of it as a shrine to life?

I want to finish these paintings before I die. But I want to die before the Musee is opened to the public. And I did.

On December 5, 1926, at the age of eighty-six, in my bed in my beloved Giverny, I took my last breath of air and found it redolent of vibrant colors—blue-green, burnt orange, canary yellow, violet and lavender, rose and vermilion, all pulsating—colors metamorphosing from their most brilliant in the luminous bright daylight to their gradual attenuation as twilight and nightfall came upon me, and, as is the nature of death with its tenebrific inevitability, displaced the vital forces of life within me.

CHAPTER 12

Now that we're back in Paris, it's the Colonel. How many times have I said that? No more tangents. No more side-trips. This is the pivotal guy, the guy you're supposed to be writing about. Keep reminding yourself of what Josiah suggested. The air that Picquart was inhaling at the time, begin to breathe it in.

My upbringing as an Alsatian Catholic and the career I chose as a military officer predisposed me towards a disdain for Jews. After the trial that found Captain Dreyfus guilty of treason, I watched his public humiliation as they ripped off the trappings of his officer's insignia. I thought, quite rightly though somewhat maliciously, 'Just like a Jew. Even now he must be calculating how much money he lost when he went to the tailor.'

Within my circle, it was axiomatic to believe that there is not a Jew who doesn't have a few convicts in his family. As Dreyfus's teacher, I never took kindly to him, and during General Staff meetings it was difficult for me to veil my dislike. With good reason, it turns out. He was a traitor to our beloved Republic!

The literary critic and poet, Charles Maurras, said it best when he said, "Jews are not true Frenchmen and are therefore unworthy of the trust the Republic put in them. Those misguided people who are defending that traitor are staining the honor of French justice and of the Army, just as Dreyfus has done."

Yes, indeed, everyone understands what honor means. Honor is an absolute. There should be no doubt in anyone's mind about the importance of retaining one's honor, personally and collectively—our raison d'etat as a country with our beloved French Army as its protector. There should be no ambiguity here. His despicable behavior tainted us all!

My name is Colonel Georges Picquart and in 1896, after the death of my superior, I was appointed Chief of Military Intelligence of the French Army. Ambition has been my constant companion, and achieving this position, one of my major accomplishments. My superiors, in their unquestionable wisdom found Captain Dreyfus guilty and that was good enough for me, except that—except that—I pause because the evidence against him seems meager. Anyway, he's a Jew, so what could you expect of him, or for that matter, of us?

But now that I'm seeing all the intelligence reports, unfiltered, it's becoming clear that military secrets are still flowing into the German Embassy. It appears that Dreyfus had an accomplice. Ah, hah! Traitors are a despicable lot. Dreyfus shouldn't have been sent to Devils' Island but shot immediately! I need to check all the past documentation to see if I can spot his accomplice. I'll get that piece of merde! I'm smarter than all of them.

By the end of the day, however, just before my eyes began to glaze over, I noticed something suspicious. Handwriting in the bordereau, the letter irrevocably implicating Dreyfus, was remarkably similar to letters written by one of our officers, Commandant Esterhazy. It seemed unbelievable at first—I sat there pondering. As a good intelligence officer, I knew that my pre-conceived notions had to be dismissed. So amongst other things, I decided to look for motivation. I checked Esterhazy's finances, and to my astonishment, they were a shambles! Gambling, dubious liaisons, mistresses, huge debts, shady business deals—the makings of a spy selling secrets for debt relief? Typical! How dare he? I see how superior I am in so many ways.

And Dreyfus? From a well-to-do family, a loving father and husband, living modestly but comfortably. There were no financial improprieties. Since money then could not have been his motivation, what was?

Upon further investigation, however, Esterhazy was considered a friend of Jews, often acting as their second in duels, protecting their honor. Then I discovered he was a friend of Maurice Weil, a corrupt Jew, like all the others of course, peddling influence in high places, who presented Esterhazy as a friend of Jews. Not only that, I discovered that the Grand Rabbi came to Esterhazy's defense for having defended Jews from scurrilous attacks. With that kind of approbation I was confused, but soon I discovered that this kind of behavior turned out to be yet another source for quenching his craving for money. But what did this have to do with spying? Not everyone who needs money becomes a traitor.

My commanding officers asked me not to continue with my investigations. I've always been respectful of my superiors and didn't want to be insubordinate. They warned me about those devious Jews, about the machinations of the Dreyfus family to help exonerate him. If I continue to pursue this investigation against Esterhazy, am I going to be accused of receiving bribes from them? Everyone knows they use their prodigious amount of money to corrupt the irresolute and vulnerable. After all, knowing how I've always felt about Jews, if I now assume a posture that can be perceived as helping Dreyfus, that I've suddenly changed my mind about him, surely some will think it must be because I've been bought.

My superiors have said implicitly, well almost explicitly, that if Dreyfus were found innocent it would be devastating for the honor and standing of the French Army. I'm troubled by their hints to let it stay buried. He was found guilty and sent away, that should be good enough. And yet, could this be a massive cover-up? I have to be respectful of them and the Army of course, but if I pursue this matter, I may find that I might lose that respect. The Army has been my life. If I lose respect for its institutions, I would lose respect for myself.

At the war college I studied deontological ethics about the nature of duty and right action, about moral obligation, which was all well and good. I knew about duty. The part that always troubled me, however, was that it indicated that duty, right action, and moral obligation were *without regard to the goodness or value of motives or the desirability of the ends of any actions.*

How could they be moral, how could they be 'right action,' if the goodness of the motives, or the desirability of the ends are excluded? Right action, goodness, and morality, like honor, are absolutes.

Are we not messengers of God's words? God is the source of morality. Who else besides God makes those determinations? Who else could define those concepts? In the eponymous Kantian Ethics, he wrote that compassion in helping someone doesn't qualify as a moral action—only helping someone out of a sense of duty qualifies—that compassion implies an emotional component that is morally unacceptable. Motivation has to be part of the equation for a morally sustainable act, but motivation without emotion. Morality has to depend on an act of will. Kant argued, therefore, that the maxim should be that the Good Samaritan behaves morally only if he believes that it's his duty to do so.

I struggled with that at school too, but since duty has always been my calling and I never had a personal conflict with that concept, I stopped thinking about it. Except, and there's always an 'except' with me, if there's a duty to always tell the truth, yet at the same time, there's a conflicting duty to protect a friend or the Army, Kant doesn't show me a way out of the dilemma.

How dare I argue with such a towering figure as Immanuel Kant? Yet, when he says that truth, compassion, sympathy, and pity are irrelevant to morality, that they are in conflict with duty, it sticks like a bone in my throat.

It's stone cold in this room. Why are the palms of my hands so moist? Why do I feel a bead of cold sweat gathering on my brow? This gardenia on my desk has wilted and smells putrid. I told that baboon I needed a fresh one every other day.

The big question that looms before me now, the very big question that will help define me as a person I can respect, Kant aside, is whether my duty to tell the truth supersedes, or is superseded, by my duty to the Army and my country. Am I good enough to let the truth prevail? Do I have the mettle to stand by my convictions?

Ahh! It was such a heady time to become Chief of Army Intelligence and how quickly the euphoria wears off. I cannot skirt my responsibility, but by ignoring it maybe I can. That, however, would be out of character for me.

Must I act according to Kant's categorical imperative, to act in such a way that, if it were in my power, my act would qualify as a universal law, that it would be beneficial to mankind? Even if it's inimical to the Army and the State?

There's always a price to pay.

To hell with Kant! I was raised to tell the truth, not out of a sense of duty which can be defined any which way, but because it's the right thing to do!

By what authority do I know it's the right thing to do?

My own, by God!

Ahhh! The fragrance of fresh gardenias seems to clear my sinuses. Ever since I was a young man, even a whiff seemed to help me compartmentalize complex issues, to sort them out clearly. To others it was cloyingly sweet, but to me it was perfect, never failing to have a salutary effect on me. This time though, I'm unable to sort out the issues clearly. I can't determine whether I'm on an uphill or downhill trajectory.

I'm not that far into my investigation that I can't put it away without damage to my reputation. Yet our agents report that the Germans are still getting some of our secrets. There's somebody else inside us. Some tubercular worm.

I read an article in *Le Matin* that unsettled me further, about a classmate of Dreyfus, Bunau-Varilla, who presented the newspaper a photostat of Dreyfus's putative incriminating letter to the German attaché in Paris, alongside a letter Dreyfus had written to him a few years earlier. There was no resemblance in the handwriting whatsoever.

Edouard Drumont, his anti-Semitism pluckingly ripe, wrote a pamphlet, *La France Juive,* denouncing Jews. It sold 200,000 copies! He later formed the *Catholic La Libre Parole* and the *National Anti-Semitic League,* condemning the army for allowing Jews in its midst. He became the leading spokesman for all those who hated Jews, all *those who could never accept that Jews could be Frenchmen as well.*

The General Staff wants me to drop the investigation. That elephant, living on my shoulders all these years, has come to life again. Polonius's recommendation to Laertes. Others through the years have struggled with that command. The question, forever unanswered, is which "self"? My disdain for Jews? My loyalty to the Army? My love of France? Obedience to my superiors? My allegiance to the truth? They're all part of my "self." How "true" to my "self" can I be? Must I establish a hierarchy of 'selfs,' a hierarchy of values?

Am I about to slip on ice and break my neck?

I can't let an innocent man rot away on some island while the guilty wallow in their squalid success. I don't even view the matter, as some have suggested, as being an immense moral responsibility. For me, it's a simple decision. Innocence is just that, while guilt is just that. I can do no less.

But, is that my only motivation? If I were to expose Esterhazy for being the traitor and thereby exonerate Dreyfus, it would be, as a counter-intelligence officer, the premier coup of my life. If I did not, sooner or later, Mathieu Dreyfus, that redoubtable brother of his, with all his friends and money, is bound to uncover the cover-up and expose my superiors, stealing my thunder, stealing from me what rightfully should be mine, if I did my job right. What would happen to my reputation if someone other than I, the Chief of Intelligence, solved the riddle?

Before I leave for the day, I'll ask my aide to get an entire bouquet of gardenias, to have them on my desk tomorrow.

I let my quandary lie fallow and continued to amass more evidence against Esterhazy. During that process, I discovered that nothing was lying fallow after all, for my subconscious had already reinforced its earlier decision.

I persisted in presenting my case to my superiors, to have Esterhazy charged with espionage, which, by implication meant exonerating Dreyfus. Some of my superiors, through their facial movements, their eyes, their raised eyebrows, their smirks and sly smiles, led me to believe that they doubted the purity of my motives.

I knew I was on the right track about Esterhazy's guilt, and about what I now suspected was the General Staff's conspiracy to frame Dreyfus, when in the late fall of 1896 they advised me, in a beautifully nuanced performance letter praising my skills and intellect, that I was to head a special mission to the Eastern Front, the Alps, and finally to Algeria and Tunisia. Those North African countries had the reputation of being amongst the most dangerous of assignments.

Commandant Henry replaced me. Henry??

Especially attuned to danger, abroad I found that my senses were even more highly sharpened, only this time, I was especially wary of what was going on behind me as well.

I survived. During a brief leave to Paris in April 1897, I came to the crushing conclusion that in addition to my superiors, many of my comrades had become my enemies. I worried that key documents had been destroyed or squirreled away. The General Staff commanded me to return to North Africa, but promised I would return to my prior duties in December. That promise was not worth the price of a week old baguette.

This was worse than I thought.

Intelligence Officers are trained to be suspicious of everything, characteristics that come naturally to me. During my leave, in anticipation of a dire ending, I wrote my last will and testament stating the reasons for my belief in Dreyfus's innocence and Esterhazy's guilt, that in the event of my death, it should be handed *personally* to the President of the Republic.

In June I met with my friend and lawyer and told him everything, holding nothing back about my discoveries. He asked me whether I had been in touch with the Dreyfus family to which I responded, that I refused to have anything to do with the family, that I neither liked them nor trusted them, that I had no intention of cooperating with any Dreyfusards, and that they were frustrated by my lack of cooperation and my dislike of them. Not only was that a true representation of the situation, but also in back of my mind, I knew there's always a conflict between appearance and reality, so I told him that I never wanted there to be even an appearance of impropriety.

That didn't matter—the truth didn't matter. Many of my superiors, having railroaded Dreyfus, were certain I had sold out to the Dreyfus family. To prove their premise, they processed my accusations and put Esterhazy on trial on January 10, 1898. They called me to testify, but insisted that I wear my sky blue jacket typical of Algerian sharpshooters rather than the black jackets of the other officers. I appeared like an inappropriately dressed iconoclast, an outsider, an untrustworthy, disrespectful officer.

The mood during the trial was tense, fear and anticipation almost palpable, small groups whispering to one another suggesting shared secrets, everyone avoiding me as though I had returned the leper. The General Staff, ramrod imperious, was afraid of having my deposition made public, declaring that military witnesses and experts testify secretly, away from the scrutiny of the press, to suppress any indication that the Army had ever made a mistake, proving to me once again that my original theory of a conspiracy to frame Dreyfus was sound.

I was unwilling to display fear, so with little modulation in my voice, as though delivering an academic paper, I testified about the facts leading to my accusation of Esterhazy, boldly naming members of the General Staff I thought were implicated, knowing full well that at that moment, I was committing suicide.

I was interrogated so fiercely that one of the magistrates, Commander Rivals, intervened saying that since I was being made to appear like *I* was the *defendant*, I should be permitted to present everything in my defense. That motion was vetoed.

The trial lasted two days. When at 8:05pm the judges rose and repaired to their chambers, everyone in the courtroom rose with them. I proceeded to go to the men's room, but all the other officers sat down. I too sat down. The only tension in the room seemed to be mine.

At 8:10pm the doors of the chambers opened and as the judges went to their seats, the public was allowed to enter. My throat was Sahara-dry.

Commander Esterhazy was acquitted!

Above deafening applause, I could hear, "Long Live the Army!" "Long Live France!" "Death to the Jews!"

In a continent dominated by German Chancellor Bismarck, France was just a meek presence. The memory of the 1870 Franco-Prussian debacle was ever-present, our hatred of the Hun manifest. Yet, our blue-coated, red-pantalooned Army, guarding our most precious ideals, had been for me the beacon on the hill.

Prevalent amongst those officers present is the belief that Esterhazy's guilt is unimportant by comparison to maintaining the illusion that the Army of our Third Republic is the untarnished guardian of those things we Frenchmen hold dear to our hearts. Love for the Army is paramount. In addition, nothing can be allowed to sever or even blemish the bond between Russia and France. Our Franco-Russian Alliance must prevail. The bulwark against Germany!

Upon leaving the courtroom, Mathieu Dreyfus, Captain Alfred Dreyfus's brother, made his way towards me. He extended his hand but I refused to extend mine. He thanked me for my previous help in trying to exonerate Alfred to which I tartly replied, "You have no reason to thank me. I was obeying my conscience."

I was crestfallen and left with a quick stride as though I had won the day, but overwhelming me, though imperceptible to the outside world, was a new attitude towards my beloved Army, one that reflected an altered view towards my corrupt, anti-Semitic superiors. They who were willing to compromise their integrity, honesty and honor a second time, to perpetuate their first blunder, betraying the ideals of our nation, and tangentially, Napoleon's assistance to the Jews. For them the honor of France had been preserved! Suddenly, the protean nature of honor was put into sharp focus, a concept that I was now seeing as having contradictory elements. That word for me was becoming bereft of meaning. I imagined my superior receiving an invitation to a ball requesting "the *honor* of your presence". What nonsense! The *honor* of having a lying, deceitful, perjurer?

What merde!

France had been the first European country to award full civil equality to the Jews. There were always those in greater or lesser numbers in every society, though mostly greater in ours, who believed that with full equality, Jews, that foreign and menacing force, were determined to take over the government. Much of our press and the public were calling openly for "Death to the Jews!"

At one time, the newspaper, La Libre Parole predicted that the Jews, by presuming to consider themselves the equals of Frenchmen and thereby competing with them, were preparing the most fearful disaster that ever marked the tragic history of their race. For the anti-Dreyfusards, made up of rabid anti-Semites, much of the media, the monarchists, the clerics, and the numbed and ill-informed citizenry, Esterhazy's verdict was vindication of the purity of the Army.

The Dreyfusard movement, drowning in despair, dropped to the bottom of a polluted chasm.

I was crippled by the verdict. I saw the architecture of my life, my sense of fairness, of justice, and of my naive belief that we are beholden to higher values, crumbling. My focus was off. Vertiginous and immobilized, I couldn't escape the gloom that enveloped me like a tightly woven veil.

The following day, I was arrested.

On January 13, 1898, three days after the verdict, I was shocked to read Emile Zola's "J'Accuse" published in the *L'Aurore* newspaper. In two hours, it sold 200,000 copies. It was a systematic disclosure, in detail, with a timeline, of all the calumnies directed at the innocent Dreyfus.

Zola supports my thesis? But I knew him to be an anti-Semite. His novel, "L'Argent" was, as I remember, about Jews and their financial conspiracies bringing down the Union. He viewed Jews as stubborn, cold-blooded conquerors, determined to gain sovereignty over the world. And, in the wake of our defeat in the Franco-Prussian War, didn't he write the novel, "La Debacle" in which he talked about "those low, preying Jews"?

He had not been alone. All the intellectuals seemed to be alarmed at the rapid rise, economically, scientifically and culturally of all those high achieving Jews of France. Did he too ignore his fundamental beliefs to set sail, as I did, with truth as his North Star, towards reversing a grievous error? What was behind his change of posture? Was it because he was anti-clerical? Anti-Jesuit? Anti-militaristic?

Archconservative Catholics, provincial petit bourgeois, the Beaux Arts, the academies, the Conservatoire, all had become anti-Dreyfusards. Was it because the people he hated had become anti-Dreyfusard, thus he had to become a Dreyfusard?

Are we defined by the enemies we've made?

Or was it because Zola was trying to fight for justice abstractly, or in some inconsistent way, support Jews specifically and generally, as underdogs? Was he setting sail under false colors, or was he indeed a man of justice?

Don't ask me anymore about what honor means. I'm no judge of that. I'm the son of our Revolution. I believe in our cry for *fraternite and egalite* and in the blessed Bill of Rights of those Americans. I know I shouldn't generalize but I just don't like some ethnic groups—especially

Jews. I know that it subverts my concept of *fraternite and egalite,* but I can't help how I feel.

What I can help, however, is to abide by what I believe is fair and just. You can call it honor if you will, but I must come to the defense of someone who has been unjustly convicted. If I were to do nothing, then along with those pernicious perpetrators I would be conspiring to ignore one of the Ten Commandments, "Not To Bear False Witness."

So one may think I'm doing the honorable thing by defending someone who has been railroaded to Devil's Island, but the Army, in their infinite wisdom, thinks it is doing the honorable thing by maintaining the belief in the infallibility of the army chiefs, and by extension, our nation.

When a word means opposing things to different people, how can it have any meaning? For me, then, there can be no such thing as honor.

Finally—yes—eschatologically—I must tell you that when we die, God in Heaven won't make any distinction between any of us anyway. He's always been ambiguous and feckless. Up there, there is too much contriteness for me—too much sweetness and forgiveness and understanding—too much sanctimonious merde.

There in **Hell**, however, there is no ambiguity—no ambivalence.

There, they're decisive!

There, they're Manichean!

There, they don't mess around with understanding and forgiveness.

There, they dump the jetsam of self-delusion, the dross of excuses, the rationale for misbehavior, and with absolute clarity, see right through the rubbish that infects our lives.

There, in **Hell**, is where true judgment will come from.

That's why I say to the General Staff: **TO HELL WITH YOU!**

Zola's "J'Accuse" raised the Dreyfusard movement to its apogee. He fought the army and the nation with his magic pen, his penetrating analysis, his eloquence, his sense of drama and purpose, his unrelenting will, his determination to right this grievous wrong, to cleanse the army of its prejudicial stupidities. He was responsible for convulsing the very ground beneath France. It aroused throughout the world even more attention to the rupture of our exalted foundations.

Amidst the cacophony of criticisms, many applauded and praised his courage to speak the truth against so formidable an opponent—as they did for me as well. But how can you praise someone for speaking the truth—for behaving justly? I'm no hero and neither is Zola. No one should be applauded for doing the right thing. That should be expected.

I was accused of passing on secret documents, of forging a document to frame Esterhazy, and was imprisoned by my beloved Army and discharged. I shuddered. Zola was charged with libel, found guilty, given a one-year prison sentence and fled to England with his mistress and two children.

Okay, Sally, this is all you're going to get from me. I hope you got what you came for. I've told you all I want about the story. I hope you now realize that your search for the meaning of honor is dubious, indefinable, protean, and like the fog, without borders, ungraspable, so you've been journeying on a fruitless quest.

And add this to your search for the nebulous, my dear. If you give *honor* the meaning of telling the truth no matter what the consequences, you've got two others who qualify for the *honor of being honorable*, Cavaignac and Cuignet. In an effort to dispel any doubts about Dreyfus's guilt, the new minister of war, Cavaignac who, along with a personal friend of Commandant Henry's, Captain Cuignet, both believing in Dreyfus's guilt, opened up a new inquiry in 1898 and were shocked to discover multiple forgeries. Their discoveries ultimately helped exonerate Dreyfus.

Both of those men demonstrated allegiance to their consciences—not to their prejudices. In a sense, you can say that for what they perceived to be a higher calling, they betrayed who they fundamentally were. *Ahhhh—those germs of propensity.* Yet, ironically, Cavaignac continued to believe that he had to destroy the power of the Jewish Syndicate.

He was the very one who imprisoned me.

For the French Army, honor meant many other things. They had to protect the exalted myth of the infallibility of the Army, and did so by employing conspiracy, duplicity, cover-ups, unwillingness to admit errors, and worse, no attempt to correct those errors, all in the ideal of protecting its honor and that of the nation. Is that concept not an ironic oxymoron?

Remember, Sally, your mandate from Adam is not to tell the story of Dreyfus. You know the rest of this convoluted saga—that a member of the *Legion of Honor*, my replacement, Commandant Henry, whose testimony was crucial in the first trial of Captain Dreyfus, was found to have committed the key forgery that helped convict Dreyfus. Henry was found guilty and sent to prison. The next day, he cut his throat.

Esterhazy fled to England and eventually pleaded guilty to spying—of being a forgerer as well. Later, in 1903, the former Military Attache from Germany to France, Colonel Schwartzkoppen, admitted that Esterhazy was the spy who gave him French military secrets.

You know what that self-righteous wit, that superficial snob, that haughty author, Oscar Wilde, said to Esterhazy, his new acquaintance, when he admitted his guilt to him? He said, referring to Dreyfus, something like, 'It's always a mistake to be innocent—to be a criminal like you takes imagination and courage.'

How insulting to those of us who risked our lives, our reputations, our careers, our liberty—the well being of our friends and family!

I was imprisoned for eleven months. Zola, exonerated in June 1899, returned to France. At around the same time Zola returned, I was freed and discharged.

On September 29, 1902, the Army murdered Zola.

There are people who deny it, but rumor has it that someone tampered with the chimney of his fireplace thus blocking a proper draft. With a fire roaring in his study as he wrote, carbon monoxide accumulated and he succumbed to asphyxiation. Rumor once again has it, that the following day some workmen were seen repairing his chimney.

I can't prove that thesis.

Zola was finally disinterred and buried in The Pantheon, a deserving place for what he had accomplished—for his eloquence, for his unrelenting courage, for his commitment to justice, for his indomitable spirit. Being buried in The Pantheon assured that France took ownership of his Frenchness.

At that ceremony, though we were standing under a battleship gray winter sky with a fierce, freezing drizzly wind blowing in our faces, it seemed, strangely enough, to be a perfect cerulean sky, embellished by a few cottony cumulous clouds and a balmy breeze, the model surely for artists like Boudin and Monet.

The battle between the Dreyfusards and anti-Dreyfusards continued unabated. An over-whelming body of evidence was accumulating in favor of Dreyfus, and on July 12, 1906, the courts annulled the results of the second trial, thus freeing Dreyfus and restoring his honor.

Despite my struggle with its meaning, restoring honor to his name meant for him and for me—everything—our credibility, our honesty, our integrity, our patriotism, our respectability, our probity—indeed our very word—our commitment never to renege on a promise nor ever to bear false witness—our belief in a transcendent France rising well above the imperfections of a few, even though those few sometimes become many, our belief that justice will ultimately prevail.

After twelve punishing long years, on July 20, 1906, in a tear-evoking ceremony that had the principal players trembling with emotion, Dreyfus was fully exonerated and officially rehabilitated. He was restored to his rightful place in his beloved Army, awarded the Knight of the Legion of Honor (that word again), and promoted to the rank of Major.

I was reinstated into the Army and later became a Brigadier General. Then Minister of War.

But what a price he paid!

What a price I paid!

What a price Zola paid!

What a price France paid!

Unlike many of my friends who blindly accepted as incontrovertible whatever was written by that towering intellect, our old friend, William, I did take issue with some of his beliefs such as, *All's well that ends well.* As though, he believed, we can quickly turn off such nightmares, such searing pain and loss, such longing for what might have been—such regrets—to suddenly forget and smile once again. Not so fast, dear William. It's never that easy. The memories—the anguish—they persist—and linger—and linger.

I behaved the way I did, you must understand, Sally, to please no one but myself. As we traverse the trajectory of our lives, like some comet never to return, I know that soon we will be forgotten by our children, and known to their children only as Unknown Soldiers, so I take some solace in knowing that between 1888 and 1889, there were a few artists who made allegorical lithographs of me, such as *An Homage to Picquart.* Artists like, Vallotton, Sunyer, Petijean, Luce, Georges Pissarro, Gumery, Hermann-Paul, and others. One, the artist Lucien Perroudon, even did a fine etching of me in uniform.

Six newspapers had run petitions on my behalf, collecting over 30,000 signatures of people who believed in my innocence. Among those were the artists, Claude Monet and Edouard Vuillard. It's good to know that I am not alone in the universe.

Does the name Galle sound familiar to you? Emile Galle, the celebrated decorative artist who, like Tiffany, added a new dimension to the arts? He was a passionate Dreyfusard who designed two breathtaking vases as well as a table adorned with symbols and inscriptions that allude to Dreyfus. On the vases there is a pattern of elm trees, an ancient symbol of affliction, delicately layered and etched in the Arte Nouveau style. On the table there's a Latin inscription from Isaiah, "Just as the garden brings forth its seed, so God will bring forth justice."

Remember your Greek mythology, Sally? Remember Themis, the blindfolded Titan of order and justice?

I always believed in her, never having doubts about her authenticity, but there were times, I must tell you—there were times—when I questioned everything I had ever believed in. My world was crumbling right before me. It took all my will to keep Themis on my shoulders. Never forget that I was wedded to the institution of the Army, the idea of the Army, the *elan vital* of the Army! I was crippled by my disillusionment in what I had once held so dearly in my heart.

I was known as a multilingual, exceptional intellect—an accomplished musician and pianist. Before this debacle, I used to entertain my family and friends with Chopin and Mozart and our contemporaries, Debussy and Ravel. But after I became immersed in the Affaire, I could no longer play the music we all loved, nor could I play any longer for others.

In my increasing isolation, I played Bach's music almost exclusively. His music is the music of solitude. The Goldberg variations, the Chromatic Fantasia and Fugue, the Italian concerto in F, the Partita #6 in E flat, his English Suite, and many others. I played them and struggled with them. I needed them for their contemplative nature, for their profound understanding of the human condition, for their poignant lyricism, for their elegiac dolefulness, for their wordless comfort—and for much, much more.

It was for me—solipsistic solitaire.

His music, ah, music, that numinous language of communication that transported me out of myself. As I soared aloft, outside of place, outside of time, it enabled me to look down on what was happening during La Belle Epoque with its many high achievers and, yes, its many demagogues. I couldn't let go of the intractable, life altering, life-destroying problems we faced, and in some subliminal way, my mind kept working on solutions.

I now sneer at the misnomer used to describe that period. No, Sally—it was not *La Belle Epoque*—rather—it was ***La Helle Epoque***.

Like the fragrance of gardenias, music was more than a palliative, it cleared my mind and helped me sort out the pieces of life's puzzles. In my increasingly self-imposed isolation, I went to many concerts, and after hearing Mahler's Symphony #8 for the first time, I knew that that was all of heaven I would ever get—or want. He, along with Bach, by bringing the divine to earth, introduced me to heaven, or was it perhaps, that they opened the doors of heaven and lifted me up with their music—for a glimpse.

Later I formed The Mahler Society.

After this horrific, harrowing ordeal was over, I tried to return to my old ways, but something had happened, some mutation—an inability to breathe deeply—a reduction of oxygen in my lungs—a slowing of my pulse—a lowering of my spirit—an inability to smile easily—an attenuation of my joie de vivre.

Even though Dreyfus and I were reborn, it was a different us. Oh—how different.

And there, my dear Sally, my tale ends.

One other thing you should know. On January 18, 1914, the day before the First World War began, I was riding my horse in Amiens and had an accident—and died.

You should also know that in my will I had requested a civilian burial, that there be no flowers, no wreaths, and no speeches. My ashes were brought back to Paris by my family and placed at the Cimetiere de Pere Lachaise.

On September 23, 1919, shortly after that Great War and the re-conquest of the Alsace, my ashes were transferred to Strasbourg and relocated to the Saint-Urbain Cemetery in a ceremony that was with full military honors.

Oh, General Picquart, before my baby comes, I promise you that I will visit your gravesite where your ashes have grown cold. I will weep for you with pride and awe. I will weep for you for the courage and strength you demonstrated on behalf of truth. I will weep for those glorious days of yours in which you remained resolute in your determination to uphold exalted principles. I will weep for you for the enormous sacrifices you made. I will weep for you for enduring the calumnies of dishonest people. I will weep for you, General Picquart, and honor you always with my profound respect.

And, in the Jewish tradition, I will put a stone on your noble remains.

CHAPTER 13

Scene I
Fade in:
Exterior: St. Urbain Cemetery Strasbourg, December 1, 1950, blustery, wintry morning, wind blowing rain sideways. Camera slowly zooms in on a woman's umbrella slanted against the wind, failing in its mission to keep her dry. Fallen leaves, adding to the melancholy, sweep over many tombstones that show the mottled effects of several decades of decay. Undeterred by the weather, she's seen examining each tombstone, finally stopping at a pillar upon which is a marble urn.

Rachel Sarfatty
(speaking softly)

Ah, finally. There you are, my friend. Soon you'll have an Anniversary. What will that make it? Let's see, Brigadier General Marie-Georges Picquart, died January 18, 1914. Did you, thirty-seven years ago, think there would be some of us who remembered who you were, what you once stood for, and what you still stand for?

When you think of Rachel, picture a woman who suggests by her walk an age of early thirties, little else. Her heavy coat and large woolen hat mask many of her features for now.

I once told you that before my baby comes, I would visit your gravesite, that I would weep for you with pride and awe, and honor you with my profound respect.

And, as in the Jewish tradition, I'll put a stone on your remains.

As she looks for a stone, a uniformed ghost appears over the marble urn and in a barely audible whisper, says,

Ah, my acquaintance of so long ago—I thought you knew—I never did like you people. If you don't mind, I don't want any reminder of your visit—please don't."

Camera fades slowly back as Rachel lowers her umbrella and removes her hat.The ghost disappears. Rain pours down her face—a look of disbelief veiling her cobalt blue eyes. She picks up a stone and bounces it in her hands, leaving the viewer to guess whether she's going to smash it hard against the urn, or ignoring his request, lay it gently on top. With the stone still in her hand, she looks at the urn. We hear her whispering.

Oh, General Picquart, your life was a gross incongruity, but contradictions and inconsistencies are part of the human experience. Behavior follows unpredictable and irregular pathways and life can be a paradox. Monsieur Le General, I want to share this cold rain with you, to let it chill my bones like it chills your ashes, to taste its icy indifference. I want you to know that I too am riven with contradictions. So it was with you, sir, who, for a few luminous years, gave exalted meaning to your entire life and irrevocably altered the lives of others—and for that, whether you like me and my kind or not, I will forever honor you.

As the wind lashes rain at her face, it mixes with her tears. Camera slowly fades away as we see her, stone still in hand, become aware of many other stones scattered on the pathway in front of his site. She gazes at his name and then at the urn. We hear her say,

It seems you've had other visitors.

She hesitates for a moment, undecided between placing the stone on top of the urn or on the pathway—or to throw it away. She places it on top.

Fade out.
Flashback. Screen shows 1894.

Military courtyard. Soldiers in full dress uniform milling about, waiting.

Is that the best place to start? Make it all a flashback? I've got to let my brain lie fallow for a bit, to percolate in its subterranean depths, to see what emerges. Then I can continue.

CHAPTER 14

Claude Monet and Cezanne mentioned Edgar Degas more than once. Let me see what kind of a man he was.

Some of my best friends are Jewish.

Were.

How can I explain? Is there an explanation that because of inherent contradictions illuminates rather than confuses?

I look for consistency always, but like a bird flitting from one branch to another, I find it elusive, always difficult to focus on or grasp, or gusts of wind blowing this way or that, or rip tides in opposition to a current's normal flow, or during the Perseid showers, locating from whence come those meteors in their coruscating descent.

As an artist, perhaps I am entitled to inconsistency, to inconstancy, to illogic, to spuriousness, to casuistry, to prejudices, to unkind emotion—to faithlessness.

Betrayal should be included in that description because I'm also a back-stabber. But I refuse to judge myself. I will leave that to others. My art is the only thing that matters. My sole criterion is whether it satisfies me. I am, as have been my colleagues, past and present, who I am.

And, I don't need anybody bringing me cassoulets.

Take it or leave it.

To hell with all of you.

"What?? What the hell are you doing, Sally?? Why are you writing about Degas? Your focus should be on your screenplay about Picquart!" Josiah demanded.

"Take a deep breath, please," I said, trying to lower the energy in the room. "I'm getting there, I wrote the opening scene and now I'm pondering whether that's the way to start, and if not, where? Don't worry. I'll get back to it soon."

"When? You're taking notes on all these other guys, all these ancillary figures, and not focusing on *The Man*! This is so unlike you, Sally! Has the baby altered your brain cells?"

"Listen, please," I said trying to mollify him. "Sit down, let's have a glass of wine and I'll explain everything."

"I don't want to sit down and I don't want wine. What I want is your attention. You're delaying finishing your job. Have you forgotten why you're here? I'm fed up with what I'm doing *and with the damn French,* AND with your delays. The sooner you finish your job the sooner we can get the hell out of here!"

"Bad day?"

"That has nothing to do with it. Don't change the subject!" I sat quietly, looking at him sympathetically. "I'm working with a bunch of ungrateful people whom I can't stand, okay!" he said pouring himself a glass of cheap chardonnay.

"Did you go on the set again as Mr. Omniscient?"

"Don't lay that on me, Goddamnit! You know me better than that!"

After a long pause during which I said nothing, he added, "Well, maybe a little, but they started it with their arrogance. They were shooting in the dark, you couldn't see the actors' expressions, they were moving fast and you didn't know what the hell was going on in the scene. It looked like a bowl of charcoal-gray Jell-O. It was all mood and no substance. It was frenetic—it needed more definition, more reaction, more whatever. It just wasn't working for me and I told them so. Goddamn it, we needed more light. It was so dark and shadowy, it was claustrophobic."

"Maybe, honey, they wanted that. In Hollywood we tend to spell everything out. Maybe they wanted the audience to guess at what was happening, to imagine, to .... "

"Enough, please," he said raising his hand like a stop sign. "They're resistant to suggestions. I tried and lost with the flowers. They insist on doing it their way and won't listen to alternate views. And they treat me with a haughtiness that's insulting—like I'm an alien intruder."

I sat alongside him, wrapped my left arm over his shoulder, squeezed a little, and said, "I remember listening to the congressional hearings as General George Marshall was explaining the benefits of his Marshall Plan. When the question was asked about what kind of reactions to our largesse we would get from Europeans, he said, *'Oh, they'll probably hate us for it.'* That astonished me.

"Yeah, I remember that too, but unlike you, I wasn't astonished. Beneficiaries hate their living benefactors. Nobody appreciates being placed in the subordinate position of being a victim with his hand out."

"Yes, but we also baled out their asses during the war."

"All the more reason for their attitude. They were the fallen and papa had to come to their aid. Their sense of inferiority, their neediness still prevail, thus their know-it-all response. I'm getting sick of it!" he said, cradling his head in his hands.

"Honey, don't despair. I'll be getting beyond the opening pages very soon, I promise. It's just that now that I finished my research on Picquart, I need to let him rest for a few days. In the meantime, Monet mentioned Degas, so since I need a break from Picquart to let my subconscious take over for a bit, I decided to take on Degas and find out what kind of a guy he was."

"Well, stop it already. You've told me fifty times about this giant quilt of yours."

"Okay, okay, honey," resigned to his impatience, "I'll stop with my stories, but just one thing. I know how much you love Mark Twain—he too had an opinion."

After a moment in which I thought he was not paying attention, he looked up at me and asked, "Mark Twain?"

"When he lived in Vienna from 1897 to 1900 he railed against the anti-Semitic press in Austria and in France, and weighed in on Dreyfus's side."

"So? Forget about all these guys! You've got an assignment! Finish it already! Let's get the hell out of here, for God's sake!"

"Please, I don't need this kind of pressure, Josiah!" I said mirroring some of his exasperation. "I'm in the place where this all happened. To do justice to my script, I need to examine it from all angles."

"Finish it at home then," he fumed.

"Aren't you listening? This is where it happened. I can't do it from home. I need to be in France," raising the pitch of my voice.

"Why the hell so?"

"Would you have been satisfied with seeing just a picture of *Victory at Samothrace*, or *The Venus de Milo,* or *The Mona Lisa, or Notre Dame Cathedral?* Seeing it in vivo is amazing, enriching, evocative, inspiring! They're awesome! There's no substitute for the real thing. That's why I need to be here, Josiah," I said with a mixture of anger and pleading.

He rose from his chair, headed for the door and shouted, "Well, don't let me interrupt your reading then! Do it while you eat. By yourself! I'm going out for dinner!" he said slamming the door behind him.

I was immobilized. After awhile, I told myself to take a deep breath. Finish his wine. It won't kill me. Good Lord, he's never walked out on me. How can I get back to work when I'm so rattled? I've got to. The sooner, the better. Take an even deeper breath and let it out slowly. Let me finish with Degas, then I'll work on the screenplay. But I'll definitely end with Degas.

Like my friend, Auguste Renoir, whose sister-in-law was Jewish, and who at an early age had apprenticed himself to a porcelain maker named Levy, I had many Jewish friends.

That's how you get to despise them.

While Claude Monet and Camille Pissarro fled to London at the start of the Franco-Prussian War in 1870, Edouard Manet and I joined the National Guard. True patriots, Manet and Edouard Degas.

Through the years my allegiance to the Army never flagged. For me it represented my beloved France and like a mother hen, any criticism of the Army was criticism directed at my family, and therefore, directly at me, so I reacted indignantly.

In 1871, I was commissioned to paint a double portrait of two close friends, Rabbi Aristide Astruc and General Emile Mellinet who had distinguished themselves as relief workers during that debacle. I tried to evoke the humanitarian bond between them and their commitment to those they served. To convey their warmth and kindness I concentrated on their eyes and the corners of their mouths—a little like Leonardo's *'s'fumato.'*

Unlike Monet's sanctimonious entreaties about separating art from politics—about its neutrality—during the siege of Paris, Manet executed a print depicting hungry citizens queuing up in front of a butcher shop. That was one of many political paintings that expressed the profound effect the war had on him. On all of us. In Paris, during the Universal Exposition of 1878, he painted a street scene emblazoned with the beautiful white, red and blue of our French tricolor flags. It was a joyous, spirited scene, but as the eye travels to the lower corner of the canvas, one can see a struggling figure of a man on crutches. It tugs at my heart. It was testimony to those of us who could not forget the consequences of war or the lingering pain of that defeat.

I need to remind Monet that during our World's Fair of 1898, he himself had not distanced himself from politics—something he clearly demonstrated in his painting, 'Rue Saint-Denis, Celebration of 30 June, 1878,' in which, like Manet, he shows a street scene festooned with French flags, but on one of the flags he painted, 'Vive la Republique.'

Is that not politics?

I asked myself much later whether it was politic for me to have painted so many Jewish subjects rather than non-Jews? Was it self-interest on my part that in the 1870s and early 1880s I painted portraits of Henri Michel-Levy, Alphonse Hirsch, Madam Hayem, Ernest May, and my old school friend, Ludovic Halevy, a Jew who had converted? Was it that they recognized talent in me earlier than others? Or was it that they had a corner on all the money in France? Was it because I wanted some of it? Was it because my ferocious anti-Semitism hadn't recrudesced yet?

Quite close to impressionist circles were many Jews, one of whom, Moise Dreyfus, was known openly as belonging to the Alliance Israelite. Mary Cassatt, who seldom painted men, did a fine portrait of him. Through the years she and Manet painted many Jewish subjects, never once displaying anti-Semitism.

Nor did I—overtly. One can never be sure of others—covertly.

I don't much like aspiring women either, or over educated women. Who needs them? Like all those suffragettes, they are useless to society. Better to paint women dancing and displaying their womanhood on stage, or doing their daily toilette, or in the bedroom or kitchen—something basic, honest, primitive—not pretending to be what they weren't intended for. I hate when they aspire to intellectuality.

Renoir's position on women was like mine, only more so. He told his son, Jean, that he prefers women who didn't know how to read or write, so it follows that he detested high achieving women like lawyers, writers and politicians. He was content to portray them with voluptuous breasts and sensuous thighs—pink skin—ripe—desirable—eager for penetration.

On the other hand, I respect talent such as Berthe Morisot's. And, as for Mary Cassatt whose career I did nurture a bit, I would never admit that a woman could draw so well.

Renoir, as a portraitist, had the best record of all of us, and in his early years, he never betrayed himself as the incorrigible anti-Semite he was. He befriended one of the many Jewish lovers of art, Charles Ephrussi, who introduced him to Louise Cahen d'Anvers, wife of a Jewish banker, who then commissioned Renoir to do a trio of portraits. Ephrussi was even included as the top-hatted participant in the rear of his painting, 'Luncheon of the Boating Party.'

He was glad to have met Paul Berard, a rich Protestant, who commissioned him to do a gallery of family portraits, and much to his great pleasure, Berard became his devout and most important patron. That gave him the justification for dropping the Cahen d'Anvers family for, as he explained in a letter to a friend, he wanted to wash his hands of those Jews and their stinginess.

My old friend, Ludovic Halevy, the writer, librettist, and engaging boulevardier, a Jew who had converted to Catholicism, never denied his

Jewishness which irritated me, but he was indeed an old, old friend of mine, one at whose house I used to have lunch several times a week and dinner every Thursday night. Mrs. Ludovic and the children treated me like a member of their family. His conversion, he once explained, was based on Heinrich Heine's discovery that having been born Jewish, it seemed that baptism was the ticket of admission into European civilization. That logic led him to convert. As though, through some impossible alchemy, conversion could wash away the indelible stain and stink of being born a Jew. So I always saw Ludovic as a Jew, not a Christian. My love for him, however, was an incongruity that made no sense to me.

Their walls were graced by many paintings and drawings I did of the family. One of them showed a red ribbon glowing like a red-hot coal on Ludovic's lapel, the symbol of the well-recognized Legion of Honor bestowed upon him for his many achievements. His son, Daniel, worshiped my art and became an ardent supporter of mine, but, regrettably, as I should have expected, he, like the rest of the family, became ardent Dreyfusards. You know how those Jews always stick together. Nonetheless, the whole family continued to treat me affectionately.

At the height of that abominable Dreyfus Affaire one of my models expressed doubt as to his guilt so I screamed at her saying that that made her a Jew, an accusation she denied. I didn't believe her so I told her to get her clothes on and get the hell out. Later, it turns out, I discovered the model was Protestant, but it was too late to make amends. That's difficult for opinionated people.

Once, in 1885, I stayed at Zola's house, but after 1894, as the polarizing disaster of the Dreyfus Affaire evolved, I broke off my relationship with that childhood friend of mine, as I did with Camille Pissarro, that friend, that companion, that man I loved as much as an appendage. About nine years older than I, he had been my mentor, my therapist, my supporter, my inspiration, and above all, my dear, dear friend.

He was one of the first to buy a painting of mine and called me the greatest artist of the time. I had no outright hostility towards him, but I had a general anti-Jewish, stereotypical attitude about them—you know, about their 'traits.' It was not dissimilar to the beliefs of most of my fellow Frenchmen.

My beliefs, like Louis Pasteur's little creatures, were germs within us that sometimes grow slowly and sometimes rapidly. We all have those germs, often in conflict with each other—some expressing abhorrence while others, love and support. Why one triumphs over the other, why one emerges while the other remains quiescent, is a question for theologians or philosophers to ponder.

Unlike Zola who celebrates his determinism ostentatiously, I'm a quiet determinist who celebrates it by acting the way I do. Those little germs within me, I call them *germs of propensity*, were there when I was born, and I can't do anything about it. And that's that!

Those other germs about love and tolerance, those urges to review pre-conceived notions and all that other blather are there within me as well, but I exercise my free will to keep them quiescent. Comparisons between people are odious so don't ever compare me with that piece of merde, Picquart.

It was impossible during the latter part of the nineteenth century to be an artist and not come into contact with Jews. Pissarro, that cursed Jew, called me a ferocious anti-Semite, and frankly, I had no use for Dreyfusards, so I had nothing to do with him or Signac and those other supporters. Besides, Pissarro was an anarchist and anti-clericalist, and I was growing more and more Catholic, the only true faith as everybody should realize, so in my growingly caustic ways, I said to hell with him and all the rest of those fellow-traveling Jews. Two of the most divisive concepts on the planet drove us apart—politics and religion.

The concept of *honor,* as nebulous as that word is, compels me to say that I wasn't always this way, or didn't overtly behave this way, despite what I said earlier. Honesty, integrity, sincerity, self-respect, they all force me to explain how I evolved into what I am today.

During the 1850s, the artist, Jacque Emile Edouard Brandon and I became close friends. He was, like Pissarro, a Sephardic Jew. Where do they come from, these Jews? And why am I attracted to them, at least in the beginning? Good enough to win a medal at The Salon in the 1860s, he even exhibited with the rest of us Impressionists in 1874, but I dismissed his work as academic. We drifted apart. Did I do that deliberately?

My once-revered friend, Ludovic Halevy had introduced me to his cousin, Genevieve, the Jewish widow of Georges Bizet. She was now married to one of Rothschild's lawyers and ran one of the most intellectually stimulating salons in Paris at which prominent people were privileged to attend. many of whom were Jews. Charles Ephrussi, founder of the Gazette de Beaux-Arts, Ernest Reyer the music critic for Le Journal des Debats, Charles Haas, the elegant model for Marcel Proust's Swann.

Maybe Ludovic was justified in rejecting my monotype illustrations I created for his satire, La Famille Cardinal, about stage mothers, ballerinas and women with questionable pasts. Though I hadn't done so before, in nine of those I did paint him as having those typically physical Jewish traits we know them to have. In a way, I may have demonstrated passive aggressiveness in those drawings, especially when I depicted him leering into the top and bottom of those skimpy tutus worn by ballerinas who were often appealing enough to make extra money when not dancing or rehearsing.

Despite the depth of our friendship, I was miffed when he rejected them. That didn't stop me, however, from dining at his house as before. After all, I was considered a member of the family. On several occasions, we had discussed the Dreyfus Affaire. Well, perhaps more than several times, and though they knew I was an anti-Dreyfusard, I didn't realize how overt my anti-Semitism must have appeared. Daniel told me that from now on, we were not to discuss the topic.

It was during the period when the Dreyfus Affaire was on everyone's lips that something drastic occurred. I remember the date very well—seared in my memory. During dinner on Thursday, the 25th of November in 1897, I was unable to participate in the lightheartedness of the banter, remaining tight lipped—jaws clenched, silent, while they questioned the probity of the army, its venality, its continued dishonesty, fraud, and anti-Semitism. My Army with its traditions and virtues! Why, they represented my beloved France! How dare they! As soon as dinner was over, I got up, seething, ready to erupt, and without saying a word, stormed out the door, and thus broke with my childhood friends and disappeared from their lives. I even stopped visiting Madame Strauss's salon that I had found as intellectually stimulating as being with the Halevys, but they too were all a bunch of insufferable Dreyfusards.

It tore at my heart.

So I ask myself, why?

I can't answer that. Was the Dreyfus Affaire the catalyst? Yes and no. One year after it began in 1894, with my eyes already beginning to dim, my housemaid, Zoe, would read two newspapers that I resonated with—Drumont's La Libre Parole and Rochefort's L'Intransigeant, both justifying their anti-Semitism, both crying out, "Kill the Jews!"

Perhaps I had a substitute heart for the one I had broken. Those Pasteur germs fulminated within my substitute heart. What I heard made sense to me.

Why?

I don't know myself! Jews had been friends of mine. I knew better than to accept those scurrilous remarks, but those *germs of propensity* took over, and grew. I hated the Jews, those anarchists, those liberals with foreign thoughts, those moneylenders, those with dreams of taking over the government of France! Who knows why there was within me the predilection for the germs I had, and why those were the ones who triumphed?

Who knows? This is not science or mathematics with a logical explanation or solution. I've got to stop trying to find the one true cause of my vocal, some say rabid, anti-Semitism. Maybe there wasn't only one true cause; maybe it was a series of causes, culminating, as Stendahl wrote, in *a crystallization.* Yes, that's a better word then recrudescence. It was now easier to congregate with friends of similar hates, to reinforce our beliefs, to wave our mutual flag. And wave it we did.

We cheered when on July 13, 1898 that prick Picquart was arrested, that betrayer of his country, that sanctimonious prig who only respected his own values and to hell with the honor of our Army and our country. But then on August 13, 1898, Lt. Col. Henry was sent to prison after admitting to forging the document that convicted Dreyfus. He soon committed suicide. Merde on that suicide. For me it was no less than a *patriotic forgery.*

In December of that same year, one of my favorite newspapers, La Libre Parole, started a campaign to raise money for Madame Henry. I'm delighted to say that more than 25,000 Frenchmen sent money. Together they published some of the letters that accompanied the donations, and I had them read to me in their entirety. More than once.

"For God," read one, "the Nation, and the Extermination of the Jews!"

"For the expulsion of the Jews," read another.

From a worker at Baccarat Crystal "who would like to see all the Yids and Yiddesses and their brats burned in the glass furnaces here."

From a military doctor "who would like to see vivisection practiced on Jews rather than rabbits."

From some officers, "to buy nails to crucify Jews."

From another, "to make a dog's meal by boiling up certain noses."

It had reached epidemic proportions!

With the printed word stoking the flames of anti-Semitism, raising the latent to the active, I joined the choir, but I was able to compartmentalize my views. That was comfortable for me. On the one hand, I could particularize my affection for my Jewish friends, what few remained, and not think of them with the same venom. On the other hand, I was able, *abstractly*, to hate all Jews.

Contradictory, I ask myself? Of course! I was able to separate the two. I know, I know, both rational and irrational at the same time.

So what? Did it affect the most important thing in my life, my art?

No, not at all!

At about the same time I discovered that that coward, Monet, dismayed at what was happening to Dreyfus and Picquart, left for England once again. That man has no loyalty to the Republic, only that he was fed up with the way Frenchmen were excoriating the Jews. He always did have affection for those holier-than-thou Englishmen. They had harbored our dissidents time and time again. They even harbored Zola when he was convicted for libel in 1898. Monet held English culture in high esteem. He even sent his son there to study English. In fact I was told that when Monet returned to France he insisted on having a full English breakfast every morning.

What kind of a Frenchman is that?

Why would he believe a Jew and Col. Picquart and not The Army is a puzzle. It seemed so clear that Jews are disloyal while the Army is the protector of the realm. And I wasn't ashamed to say so. Often.

One evening in 1907, I was invited to a dinner in the cellar of Vollard's gallery, which, along with other famous galleries like Durand-Ruel's, was on Rue Lafitte, and which had, at the turn of the century, become known to young artists as *our second Louvre,* a place where one could see a Cezanne hanging alongside a new Picasso, or alongside one of mine.

One of the guests, Pierre Bonnard, decided to render a painting of the event. Redon was there, Forain, Count Harry Kessler, and amongst several others, Vollard's fellow art dealer, Bernheim. I know that guests have a responsibility to the host to maintain an air of congeniality, but I couldn't refrain from remarking at one point that *he, Bernheim, was a Belgian Jew and a naturalized citizen—that these people aren't of the same humanity as us.* Of course, lively contention should be welcome at dinner parties as well, but when I said that and other similar things, it did sour the atmosphere.

To hell with him! With all of them!

Bonnard, Vuillard and Vallotton were all Dreyfusards, while Maurice Denis, also a gifted painter, whose patrons were mostly the Catholic right, was an anti-Dreyfusard. I remember that in Denis's journal of 1899, he had made what some thought was an ugly distinction, but which I thought was an accurate one, between his own art which he called *le gout Latin,* the Latin taste, and *their* art which he called, *le gout Semite,* the Semitic taste.

I made it a point *not* to attend Pissarro's funeral on November 13, 1903.

When Ludovic died in 1908, however, I did pay my respects to the Halevy family. His son, Daniel, remained a loyal advocate of my work, and despite my incorrigible anti-Dreyfusard stance, seemed still to adore me. I remained his childhood hero, so he too was able to compartmentalize. When I picked up the shovel to add dirt to Ludovic's descended coffin, I wondered, if stirring in his coffin, he felt that I had betrayed him. Betrayal and indifference are among the greatest of human hurts. I was a member of that family, but my hatred for the Jews prevailed, and when I left abruptly that night, he must have felt that I had stabbed him in the heart. I hope not. I guess I could have pretended to remain his friend, but I was caught up in my own narcissism, my own political priorities, my own hatred.

We metamorphose. We survive. Kappuras, as he would have said in that bastard, abrasive Yiddish of his. *Let it go—don't be shackled to the past—screw the past. Get on with your life.* So, I had to get on with my own.

We lose some friends and gain new ones, but I was becoming more and more isolated, and I had little need for friends. If you were to ask me, I willfully cultivated the image of a curmudgeon. People often referred to me as that *terrible Monsieur Degas.* Why should I have people disturbing my solitude? Why should I like children, dogs and flowers? What's the benefit in that? Why pretend otherwise?

I have my art. That's all that matters.

At one time, when Emile and I were still friends, he said that artists have obligations towards society, not merely towards themselves. Screw Zola!

So, in the final analysis, I don't know what the hell *honor* means, and frankly I don't give a rotten tripe! Well, now that I think about it, perhaps *honor* means being true to one self—or rather, true to one's gifts, without bending to public or private pressures—being honest and uncompromising with those talents we've been blessed with. Though others, like Pissarro and Cezanne, influenced me, I nonetheless kept true to my own vision, and that was the honorable thing to do.

One more thing I need to say—to round out this thing in my head as I age and become reconciled to the reality of having more of the past and less of the future. Beyond those of my contemporaries who have responded favorably to my work, should my work survive my generation, what do I care about those biographers who get a perverse pleasure in poking their noses into my personal life, my political opinions, my attitudes, the ambiguities and contradictions of my life. What business is it of theirs? Of what importance can it be?

The only thing that matters is whether those as yet unborn will respond to my creative Output, will understand it, will be enriched by the way I saw life.

All else is irrelevant!

On the other hand, if my work does survive me, I won't be around to enjoy their enjoyment so who gives a damn about those as yet unborn?

As I lay on my deathbed in the descending darkness outside, or is that darkness in my head? I see fading, raggedy tutus, disembodied, rapidly twirling and twirling, my head spinning along with them, but soon, we all slowed down to stillness.

CHAPTER 15

"Thank goodness! You're finally home. I was beginning to worry, Josiah," hugging him tightly, tears welling in my eyes. "No, not beginning to worry—deep into worry. Please don't do that again—it's very upsetting to your baby."

He pulled himself out of the hug, looked at me intently and asked, "Which baby?"

"Come here, my love," pulling him to the couch. "Our baby wants to tell you something. Here, put your hand right here, he's been asking for you all night, wondering when you'd be coming back, kicking me until it hurts for what I said, for what you said, for what was left unsaid."

He placed his hand on my stomach and said indifferently, "I don't feel anything."

"Then keep your hand there until he wakes up again. Knowing him, it won't be long," barely managing a smile. I kept looking deep into his eyes, waiting for a sign of affection, not bothering to dry the tears falling down my cheeks.

Without saying a word, as if nothing had happened, his hand worked its way up to my breast while he kissed me gently on the mouth, removed the straps of my nightgown and gently kissed the areola of my breast. I was surprised at the sudden transformation, and relieved, but puzzled. After all of that?

A moment later, he said quietly, "I had dinner at a small bistro called Suite Bergamasque, a place I've never seen before. It was surprisingly quiet, and since I didn't have your non-stop conversation, I just ate and listened, not to the whispered conversation at adjoining tables, but to the music. It was not background music because it was loud enough to be enjoyed while dining—more like a muted concert, not intrusive yet clearly intended to be listened to."

"What did you eat?" I asked, wondering where this was going and why we were skirting important things.

"Sweetbreads, first time, not bad, but that's not the important thing. It was the music, a piece I hadn't heard before. I asked the waiter, who happened to be the chef and owner, which shows you how small a place it was, what I was listening to, especially that long, haunting solo passage that sounded like an oboe or an English horn, and he said it was Debussy's "Gigues," part of his "Images," and that the instrument I had heard was neither one, but what he himself played, *the oboe d'amore.*

"Being a Frenchman, he called it, the *oboe d'amour.* He excused himself for a moment, went to the back and brought out this exquisite instrument—like an oboe, but with a small bulb at the end. And to my astonishment, but not to anyone else's, he started to play."

"And I missed that?"

"Well, you were busy reading—or writing?"

I didn't want to go there, so I asked, "What did he play?"

"While everyone remained silent, he played the oboe d'amour solo from Maurice Ravel's "Bolero," and played it so luminously that I scarcely took a breath. It made for such a special evening, Sally. I'm sorry you weren't there."

I was now hooked. "So this is a restaurant that has dinner concerts?"

"Not really, but yes. He had to get back to the kitchen so it didn't last long, but when he put his oboe away we applauded. He bowed slightly and disappeared. Soon the recorded music came back on and I continued eating, but remained transfixed.

"I want to take you there soon. The experience was so unexpected and so much fun, that ... " and before he could finish his statement, I interjected with, "That you didn't miss me at all. Is that what you were about to say, my love?"

Without answering me, he looked into my eyes—deeply—beyond my eyes—to some hidden beyond, looking with such intensity that it made me shiver. I gasped, "Josiah, please say something," my tears beginning to well again.

He held me and said, "You're shaking, Sally. What are you afraid of?"

"That look—that look scares me—it seems so final—so irrevocable, like you .... " choking up, unable to continue, my tears burst over their thin boundaries again and rolled down my cheeks.

"Sally, Sally, what's the matter? I was just about to say that after our argument and the experience at the bistro, I realized that you are your own woman, that I can't stop you from doing what you want to do, that if you need to explore all these other guys, go ahead. That if you don't finish your screenplay, it's okay with me, that I shouldn't try to pressure you anymore. That's what my look was all about. Understand?"

I sighed with relief, and let my tears roll into my mouth. I couldn't speak and kept in his embrace. I remained there for a long time wondering how he could make such a quick u-turn, how it takes me forever to do the same. I have so much to learn from him. Is that kind of behavior learnable? Was there something else behind this swift turn-around?

He kissed my breasts again and whispered,"You know the areola should really be called the *aureola* because it is *burnished gold*, a golden halo for your nipples."

I was really moved by his tenderness. "Your breasts are especially beautiful tonight, bijou, full and soft, exquisite to the touch, with a unique fragrance that I could recognize blind-folded."

I laughed for the first time this evening,"Oh, yeah—everyman's fantasy. A blindfolded 'guess-your-mate' contest with dozens of females, breasts exposed."

"What a great idea! Until we can organize such an event, I want to play a solo for you with my built-in *oboe d'amour*."

He slipped the top of my nightgown off, and asked, "Concert, ma'am?"

"Sound like a great idea," I beamed at this unexpected turn of events. "Yes, a duet."

It was a delightful ending to a terrible day. But twice during the night, he gasped and shuddered. During the second episode, I woke him and asked if everything was okay—why the gasp and shudder? He grunted, said he was unaware of it, turned over and went back to sleep.

The following morning as he whipped his brush in the antique porcelain Arte Nouveau shaving bowl I bought him shortly after we arrived in Paris, it slipped out of his hands and shattered all over the bathroom floor. The bowl had a finger handle curved like a stylized ear. On one side of the bowl was a painting of a dragonfly in shimmering iridescent cobalt blue and all its complementary shades, while on the other, an iris painted in a stunning iridescent bluish/green/gold color that, like a hummingbird, changed colors each time there was a change of position. It was one of our few treasured possessions.

The style was no longer popular in France so when we saw it at the Parisian *marche de puce,* the flea market, we wondered how a thing of such exquisite beauty could go for so few Francs.

With a sleepy voice, I asked, "What was that?"

"Damn, honey, I didn't want to wake you, but I have to be on the set early—to sit around all day contributing nothing. I'm so sorry. Can you get back to sleep?"

"What broke?"

"My shaving bowl, my irreplaceable shaving bowl. Damnit! It was a great gift, and it's all in pieces. So sorry, Sally. Can you try to get back to sleep?"

"Only," I said, lifting my head from the warm pillow, "if we can have an encore of last night's performance of that delicious duet."

"I can't, sweetheart, I just can't. But the day won't end without a repeat performance, I promise."

Delighted, I said, "I won't let you renege, no matter how tired you are. Guess what, Josiah? I figured out the mystery behind his 'Bolero.'"

He chuckled, "What mystery?"

"Ravel's muse was Aphrodite!"

"Of course, I should have guessed. I won't be too tired for a reprise. I have huge reserves of energy, and I'll make certain my *oboe d'amour* remains in good working order, but it's your responsibility to keep it in tune," he said wickedly.

I sat up, saying nothing, but remained with a bemused smile on my face. After a moment, I said in a light-hearted voice, "I know how to do that."

"Honey, sorry to ask you, but I have no time to pick up the broken pieces. When you get out of bed, be careful where you step. But do me a favor, put the shards in a bag, dig a hole in the garden, and bury them there, and be sure to include a note. It'll be fun to wonder how some future archeologist will interpret that."

The smile on my face remained. He approached to kiss me goodbye and I said, "Just so that you won't have to ask, Josiah, I think I know what next to do with the screenplay, but I'm going to let it rest for a day or so. In the meantime, I'm going to the library, and I'm really glad you won't be pushing."

He sat alongside me with his arm around my shoulders and said, "Actually, we're both trapped here until your seventh or eighth month and then we can escape from this place, but if we can't, we can't. So be it. We'll stay in France. Don't worry, I know you'll do what you have to do."

"Even though I don't know whether what *I have to do* is the right thing to do?"

"Gotta' go. Have a bonjour day," he said blowing me a kiss.

Slow to anger, a long fuse to the bang then quick to bend. "If you don't finish, we'll stay." Is this for real? Does he really mean what he said? Does the rapture of music always mollify? The rapture of sex?

CHAPTER 16

The prescience of the person recommending that Jews be incinerated in Baccarat ovens continues to haunt me. Ughh! Would Degas and Cezanne have helped? Mon Dieu! Where has this quest taken me?

I went to the library to see if anyone had ever written a play about Picquart. None. I was in the 'P' section and found a book on Pissarro. He was mentioned often, and since we were both Sephardic, I thought it might be interesting to get his reactions to all the goings-on. I borrowed the book and planned on reading it while preparing my next step.

All artists are anarchists! They have to be. I happen to be an official one. Camille Pissarro, a humanist-anarchist, if you will. It's probably my heritage, Sephardic—my search for a simpler, utopian life—rebelling against those who exercise authority over my flesh and soul. We've had our fill of authority, my people and I. With rare exceptions it meant loss of life, dignity, opportunity, community, potential, peace—even of a place to bury our dead. I ask for no forgiveness for my attitude—certainly not understanding—I detest sycophancy. When you see before your eyes your loved ones beaten to death or burned, you'll know what it means to be considered vermin. So don't be surprised to learn that peace for me is ephemeral—that peace is only prelude. I'm a bird at a water fountain, every sense heightened, always on guard for the unexpected.

So much for my political anarchy. My artistic anarchy is something else, something I share with all other artists, that of doing only what each of us thinks is best. Diffidence has no place in my life. If sometimes I appear truculent in my approach, so be it. There is no room for compromise in art.

For all artists, solipsism is our North Star! C'est tout!

Cezanne and I had been friends for decades, through the eighteen sixties, seventies and early eighties. We painted alongside one another, competitively, amicably—coming under each other's influence, inspiring one another to realize the impossible.

During the last few years of the eighteen seventies, Paul implored me to move with him to southern France to explore the landscapes and sea that were an inspiration for much of his recent work. He was certain that I too would find new ways of exploring my art. Family considerations prevented that, besides I didn't care for the sea. He had that kind of freedom. He had money, and I, none.

In 1881, it was in the small towns of Pontoise and Auvers-sur-Oise, northwest of Paris where we lived only a few blocks from one another. We painted no more than a few meters apart, each viewing the outside world through the prism of his inside world. We encouraged and challenged each other to explore the geometry of spaces. All those shapes, those colors, the changing light, the changing shadows, the changing perspective between foreground and background.

The raging sun—no less raging than a raging storm—glistening crystalline air shimmering like the sea—windmills like rooted giants faithfully carrying out their tasks—orchards resplendent with colorful blossoms beckoning thousands of suckling bees—bosomy hillsides—hundreds of trees through which I saw, like polka dots, red tile roofs—yes, it was there I rescued Paul from despair. It was there that I helped the other Paul—Paul Gauguin. It was there I urged my son, Lucien, to paint, despite his mother's entreaties to learn a different craft so he could earn an honest wage. Yes, it was there that I was at my happiest as an artist.

A heady time it was!

Some said that Cezanne and I seemed to maintain a psychological investment in one another. I agree. Our works were similar, yet radically different. We continued to paint side by side during the years 1881 and 1882, ostensibly as friends, but his comments, ever so subtle, implied that what I had painted in the late eighteen sixties and early seventies was superior to what I was doing in 1881, that if I had painted today as I had painted then, I would have been the strongest of the Impressionists.

What does that tell you? That goes straight to the jugular of one's expectations of being better today than yesterday, of growing as an artist.

We loved each other. More than brothers. But brothers can offend.

How does one get over a wound that pierces the heart?

Maybe that was the beginning of the end of our deep friendship. Maybe there was something else. Maybe it was in 1885 when he broke with his childhood friend, Emile Zola.

After all, we had worked together, on and off, for over a quarter of a century and though our works looked similar, the discerning eye could notice profound differences. Amongst the many, my chromatic scale was made up of brilliant, luminous colors while his, more monochromatic and muted. During the eighties, it seemed that Paul attempted to capture what I was doing in the seventies, and surprisingly, despite my wound, I found myself attempting to capture *his interpretation* of what I was doing then.

Go figure. I hated him for that!

Besides, that ubiquitous Dreyfus Affaire loomed over us like a typhoon—disrupting everything. No one could escape its presence, its tentacles, its primacy as a topic—its profound implications as to what it meant to be French—to be just, to strive to be something more than what we were.

Earlier, when we painted together, we seldom spoke, just looked at our subjects with penetrating eyes, sometimes peering over the other's shoulder. When the Dreyfus case broke, we began snarling at one another.

How could we let that supersede what we once had had?

Our friendship should have transcended politics, but politics inexorably wormed its way to the top. How could it not when your friend hates your religion and ethnicity? I was crushed. Paul was crushed.

It was inevitable. Like an arrow, we knew where it was leading but were powerless to alter its trajectory. Where was our free will? I'm Jewish. I don't believe in fate, in its pre-destination, in its determinism. Despite that, it doesn't prevent me from making predictions. When

I said that peace is only prelude, I had the nagging premonition that this dreadful Dreyfus Affaire portended something pernicious, on a vast scale—beyond our borders. On the micro scale, however, this Affaire, like a perverse enzyme, broke Paul and me apart, and couldn't put us back together again. Like Humpty-Dumpty—irremediably broken.

Life is about learning to mourn, to adapt to loss, to embrace the hour.

I heard our door opening and got up to greet Josiah. "Hey, pleasant surprise! Glad you're home early. I tried reaching you but couldn't. You'll help me fix something for Adam who *finds himself in town and wants to pay us a visit.* How the hell do you suddenly *find yourself in town?*"

"Damn!" he said. "I wanted to spend a quiet night with you. Alone! We had a date. Doesn't he ever give us more than a moment's notice?"

"Maybe he's trying to catch us inflagrante, or, as I suspect, to catch me unprepared."

"Are you?"

"Yes, and no."

"Why don't we go out to dinner, like that place with the *oboe d'amour* owner? Why the hell do we always have to entertain him at home? Let him pick up the tab for once."

"I did recommend that bistro, but no matter how much I tried, he insisted we eat here, *so we can talk at leisure and I'll bring a bottle of French wine, blah, blah.*"

"So what are we feeding our guest of honor?"

"What is that Japanese fish with a poisonous organ that has to be carefully extracted by experts, otherwise ... ?" I asked, slashing my finger across my throat.

"Fugue something."

"Yeah, something like that, but after the last episode, he 'll bring his own royal taster."

"Fugu, that's it. That'd be perfect! I'll prepare it with my own clumsy hands."

"Please wash the romaine, Jo, and I'll get on with the entrée."

"Let's add anchovies, pretend it's fugu."

"Good idea. I have a strong longing for salt anyway."

"Was that a knock on the door? Already?"

"My hands are wet. Please go."

"Hi, Josiah! Howyadoin?" Adam asked real friendly-like.

"Fine, Adam, nice to see you again. It's been what? Four weeks or so?" Jo asked.

"Three and a half weeks actually. Hi, Miss homemaker, how's the chef?"

"Be right in."

I sat alongside Adam and said, "Oh, Jo, please get the cheese knife." Then mimicking his greeting, I said, "So, howyadoin?" deliberately omitting his name.

"Great, actually," he said as he sipped the wine. "This wine is pretty good, for a French product, don't you think?"

Was he trying to provoke so early in the evening?

"You must know," I replied, "the French are known for their wines and cuisine, while Italians are known, less tangibly, as lovers." I winked at Josiah and said, "You know, like their *oboe d'amore*?"

Adam noticed the wink, "A private joke?"

Jo, suppressing a smile, said, "The French refer to it as the *oboe d'amour.*"

"O.K. I won't go there." He turned serious and mumbled through a piece of cheese, "So Sally, my dear, I'm dying to find out. How's the script coming? You only have a few months before you'll be otherwise engaged."

I fired back, "Did you know that the very first docudrama film *ever made* was in 1899 and that it was about the Dreyfus Affaire? And the second, in 1907, was by Pathe News, also about the Affaire? And that after their initial showings, violence spilled from inside the theatres onto the streets? The Dreyfusards and anti-Dreyfusards were at each other's throats, so the French government banned the further showing of both films.

"And to this very day in 1950, France prohibits the film industry from producing or showing any film about the Dreyfus Affaire? How about that for film censorship? That from a country that claims ownership to liberty?"

There was an audible sigh. "If you remember, I told you that first, but I also told you that your screenplay was to be about Colonel Picquart and the nature of honor. And now you're talking about films concerning Dreyfus. Are you still straying off target?"

"Adam, they're all of a piece. There are so many other voices that ... "

He interrupted, "You've told me that before. If you can't focus on one person but continue to hear other voices, if you can't channel your thinking, if you can't focus on the subject, Sally, I wonder if you're up to the task," his green eyes said without flinching.

"Damnit, Adam! Of course, I am! I'm just telling you that it's not just a single event about a single person! It's not a single ember—it's a raging fire that has to be tackled from all sides. I've told you that before."

"Well, if this 'fire' is more than you expected—more than you can handle—perhaps we should call in another fireman. What do you think?" he asked taking full swigs of wine.

I reflected on what he said, swallowed hard and visibly, trying to be calm, "Adam, it's not bigger than I am, but I need a little more time to immerse myself in the culture of the time. I want you to know that I'm getting there. I absorbed a great deal of material about the lives of ... " and before I could continue, he interrupted, and asked in a loud voice, "Sally, Goddammit! In all these months, have you written anything at all?"

More loudly than I had intended, I said, "Yes, I have! Here," handing him a thin folder.

He emptied his wine glass, looked inside and muttered, "Barely two pages, huh? Forgotten, have you, that one page equals one minute of screen time?"

I remained silent while he read the script, looking defiant.

Between clenched teeth, he said, "Sally, I don't like ghosts in my films. Matter of fact, I hate them! Get rid of it!"

"We have ghosts in our horror movies."

"This is not a horror movie!"

"But Adam, Shakespeare has ghosts in his plays. Why can't I?"

"When you start writing like Shakespeare, I'll accept ghosts. Until then, NO! You get it? NO!"

"But Adam, it's not that they're going to be in the rest of the story, just in the beginning—to set the stage—after that ... "

"Sally, I'm not here to argue with you—and maybe," he said in a patronizing way, "you should see a therapist and talk to him about all these other voices you keep hearing in your head."

I felt the blood rush to my head and wondered what to say when he continued, "Do as I say. If you can't get more than one and a half stinking pages, you're out of here! Understand?"

He pointed his finger at Josiah and said with a look of disgust, "And that goes for you too. You're some pair, you two. "So ... " pausing a long time with that 'so,' his clenched jaw said to Josiah, "do your parental duty—get her focused on her work!"

Before I could respond, Josiah shouted, "How dare you talk to my wife like that? Like she's a child? Goddamnit, I resent that! She's a conscientious writer, and you've always gotten the best she has to offer. Just give her some space, and don't ever talk to her like that again, you understand, Adam?" He had just tread on icy ground.

Adam got up, went to the door, lowered his pitch to almost a whisper, "Sally, perhaps your best is not good enough, and Josiah, from what I hear from the French, your best doesn't seem good enough either. So finish the wine, enjoy whatever dinner you had planned, and get back to me *very soon* with an outline, or with a screenplay that doesn't read like a childish ghost story," and slammed the door behind him.

A second later, there was a knock. I opened it.

"As for you, Josiah, get with the program. Don't be in the resistance movement. Join the French. Don't oppose them. Get in the groove or you'll find yourself in the same boat as your wife! Get it?" He slammed the door again.

We were stunned. "Well, that's an appetite suppressant," Jo said.

"Honey, my head feels like Jell-O. I can't think. I'm numb."

"I can't think either. Turn off what you're cooking and let's go to that bistro for dinner. I'll ask him to play something. That should help clear the senses."

"Deal."

The owner was out ill. His policy was to prohibit anyone from touching his precious record player, since, as the waitress explained, parts were difficult to come by—you know, so soon after the war—pardonne. In total silence, we picked at our food while staring lugubriously into each other's eyes.

We got into bed, pecked at each other's lips and tucked ourselves in. In the morning, still dazed, I fixed Josiah coffee and a warm croissant. "Honey, they don't know about cereal in this country. When we get home, I'll make a proper breakfast for you," I said forcing a smile.

"Yeah, bacon, eggs, and well-done hash-browns. See you tonight," he said still chewing his croissant.

At the end of the day, he came in and starting talking immediately, "Honey, let me tell you about my day," kissing my cheek. "I'm starved. Let's eat."

I laid the salad down. With a mouthful of salad he roared off, "The director, that tyrant, was verbally abusing one of the actresses. What he said was correct, but he was so insulting he left her sobbing. She sounded, he said, like she was reading a textbook, like she wasn't fully invested in the role. He was denigrating her in front of everyone, using cuss words I've never heard.

"Normally, I wouldn't have interfered, but this time, I pulled her aside, and in imperfect French, I picked up on his word, 'invested,' and said that she was not yet a *stockholder* in the movie, that she was looking at it from a distance, like an outsider. I understood why she was crying at his behavior, but I also explained to her, quietly and gently, what the director wanted from her, but that he had done it in a totally unacceptable way. I explained the pressures the director was under, not to take these attacks personally, to let them slough off, to be impervious to them, to get down to what was critical–inhabiting the character."

"Josiah, that's what you were known for. You mean you never did the same here?"

"Well, no. My job is not to be an assistant director, but to learn about the grit of the French films, the hand-held cameras, the angle shots, their freedom to let actors have lengthy intelligent discussions, but I never permitted myself to actually help in directing them. That's not exactly true. Several times I didn't accept their ways and spoke openly about it, unsuccessfully."

"Do you suppose that's what Adam was suggesting?"

"Damn Adam!" he shouted taking a big bite out of his baguette like it was Adam, and to wash it down, a big gulp of wine.

I didn't want this leading to a sour stomach, so rather than pursue the subject, I said, "Sorry to hear about your day. Wanna' hear about mine?"

"Sorry, honey, I was rambling on. I do, but just so you know, after our conversation, she improved, and several people came over to chat. So tell me about your day, and how you've come to terms with what that bully had to say."

"Well, I was determined to remove Picquart's ghost and rewrite the opening scene along more conventional lines, so I went to my typewriter and stared at it all day—and it responded in kind. Worse. I never even inserted paper. Like a Rodin sculpture, I was rooted to the spot. Immobilized. I never had lunch. What thoughts I had, kept wandering in and out in a desultory way. I was unable to focus on any one thing for more than a fleeting moment. It was an awful morning, Josiah."

He came over to my side of the table, put his arms around me and whispered, "It'll sort itself out soon. Just you wait. At least I have a place to go and that in itself is distracting. You, unfortunately, have nowhere to go. Be patient, you'll knock 'em dead soon."

I dried my tears and said, "Thanks for the vote of confidence, my love, but I didn't finish telling you about my day. Since I couldn't get my brain around Picquart, I decided to read the book I borrowed from the library, a book about Pissarro, and found that I was able to write something about him, yet not about Picquart. Go figure."

"Hmn."

"Just got an idea, Jo. I loved Giverny. Monet's Japanese bridge, that gorgeous lily pond, all those lovely flowers. If I went there it might help revitalize my spirit. Would you be upset if I went away for a few days while I refocused? By myself?"

"Away from me? Hell, Sally, I'm not the problem!"

"No, my dear, dear Josiah, you are absolutely not the problem! But I need to get out of this apartment for a few days. Adam sullied it. I just need a few days of Monet's rejuvenating magical potion."

"Wait, you hated that cottage. There's no phone there. You'll be alone. You're pregnant. What if something happened?"

"Being pregnant is not being ill. I'm not an invalid. I'm strong and healthy, like one of Monet's poplars. Please don't worry. I'll just be away for three or four days, that's all."

"You don't even want me to visit?"

"Josiah, please, I'll be home before you know it. This has nothing to do with us. You are, Sacre Dieu, a blessing to me. I've just got to think about what my next move is going to be. Right now, solitude is what I need. Can you be okay with that?"

He looked puzzled and disappointed. "I'll make arrangements with the producer."

The thought of going to Giverny was energizing. I needed a change of venue.

I sat on the bridge overlooking the pond and thought about how Monet may have seen rain coming down in rainbow colors, but the rain pouring down on me is gray and black. Maybe Monet saw the Technicolor flowers enhanced by the rain, but all I see are droopy, funereal looking flowers. Maybe Monet saw his stately poplars and willows enjoying the rain, but everything I see is washed out. The only thing I see is the truth of willows weeping.

I got a chill on the bridge. The lilies look like they're drowning, the muddy flowerbeds with dispirited plants, impassable. This rain has got to stop soon. Two days of relentless rain are about all I can take. The wood is too wet to make a fire so I can't even sit staring at the flames, nor even contemplate those roaring in my head.

I'm a mess!

I can't read and I can't write. I have nothing to say!

One more day of this and I'm outta' here.

Three days of rain. I'll give it one more day, and then I'm outta' here!

"Josiah, my love, I'm so glad to be home with you. Four days of rain without you cannot compare with four days of rain with you. Normally, rain gives me a lift, but not this time. I should never have gone. I accomplished nothing. I still don't know what the hell I'm going to do. My mind is a pot of big boiling bouillabaisse."

He held me in his arms and said, "It's amazing, my dear, dear Sally, that just a few years ago, we were total strangers and now I find I can't live without you. How does this integration happen so fast?"

"Ah, the numinous magnetism of love," I said struggling to unbutton my blouse. "How about a duet?" my eyes sparkled.

"Yes, indeed. After a few days my *oboe d'amour* gets out of tune, but I know you'll return it to its perfect pitch," he said through kisses.

Later, with the afterglow beginning to wane, Jo said, "Honey, now that we're finished with all that good stuff, let me tell you that while you were gone, I heard from Adam. He's given us some advance notice this time. He's coming next Wednesday afternoon. Not for dinner. For a meeting only. The tingling in my body vanished. I let my head collapse on his chest, and said, "Oh, merde!!"

"That's what I thought you'd say. The burden, if it's any comfort to you, is on me as well. Both of us might be on the auction block."

"His tone telegraphed that message?"

"Yup! Very businesslike. No attempt at congeniality. Straightforward. I'm coming, be home. See you. That was it."

"I just lost my appetite."

"You have to eat something, if not for you, for him—or her. Let's heat up the potato/leek soup I brought from the set. It's nutritious and will get her enjoying exotic tastes at an early age."

Wednesday finally came. When I heard the knock, my heart raced from 60 to 120. Josiah looked at me and went for the door. I was filled with dread.

"Hi, Adam. Right on time. Can I get you coffee, a glass of wine?"

"Nothing." Turning to me, he asked matter-of-factly, "Hi, Sally. How's your baby feeling?"

"About as well as I am."

He sat down on the couch and said, "Before I get to you, Sally, I want to apprise you, Josiah, of something disturbing that happened the other day."

Startled, Josiah asked, "What could that be?"

"The director complained that you deliberately interfered with his duties. You pulled aside one of his overly emotional actresses, put your arm around her, whispered something, and broke the moment. You behaved like a patriarch or father confessor. You stole his authority! Don't you know better?"

"Is that what he thought?" Jo asked in disbelief.

"You haven't grown much either during these past few months, have you?"

"Adam, that's what happened, but I defused a highly tense situation. I helped everybody get back to work without all that damn static in the air."

"That's not what I heard, and his word matters. Maybe he wanted that tension in the air. You pissed him off! Don't make me remind you that you're his guest, not the other way around. Next time, remember your goddamn place!" Then in a stage whisper, murmured, "You're both driving me crazy with your incompetence and your insubordination!"

Josiah, red in the face, got up and hovered over Adam. "I don't know what the hell has gotten into you since we've been here, but it's like we're dealing with a schizoid personality. At home you were one of the most well liked, considerate producers, but here you're behaving like a Mafioso bully. We haven't lost our civil rights in France, have we?" he bristled. "How about thinking of us as innocent until proven guilty instead of the other way around?" I saw his jaw muscles rippling.

"Sit down. I don't like people standing over me. I'll be able to answer that more accurately when I find out what your wife has been up to. Sally? What have you been up to? Got anything for me? Anything, that is, besides a ghost story?" he asked with such scorn that I shivered.

"Here," I said, giving-throwing the same blue folder.

"What the hell is this? It's the same child's merde as last time, the same damn thing! Goddamnit, Sally, did you think I was joking when I asked you to get to work and give me something besides this same one and a half page piece of stinking shit? What the hell have you been doing for the past week? Visiting L'Orangerie and the Louvre?"

"Adam," I said with deliberate softness, "You're right, I am sight-seeing in Paris. I'm visiting the libraries, the cemeteries, the monuments to those whose lives were affected by the Dreyfus Affaire, examining their disparate versions of honor and integrity, the houses and apartments where they lived, the scenic areas in France where they painted their magnificent works, created their magnificent compositions, the bistros where they used to spend time with their fellow high achievers discussing art, politics, philosophy, the science of light, books, poetry, visiting the museums housing their work, listening to their music in concert halls, studying the language, and trying to get first hand information from those participants still alive."

I barreled on, "Yes, Adam, all those things and more. I've allowed myself to become, during that troubled time, a citizen of that society, becoming aware of its inconstant—its incoherent—its incohesive—its conflicted eidos. I allowed myself to become part of La Belle Epoque—the era that for people like Picquart, became *La Helle Epoque*. Yes, that's what I've been doing, Adam. I'm guilty, your honor, with an explanation."

"This isn't a court of law, so don't give me that bullshit. I didn't send you here to become a scholar on La Belle Epoque and cut out that crap about it being La Helle Epoque. That's your poetic license at work, more bullshit. You're not here to teach a class, you're here to do one thing only, about one man only, and since I'm the professor doing the grading, you're getting an 'F'. And, *I'm the one paying for your ineptitude!"*

"So," turning to Josiah, "to answer your question, you are guilty, not before you were proven innocent, but after you both proved yourselves guilty!"

Before Josiah could answer, I got up, looked down on him, and spoke softly once again, hoping to assuage him, "Adam, please understand us. Josiah did the right thing in grounding all that electricity on the set. How can you expect the best from actors when the director brings out the worst?

"As for me, my mind is a hodgepodge of conflicting ideas each trying to emerge on top. I know my mind is in disarray, but please understand, I'm taking this very, very seriously. I'm not loafing on the job," and seeing him ready to shout, I said, "Let me continue to explain, please ... "

But before I could, he interrupted angrily, "I know what the hell is happening. You've explained it quite well. It needs no further explanation. Your work, *or absence thereof*, is telling me what's happening. Zero. Nada. Zippo. Rien. Nizente. Bupkes. That's what's happening," raising the volume of his voice with each successive word. "Is there any grade lower than 'F'?"

With clenched teeth, Josiah said quietly, "Adam—you—can—leave—now!"

Not making any effort to rise, he asked, "Why? Isn't this meeting getting anywhere for you? Have you failed to get my meaning—the two of you? Have I left anything out? What other clarification do you need? Your stay here, so far as all of us are concerned, has been non-productive, and I've told Pete as much." Still truculent, he hissed, "Nobody here likes you or thinks you've made any contribution to their craft, nor that you've learned anything from the French style of movie making. The only thing you seemed to have learned is pidgin French."

"Why don't you fire us then?" I asked thrusting my chin pugnaciously.

He ignored the question and said, "Sally, my dear, you were supposed to be writing about Picquart's radical pivot and what that had to do with his sense of honor ... "

"Adam! That's what I was trying to get past your pre-conceived barriers before. Honor has different meanings for different people making its definition *mushy and ambiguous*. Picquart didn't give a damn about honor—*just justice! That's why he made his 180 degree turn*! The deontological notion of duty, if you will, which for some framed the concept of honor differently from the way others viewed it—the way his superiors and other anti-Dreyfusards saw it—made any definition ultimately meaningless—*for them, honor was everything—justice nothing*!

"Picquart, himself, views honor differently from the way his superiors and other anti-Dreyfusards did."

"Sit down!"

I obediently did, but later regretted it. I went on a bit more softly, "It's not as simple as you would have it, that's what I'm trying to sort out in my muddled head—how to reconcile all the points of view of honor into a cohesive whole. Do you get that?"

"Don't lecture me, Sally! This is not the Sorbonne and I'm not one of your Goddamn students! I don't want to hear what philosophers have to say about *dentistry* or whatever you called it, so don't try to bamboozle me with some esoteric, philosophical babble! I'm not interested in how others view honor—*only how and why Picquart reversed his core beliefs and what that had to do with his sense of honor."*

"You're not listening—you don't understand—forget about honor, Adam. I now understand the rationale behind his change of heart."

"The only thing I understand is that you're both failing in what you set out to do. It's costing a bloody fortune to have the two of you here, and so far we have nothing to show for it. How does that make you feel?"

"Shitty!" we said simultaneously.

"Well, where's the *honor* in that?" he asked. "Before you interrupted, I was going to ask how what you haven't done *squares with your sense of honor—of justice*? Don't you think you've betrayed those principles?"

I jumped to my feet and shouted, "You know what, Adam, you can take this job and shove it up your culo, or as they say in Italian, you can shove it up your asino!"

He remained seated. "'Asino' means ass—like in donkey."

"That works, too, Adam!"

"Does that mean that you, Josiah, are quitting as well?"

'It sure as hell does, only I'll use English. *You can shove my job up your ass as well! Now get the hell out of my house. You know where the damn door is."*

When Adam slammed the door behind him, it jarred the building leaving the tympani sound reverberating through the walls—and through our bodies. After a few minutes, still dazed, I asked, "Was I dreaming, or was that real? Was that a terrible movie we just saw?"

"It was a movie, Sally. And we just walked out."

With dull eyes, we just gazed at one another. After ten minutes of so, I asked, "How about some chamomile tea with honey?"

"Yeah, anything to moisten my mouth."

I put up a big pot of water, like for drowning.

"Ouch! I burned my tongue," I shouted.

"That's not the only thing we've burned. You know those bridges?"

"Yeah—at both ends, leaving us stuck in the middle. You think we over-reacted?"

"Maybe—maybe. It's just that he hit our 'fight or flight' button." And, with a hint of remorse, he said, "but instead of choosing one over the other, we did both."

"We're grown ups, Josiah, maybe one of us should have exercised some restraint over our youthful impetuosity," I said nodding my head from side to side, "and held the other back from committing a serious blunder."

"But we were both offended by his allegations, and his tone. How could we have retained our self-respect if we let him shit all over us?"

"There's so much at stake, Josiah. We're in a foreign country, our baby is due in about three months, and we're out of work. The tornado has scooped us up, my head is spinning, and I see no horizon on the horizon."

He came over to my side, hugged me, and forced me to smile when he said, "Sweetheart, even if I have to kill pigeons, you'll always have something to eat."

"I know I can rely on my fearless hunter, but honey, if it were within your power, would you rewind this film and re-edit?"

"Hell no!"

After a few moments, he said, "I think."

"So you think we should reconsider? Maybe I should call him, say I'm through with distractions, that he'll have twenty pages within ten days?"

"And what would I tell him?"

I couldn't answer him. I slouched on the couch feeling smaller and smaller by the moment.

I can't remember the next two days. We went through the mundane parts of our lives hardly speaking. On the third day, when we were chewing on the bones and cartilage of a roasted chicken, our comfort food, I asked Josiah, "Do you suppose there was a grand design to all of this?"

"You mean, it was Adam's intention all along?"

"Like getting us out of the way for some reason?"

"Like HUAC?"

"Too far-fetched."

"Yeah, maybe. He's gone. You're gone. I'm gone."

"Can't be—that's another screenplay."

CHAPTER 17

Barely two weeks later, the phone rang. "Hello?"

"Surprise, Sally. It's Adam," the voice on the phone said.

"Who?"

"Forgotten me, already?"

"Josiah, stop horsing around. That's not funny."

"It's not Josiah. It's really me, Adam," the friendly voice said.

"Josiah, stop it already. I know you've got a good ear, but don't remind me of that horrid man. Tell me why you called. I'm right in the middle of an important scene."

The voice said, "That's sounds promising. Sally, my dear, the Italians make hundreds of cheese, but not feta. Whenever I ask a restaurant to prepare a plate of white spaghetti with feta, they end up adding something else that's not even close—like ricotta which is quite bland. Do you know ricotta?"

"Adam, or Josiah, whoever you are, get to the point, please."

"It's really me, Sally. Adam—like in Adam. I want to talk to you guys over a plate of your pasta and feta. Can you feed a poor hungry man who's salivating as we speak, this evening, say about 7:00pm?" All said with such sweetness, I wanted to puke.

"What the hell for?"

"Not on the telephone, please. I promise it won't be the kind of evening where I end up slamming the door on you, believe me."

"I can't promise the same."

"Allow me to take that chance, please."

"Make it 6:00pm. I'm hungry all the time. I can't wait 'till seven."

"See you at six."

After I hung up, I left my hand on the phone trying to figure out what the hell he was doing and why the hell I said yes. I dialed Josiah and was glad to have reached him so quickly. "Honey, can you get off at around 4:00 this afternoon," I asked as if nothing had happened, "and pick up some feta on your way home, please?"

"Sally, you feeling okay?"

"Yes, it's just that we have a surprise dinner guest who asked for our cheap-host dinner."

"You're kidding, right?"

"Serious."

"Adam?"

"Yup, the one and only, Adam Lapidus, aka, prick number one!"

"Merde! I won't be able to leave early. It's a new job and I'm trying to impress them with my work ethic, but I'll try to leave at five. A pound, you said?"

"Yeah, and half a pound of pitted olives."

"I can't stay on the phone, but I'm dying to find out why he's coming. Wish I could go home right now to prepare our strategy for this surprise encounter."

"Nothing to prepare. We've had this stuff percolating for awhile. Let's see where our impulses take us."

"Impulses with restraint."

"We'll see. Jo, how in the world did something as lovely as a prick become a pejorative?"

He laughed and said, "Maybe we'll discuss that with him."

When I hung up, I stared at the phone and heard myself echoing Josiah's, 'Merde!' How am I expected to get back to work now? That shit-head, barging in on us right now after two weeks of fear and worry. What the hell can he want? He's certainly not the groveling type, nor the supplicant type, nor the mea-culpa-I-blundered-so-please-forgive-me type.

I'd better prepare the salad. The next scene in this newsreel should be interesting.

An hour later, there was a knock, never a welcoming sound with its dull thud, and now even less welcoming. "Bonjour, Mr. Lapidus," I said opening the door, not bothering to extend my cheeks or my hand.

"I guess I shouldn't have expected your smile, Sally," he said with his green eyes somewhat dulled, "but I do miss it."

I didn't buy it.

"Well, you know, Mr. Lapidus," I said glacier-cold, "it has to be earned."

"My first name, you'll recall, is Adam. May I ask you to call me that please, so this conversation can start off on a less formal basis? May I come in?"

"Yes, of course—Adam," I said, saying his name almost like a reprimand.

"Where's Josiah?"

"At his new job," I said letting that sink in, "he usually gets off at seven but I asked him to come home at five. As you can see, he hasn't made it yet."

"I'm not offering anything to drink or eat before dinner because as soon as he comes it, we're sitting down to dinner."

"How's the baby?"

"Spirited!"

"It's in the genes, isn't it?"

"You got that right," I said, "as is survival as well!"

"When's the due date?"

"January 15th, 1951."

"An auspicious date."

"Any day it's born will be auspicious!" My responses sound like they're ending with exclamation points. I'd better be less truculent; otherwise I'll have no room to go up.

"Ah, I hear footsteps," and went to the door. "Adam Lapidus is here," as though he knew other Adams that could be mistaken for The Adam.

"My hands are dirty, Adam. Be right back," he said without a hello or a smile. When he came out he went straight to me and gave me a prolonged kiss. He nodded to Adam but didn't bother shaking his hand, and sat down on the couch. Good for Josiah. That'll show the bastard.

I tidied my blouse and said, "O.K., the dinner bell has rung."

We sat around the table. I lit the Sabbath candles, said the prayers and followed that by a shallow, "Shabbat Shalom" to Adam. I bent over and kissed Josiah hard on the mouth. Now he knows for sure I'm Jewish.

Without expecting to, without thinking about it, without intending to, without preparing to, without asking Adam to explain the purpose of his visit, without even giving him a chance to initiate the conversation, I bulldozed him with, "So, Adam, this was a Machiavellian plan of yours, all along, wasn't it?"

He looked surprised at the sudden attack and stopped chewing while I continued, "You know, you should keep your windows closed when you're angry and spiteful, and whatever else was going on in that conniving head of yours because as I was passing your office one day I heard you excoriating me to someone. It sounded like I was going to get axed. What you said worried me terribly until you invited me to Paris to do this cockamamie project of yours," I said without taking a breath, not imagining that I would be so pugnacious. "Firing me was not classy enough for you—no, you promoted me to a job designed for failure—making my life so miserable, I would fire myself."

Josiah stopped eating as well. I continued with fork in hand pointing at Adam in an accusatory manner, "You knew all along, didn't you, that this was the kind of project that couldn't be about one man alone, that like all biographies, there are many players involved, and in this case, those players turn out to be *The Crown Jewels of France!* I originally bought that crap of yours that I could isolate this guy and write about him only."

With the salad wilting before us and the pasta overcooking, I went on like a lioness, "You hoped all along, didn't you, that I would be so intellectually stimulated, so fascinated by the subject that it would force me to investigate the entire matter which would overwhelm me, and that I would be delayed, and troubled, and a mental mess. And you did that," I yelled at him, "knowing I was pregnant! You son-of-a-bitch!"

Before I gave him a chance to respond, I rose abruptly, said, *FANDUGU,* and walked over to the boiling pasta, picked it up but forgot to turn off the flame. The napkins I used for the hot handles caught fire and I dropped the whole pot, splashing boiling water and pasta over my legs. I screamed and slumped to the floor.

Both men jumped out of their seats. While Adam grabbed the napkins and tossed them into the sink, singeing his fingers in the process, Josiah dried my legs and helped me to bed. He went immediately to the medicine cabinet, got a jar of Vaseline, and proceeded to gently smooth the viscous ointment on my rapidly reddening legs.

Adam knocked softly on the open bedroom door. "May I come in?" I was sobbing but managed to say in a surprisingly loud voice, "No! Stay the hell out of my bedroom!"

He went back to the couch and cradled his head with his hands. Despite the searing pain, I was sure he was thinking: *Merde. This is not going the way I planned. It's a disaster. Should I go or stay?* He got up and walked to our bedroom door again. "Do you want me to call a taxi to take you to emergency?"

Josiah said, "The hospitals are not that great. Let's wait a few minutes and see how bad this is."

"But she's pregnant—shouldn't you ... "

"Now you're aware that I'm pregnant? NOW? You Prick!"

He knew better than to give me that crap about being respectful, so ignoring the insult, he said, "I want you to know that I'm not ashamed of what I did."

"What? Your timing stinks, Adam!" I yelled. "But thanks for confirming my suspicions."

"I think you've got a novel aborning, and you should proceed with it. You've got what it takes, Sally. Stay in France. Finish your research, write your novel in the very place this happened. Write about those crown jewels of French culture and their perspective on that seminal event that occurred on their watch."

As he got to the door, I shouted in a scalding voice, "What the *FUCK* do you think I'm doing?"

CHAPTER 18

"Honey, the red on your legs is deepening. We're going to the hospital."

"No, not yet. I was more startled than burned."

"Yeah, among the many startling things that happened tonight. It's red all over. I'm calling a taxi."

"Guess you'd better. Believe me, Jo, I had no idea I was going to explode like that. I intended to find out why he came here, but suddenly I got ... "

"Volcanic!"

"Yeah. Still."

"The bastard had it coming, but I was curious too."

"We'll never know."

I was barely able to walk into the clinic. The nurse looked once and pointed to the chair near the doctor's entrance. "I think we're being put near the front of the line, Jo. Being pregnant has some benefits."

I told the doctor in English what had happened. He touched it gently with his gloved fingers, and said, "Merde," knitting his thick eyebrows together, thinking, perhaps, that I didn't know what that word meant. That was not reassuring.

When we got home I said, "That cream must have anesthetic in it. The burning sensation has lessened."

"You're going to blister. When they pop, we gotta' make sure they don't get infected."

"With you ministering to me," I said trying to add some levity to a terrible evening, "I know nothing bad will happen. You're my protector, my healer, and favorite voodoo man."

"I could have used some voodoo myself tonight."

"My legs won't prevent me from writing or reading," I said trying to be cheery, "so tomorrow morning, I start again."

"Listen, sweetheart, we've got about six-eight weeks before the baby arrives so unless you want a French baby, you only have about four weeks to finish your research. We shouldn't be traveling during your last month. Think you can button it up in a month?" quickly adding, "if not, we'll stick it out until you're ready."

"I don't know. I'll try. No French baby for me though. I don't want to deny my mother the pleasure of having her oldest child give birth, besides, I'll need all the help I can get. And in January it's warmer in California than in Paris."

He tucked me into bed, a ritual I loved, and asked, "How are we going to celebrate Thanksgiving? It's just a couple of weeks away, and since turkeys are indigenous to the New World, they probably don't even raise them here yet. Have you ever seen it in a shop?"

"Never. We'll get squab and pretend."

"If worse comes to worse," he quipped, "I'll kill pigeons for us. Better still, honey, let's go back right away. We're both depression babies. Jobs will continue to be sporadic and our savings are dwindling fast. Let's tell the landlord we're leaving in a week or so. Whaddaya say?" he asked without expecting any resistance.

"Honey, I'm washed out," I said with a yawn. "Let's leave that for tomorrow, okay?"

After a restless night trying to get into a comfortable position with a basketball belly and bandages on throbbing legs, I came to the table the following morning groggy, yawning repeatedly, and as those things happen, Jo started yawning. I sat down to a breakfast he had prepared and while sipping my coffee slowly, I said, "Jo, listen, I've been measuring things and I think I want to have the baby here."

"What?"

"I know I should be home with my mother, but I feel like a mother here in France, a mother to all the characters I've been writing about. I can't leave until I'm finished writing this book, I don't think," I said tremulously, giving myself a way out.

"I was only kidding when I said I'd kill pigeons for you. What the hell do we do for money while you indulge yourself?"

"Please, don't be angry. I'm not indulging myself. Don't use that word again, okay? I feel so committed to the project, to my characters, that I don't want to budge from the place where their saga unfolded and played itself out—not until I'm finished."

"And what about your commitment to me? To the baby? To your mother? To how I'm going to support you? What does your conscience say about that, my dear?"

After yesterday's stressful day, I tried to stay calm and said, "Honey, we've got some income coming from the apartment buildings in Santa Monica my family and I own, so we can live on that until I'm finished," I pleaded, then paused before I threw out, "about a year or so ... "

"A year? And what the hell am I supposed to do in the meantime?" he said raising his voice, forgetting that I was suffering from the burns and my own deep conflict, but he went on, "France is still recovering from the devastation of the War, and their fledgling film industry doesn't need me, and even if they did, it would pay enough to buy the shot for killing those pigeons. And I'll be damned if I'm going to sit around waiting for those monthly checks, so forget it."

"Wait a second, Jo, last night you said if we have to stay, we'll stay. What's going on?"

"Well, that was last night. Today is today."

"Why are you running hot and cold?"

He just shook his head from side to side, didn't answer, so I went on, "I have a career to think about, Josiah. A novelist's career, maybe. I hope. I'm on to something and I want to pursue it. Maybe not a year—six to eighth months. Please."

"So I don't matter? What about *my* career? It's not as a househusband, I guarantee! If you're better in a couple of days, we'll start packing," he said leaving no room for discussion.

He saw my head no-nodding, and continued, "We're married. You're having my baby. We're strangers in a foreign land. We've got careers to pursue. I can't pursue mine here. You can write anywhere. In the toilet. In the bedroom. In the park. And above all else, in Santa Monica! So get over this urge of yours to stay. We're not staying. Is that clear??"

"Stop yelling at me, Goddamn it! I'm not your child or your slave! Get off that Napoleonic high horse of yours and try to understand my need to stay, to round out this project, to fulfill my new dream," I said, tears beginning to well.

Tense from what had happened, he lost it. "You know what the goddamn problem is with you, Sally? You were hired to write an original screenplay, but I realize now that you can't write a screenplay from scratch. You're incapable of it. That's your problem, Sally. You're not an originator, you're an abstracter! You need to distill the essence from a novel—the key issues—the engine driving the plot—*that* you're good at—*that's* where you're at your best—but starting from scratch? You don't have that ability. That's why you're writing your own novel, to lay out all the permutations so you can extract its essence, and then you can begin," he kept shouting while pacing the floor. "You need that intermediate step, don't you? You're taking money under false pretenses! Adam was right all along. You stink at what he hired you for!"

I got up and put my nose close to his. "I don't give a shit about your analysis, Dr. Freud! Maybe you're right, but what the hell does it matter? Right now, it's the novel that's grabbed me. That's what I'm determined to finish. Who knows about an eventual screenplay?" And at the same pitch, I yelled, "I'M DETERMINED TO FINISH IT HERE! IN PARIS!"

"Sally, I'm going back. With or without you. *Got It?"*

I softened a bit and said, "Honey, bear with me. I'm all confused. You told me that it was okay to stay and finish up here, if that's what I wanted, and you recently repeated it, and now you've made a one hundred and eighty degree turn. What gives with your stupid ambivalence? Are you going to change your mind again tomorrow?"

"Sally, I'm determined. We're going back together. Start packing."

"I'm not going, Jo. Take it or leave it!"

"Oh, yeah? It's my baby you're having. I'll be damned if you're going to have it without me!"

"Then you're staying?"

"No. You're going!"

"Hell, I will!"

"Well, screw you!"

Before the door slammed, I yelled, "Good riddance!"

He returned immediately and barreled on in a tone filled with disgust, "I want to remind you that you're writing about the dead, Sally! The DEAD! We're alive. We're the ones that matter. You, the baby and I, not those long dead characters you've been buried with all these months. Disinter yourself. Get out from their clutches, rejoin the living, Goddamn it! We're more important than those guys! Once and for all, start packing!"

"They're not dead to me! And, don't tell me what to do, Josiah! I'll do what the hell I want! Remember that!" I said sticking my chin way up.

"Now I realize what I did," he said moving his head from side to side in disbelief. "I married a nut case! I see what your problem is. When we went to Dieppe to visit the statue of Saint-Saens and discovered that a bomb had destroyed it during the war, you wept, as though it had been your statue or mine.

"And when we visited Zola's tomb in the Pantheon, you burst into tears, as though it were *you* who had been buried there—or *me*. Why, it seemed like you were weeping at *your own burial sites!*

"The same thing happened at Giverny. You were transformed, transmuted, transmogrified," stuttering through the words, "into Monet. And as you placed a stone at his doorstep, you sobbed like you sobbed when you placed stones in front of all those other gravesites. Why, Sally, you've been placing stones on your own gravesites! You've become all these people, Sally, individually, collectively. You are crazy, you know! Projection is one thing, empathy another. Identification, yes, but you—you're out of control. I married a wacko!

"You know what else just flashed before me," he raged on ignoring my sobs. "A story you told me soon after we met, about one of your lunatic ancestors in the thirteenth century who experienced a mystical vision, and set out from Spain to Rome where he planned to complain to Pope Nicolas III about Christianity's treatment of the Jews. Then that crazy relative of yours tried to convert the Pope to Judaism!"

"That was over seven hundred years ago," I said with tears flowing, "and the man's name was Avraham Abulafia. I have no way of knowing whether he was my direct ancestor or not. He spelled his name differently. And I'm not trying to convert you, sir, I'm just trying to help you understand my point of view."

"You mean you're trying to *convert* me to your point of view!" he snarled.

I got up and walked to the bedroom, my body shaking. When I turned to him to speak, I knew he could see my chin tremble, tears meandering down my cheeks. "Josiah, you're right on all counts. I *am* out of control," I said with a quivering voice, "I don't know what's happened to me here but I'm on a journey of discovery and it's fascinating.

"I'm not the person I once was. I am living the lives of others—trying to give unfettered voice to their inner selves.

"Through some weird alchemy, I've become many someone elses. I don't know who I am anymore. And for the time being, I can't let go." And then added softly but firmly, "Nor will I."

I sat on the edge of our bed and said, "Come here, please, Josiah. You've got to help me. I feel like a teenage girl trying to discover who she really is—who she wants to be—to settle into one's own skin—to be comfortable with herself. Sweetheart, I'm a mess. I can't seem to separate—it's become a compulsion of mine, an uncontrollable passion. I've got to stay and finish the job. Haven't you ever been obsessed by something?"

He remained at the doorway and didn't make his way to the edge of the bed. He said, "Yes, a long time ago," and paused with a distant look in his eyes. "But yours is more like a sick compulsion. I can't help you if I don't understand. And I don't."

I looked at him with surprise, confusion, dismay and profound disappointment. He then said, "So that's it then?"

With my chin lowered, still trembling, still crying, I said, "Looks that way," unable to believe what was happening. How did it get so far?

He opened the door and, in an audible whisper, said, "Some *man-of-the-house* I am."

About 2:00am, I heard the key gently turning the tumblers and, ignoring the pain in my legs, I rushed to the door. When he saw me he was momentarily startled.

I looked longingly at him and watched as his briefly shocked eyes quickly turned into a look of despair, of mournfulness, of melancholy. Overwhelmed by the pitiful sight, a cascade of uncontrollable tears rushed down my face. I hugged him around the neck so tightly that neither one of us could speak for a moment.

I soon let go, cradled his face in my hands and looked at him as lovingly as when we had first made love. "Oh, Josiah, you're the love of my life! I missed you so! I thought I was going to be struck dead by a lightening bolt—to penalize me for my cruel statements, my horrible shouts, my juvenile behavior, my petulance, my selfishness, my egotism. We're not going to be separated, we've got to work something out. We will, I promise," the tears flowing still.

He took me to the sofa, and asked softly, "What's to work out, honey? You want to stay and I want to go. How do you reconcile the two? Before you tell me, how are your legs?"

"I don't know. The bandages are still on but the pain has returned, and when I peeked, they were very red. About your first question, here's what I've been thinking, so tell me what your reactions are, after you hear me out," I said gently hoping to soften my earlier comments.

"You were absolutely right about my need to write a novel before a screenplay, and because I was so angry at the time, I didn't admit it to you. But after Adam gave me all his bullshit, there was an explosion in my head illuminating everything. That's when I yelled at him that a novel was indeed what I was writing. That shout confirmed what I must have felt inside.

"You see, Josiah, I need to finish my novel in the place where it happened. But I don't want to be separated from you. I'll ask my mother and brother to send me my portion of the profits from our apartment buildings. That should be enough to help us live modestly."

"How does that differ from we talked about earlier? And may I know what your plans are for me, my patroness?"

"There are burgeoning film makers all over Europe and you can act as a consultant, sort of a roving consultant to help them develop their skills, and if someone wants to hire you full time, fine."

"You're out of your mind, Sally. I was and still am an assistant director. I'm not going to fly under false colors and tell people I'm something more than I am. With my limited experience, no one is going to hire me as a consultant, so give that thought up," he said, waving his hand dismissively.

"With that first film company, you were quite useful, you gave them many good suggestions. You even rewrote the dialogue to give it an ambiguous ending leaving the audience wondering whether it was murder or accidental. And you lightened the mood on the set. All those good things."

"Yeah, right, so much so that the director complained to Adam and I got fired."

"You quit!"

"You remember what Adam said about how I undermined the director's authority. I would have been fired if I hadn't quit that night. Stop being naive, please. I'm not qualified to be a consultant because I'm still learning. I'm not a bullshit artist. Right now, I have no interest in pretending to be what I'm not. Not like you!"

"That's cruel. Are you saying I don't have what it takes to write a novel?"

"Right now, I don't know what you have. You're doing something for the first time and you could do it at home while you're nursing our baby. But no, you've got to pretend that you can only be inspired by being in the place where your lovers once lived. That's all merde, Sally! If, in the future, you were planning a novel about the Civil War, would we be moving to Gettysburg? Or the Peloponnesian Wars, would we be moving to Greece? Or how about the First World War, the trenches?" he asked with disgust and impatience.

"Just this once. I promise. I need to be here," I pleaded.

Triggered, he sat back, and with quiet vehemence said, "You know, my dear, I think I have you figured out. You've fallen in love with ghosts. You're making love to all of them. They're giving you orgasms I'm incapable of giving you. You'd rather be with the dead than with the living. They're not threatening to you, they don't make demands, they accept you as you are, their love for you is unconditional. In return you love them unconditionally. If Freud were still alive, he'd write a chapter on you alone, maybe a whole book." he said, turning away from me as tears began trickling down his face.

I cradled my face in my hands, wept loudly and said, "Josiah, my mind is like a pot of stew, all those ingredients bumping into one another, with nothing emerging on top. Can you be patient with me for awhile longer?"

"The unambiguous answer is, NO! I'm going back with or without you, and I want to know right now, not tomorrow, right now, whether you're going to come with me."

I looked at him with a puzzled expression, unable to speak. He continued, "You act like we live someplace on the Steppes of Central Asia. We live in Los Angeles, remember? The libraries at USC, UCLA, and our own huge downtown library? These are not places with a few hand-me down books donated by The Salvation Army. These are major institutions. Why can't you continue your research there, for god's sake?"

"I need to go to bed now. Are you coming?"

"No. The couch will do tonight."

"Good idea," and slammed the bedroom door.

An hour later, I got up and sat on the couch. Nudging him gently didn't work so I whispered in his ear, "Josiah, we need to talk. Wake up, please." I had to repeat that three times.

He opened a sliver of one eye and said, "Sally, I'm exhausted and can't think right now. I've been walking the streets all night trying to get a handle on this—trying to sort out everything, and right now I'm too tired to talk and certainly incapable of making any decisions. I need to sleep. We'll talk in the morning," he said, yawning in my face.

I just sat there, troubled. He opened the sliver again and said, "Honey, please get up. You're sleeping there," pointing to the bedroom. "I'm sleeping here."

"Aren't you getting into your pajamas?"

"Tonight my clothes are my pajamas."

I slowly got up and started towards the bedroom door. I turned to see if he had changed his mind and saw him stretch out leaving his feet dangling over the side. "Sure you don't want to change into your pajamas?"

"Enough with the pajamas already." He pointed once again and said sleepily, "You, there. Me here. Sleep. Right now. Get it?" and turned his back towards me.

Sleep eluded me all night so as soon as I saw a hint of daylight, I got up.

"Mmm, that coffee is better than an alarm clock," he said still stretched out on the couch.

"Not really. It's my third batch. You slept through the first two," and came to his side.

"What time is it?"

"12.30."

"PM or AM?"

"Today, I don't care," and sat alongside him, brushing his hair away from his forehead with my fingers.

I had been awake all night figuring how I was going to approach him in the morning, but quite unexpectedly, I said with mist fogging my eyes, "I love you, Josiah. I never knew how much until I threw you away. How stupid of me not to know that until I almost lost you. God, is that the only way to learn?"

"Gotta' pee," he said rushing past me.

He had just broken this important moment so, bewildered, I just sat there. I then got up, poured him coffee and put the French toast up.

The smell wafted into the bathroom. "Smells great, Sally."

That sounds promising. "Your coffee is poured and the toast will be ready in a couple of minutes, with your favorite jam, to sweeten your stomach and your spirit, ha, ha," I said in a tone that recognized its banality,

Without commenting, he sat down and slowly picked at the French toast. That surprised me since he usually wolfed down his food. I said, "Glad you're eating slowly, Josiah, it improves digestion."

"Sally, today nothing will improve my digestion, or disposition."

I realized there was no good way to segue into what had kept me up all night, so I took a spoonful of jam and began, "I've got a plan for us. Are you open to hearing it? Please say yes. I've been rehearsing all night long. But first, how'd you sleep last night?" regretting the question since the couch was lumpy, and sleeping with dangling feet is not a recipe for rest.

"At first, I looked for a restful place for my body, and my brain," he said emphasizing the word, *brain.* "I felt like a restless stone skipping the surface of a pond, but soon sank deep within its waters, resurfacing only when you woke me in the middle of the night," looking at me with disbelief, "but, fortunately, I fell right back to sleep."

"Great. Sleep," I said looking for some agreement, even a superficial one, "that great resuscitator!"

"And you?" he asked, his voice showing he really didn't care. But he remembered my burns and asked, "How're your legs?"

"Not so good, and as for sleep, for the past couple of days, it seems I haven't slept at all."

"Oh, yeah, I believe that," he said unconvinced, knowing how much I needed my sleep.

"Stuff yourself, Josiah, no major decisions should be considered on an empty stomach."

"Or on a sleepless night either."

"Adrenaline and caffeine are good substitutes."

I tried to muster enough enthusiasm to be contagious and said, "O.K., here's my plan. It's mid-November—we'll leave right before Hanukkah/Christmas. That'll give me about a month to do some research—in situ—to walk the same streets as my characters. Then I'll have a month at home before the baby comes."

Not sharing my enthusiasm, he asked with his mouth full, "And what the hell will I be doing in the meantime?"

"Keep looking for day jobs in film, and whatever money you bring in would be welcome. If not, see Paris, walk along the Seine watching uninhibited lovers, look at Notre Dame the way Monet did, in the morning, at twilight, in the rain, in the fog. Visit The Jeu de Paume, go to the top of the Eiffel Tower, sip coffee in The Tuileries. Drink it all in, Josiah," I said with increasing enthusiasm. "Who knows when we'll be returning. I promise to gallop through my research, and we'll be on our way by mid-December. Guaranteed. Sound like a plan?" I asked, displaying my dazzling smile which in the past had originally won him over, and which, he had said more than once, had always made him wet down there, but, as I looked at his face, none of that.

With a hint of disgust in his voice, he barked, "So now you're a pimp for Paris?"

"Ohhhh!" I gasped, jolted.

"Oh, you didn't like that, huh?" he asked. "One other thing, Sally. You have the ability to recover quickly, but I'm in shock at what happened and, with what now sounds like your change of heart," he said coldly. "It takes me more time to recover—takes me more time to digest everything. I've hardly opened my eyes, I'm half asleep, and you come up with this. You're timing is always off. Can't it wait until I'm through with breakfast? Otherwise I'm going right back to sleep."

I forced myself to ignore his nasty comment. I was very disappointed. "Of course, finish your breakfast. Funny, Josiah, I always thought that it was you who recovered quickly and that it took me forever. But, please, just tell me whether my short-term plan is plausible. Tell me it's not a bad idea. Tell me it's okay with you. Some reactions please, otherwise I won't be able to sleep again tonight. The baby needs to sleep—your baby—both your babies—tell me something," I pleaded, on the verge of misting up once again.

He got up, came over to my side of the table, kissed me coldly on the forehead and said, "Sounds like a magic plan of reconciliation."

"Are you being sarcastic?"

"I can't register any feelings right now. Except fatigue," he said through a yawn.

"What?"

"Let's not argue, okay?"

"Josiah, what are you saying? I'm making up with you. I'm admitting what a selfish fool I was. It was a venial sin, that's all. It's undoable. I'm undoing it! We're together. We'll always be together. Why are you separating us with such coldness?"

He sat back on the chair and said quietly, "Yesterday, my dear, we got so close," and extending his arms wide, said, "to getting so far. I can't get over that. Like an earthquake, you shook the very foundations of our relationship. When my very moorings are loosened, it gives me pause, about how strongly you really feel about me, about how your career comes first—*before me*. That's a hard realization to get over, Sally. It's hard for me to swallow. And, it seems you're still thinking that way, so please, I'm still reeling from the ease with which you were ready to throw me into the River Seine. And right now I'm suffering from a power outage—there's no current going through me. I'm still numb. Would you pour me some more coffee, please?" he asked flatly.

"Oh, my God, Josiah, I'm so, so sorry! You've got to forgive me! I beg you! I understand why you feel that way, but believe me when I tell you with all my heart that I didn't want to throw you overboard!" I began to sob.

"Aren't you the one who's always preaching about how our actions speak louder than our words?"

"I didn't take any action, honey, they were just words."

"But your intentions were actionable."

"Oh, my God, Josiah," I repeated, sobbing, despondent.

"Stop calling for God, Sally. He's not around, and I don't know when he'll return, if ever. Remember, he left right during the war and hasn't been seen or heard from since."

My body folded upon itself with overwhelming sadness as copious tears fell. I managed through my sobs to ask, "Which war?"

Wet with mascara-darkened streaks, my face must have appeared like a mournful, weathered cemetery sculpture—one that had died more than once.

"'Which war?'" he asked, "Can't you guess?

"You've broken my heart, Sally. Our lives are not on film—we can't go back and edit—we can't take out the parts we don't like and start all over—this script cannot be changed. Life is not a dress rehearsal. You wrote the script, sweetheart," he cynically addressed me, "you said what you said for better or for worse, and right now it's for worse. I don't know if I can ever get over this," despair etched over his face and in his cracking voice. "I now know who you are, Sally, and where you live."

I had never witnessed such a funereal expression on his face before. "Josiah, I've broken my heart too," speaking between sobs, "but even worse than that, the heart of the only man I've ever loved. Let's leave right away. You say metaphorically that *you know who I am and where I live,* and I tell you that I finally discovered a major part of who I am, and that is *as your wife*, and where I live—*beside you.* Be patient while I struggle with the rest of me. Let's go home in the next few days. What do you say?"

Before he could reply the doorbell rang. We had puzzled expressions on our faces. Jo asked, "Who could that be? It's not that shit-face again. Can it be?"

"Geez. Not now. I'll be damned if I'll let him in!" I bounced up with surprising alacrity and said, "I'll check. Finish up." I knew I must have looked awful so I took my handkerchief, started drying my face and took big gulps of air to try and quell the flow of tears, pausing for a moment before opening the downstairs door.

I came running up the stairs as best I could, and shouted, "Surprise! Three letters. One from Universal Studios, one from Warner Bros., both addressed to you, and the other from Peter Nathan at Twentieth Century Fox, addressed to me," I said, hoping they were bearers of good tidings.

"Sounds exciting," he said with a burst of joy.

I waited until he read his first.

"Hey, look at that. Universal wants to meet with me when we return—about a director's job, and so does Warner Bros. No offers, just talk. What a great response to those letters I sent after Adam forced us to resign! That's invigorating. The wake-up call I need," then added, "besides your coffee, that is," he said, smiling for the first time.

I read mine. "This one from Pete is not so good. Let me read it to you."

"Sally, hope you and your baby are thriving, immersed as you are in the high culture of France, and best of all, warm, flaky croissants on every corner, and sour-dough baguettes.

"I wasn't much surprised when Adam told me what had happened between the two of you—actually, the three of you. After all the years you spent with us, this change might help you explore other facets of your talent.

When you return, call me so we can have lunch together, a long lunch, when you're not busy nursing your newborn, of course.

"On another matter, it looks like HUAC will be sending you and other writers on our staff, past and present, subpoenas to testify, so you'd better plan on being back here before the end of the year. From what they're telling us, hearings will probably begin in January or February of 1951. If you stay there, they do have the authority to call you back home, though they didn't do it for Bertolt Brecht and some others, but they do have that option.

"Please know that we'll make available our archives so you can revisit all the films with which you were involved. That should help prepare you for any untoward questions about how you inserted 'communist propaganda in those films.'

"It's come to that, and we're all up in arms against these spurious allegations. Try to recall, as well, any questionable political conversations you may have had with anyone, just so that you're not caught unawares.

"Sorry to burden you with all this garbage when you're so close to giving birth, or have already done so, but there's an epidemic across the country, proving once again that joy is ephemeral and strife never far away—like the opposite sides of the same coin.

"But, we endured the Second World War, so this too we shall overcome.

"Best to Josiah. I'm sure he doesn't have anything to worry about with HUAC, but I want to have him for lunch as well—separately.

"Adieu, Pete."

Bewildered and disturbed we just sat there looking at one another without saying a word. Josiah spoke first, "It looks promising for me, sweetheart—on all counts," he added, "but somewhat frightening for you. That worries me. I don't like what that sounds like," he said, his India ink black eyebrows knitted together.

Pleased at his appearance of concern, and his tender use of the word, *sweetheart,* I said, "I have nothing to worry about! I wrote B Movies, small ones only, horror movies, science fiction, noir stuff, nothing with a *message,* let alone a *let's-go-communist message.* I have nothing to hide. Let them see my films. They'll know then."

"But you know what happened in 1947—innuendos, suggestions, implications, associations, all the stuff without merit that condemned a whole bunch of people and that can easily condemn you," Jo said. "Who knows what innocent remark you may have made that somebody may recall and possibly misinterpret."

"I'll be okay, you'll see. I'll be safe at home plate. Home plate, Josiah—home plate," I said sporting a relaxed smile. "Actually, this makes all of our conversation moot, doesn't it?" hoping this would end it all.

"Not really, Sally, it doesn't quite take us off the hook—emotionally, existentially. You were *ready to throw* me away, like a mere bagatelle. You said it and behaved that way, so this news is just surface news, that's all. How can I forget that? Ever? It hurts me to my very core."

"Je le regrette, mon amour," I said licking the tears from my lips, "je le regrette profondement!"

Unmoved by those tears, he continued, "Remember our friend, Omar Khayyam? How often, when I was courting you, we used to throw quatrains at one another? Remember the one about the moving finger?

The moving finger writes, and having writ,
Moves on. Nor all your Piety nor Wit
Shall lure it back to cancel half a line,
Nor all your tears wash out a single word of it.

"Sally, you see, it can't be undone," he said on the verge of tears.

"My God, Josiah," I jumped in. "What in the world are you saying? That poem is about accepting what has happened in life. It's fatalistic. It's existential. It's about accepting those things over which we have no control. It allows for no redemption, no recovery. But you and I have control over what has happened. I blundered. I made a mistake—not an irrevocable one—not an irreversible one!

"Don't make me grovel! Goddamn it, Josiah! Are you burying me? Are you burying us? Stop being so goddamn self-righteous and sanctimonious. You're not the Pope!" I yelled.

Without saying a word, he looked at me coldly and impassively. Breaking the silence, I said with an overwhelming sadness, my shoulders slumped over, "For the first time I see a cruel streak in you, a stubbornness, an unforgiving rectitude. It's not flattering at all."

Softly, I said, "I now know the totality of who *you are*, and where *you live*!"

"Well, Sally, you've brought out the worst in me," he said unashamedly. Then added, "You never know the totality of anyone—ever. Even for a busy body with an inquiring mind like you," he said softly looking at me with a hint of a dark facet of his life. It left me puzzled, and even though I was indeed a *'busy body,'* I was involved with more important things at the moment to probe.

I rushed to his side and cradled his face in my hands, "Ohhhh, no!! Josiah, my love," I said passionately, lovingly, "that hurts me to the core. I want to bring out the best in you always, never the worst. You're my husband and I want you to remain so for the rest of my life. I never want to lose you. The thought of a life without you leaves me numb!" and then I broke down with uncontrollable wheezing sobs barely squeezing out the words, "You must, you must," I couldn't finish. For the first time in my life, I saw him crying, his face now less stolid.

After a pause, with a subdued tone, I continued, "Listen, my dear, I don't think we should prolong this brief episode in our lives. I do want to remind you, however, that you too were ready to throw me overboard as well. You were ready to go back without me."

"Only after you were determined to stay," pointing his finger at me, "only after you agreed to the separation."

"No, I never did."

"Oh, yes you did!"

I jumped on his lap, heavier now with the weight of two, and said with tender ardor in my voice, but with no tears this time, "Josiah, mon amour, m'inamorato, my only true love, my first and last love, my Olympian love ... ." Suddenly I paused, my profound seriousness waned, and smiling, continued with, "my Rubaiyat love, my Romeo, my Tristan—" and broke out laughing.

He laughed too and said, "That sounds like so much schmaltz, treacle, saccharine, nectar, honey, gooey molasses, and syrup … "

We continued laughing and hugged each other as hard as we had ever done. As we remained in that position, I expected a hardness to swell beneath me, but it wasn't forthcoming. Disappointed, I assured myself that it would come and said, "We've reached the point where we can't anymore, for the sake of our newcomer, but be patient and detumescence will soon be yours."

He grunted, "Geez, you're too heavy for me. Sit on the couch, please." Then to my surprise he asked, "In France or the USA?"

"Do you need reassurance? Honey, just so that you understand once and for all," I said looking deeply into his eyes, "with or without those letters, I will never let you go. I will never think of that as a possibility ever again. It will never be an option." Then changing into a wicked expression, I added, "Unless you stray, and then all bets are off."

"Like you've strayed with Monet, and Pissarro, and Degas, and Cezanne, and Zola, and Picquart?" he asked with feigned suspicion.

The change of tone relaxed me and I said, "I must admit, I have taken them as lovers, Monet, Zola, Picquart, and my fellow Sephardic, Pissarro. Yes, but not Degas or Cezanne." Bemused by the thought, I went on, "On the other hand, I should have taken Degas and Cezanne. The energy of their certitude—yes, that can be a turn-on—but their hatred is a turn-off. What is it about hatred and anger that leave no room for ambiguity, for ambivalence? All that passion. Ahh, to know genius with attitude—that must be something, huh?"

"You know, of course, ma cheri, that I knew all along," he said, "no spouse is ever unaware of infidelity."

"You've caught me *in flagrante delicto*. But, your honor, there were mitigating circumstances—I fell in love with the dead. I know now, the living are better. Forgiven?"

He paused, and I saw on his face that he must have been wondering whether to continue this badinage or awaken the elephant in the room, but thankfully, he decided to put everything on the back burner, I hoped forever, but that look on his face told me that maybe it was only for the time being.

"Forgiven by reason of inherited insanity. I knew I had married a wacko, so there's contributory negligence. Case dismissed!" Our kiss lingered until we both had to gasp for air.

CHAPTER 19

"One more week, Josiah." I have to finish up with Zola—last one—promise."

With an air of hushed solemnity, I was disinterred in 1908 and re-buried in The Pantheon—where I belonged in the first place. The place for those few Frenchmen who have sustained the ideals of what it means to be *French*, those who have raised the concept of *Frenchness* to enviable and emulatable heights. This was the way my beloved France repaid me for having saved its integrity. Others would have called it saving its *honor*, but that word means nothing to me. Integrity, however, does.

The exalted cry of the French Revolution had devolved into a tyranny that we're still condemned to suffer through. Yet there is some hope, some progress made by those of us who have tried to keep French Civilization afloat.

As for me, Emile Zola, too much already has been said about me, of me, around me, underneath me, in a whirligig of conflicting opinions, and it's time to speak up for myself. Yes, I did sacrifice my fortune, my reputation, my allegiances, my friendships, and ultimately my life, not for *honor*, whatever the hell that means, but for one guiding principle, not a deontological one—damn the philosophers for that one—but for justice based on truth, not as adjudicated by the feckless, but by The Truth! That's my moral imperative! That is my duty as a sentient being! That's it. The quiddity of Emile Zola!

All else is mere merde.

If you must know, I didn't give a damn about Captain Dreyfus. I didn't much care for Jews anyway, but he was an innocent man suffering the most horrible of tortures for a crime he did not commit.

Our exalted concept of *Frenchness* was sullied, I hope not irrevocably. The Army—Mon Dieu, our beloved French Army continued to commit injustices to preserve, as they blindly put it, their *honor.* More merde! What a price we all paid for that!

When *J'Accuse* was published, it was as though a celestial ball had rung, sending crystalline peals of revelation reverberating throughout the world. French-speaking Canada and Russia denounced me and praised the Army instead. The Pope of the Ralliement, Leo XIII, kept quiet but allowed the Jesuit Review, La Civilita Cattolica, to rail against the Jews. The plot, it said, was hatched at the Zionist Congress in Basel to deliver Jerusalem—that the over-arching problem was the *Constituent Assembly of 1789* granting Jews French citizenship—that that law must be repealed!

I received letters of congratulations from over thirty thousand supporters. A concerned San Francisco Examiner worried that "Zola May Be Cast Into a Dungeon." Even Mark Twain, writing in the New York Herald, said something about how cowards and hypocrites in military and ecclesiastical circles propagate every year by the millions, but that it takes five hundred years to produce a Joan of Arc or a Zola.

In the early days of my trial, there was a steady stream of supporting telegrams from America, Britain, Japan, Peru, Rumania, and one from Belgium containing over a thousand names. At the end of the first day, that rabid anti-Semite, Drumont, had whipped into a frenzy the crowd outside the court building. A thousand people stormed the courtyard of the Palais de Justice, screaming for my blood. Had a special police van not been summoned at that very moment, I would have been torn apart. When I was found guilty, fined 3,000 francs and sentenced to one year in prison, The Chicago Tribune wrote, "Such a farcical perversion of the methods of justice could not be conceived as occurring in England or America, probably in no other country where courts exist, except in France or Spain."

The Daily News of London wrote off France as being, " ... virtually in the hands of a military government."

Budapest's Pester Lloyd asked, "To what low depths must the nation have sunk which casts Zola into prison?"

The Berliner Tageblatte wrote that, "Yesterday, the French Army won its first victory since its defeat in 1870."

The Bee of the District of Columbia, a black owned newspaper, wrote, "French justice seems to have fled to brutish beasts, for the verdict is simply an expression of the prejudice and race hate of an uninformed and inferior mob."

World opinion for the most part supported me, however, thousands of Catholic children learned to call each of their chamber pots, "a Zola."

I escaped to England and spent a year there.

Dreyfus, much to his credit, behaved in his public dishonor, honorably. For him the loss of his good name meant that the honor of his family had been tarnished, a condition worse than death. His determination to stay alive, to prove his innocence, erased all thoughts of suicide His wife, Lucie, showed me one of his letters written from his wretched solitary confinement on Devil's Island, on tear stained paper. In response to Othello's question about what Iago meant by his manhood, honesty and wisdom, Dreyfus quoted him in his letter,

'Good name in man and woman, dear my lord,
Is the immediate jewel of their souls.
Who steals my purse, steals trash; 'tis something, nothing;
'Twas mine, 'tis his, and has been slave to thousands;
But he who filches from me my good name
Robs me of that which not enriches him
And makes me poor indeed.'

"And, I tell you my dear love," Dreyfus continued in that letter, "that I need no longer look up the passage. I know it by heart—deep in my heart. I know that one day justice will be served, that I will be exonerated, but living here, without you and the children, disgraced, humiliated, and dishonorably discharged from the Army which I loved and respected all my life, takes a will, a spirit, a hope, all of which are difficult to sustain on a daily basis, even on an hourly basis. The incongruity of it all, the compromised and faulty decisions of my superiors, the collective lies, my exalted belief in France's commitment to truth and justice—where had it all gone? Were it not for my longing to embrace you and the children one more time, in a prolonged embrace, a sustaining dream that gives me breath, gives me strength, gives me life, I would cease to exist."

When Lucie saw the disturbed look on my face, she understood the source of my discomfort. Before I could utter a word, she said, "Before I read another word, Monsieur Zola, no heart can be insensitive to those sentiments, of course, but I see in your eyes more than just sympathy for his plight—something else. Alfred is too well-educated not to know what a villain Iago was—that he was devious, deceptive, duplicitous, disingenuous—yes, all those descriptions are valid—that he meant not a word of what he said—that it was not a reflection of his inner philosophy but a show of contempt for Othello, knowing that he would take his pious sentiments at face value. Alfred, of course, was focusing solely on the merit of Iago's words."

"I'm glad you explained, my dear Lucie, because certainly Iago always pretended to be what he was not. *Esse quam videri*—to be, not to seem, but for him, to *seem* mattered. Yes, I'm certain Alfred has the true measure of Iago.

"But I must tell you, good sir," Lucie said after a pause, "Iago is the standard bearer, the Polaris, the guiding light of the French military. And when he says, *O world: To be direct and honest is not safe,* he found a ready audience in the military, but no resonance with Alfred. Oh, no, not my Alfred. He continues to be *direct and honest*, believing, as we all do, that his honesty will eventually exonerate him."

I nodded in hopeful agreement, but I had to stop reading those letters.

Until Lucie brought me another batch.

They were filled with disturbing comments " ... promising to bear up until I'm vindicated, to go on living. The oppressive heat—the interminable monsoons—the insects, my body covered with bites and sores—feverish, colicky, unable to eat even the occasional piece of rancid meat, my body quickly deteriorating to the extent that my guard called a physician who brought me some canned milk. My teeth have loosened, my hair thinned, my clothing sags from the lack of nutritious food. The relentless pounding of the waves that at one time, during happy times, were an anodyne, but now, more like spikes in my head.

"I am breaking apart. I have begun, my dear Lucie, to rot.

"I remember what that insufferable, anti-Semitic Schopenhauer once said, "*If God created the world, I should not wish to be God.*" He failed to mention that God did not create the world, but *Hell* instead—that inner-world, the world of *Hell* that I now occupy.

"In my diary I wrote that the piece of merde who committed this crime will one day be exposed, and if I had my hands on him for a few minutes, I'd torture him the way he has tortured me. I would then cut out his heart and guts and testicles without pity, and feed them to the snakes. Revenge, my dear Lucie, is nourishing me, it gives me hope and keeps me alive—that, and seeing you and the children at least one more time."

Another letter described " ... that after seventeen months, I was put in irons. Can you believe that? Lying on my back I was immobilized by four bars placed in wooden blocks at the foot and ... "

Enough, I told Lucie! I'm not writing a novel about your husband. I don't want feelings to enter into my expose. Just the facts without emotion. We'll damn them, and vindicate your husband with the truth—not with sympathy.

I returned the batch of letters, but on one, my eye caught the name, Cyrano. I knew that Edmund Rostand was a supporter of Dreyfus, so I pulled that one back. To my astonishment, shortly before I wrote *J'Accuse* on January 13, 1898, I had gone to see the opening of, *Cyrano de Bergerac,* and while the performance was going on, I couldn't help fantasizing that Cyrano, with his integrity and sword intact, might have joined us Dreyfusards in combating the conspiracies unfolding before us, slicing right through them! Lucie had been at the opening as well, and must have written him about it, because in one of his letters he dreamed of Cyrano, with his liberating 'Excalibur' sword coming to his defense.

So much for delusions and fantasies.

But hope is a powerful oxygenator and sustainer!

Yet, among the many humiliations surrounding this Affaire, Dreyfus wrote " ... that the night before the assembly when I was going to be stripped of my braids and my rank as an officer, I had to grind down my own sword, a great dishonor, to make it thin enough so that my superior officer, in the final act of my debasement, could break it easily across his knee."

Among those defending Dreyfus, many had never met him, and even if they had, there would have been no surprise at the outcome because when he testified in 1899 during his second court-martial, August 7th through September 9th he was colorless and unsympathetic, his speech flat and un-modulated. It was an abominable and disgraceful trial, one in which race and religion played a divisive role. At those critical moments when eloquence could have persuaded, he was furtive, unappealing, and unemotional. We all knew how much he had suffered, and though the details were compelling, his delivery was not. Though thousands had requested that he should be given a chance to tell his story, he failed to win over the judges and audience, once again demonstrating the crucial difference between style and substance.

At the trial I saw a great actor from the Comedie Francaise who wrote to me,

"That had he been Dreyfus, he would have swayed the audience with his delivery and eloquence, and, as he walked the fourteen Stations of the Cross on his way to Calvary, would have had everyone in tears, thus easily winning the day. But what we heard was something as effete as one who had been robbed of his goat."

On the other hand, one of our rising young philosophers, Julien Benda, wrote in the newspaper La Revue Blanche:

> *"By the sobriety of his conduct, by the austerity of his attitude, by the dryly scientific character of his defense and even of his indignation, by that famous atonality of his voice, by the absence of all that which*

certain people call 'charm'—in a word, by the lack of all those means appropriate for exciting sentimentality—Captain Dreyfus has come to symbolize naturally, and in all its purity, the cause of justice."

He was found guilty again, but this time with '*extenuating circumstances.*' Given a sentence of ten years, but with an allowance for the five already served, his sentence was reduced to five. Public expressions of dismay rained down from most of the world. Queen Victoria wrote that she was too horrified for words at the monstrous and horrible sentence.

From coast to coast throughout the USA meetings and demonstrations were held. William James wrote that he was glad that he belonged to a republic. The attorney general of Montana said that in addition to the unexplored regions of Africa, we should send missionaries to France as well. A decorated Colonel from Kentucky said that it was too late to save France—that it was suffering from an incurable disease. A congressman from New York said he would offer a resolution withdrawing American participation at the Paris Exposition of 1900. Chicago imposed a total boycott on French products. Anatole France, referring to the sentence, wrote to Clemenceau that the judges had committed an unpardonable blunder.

Everyone was exhausted by the prolonged agony of this hapless Jew. Granting a pardon seemed like the expedient thing to do but we urged Capt. Dreyfus to reject it because that would have implied that he was indeed guilty, his reputation tainted still. His wife told me he was not looking for clemency—he was looking for justice! Liberty was nothing to him without honor. But he was a broken man, physically, malaria stricken, needing a cane to support his once shackled wounded legs—skeletal, physically and emotionally.

World opinion mattered to me. If the proposed amnesty law passed, it would deny judicial redress to us—Dreyfus, Picquart and me. All the charges against the real culprits in the conspiracy would be nullified.

Picquart remained unmoved by world opinion but with convictions of forgery and betrayal of duty, his reputation had been tainted as well. In September, upon first meeting Dreyfus, he tried to dissuade him from accepting *'a pardon—transgressions forgiven,'* explaining that that would imply guilt. When Dreyfus decided to accept the pardon he offered his hand to Picquart. He refused to shake it.When Picquart left, Dreyfus fainted.

Dreyfus had now left the company of the Dreyfusards.

The amnesty bill was passed on December 17, 1900, but that wasn't the end of it. The Dreyfusards and anti-Dreyfusards remained at battle stations. The flames of partisanship continued to sap France's elan vital. Passions remained at their apogee with the Dreyfusards attempting to disqualify the verdict at the second court-martial in Rennes, while those opposed, pointing to his guilt, continued with false testimonies.

He finally got the reprieve he sought—we sought. On July 12, 1906, the Court of Cassation, France's equivalent to the American Supreme Court, annulled the Rennes verdict and declared the poor man innocent of all charges. No matter how descriptive I was, or as penetrating as others were on both sides, no words could convey the full spectrum of emotions evoked during that period, nor the depth of those emotions that manifested themselves in the unpredictable events that brought out the best and the worst in people. The participants anguished throughout those years, twelve excruciatingly slow years. 4,380 tortured days. 105,120 painful hours—drawn out like taffy—impossible to forget.

Ahh, if only we were able to will *selective amnesia.*

When Dreyfus attended the ceremony placing my remains in The Pantheon, a fanatic shot him in the arm. He was caught and tried. A Paris jury *acquitted him. Unanimously!*

My friend Picquart once said, it was *La Helle Epoque!*

I cared for Colonel Picquart. There was a man who sought justice. Hang those above and below him who refused to do the right thing. I too could do nothing less. That was the only thing to do—to do justice—to bring the real truth to light—to right a wrong. That for me was what my idealized France stood for, should have always stood for, but often did not. To quote the damn Chinese who always have a pithy, worthwhile saying for everything, *the journey of a thousand miles begins with a single step.* True, we French have taken many steps, but there are thousands yet to take. Yes, I must admit, the very eidos of French culture was in disarray—it was amorphous, incoherent—it lacked a center of gravity—it was afloat in a sea of chaos.

It does give me pause.

Was I always insufferably right? That makes for few friends and helps lose many. And I did lose two of my closest, Paul Cezanne and Claude Monet, though that had less to do, I believe, with the Dreyfus Affaire, but more about what I had written in my book.

Damn! I was right! We're condemned by our genes to be no better than they permit us to be! The artist in my book L'Oeuvre aspired to something greater, but his nature condemned him to mediocrity, and so, unable to deal with that realization, he committed suicide. If Claude and Paul had suspicions that I was writing about them, well, maybe there was some truth to that.

Because of that, I managed to destroy the close friendship that I had enjoyed since childhood with Cezanne. So be it. That was justice for me. To tell the truth at all costs. Sounds Kantian, doesn't it? Well, it is. After my book was published, Monet wrote to me that enemies of the Impressionists would be using my book as a cudgel to beat them senseless. Well, that's the price of truth! Get used to it!

But as I think about it, there was another truth about the schism between Paul and me. As an avid Dreyfusard, and one of the major irritants against the Army and its sycophants, I was irrepressibly resolute in my determination to have that hapless Dreyfus, after the nightmare he was enduring, exonerated.

My friend, Paul, however, was, I regret to say, an anti-Semite, and as could be expected from the many other anti-Semites throughout Europe, an anti-Dreyfusard. Politics often guillotines relationships. How could we have been reconciled when I believed in Dreyfus's innocence while Paul knew in his heart that all Jews were capable of treason? After all, he used to say, that this people without a country could never become true Frenchmen—that they were an alien people pretending to be French when in reality they were interested only in converting France into a Jewish State. One of his favorite expressions was, *'those perfidious Jews.'"* And of course my book was also to blame. Such a pity!

I loved that man, but those two inflammatory issues damned us, old, old friends, from continuing to have a future together.

With the arrogance and certitude that inhabits youth, I believed that art was supposed to reflect the times in which the artists live, and so I tried to remain true to that vision. Isn't that why I wrote, 'Nana' and 'Germinal' and others—to reflect the corruption and perversity of society? But as a corollary, if life is sordid and corrupt, why then do we expect our artists to behave in an exemplary way—in an uncorrupted way?

So were those Impressionists whom I extolled from the beginning, whom I unconditionally supported critically and publicly, were they reflecting our times? Absolutely not! With subtle and bold splashes of color, with harmonized geometries, with voluptuous women and landscapes, with their extraordinary palettes and carving tools, they transcribed on canvas and stone, the music of our senses, and managed to embody nothing about the ugliness and toil in society. Only its beauty.

The whole lot of them failed in their task of reflecting our times.

Two years before I was murdered, I must admit, I began to think that Paul and Claude did exhibit unbelievable truthfulness in their work—actually—genius. Like me, they penetrated very deeply within themselves to help them perceive more clearly the world outside.

"Imagination," Kant wrote, *"is a necessary ingredient of perception."* Weren't we all seeing with a third eye? That *je ne sais quoi* that permits us to see beyond what we see. Weren't we all of a piece?

Paradoxically, over time—as a determinist—how could I deal with the malleability of truth—with its mutability—with its slippery and protean realities—with the way culture affects our behavior, attenuating or enhancing our gifts—how our gifts affect culture? Above all else, justice must prevail. The honor of justice.

For God's sake, let me rest in peace!

Ah, my dear, dear friend, Emile, for your commitment to justice, for your unwavering support of the innocent, for your indomitable spirit of defiance, for your respect for humanistic values, for giving us the courage to pursue those values that help keep civilization afloat—yes, good sir, I will place at your tomb a stone wet with my tears to let you know that an appreciative friend had come to pay her respects—to honor you—for as long as she lives.

CHAPTER 20

A week later, while Josiah and I were sharing our third croissant smeared with elderberry jam, we talked about how so many big things were lost during the Second World War, things that seemed so impossible to repair—all that infrastructure—shops, homes, buildings, electric grids, water mains, sewers. Where does one start? Yet biting into a flaky croissant—a recipe not lost—an oven repaired—butter churned—flour ground—skilled hands, warm and loving—hearts eager to resume—small kinds of infrastructure not beyond repair—they give us hope that if repair is possible on these little things, repair on the larger ones could not be far away.

Josiah was reading the entertainment section of Le Figaro while I, the book section, when suddenly I made him jump. "Josiah, they're reviewing a book about the musical history of Vienna, so before we leave for home, whadya' say we go to Vienna for a few days," I said with a look on my face that belied the pain we had recently gone through, "and on the way, we can visit General Picquart's tomb in Strasbourg. We have little time left, and the past few days haven't been the sunniest," I said rolling my eyes, "so let's get a fresh start and breathe in the magical air that stirred the blood of those musical giants. How's that sound?" I asked as though the argument had never happened.

Maybe Josiah is right—that it takes me a short time to recover—even if I have to pretend. That helps sometimes.

"Are you up to traveling, Sally, with that huge belly? And you're still walking with a slight limp. With a big trip coming up, I don't want to tire you unnecessarily."

"To paraphrase Cyrano, my dear, *despite a protuberance that precedes me by a quarter of an hour,* I'm still strong, and it's not such a long train ride. I'm anxious to go, so let's, okay?"

"No research—that's the rule, okay? Just touring and concerts. Deal?"

"Deal."

The polished brass door handle of the pensione was of a beautiful curvilinear dragon. Upon entering the lobby, we looked at the hanging arte-nouveau lamp festooned with clusters of grapes, layered with shades of purple, signed, *Daum Nancy*. Our eyes then moved to the receptionist's desk and the gold-framed mirror behind her, both of which showed the same curvilinear design typical of the turn of the century. Josiah turned to me and said, "What a charming place."

"Yes," I said, happy at his lightened spirit, "and unscathed by the war. If we had the wherewithal, Josiah, I'd buy this entire lobby, door included, and ship it home."

While he was paying for the first night, I noticed a sitting room with hundreds of books on the shelves. Unable to contain my enthusiasm, I asked the woman behind the counter, "How is that you have so many books here?"

"People come for music festivals, long time, leave books, owner buy books on composers, history, libretti, some English—you take." We smiled and noticed her stern look when she said, "Must give back!"

We carried our bags up one flight of curling stairs, Josiah the heavy ones, and I a bag of tangerines and apples we bought on the way. We were pleased to discover a room with the same arte nouveau motif. The head and footboards, as well as the bedposts, were carved in those exquisitely delicate curves typical of the period. The bedside tables had small lamps with hemispheric shades, like mushrooms, crafted with a mosaic of leaded green glass that bathed the room in a soft emerald-green glow.

After inaugurating the bed, cautiously, we showered, but found it difficult to leave. We had to because we had bought tickets to a concert, and we were hungry.

We found a small restaurant near the hotel, and much to our surprise it too was designed in the arte nouveau style, not a straight line nor right angle anywhere, swirling elements of metal over carved wooden panels, lamps with dazzling colors of dragonfly designs, of peacocks and their feathers. I held my breath for a moment. While waiting to be seated, I turned to Josiah and said, "At one time, when I thought of arte nouveau all I could think of was Tiffany. When we got to Paris, we saw the exquisite Metro subway and some beautiful buildings, but I had no idea it ever got as far as Vienna. Look at how charming this place is also," I said squeezing his arm. He nodded.

The food, however, was not as charming. Scrawny overcooked chicken in an undistinguished light sauce, wilted salad greens, overcooked mushy cauliflower with no seasoning, lukewarm mashed potatoes, all in all, not a place we were going to revisit. But the silver-plated salt and peppershakers with their exquisite arte nouveau design were a knockout. "Jo, these things look like they're going to be airborne any minute. I love them, don't you?"

"I've never seen anything like them," he said fondling them, "if they were made of sterling they would belong in a museum. I wish the food matched the beauty of this place."

"Jo," I suddenly gasped. "Don't look now, but the couple right behind you—the woman just slipped the pair of shakers into her purse. That's terrible! What should I do?"

"Well, don't go bopping her on the nose. Look the other way. It's not the first time stuff was pilfered from a restaurant or a hotel. Just mind your own business and don't make eye contact, okay? I don't want to make a scene."

"I need to go to the ladies room—hold my place, okay?"

I walked away and heard him say, "Oh, geez!"

"Sir?" I asked the man in the tiny kitchen, "Are you the owner?"

"Yes, fraulein, how can I help?" he asked in an unmistakable German accent, wiping his hands on his apron.

"The couple sitting next to our table, well," I hesitated, clearing my throat several times, "they took a pair of your beautiful salt and pepper shakers, and I think you should know about it," regretting it the moment the words left my mouth. I was making a scene in a foreign country—just like an American. I should have paid attention to Josiah. I stayed in place, shuffling my feet, eyes furtively looking at my shoes, then up to his eyes.

"Fraulein, don't worry, please," he said with a broad grin. "We '*sell*' a lot of those that way."

"What? They stole them, sir. You didn't sell them."

"Oh yes I did. We charge a very good price for them, a higher price than if we had them on display. We *'sell'* many more this way."

"Excuse me, sir, I haven't made myself clear. Let me repeat ... "

"Don't bother, please. True—they took them—but they just got a bill for the food they ordered—with a charge for those shakers. They'll be shocked, but too embarrassed to say anything, so I will have *'sold'* another pair. Every month, you'd be surprised at how many I *'sell'* that way. My nephew runs the silver plating shop down the street, and it's become a very good side business for us."

When I finally got the picture, I broke out in a laugh, touched him on the arm, and said, "Sir, that's enterprising of you."

"Well, after the war, we have to make a living any way we can, even when we have to tap into the dark side of people."

With the smile still on my face, I walked to our table and told Jo. When he guffawed aloud, the other guests turned to look at him.

When we paid our bill, the owner came over with a package. "Fraulein, for your gracious honesty, I present you with a gift of those shakers to enjoy when you get home, and for the pleasure you will get every time you tell this story to guests."

I kissed him on both cheeks. "Thank you, sir."

After hearing Mahler's *8th, Symphony of a Thousand*, and the unfinished *10th, The Purgatorio,* we walked home and remained speechless, as though words might break the spell. When we neared our pensione, Josiah, knowing that I too was overwhelmed by Mahler's romantic and grandiose expansiveness, by the sheer inventiveness of it, by its staggering complexity, quietly said, "You know, Sally, the monotheistic religions have it all wrong. There is no *one* God, but *multiple* Gods, alive and well on Mount Olympus, and extremely productive. They keep sending their masterpieces to a few selected people on earth, those blessed ones, who then transcribe them for us. Humans can't create music like that—only gods."

I said nothing to change the mood, just kept squeezing his hand. If anyone had seen us walking with these grins, the guess might have been that the moment before we had had sex.

While we were undressing, I wondered aloud why Mahler had written on the margin of his manuscript for 'The Purgatorio,' *"Madness seizes me, annihilates me.*" "But," Josiah said, "he wasn't clinically insane, or so the program notes say."

"Why do you suppose then, " ... *did he appeal to the devil to take possession of his soul?*""

Through a yawning mouth, he said, "It's those gods again. For those musical gifts, there's a price—the price of madness. Right now, I'm spent. I'm going to bed. Coming?" he asked, slipping under the covers.

"You mean those guys made a Faustian bargain?" No reply. He was asleep.

I was too stimulated by the experience, so I opened up a few of the books I had gotten from the library downstairs.

"How is it, Herr Mahler and Herr Schnitzler," I asked as we were shaking hands, "that here in Vienna, out of a population of about seven hundred thousand, and of our kind, only seventy thousand, it would have taken us so long to meet?"

"Yes, Herr Schoenberg, it is a wonder," Herr Schnitzler said as we sat down, "but finally we gather here in this coffee house that sees no difference between Jewish money and Catholic money. Thank God, if he's listening, or even cares about my offer of thanks."

Herr Schnitzler motioned the waiter and asked politely, "My dear young man, would you please bring us three coffees," then glanced at us wickedly, "and a tray of your famous strudel, so that when we see them before us, we may choose to take more than one."

"Before we go any further, gentlemen," I interjected, "we're about to enter a new century of promising new beginnings so we should start our spring cleaning by dispensing with formality. 'Herr' this and 'Herr' that, is stuffy cloth ridden with moth holes, so please call me Arnold, and," looking at Arthur Schnitzler and Gustav Mahler, I continued, "may I refer to you, as Arthur and Gustav?"

Arnold smiled and said, "Yes, of course, that would be like a fresh spring breeze."

Known for his patrician manner, I noticed Gustav stiffen slightly but only briefly. He lowered his shoulders, and said, "Yes, by all means." He then addressed Arthur, "I hadn't pictured you, Herr Schnitzler, sorry, Arthur, quite this way. Your novels and plays convey a picture of burning youth—impatient, ambitious, out of control, a passionate virility, yet as we speak, I see a calm, tranquil man of maturity. A surprising contrast. Does my candor offend you?"

I placed my hand on Gustav's arm and said, "Since our friend is the most widely read novelist and the most widely seen playwright in Vienna, he probably welcomes candor. Is that not true, Arthur?"

"Yes, I appreciate candor, but when it's accompanied by severe criticism, not so much."

Gustav broke in, "The most widely read and seen, despite your religion," he said cynically, trying not to offend, letting the comment hang for a moment. "I've seen most of your plays and read several of your novels. That's how I conjured a mental picture of you."

"Has anyone ever gotten an accurate image of a writer by reading his work, or a composer by listening to his music, or a painter by viewing his painting?" Arthur asked.

In a quiet voice, as though he were trying to hide something, Gustav said, "Do you think my music conveys my Jewishness?" He didn't wait for an answer. "I've never hidden my Jewishness in the past, but I must tell you, it's been no cause for joy. Now that I've converted to Catholicism, do you think my music will change—become Catholic?"

I leaned forward, and said, "Yes, if you add Gregorian Chants to your music, or celestial harps and angelic voices. But Gustav, how can you reject who you are?"

Arthur didn't give him a chance to respond and said in a louder voice than we expected, "Very sorry to hear that, Gustav."

"Well," Gustav explained, "I was determined to conduct the Vienna Opera, but it was an Imperial appointment—one forbidden to a Jew—so I had no choice. It's hard to believe that in 1897, in this age of enlightenment, during our revered Austro-Hungarian Empire, the conductor of our famed orchestra cannot be Jewish!

"It's the price I had to pay," he said blithely, "so I paid it. In February I accepted Baptism. Within two months, I was appointed Kapelmeister of the Vienna Opera!"

"Ah, Gustav," Arthur said, "it's a currency that has no value for me, and I'll tell you why. Pfitzner, that piece of eskremente, accused me, and all other Jews, of being un-German, of being unable to grasp the true nature of German Kulture, and, echoing the Wagnerian line that we Jews are unfit for genuine creativity, that hiding in a putative Germanness, we are wily enough to hide our true selves.

"No, my friend, the coin of conversion is worthless to me. In my youth, my memories, most of which are bitter, we had to become skilled at fencing. You know why, of course. When I was in medical school, The Waidhafen Manifesto was passed barring Jews from membership in student organizations and fraternities," and before continuing, I interrupted.

Yes, Arthur, I know that Manifesto well. And because it hurt me so much, I memorized it. 'Everyone of a Jewish mother, every human being in whose veins flows Jewish blood is from his day of birth without honor and void of all refined emotions, that he's ethically sub-human, etc. etc.' Yes, I too have suffered, my friends. Haven't we all?"

I turned my gaze to Gustav and said, "But I cannot do what you've done, Gustav. It would be like amputating an appendage of mine. I am who I am and damn those who think that conversion will make us more ethical or holier, more human, closer to God, or whatever their insidious reasons are. Let my music stand alone. It's who I am."

"Ah, but remember, my friends," Gustav said, "wasn't it just a few decades ago that Wagner and Liszt said that international Jewry was about to destroy European music? So," he continued, "you don't understand then? Buber, Freud, Rilke, Heine, Wittgenstein, suffering Jews, the whole lot of them. Why should that continue? Please understand why I converted—it's the key to the vault."

After a long pause I was the first to speak, saying wistfully, "Have you been to the Austrian Lake District? It's the place where God goes when he wants to get away from the strife in the world. Well, I was forced to leave Mattsee because it's restricted to Aryans."

Arthur, pained by the look of despair on my face, said, "That's no surprise. Everybody knows God is an Aryan!"

"And a Christian," Gustav added, taking turns looking at each of us, wanting to make sure we got his message.

I smiled politely, and continued, "We're supposed to be emancipated aren't we? Here at the turn of the nineteenth century, Jews are at the center of Viennese cultural life, journalists, musicians, artists, composers, authors—our achievements are similar to the bourgeois Catholics and Protestants, and yet no matter what we accomplish, it's never enough. Anti-Semitism is in the air we breathe, in the food we eat, in the places we visit. It's inescapable, like a poison we can't wash away. I'll be damned if I can accept that I'm tainted. To convert would be tantamount to accepting their baleful version of what they perceive to be my 'affliction.' A pox on all of them! Even if my music is never accepted, I will continue to compose as I see fit."

"You're not listening," Gustav said. "I just told you the formula for acceptance. Convert! It washes away every sin—just like that," and snapped his fingers. "Why are you suffering? You don't have to! Being Jewish is a curse! Don't be a martyr. We've had enough of those! They have *THE WAY*—their way—and we must follow. It's as simple as that!"

Arthur dismissed his plea and said, "Kandinsky once invited me to join the Weimer Hochschule and the Bauhaus. I knew they had, like so many rabid dogs, their share of anti-Semites, so I told him that the painful lesson I've learned in life is that I'm not German nor, European—but a Jew. Ritter von Schomerer, in concert with Pan-Germanism and Pan-Slavism, amended its charter to expressly demand the elimination of Jewish influence from all areas of public life, so I knew where my course lay.

"For those of us bemused and saddened by irony," he continued, "it's ironic that the Dreyfus Affaire could never have happened in Germany, in Austria-Hungary, or elsewhere in Europe or Russia. Only in France where Jews were permitted to enter the highest reaches of government and the military, could a high-ranking Jewish officer in the army have been *accused and convicted* of a crime he did not commit. In our countries, it would have been unthinkable for a Jew to have ever reached any such position in the military or the government."

"Gustav," I said, "he's right. The Dreyfus Affaire could not have happened in a country devoid of anti-Semitism nor in a country wholly anti-Semitic."

"Stubborn, the lot of you," Gustav said, raising his voice, "Had Dreyfus converted, that would never have happened! You're all *dead-in-the-head*—and soon will be in the body. We were born Jewish, and we have to adapt to the new realities. In Spencer's phrase, it's "Survival of the Fittest!" It's Darwinian! That's what his finches were all about in the Galapagos. That's what he meant when he spoke of *natural selection*. If we fail to adapt, we won't survive! That's the formula, my friends, and you've got to learn it and adapt soon—otherwise, you're both doomed—like Jews will be everywhere."

I said, "Perhaps in time, one gets used to the times."

Gustav said. "Only in the grave, my friend, only in the grave."

We parted, looked closely into each other's eyes, shook hands and said our goodbyes joylessly.

Years later, in the silence of my room, away from friends, I realized that being prescient about an unholy cause is never a prescription for accumulating friends. I, Arnold Schoenberg, have become a Cassandra. A Harpy predicting doom to everyone who would listen. Ah, would that I were wrong!

When the Nazis took over in 1933, I knew I had to leave Germany. The air was charged with anti-Semitism, and I understood for the first time why the Nobel Laureate, Fritz Haber, a Jew who had converted to Protestantism in 1893, ruefully said this year, that never before had he felt more like a Jew than now. Imagine that—forty years later that 'Jewish stink' remained! Even as a world-renowned chemist, he knew he had to get out before it was too late.

It made no difference, converted or not. Gustav was wrong. Having being born Jewish, no matter how hard one tries, one cannot live life as a non-Jew. I discovered that conversion was not a panacea, and so one must die as a Jew. All those autos-da-fe during the inquisition in Spain were visited on the conversos, not the Jews who chose to escape. For those hapless conversos, there was no escape.

My reputation was growing, as was Mahler's, but we were still, "those converted Jews." He was right—being born a Jew was a curse. But being a converted Jew was also a curse. Yes, that surprises you, I know—my hypocrisy. I too converted and I should tell you why, even though in the retelling it embarrasses me still.

On the ship coming to America, I had time to reflect on how it takes forever to grow up, a process remaining unfinished even as we're lowered into the grave. How embarrassed I was when in 1904 I attended a concert of Mahler's third symphony and afterwards invited him for coffee. We no sooner received our coffee when I motioned the waiter for another while Gustav was still sipping his first. I ordered still another. With each sip, I swallowed hard, scarcely looked at him, noisily tapped my fingers on the table in an incessant drum roll, I sheepishly confessed that in 1898, at the age of twenty four, I had converted to Lutheranism—less than a year after he had converted to Catholicism—and that, after my sanctimonious eskremente about staying true to our Jewish heritage!

My certitude of 1897 was replaced by the certitude of 1898, but this time it was for real—and I was sure, permanent.

Why did I become a Lutheran? In the assimilated circles of my parents, there was little Jewish instruction, especially about the philosophical aspects of Judaism with which I might have resonated, but since my father, Samuel, died at an early age, and I, as the nominal head of the family was left little to embrace, I sought other avenues of religious inspiration. Besides, Judaism was too nebulous, too amorphous, like grasping fog.

My dear friend, Walter Pieau, gave me Luther's translation of the Bible, and, transformed by what I read, I converted to Lutheranism. That Bible remained with me for the rest of my life. A quiet companion.

The concept of spirituality has always eluded me. Music is precise, mathematical, architectural, structured, quantifiable. But, as I listen to the music of others, as I write my own music, I am, through some ethereal alchemy, transported outside of myself to a place not real, not tangible, and like fog, not palpable. Is that not contradictory? Is that what spirituality means?

Max Bruch once said, " ... true art should elevate the soul and fortify the spirit." That part I get, but the part I don't get, the one argued in every coffee house in Europe by poets, painters, sculptors, and composers, " ... it should not intoxicate the senses and paralyze the powers of the mind."

How could it not?

Heavens! Have I not had music 'elevate my soul and fortify my spirit, and intoxicate my senses, and paralyze the powers of my mind'? Literature? Sculpture? Painting? They've all done that to me!

Hasn't my mind come to a standstill when I read a line of poetry that dazzles—that for a moment freezes me solid? Or in great literature, an evocation of a character's anguish or triumph that immobilizes me for a moment? Or upon seeing Victory at Samothrace? Or The Milk Maid by Vermeer? Or by listening to Bruch's own First Violin Concerto in G Minor?

What was he talking about?

Max, the son of a clerical Protestant family, had written in 1880, his famous Kol Nidre for the Jewish Community of Liverpool—a piece of stunning spirituality. I was confused even further when in the early 1850s Liszt and Wagner said that international Jewry was about to destroy European music.

Max is European, yet that piece is so Jewish! Would that piece written by a non-Jew, not help destroy European music?

When I heard Franz Liszt's oratorio Christus for the first time, I knew that it was about search, not discovery. It was in that search that my devotion remained, the search for spirituality—within me and within music.

When I told Gustav about my conversion, he responded with a nodding silence, mercifully sparing me from a condescending, 'I told you so', or from a lecture about hypocrisy.

And now, in 1933, I've returned to my ancestral beliefs, for how could I remain a Lutheran while the Jews of Europe are under vicious attacks against their people-hood? That would be betrayal—desertion under fire!

It wasn't an epiphany. It took me a quarter of a century to understand that one cannot go to a Turkish bath and wash off one's heritage. Assimilation is self-delusion, idol-worship. No one in Europe ever forgets that you once were a Jew.

Jewish intellectuals, eager to embrace the exalted German/Austrian culture they had admired from afar, and blinded by their idealization of that culture, were oblivious to the corrosive signs of the deep hatred Europeans had of Jews.

*Following the assassination of Tsar Alexander II, thousands of Jews, survivors of the pogroms, fled Eastern Europe. The writing was on the wall—in bold letters—***there is no future for Jews in Europe.** *So onto Vienna—their pathway to safety in Great Britain and the United States.*

On October 31, 1933 when I saw the Statue of Liberty for the first time, chills ran unexpectedly through my body. With tears suddenly overflowing, I hoped that America was not like the never-forgetting Europe.

And so, as it often is with converts, or re-converts, I became a compulsive zealot speaking and writing about the plight of Jews in Europe, how there was a systematic attempt to exterminate them, how we had to gather our resources to get them out of Europe before that happened. Many prominent Rabbis joined in that effort, but most Jews and non-Jews thought of us as Cassandras—gloomy scolds. Who wants to hear that?

People want to hear only good news!

Hitler had his pulse on historical truth. He was the only honest one. He hated Jews and knew that the entire world shared his view, that all their claims about what he was doing to them was inhumane, were so much cant, so much hypocrisy—that deep within their cultures, nobody wanted us. And he proved it when in May of 1939 he let 937 prominent Jews leave Hamburg on the ship, The Saint Louis, ostensibly for Havana. He must have gloated when the Cubans wouldn't accept them—nor the United States—nor any other country. He proved his truth and disproved theirs. He must have danced a gavotte when the ship returned to what he would ensure was their certain death.

Who the hell wants Jews?

Politicians in democracies often renege on political promises, but dictators always fulfill theirs. They must be believed. Always.

I have found, as I age, that those with optimistic, even unrealistic, thoughts, are well received. If their predictions prove untrue, only good-hearted shrugs emerge. But with us, the bad news purveyors, we're greeted with scorn. Events proved us right, disgustingly so, depressingly so, disillusioning so! Yes, events have proved the accuracy of my Weltanschauung—and regrettably—my continued Weltschmerz.

With shoulders slumped in disbelief, I wonder aloud when we as a species will finally become extinct—that it's about time—before we do any more damage.

And yet——————————and yet.

I jumped when Josiah shouted, "What the hell are you doing, Sally?" I turned around to see his scowling face. I had been so immersed in writing that I think he said, "Did you ever get any goddamn sleep?"

"Oh, nothing, nothing," I said, slamming my notebook closed and knocking my teacup off the table. Embarrassed, words stumbling out, I said, "It's just that while you were sleeping—there were these books from downstairs—I couldn't resist reading about important people—you know, Vienna, turn of the century—just until you awoke."

He repeated, "DID YOU EVER GET TO SLEEP?"

"What time is it?" I asked, mortified to discover that it was light outside.

"It's morning in Vienna. Time for breakfast," he shouted, stuttering some descriptive clauses like, "you compulsive idiot—you nutcase—you whacko. Arghh!"

I shrank in my chair, chin on my chest, shoulders at half-mast. What to say?

"You weren't just reading. You were so engrossed in *writing—not reading,*" he kept yelling at the same pitch, "that you never noticed me over your shoulder. You're on vacation—to recharge your batteries. Remember?"

"Yes, of course, it's been wonderful. I just couldn't help taking a few notes, that's all. It's quite innocent, Josiah, please don't be angry with me," hoping to make light of it.

"You're incorrigible, you know, amongst these other recently uncovered revelations," he said with thinly veiled disgust.

"Josiah, don't turn this into an international crisis. What I was reading triggered some thoughts, that's all. We can't stop thinking, you know," I said smiling, "it was quite innocent."

"Sally, that's pure merde," he snapped, "you're supposed to be taking a break from writing. We both know that writing can be injurious to *my* health, so why aren't you taking care of *me* while I take care of *you?*"

I went over to his side, put my arm around his shoulders and said, "Josiah, you're right. I am incorrigible." With rising passion, I said, "Being in Europe has been an extraordinary adventure for me, different from anything I've ever done, and I'm savoring the experience, not wanting to let go, not wanting this journey to end. I've never experienced pushing myself to my intellectual limits. All my senses are fired up, electrified, galvanized, sharpened, as though I'm on the Serengeti Plain as both *hunter* and *hunted.*

"But, I promise you my adventure is over. Until we get home, everything goes in the attic of my mind. As you know, Jo," I smiled, "I never renege on a promise. It's one of the cultural mandates of the Aboulafias!"

With the thinnest of smiles, he asked, "Oh, really? Like the one you just reneged on?"

"You can bet the Eiffel Tower on it."

"Not enough."

"And the Louvre."

With continued lightness, I added, "But one final request before we leave Paris. Let's revisit Montparnasse Cemetery and lay a stone on Dreyfus's tomb once again. One final farewell—one final tribute to one of those benighted men—the father of this convulsive imbroglio—and to these exhilarating months in France. O.K.?"

He took a long time to answer, eyeing me suspiciously. I didn't want to break his gaze, nor did I want him to miss the loving smile on my face, nor the caressing love in my eyes, both of which asked for understanding if not forgiveness.

Finally he spoke, "You know, Sally, sex is not in our gonads but in our heads—the gonads only respond to signals from the brain. I've asked myself, especially during our trying times, what it is about you that I find irresistible, appealing, ingratiating—even when you're insufferable. And you know what answer I get? Your insatiable curiosity in everything—the depth of your investment in those things. I find them sexy. And if that were not enough, I find that your irrepressible exuberance about what you've discovered turns me on.

"Funny, at school all my friends dreamt about sleeping with the girls with big boobs. But for me, I wanted to sleep with the brainiest."

I walked over, sat lightly on his lap, and asked, "Now who's the whacko?"

"On one condition."

"What? What condition?"

"Visiting Dreyfus's tomb."

"Oh, yeah."

"That you leave pad and pencil at home. You're not even to carry a purse. Deal?"

"Deal."

"Yeah, like I can trust your *'deals,'*" he harrumphed. "One other condition. No tears."

"That I can't guarantee."

CHAPTER 21

"Jo, I'm miserable—like the early weeks of my pregnancy. Ring the steward and ask for cheese and crackers. And some hot tea, lots of it. When do we dock?"

"When do we *dock*? We left Le Havre less than a day ago," he said. "But, don't worry sweetheart, you'll get your sea legs soon—as soon as I get mine."

I looked at his pasty face and asked, "Does that mean you're going to skip dinner too?"

"Don't mention food. I need to go to the bow of the ship—that's the front, right? I need to get a blast of fresh air on my face. Coming?"

"Every time I raise my head, I feel like I'm going to heave. You go, but call the steward first."

When the steward knocked, I opened the door but had to rush to the toilet.

After what seemed like forever, Josiah entered, came to my side, looked at my half-closed eyes, touched my forehead, and said, "Honey, I've been gone for an hour and you look worse—matter of fact you look terrible."

"You should have stayed with me, Josiah. Since you left, I've been dry heaving every few minutes. I finally decided to stay with my head over the potty. What little is coming out is bilious green. I don't feel well, I'm cold and clammy, I'm feverish, my eyeballs ache, and the baby is kicking non-stop. I wish you could stay with me in bed, but these beds barely fit the one and a half I am. Hold my hand, please. I'm worried, Josiah, really worried. Do I feel feverish?"

"A little. You never touched the tea and stuff. I'm calling the ship's doctor. Maybe he can give you something for seasickness."

"No, it's too late. Doctors are always being called at odd hours. I don't want to do that. Let's wait 'till morning—see what happens. I need to sleep. Turn off the lights, please. When will the captain right this ship? Are we going through a hurricane? Did we hit an iceberg? Are we sinking? Oh, my God, Josiah, I feel like jumping overboard."

"Seasickness is about as close a near-death experience as you can get, Sally, I understand, but ... "

"Or as close to a *death wish* as you can get."

He managed a thin smile and caressed my forehead, "You'll get over it soon, I promise. Just close your eyes and think of whatshisname, the Roman god of sleep. Whatshisname?"

"Somnus—the son of night—the god who never saw dawn breaking—and," I gasped, "the brother of death. Oh, my God, Josiah!"

"Merde! You would have to know mythology! You and your Latin! All I was thinking about was the sleep part. Don't worry, honey, I'll be by your side all night, on my knees, holding your hand, soothing your brow. I'll breathe sleep into your body—a restful, undisturbed, untroubled sleep—a calming, tranquil sleep. I'll tell our little one to stop disturbing her mother. Now un-wrinkle those furrows, relax your facial muscles, The Great Josiah, known internationally for his miraculous cures, is hovering over you, protecting you from Neptune's fury. Sleep my love—relax and sleep," he whispered, "breathe slowly, deeply. I promise that with the dawn you'll awake refreshed."

"I love you so, Josiah. You won't abandon me, will you?"

"Abandon you?"

"You know, when they give orders to abandon ship," I said, hoping that the word 'abandon' didn't remind him of our argument.

"With your dowry still unpaid? No way! You're going to be fine, bijou, you'll see." The look on his face told me something else. In a voice intended for children, he said, "Once upon a time, there was a beautiful scullery maid whose mind knew its place but whose heart did not. She worked in a castle where lived a kind but indifferent young prince ... " tapering his voice off as I was falling asleep.

I never heard the door open, just distant voices. "Thanks for coming, Dr. Briquehomme. She was moaning all night and when she started shaking, I decided not to wait for morning."

I felt gentle hands touch parts of my body, looked up to see a middle-aged man dressed in a traditional white lab coat, stethoscope necklace, tongue depressors peering out of his pocket, stuff that I had always found intimidating, but which I now found assuring. I couldn't keep my eyes open for long.

"From the looks of her, she's pretty far along in her pregnancy," I heard him say to Jo.

"Somewhere in her eighth month."

"Her pallid skin and very high blood pressure concern me. Sally, can you hear me? Hello?"

"Where are we?" I asked. "Don't bother answering. This bucking bronco tells it all. Aren't we there yet?"

"Sally, I'm going to move you to our emergency room," he said like he was ready to move some furniture. "Can you get up?"

"Emergency room? You don't mince words, doctor. You are a doctor, right?"

"Yes. That should be reassuring."

"Right now, only terra firma would be reassuring."

"Let's get going, okay?"

I sat up and wailed, "Whoops, here I go again. Josiah, help me to the bathroom, please." I barely made it to the potty. "Ohhhh, dry heaves again," then raising my voice as best I could, asked, "Doctor do you want to see my small offering to the sea gods?"

"Yes, please." He peered into the bowl and said, "Not much to see. Here, take this to chew on. It'll help."

"What is it?"

"Ginger—it'll soothe your nausea."

"I don't like ginger, Doctor."

"But it likes you," he said with a smile thinly veiling his troubled look. "Think of it as having an unrequited love for you."

He put his arm around my waist, raised me up and said, "Josiah, help me carry her upstairs—to the *examining* room, Sally."

"That sounds better. But words don't matter much right now. The only thing that matters is to get me into a submarine below the waves. Waves are not healthy. As a matter of fact, they're about to kill me. How come the boat was ever invented in the first place?"

Though it was one short flight up, I stopped at ever step to catch my breath.

"Before you lie down, let me have a urine sample. Josiah, help her with that. When you come back I'm going to draw some blood."

Thirty minutes later, he returned and said with the characteristically charming cadence and musicality of the French when they speak English, "Okay, with the tests I have available—urine, blood, eye pressure, blood pressure, breath—my instruments are limited of course, but I think you might have eclampsia, or preeclampsia or something called, hyperemesis gravidarum, or maybe two out of three. Whatever it is, I'm sorry to say, is a good deal more than ordinary seasickness. Apart from dehydration, you have acidosis—that means the bicarbonate level of your blood is below normal. You have a high concentration of albumin in your urine—your ocular pressure is high and so is your blood pressure. With no one around to consult for a second opinion, I'm afraid you're going to have to rely on my judgment only, but I'm not fresh out of medical school, and I've seen this several times in the past when I had my practice on the mainland. I'm rambling, I know, trying to postpone telling you that it's imperative that your pregnancy be terminated immediately," and then more forcibly said, "*terminated immediately*." He looked at both of us and without waiting for a response, continued, "and I need to put you on intravenous fluids right away. Your ankles are edematous … " he said, taking what seemed to be his first full breath.

With what I was sure was a terrified look, I choked out, "What happens to my baby? You're not going to abort it, are you? It's not going to die, is it?"

"No, absolutely not!" he said. "It'll be okay, I'm sure, just premature by a month or so. You and the baby will be okay, no doubt in my mind. I've got most of what I need right here. It's not the first birth to occur on board ship, even in heavy seas. Please take that panicked look off your faces. All three of you will be fine," he said exuding confidence. "But," he continued, "you've got to give me permission to take action right away. I've got to get to work. Right now. Shall I leave you alone for a few minutes?"

Josiah put his hand on the doctor's shoulder and held him back. He looked at me and said, "Sally, there's no time to lose. We must save you and the baby. There's no choice. I'm not going to take the chance of losing you and the baby by waiting five or six days to bring you to a land hospital. I trust Dr. Briquehomme, so let's say yes, okay?" he asked, feigning the same confidence as the doctor.

"Oh, Josiah, I didn't expect this to happen, I wanted my mother to be around, I wanted a regular hospital, on dry land, not one that's heaving like me. Oh, I don't know what to do," I sobbed.

"Honey, I can't imagine life without you. I'm so sorry for not respecting your instincts about staying in Paris. You were right all along and I was a stubborn mule. This might never have happened there, and if it had, we would have been in a hospital that didn't rock like a cradle," he said, tears welling in his eyes. "Forgive me, Sally."

With his chin quivering, he went on, "And the way we can forgive each other is by agreeing to go through with this procedure right now. You must. It's imperative. The steamship line would not have employed an incompetent doctor. Let's tell him yes. There's no time to lose," his voice choking. He looked desperate. So was I, but it was I who had to go through with this. I forced a smile and said, "Let's increase our love pie, Josiah—from two to three—here on the high seas. She'll be an American with a colorful history."

He must have seen that my look of terror and tears did not reflect my words. He put his arms around me and held me tightly, our cheeks caressing each other, our tears co-mingling. He knew he had to cheer me up if only a little, and whispered loud enough for the doctor to hear, "How can things not turn out alright, sweetheart, when your doctor sounds like Maurice Chevalier?"

I smiled, turned to the doctor and said, "Doctor Briquehomme, save us both, okay? BOTH! You hear? YOU MUST!" trying to dry my tears on the short sleeve of my emergency room gown.

"Sally, believe me when I tell you that it will be okay. I promise you! Please understand, however, that I might have to do a Caesarean Section," he said holding my hand in an assuring bedside manner, "but either way, I'll do everything possible to deliver a healthy baby and leave you a healthy young woman. I'm terrific at what I do, and you'll be the beneficiary of my skills, so close your eyes and let the IV begin to work its magic."

I floated into the painless world of anesthesia and heard Josiah quietly ask him, "Before I leave, she couldn't see your face as clearly as I could, and I just want you to know that your assurances to her failed to assure me. This is very serious, isn't it?"

"Yes, it is," the doctor replied in a whisper, "I don't have an ophthalmodynamometer to do extensive eye examinations, but one of the reasons for doing what I'm doing is that evidence points to the possibility of a hemorrhagic retinitis, so when you get back home she needs to go through a battery of eye tests. And liver tests. And electrolyte tests. I'll spell out a bunch of things for you. Now it's time to go," he said, "I'm going to do my very best. After this last war, we need all the new life we can get—especially intelligent life. You understand, my very best may not be good enough, but while you're waiting outside, don't think of the worst possible scenario. Keep in your thoughts only the best possible outcome. Now allez!"

Damn! Jo should have asked him that when I was fully asleep. "Oh, merde!" I cussed aloud. "I'll be in your waiting room," I heard him say, "waiting patiently—and optimistically." Then the doctor said, "By the way, the color of your face is making *me* nauseous. Ask the nurse to give you some ginger lozenges." That was the last thing I heard before things began to vanish.

I started my sharp descent into the India-ink blackness, wondering whether my baby will live—whether I'll live to celebrate her first birthday—whether I'll be around to celebrate my thirty-third birthday—whether I will ever see spring again—whether I'll ever smell the fragrance of pittosporum—wondering why they ever made January 1st the first day of the year—why they hadn't chosen the vernal equinox instead—whether I'll ever play a duet with Josiah's oboe d'amour—whether—whether—what is that music I keep hearing in my head—what are those floating notes in front of my eyes—why can't I grasp them? Ohhhh, what's going on?

Towards the end of our *voyage-of-the-accursed*, I insisted that Jo give me a blow-by blow about what happened while I was out there someplace. He knew, of course, that I was never kidding about those requests. The last thing I think I heard, I told Josiah, was something about the nurse and ginger.

"The nurse gave me a bunch of ginger and Dramamine which quickly made me sleepy. 'Ahhh,' I thought, 'the soporific effect of anti-histamines.' I couldn't tell how much time had gone by, but soon felt a gentle shove and heard a question I couldn't figure out at first. "'Have you ever been a father?'"

"What? What did you just ask?" trying to get my mind working again. Then suddenly I asked, 'Is the baby okay? Is Sally?'

"'You'll be delighted to hear that they're both fine! And I didn't have to do a c-section. It looked like the baby was about 34-35 weeks old, a good safe preemie age.'" "Fantastic!" I shouted and started to do a soft-shoe dance as tears cascaded down my face.

"Sally, did you ever try a soft-shoe dance on a rocking ship?"

"'Then I asked, 'Can I see them?'

"'He said, "They're both asleep, but you can peek in. Put on this mask first, please.'

"'Are they really okay? Were there any complications? Will they recover from this ordeal? Will there be any consequences? Is the *urgency* over? Is the *emergency* over?'" I peppered him as I tried getting my mask on with shaking fingers.

"'Don't you want to know the gender of your baby?'"

"'I don't care. I only care if they're okay.'" But I smiled and asked, "'Tell me, what is it?'

"'It's a healthy little girl—little right now, innocent and accepting, but they've been known to grow into feisty teenagers, and then you'll be tempted to return her to her infancy to relive the great joy she had once brought you,' raising his eyebrows as though from personal experience.

"'I turned serious and asked, 'And Sally? With all those complications, how goes it?'"

"'Surprisingly okay—considering—but she needs close follow-up the moment you get home. Her physician needs to test her for a number of things right away. I'll give you all the test results I have in my possession. She's a strong lady, Josiah, with a strong will, so she'll be okay after a while, but right now, she's going to have to stay with me for a few days, on her back, until we arrive in New York. I need to keep a close watch on them. If I can't get their electrolytes balanced or her blood pressure down, when we dock, they have to be hospitalized immediately. No trips for you until that's done. If I manage to stabilize her, you cannot dawdle on the way to Los Angeles. Understand?'"

"'Absolutely. And thank you,' I said as I choked up and gave him a lingering bear hug, wetting the shoulder of his surgery gown. 'Can I see them?'"

"Josiah, I remember you kissed me on the forehead, right? I was still in a stupor with my eyes at half-mast, but I remember how funny you looked trying to kiss the baby through your mask—and breathing her in deeply—and I thought, wow—that's how fathers bind themselves irrevocably to their daughters—that primordial link.

"You then leaned over and breathed me in as well. I whispered, 'Oh, Jo, my love, it's a girl, isn't it? Imagine—a girl from you and me—together—she's yours—she's mine. She's ours. Wow!' That much I remember.

"Oh, one more thing I remember. My hand was on your face, wet with your tears, and you whispered, 'Sally, my Rubaiyat Sally—my treasure, my fortune, the very breath of my life. I have found you again and will never let you go.' "Am I right?"

CHAPTER 22

"Sinty? It's Josiah. Hi."

"Josiah? Good to hear from you. You calling from Paris? How are you guys? Salty is ready to give birth, right?"

"We just disembarked in New York, but can't stay and visit like we had planned. Sally gave birth to a girl during a very difficult crossing. She's got to get some treatment right away, and plenty of bed rest, so, I'm sorry to say, this call will have to do."

"You sound terrible, Josiah. Are they both okay?"

"We think so, the baby was premature by a month, Sally developed all sorts of chemical imbalances that of course affected the baby. Right now they're under partial control, but we need to go home immediately. They may have to be hospitalized."

"Damn! You're going to fly, right?"

"Yeah, we can't afford to delay treatment by a six day train trip."

"When?"

"In about six hours. We have to clear customs and then go to La Guardia Airport."

"Tell me what pier you're on."

"Pier 3."

"O.K. Wait by the customs exit. I'll call Rachel. We'll pick you up and drive you to the airport. At least we'll have a couple of hours together," he said, leaving no room for alternatives.

"You sure?" Josiah asked, relieved at the convenience but troubled by inconveniencing him.

"Of course! You're my brother-in-law and the father of my niece—my very first. We'll be there in about an hour. See you."

"That's nice of you, Sinty. Thanks." he said, glad to hear that kind of spirit from someone he hardly knew.

I waddled like a duck through the customs gate when Sinton and Rachel came rushing over.

"Sinty, my little brother, you look great!" I said, and turning to his wife, "and so do you, our beautiful Rachel!"

"I wish I could say the same for you," Sinton said. "You look like you've been living in a cave."

Rachel jumped in and said, "Don't mind him, Salty, his eyes are going. He doesn't see what I see. A beautiful young mother—tired, but glowing."

"Thanks, Rachel," I said, "there's room in life for the occasional lie, but I feel the way Sinton says I look. I need to sit down with my baby. Come take a peek at the newest member of our family who's sound asleep."

"It sure looks better than my own two when they were born." Sinton said, "Mine looked like they had been soaking in brine for nine months."

With bemused exasperation, Rachel sighed, "I should have left you at home, Sinty."

"None of us in the family," I answered, "would have ever qualified for the diplomatic corps."

The first time I had seen Rachel was at her wedding when my mother, younger brother and I came to New York. I knew immediately why Sinty had chosen her. My siblings and I were not a handsome family, but she looked like a Turk, maybe a Persian, maybe it was that she reminded me of that famous fresco from the Palace of Knossos in Crete—the one called La Parisienne. With dark almond shaped eyes, a slightly beaked nose, bright white teeth seemingly illuminated from within, flowing black hair cascading well over her white gown, I thought she was more than my brother deserved. I hoped that the rest of her, the substance of her, was its equal—and his. The distance from coast to coast, however, would prevent me from meddling.

Sinty looked like a man, and through his clothing you could see that he had lifted onto his truck many sacks of potatoes, crates of carrots, onions and melons for his increasingly successful wholesale produce business. An evolutionary leap from my father's pushcart in Harlem.

"Before we go any further," Sinty said, "let's clear something up. Josiah, you keep referring to my sister as 'Sally,' but we know her as 'Salty.'" He turned to me and asked, "Did you officially change your name to Sally? Is that your 'stage' name—even though I know you're not on stage. Or, is that your Hollywood name?"

"Call me whatever, Sinty," I said, "at the studios I'm known as Sally Apple. I met Josiah as Sally Apple, but you can continue to call me, 'Salty,' but not by my birth name, 'Saltiel,' okay? Like I don't call you by your birth name, 'Sinton.'"

"Deal."

"So tell me about your health and that of the baby? Is it as ominous as Josiah suggested?"

"Maybe not ominous—maybe yes. I'm having trouble with electrolytes, albumin, high blood pressure, pressure behind my eyes, a whole bunch of things that need to be treated when I get back home."

"The baby too?"

"Some. She was sharing everything with me, of course, but I don't know for how long. Being premature by about a month, has its special concerns as well."

Rachel asked, "Was this going on for awhile?"

"No, the last time I saw the obstetrician in Paris, everything looked fine. It was a sudden onset, maybe brought on by my seasickness, maybe some emotional kick, I don't know."

"What emotional kick?" Rachel asked.

"You know, things."

"O.K., let's carry your stuff to my car," Sinty said grabbing two suitcases. He looked at me and out of the corner of his mouth, said, "there's nothing wrong with the truth, you know, it's always beneficial even when it hurts."

"Whose truth?" Rachel asked trying to lighten what seemed like a dark moment, "the absolute truth or relative truth?"

"What?" he asked.

To which she responded, "You know, truth assumes many guises, remaining relative to the one who perceives it. You know—Einstein stuff."

Sinty smiled and said, "It's tough living with a home-grown philosopher who asks uncomfortable questions."

Josiah, carrying two suitcases himself, said, "I can see already that I'm sorry we don't live in the same city."

"Josiah, if you did, you'd soon discover, that when Sinty is with his customers, the truth often remains unspoken. Right honey?" she asked quietly, eyes smiling, as she put her arm around his burdened shoulders.

He nodded briefly and with a quick glance back at us, said, "We'll get there in lots of time for you to check in, and maybe get something to eat."

"Don't mention food, okay? Day and night it was like riding 'The Cyclone.' Remember that wicked Coney Island roller coaster?" I asked and saw the three of them rolling their eyes in recognition. "The only thing that could have been worse was hitting an iceberg. I was sure we had. I'll never get on a ship again!" I said, "Never, ever. Now there, Rachel, is an absolute Truth—with a capital 'T'.

"When I mentioned that monster ride, something vague came to mind," I continued. "Let me think—while I was going under, all sorts of foggy thoughts were going through my head, but there was some music—yes, Ravel's 'Pavanne for a Dead Princess,' that melancholy tone poem of his. But curiously," I continued, "the notes were alive, floating across my eyes like silver/purple flakes. Every time I tried to reach out to grab them, they would dissipate—like when you throw a stone in a lake and disturb the reflection of the moon. It was at once beautiful and frustrating. I remember being overwhelmingly sad."

"Well," Josiah said, "that dead princess is long buried, and we've got new life right here, so erase the thought. We're all alive and well! Mostly."

We were glad to be rid of our suitcases at the check in counter. We gathered outside the airport restaurant redolent of fragrances—bread, cookies, frying chicken, grilling hamburgers and onions. I turned to Josiah and said, "For the first time in over a week, the smell of food is not making me run to the toilet. Maybe a bowl of soup, honey?"

"Yeah, that might be settling. Let's try it."

"Sound good to you too, Rachel?" Sinty asked.

To a frazzled waitress, he said, "Four soups all around. Potato/leek. It's the daily special. The only one available."

While waiting for their soup, he asked, "So how come you both got fired at the same time?"

"We weren't fired," was Josiah's rejoinder. "We both resigned at the same time."

"From your letters it sounded like 'please hand in your resignation.'"

"Do we have to talk about that now?" Rachel asked. "We only have a few hours, Sinty, and I don't want reminders of what's bad—their recent ordeal is reminder enough. Surely there are more pleasant things to talk about?" she asked smiling at each of us.

Sinty looked at Rachel and said, "My wife hates to have unpleasant subjects brought up at meal times. She claims it ruins everyone's digestion, but the question is not so much about what was on the table, but what's on the menu when you get back? You're both out of work, right?"

"But your question was about what happened," Rachel said. "To hell with the past! I liked your second question better."

"What happened to those wonderful olden days when women knew their places and never argued with their husbands?" he asked putting his arm around her shoulders. "Ah, one of the deficits of democracy!"

"The soup smells good, but the baby is beginning to fuss," I said. "I've got to feed her first."

"Now you can remove her blanket so we can get another look at your contribution to civilization," Rachel said. "Look at that skin. Oh, I can't resist touching her. It looks and feels like heavy sweet cream."

"Tell us, since she's already four or five days old," Sinty quipped, "is she opinionated? Stubborn? Before you answer that, we keep referring to her as 'the baby.' That's not going to be her name, I'm sure, so what did you guys decide on?"

"One of the traditions from your 'wonderful olden days, Sinty,'" Josiah replied, "was naming a baby after the father's side, and in this case, my mother's name was Eleanor, so we decided on Laura.

"So," he continued, "let me introduce you to Velia. And don't forget to coo."

"What?"

"Velia."

"Is this a joke? What are you talking about?" Rachel asked. "We thought you said, 'Laura.'"

I answered in a buttery voice, "Let me explain. We originally agreed on 'Laura,' but when the doctor first put her in my arms, chills ran all through my body. It was the same tingling feeling that I get when I hear certain music. Strangely, as I hugged her, the song, 'Velia' from Franz Lehar's 'The Merry Widow,' went through my head. I knew immediately that that should be her name. She still gives me chills when I gaze at her. Maybe someday she'll give chills to some young man. So Laura became Velia."

"So much for tradition, right?" Josiah smiled. "Let that be a lesson to you, Sinty, about 'the good old days.'"

"You eat, honey, I'll feed her," Josiah said as he took Velia from me.

"How come the bottle?" Sinty asked. "Can't you breast-feed?"

"My system is all screwed up, and the doctor thought it might be best that I feed her bottled milk rather than give her whatever is ailing me—until I'm okay again." I took cautious sips of the soup, then larger spoonfuls. "This soup feels good going down. I hope it stays there. My body still feels the ship's motion."

I looked at my brother and Rachel and didn't want them to think I was about to heave, so I calmly said, "That rocking sensation has something to do with the inner ear. It's called 'Mal de Debarquement Syndrome.' Usually it goes away after a few days, but in rare instances, some people are left with a balance disorder that can last for a long time. I've got enough going wrong with my body right now, I hope I get over this soon."

Sinty asked, "Where in the world did you come across that?"

"Don't ask," Jo said. "Your sister has a cluttered mind. That's a strength, but I must tell you, it's also a weakness, especially since it got us where we are now."

"Let's not go there right now," I said. "Someday, I'll tell you all about it."

"Okay," Rachel said respecting my wishes. "So what's on the menu in Los Angeles?"

"A mixed plate," Josiah answered holding Velia close to him, watching the milk disappear. "I received letters from two different studios asking me to visit, while Sally got a letter from one of the production heads at Twentieth asking her to visit—with an admonition of sorts."

"First the bad news; then the good," Sinty said. "Is this the guy who fired you?"

Jo shook his head from side to side and said, "No, he's above the bastard who *forced us to resign,* Sinty."

"That's an interesting dynamic—a producer going over the head of one of his subordinates. So what's this admonition?"

I said, "You know about the HUAC hearings—those stultifying and humiliating un-American activities of the House Un-American Activities Committee. Well, I may be asked to testify about what I wrote, what I heard, with whom I spoke, or with whom I conspired to influence Americans about the joys of communism. Stupid, but scary, isn't it?"

"Not if you have nothing to hide," Rachel said.

Without skipping a beat, Josiah said, "She's got nothing to worry about, except by association, or rumor, or hints, or doubts, or innuendo. You know, all the merde that can stick on the resume by appearance if not by reality."

Sinty assured us, as though he knew best, "You guys have nothing to worry about. You're as good as apple pie, or in this case, as good as potato/leek soup."

"Or baklava," I added.

"There is one thing, though," Josiah said with a feigned look of concern on his face, "In the interest of full disclosure, I need to tell you a story about my own political corruption."

I looked at him with surprise and thought I saw a flash of regret running through his face, as though he wished he hadn't started, wished that he could reach out and retrieve the words. He then continued, "When I was about eight or nine, we were living at 1269 Morris Avenue in The Bronx, on the fifth floor of a five story tenement house with no elevator. The fifth floor was always the cheapest, and those steps, like 'Wonder Bread,' helped 'build our bodies in eight strong ways.' We were also right next to a fire station that was called out often, at night mostly. The engine's roars and sirens made our fifth floor flat even cheaper.

"We were too poor to own any books, and though we used to get text books from my grammar school, PS 53, we had to return them at the end of the term. The library was not too far away, but all those books had to be returned too. I dreamed of someday owning a book that was mine—all mine, you understand—one I didn't have to return.

"One day, a friend showed me a book he had gotten from an organization. FREE," he said raising his voice. "Since I wanted to have a book of my very own, I wrote away for it. Within a week, I received a small book. The first time anything was ever addressed to me. I remember it clearly. The cover was a beautiful gray with bright red printing on the front boldly announcing, 'The Communist Manifesto.'

"I didn't know what a 'Manifesto' was nor what in the world I was reading, but it was a book and it was all mine! I treasured it for the longest time until it disappeared. When asked, my mother gave me a shrug."

To the bemused looks on everyone's faces, and certainly mine since I had never heard this story before, he went on, "And to give you further evidence of my continued political corruption," he said, looking at each of us quite seriously, "soon after that, I heard that the Chinese government was giving away a silk kit. Also FREE. This was great because we had no money to buy kits either, so once again I wrote away for this freebie. Soon, I received a beautifully decorated box addressed to me personally. I was feeling important. Inside this gorgeous box were some of the most beautiful things I had ever seen.

"There was a cocoon, a real one, not fake, and three braids of pure silk. One was white, like goose down. Another yellow, like corn silk. The third, golden-orange, like a California poppy. I had never seen or felt silk before, and when I put it next to my face, I shivered."

Sinty almost shouted, "Well, brother-in-law you're in deep doo-doo. You were the worst kind—a nine year old Chinese Communist!"

"That was well before the Chinese became Communist," Jo said quickly.

"Makes no difference," he said, "they're going to nail you for your youthful indiscretions. Salty, had you known this beforehand, would you have married this flaming pinko? You've made a big mistake and you're going to pay a heavy price before HUAC!! Better send him back to Paris right now. Or Moscow! Or Peking!"

I thought I saw Josiah's shoulders sag a bit. "As you can tell by her screams," I said, "Velia doesn't agree, despite her full stomach."

I took her from Jo and said, "I finished my soup so I'll walk around to quiet her down, otherwise it'll be bedlam on the plane. It's getting close to boarding time so thanks for taking the time to come down. I can't tell you how glad I am to see you. Give my love to your children, and maybe one of these days, we can all get together here or in Los Angeles. And, if my novel gets published—at a book signing in New York."

They both shouted, "Novel? Book signing?" Rachel adding, "You never said anything, you rat! Tell us everything!" They both got up to accompany me when we heard Josiah say, "Hey wait a second. I haven't eaten yet, remember?"

I turned to Sinty and Rachel and said, "Rachel, walk with me and let Sinty keep Jo company." We strolled down the corridor, and I said, "I can't tell you about the novel. We don't have time. It's just a dream right now, it's unfinished, but it's been an extraordinary journey for me, like a Rudyard Kipling adventure. Not so much for Josiah, I'm afraid," looking back at him. Rachel noticed my troubled face.

"With Velia—I'll see if I ever finish."

"Is everything okay between you two?"

"Yes, of course. We had a few bad swells together, but we're on dry land now. It's really okay."

"Glad to hear that, Salty. Really glad," she said looking at me for assurance. "While we walk to the check-in counter give me a hint about the novel."

"I'd rather not. I hate talking about something in progress; only when it's a fait accompli, if it ever becomes that, but I'll keep you posted."

We walked around as I gently rocked Velia while Rachel brought me up to date about her family. When Josiah was through eating we all walked to the gate and suddenly Josiah said, "Ah, merde!"

"What's up?" I asked.

"Flight's been delayed for forty five minutes. Damn! I really wanted to get underway."

We sat down and Rachel asked, "Since we have some additional time, I never heard about how you guys met. Was it like in the movies?"

"No, but strange," I said. "He was the assistant director on a twerpy film I wrote called, 'Twaddle,' one of my more forgettable films.

"When the film started shooting, I went on the set and noticed this serious looking guy pointing here and there, whispering to the cast members and the craftspeople and saw them nodding in agreement. Even in the subdued light I liked his face and his energy, but when I tried to have a conversation with him, he seemed so deeply immersed in what he was doing that he ignored me. When the lights went on, I saw that he had dark curly hair, big almond shaped eyes—black—and olive complexion. I was immediately smitten! But, when I tried to make some small talk, the jerk," I said touching his face, "was totally indifferent to me—as though I were transparent. I was sure that if I met him an hour later, he would have looked at me as though we had never met. That hurt me since I had never had that kind of instant reaction to anybody. When I got back to my office, I couldn't get him off my mind.

"Look at the grin on that pathetic husband of mine, reveling in my puppy love. Well, a few days later, I was on the bus going home and saw him walking, so I rang for the bus to stop. In my rush to leave, one of my shoes fell off. I turned around to get it but the doors closed.

"I was terribly embarrassed but I hobbled towards him like the Hunchback of Notre Dame, waved my arms and shouted, 'Hi, Josiah, hi. It's me, Sally. Remember? Smiling in as best a mixture that joy and shame would allow.

"When he turned around to see who was calling him, he saw this foolish young thing with a shortened leg limping towards him, one shoe on, one shoe off, sounding like a twelve year old. He looked down at my shoeless foot, and with a broad smile, asked, 'Are you the street clown? Are you getting ready to perform?'

"I scowled and shouted, quite eloquently I thought, 'Screw you, Josiah!' and pivoted on my shoeless foot ripping a hole in my stocking. I was breathing fire and smoke, and hobbled away as fast I could, teeth clenched, totally humiliated. Suddenly I felt a strong hand on my shoulders. The hand turned me around and a voice whispered, one finger perpendicular to his lips, 'You shouldn't be shouting on the street.' Before I could tell him to go to hell, he said, 'Sally, of course I know who you are. I was dentally attracted to you right away.'

That was about as disarming a comment he could have made. "What? 'Dentally?' What the hell does that mean?'"

"'You have,' he said, 'a beautiful set of teeth, all standing at attention with perfect posture. And a smile that made me quiver all over, so after you left I asked everyone about you. I even got your phone number so I could take you to dinner. Save me a phone call. How does tomorrow night sound?'

"To my total surprise, without making him suffer even a little, I quickly said, 'I'd love it,' certain my face was ablush.

"'But do me a favor," he said still smiling, "wear two shoes, okay?"

"I smiled but was too embarrassed to give him an explanation. Then something strange happened. I didn't want to leave, so looking for some excuse to stay, I ran my hand slowly over his tie saying something banal like what a beautiful tie he was wearing. All the time we kept looking intensely at one another.

"I was wearing a lovely silk scarf casually draped over my left breast. When I was finished running my hand over his tie, he ran his hand slowly over my scarf, and while saying something equally banal about my scarf, paused for an almost imperceptible moment over my breast. With a glint in his eye and an orangutan grin on his face, I saw him bobbing his head.

I was so shocked that I punched him on the nose. Not a slap mind you. A punch! I was horribly humiliated and ran to the bus stop.

"While I was waiting, he came running over with apologies about how unlike that was of him, that he had never done something like that before. A likely story I was sure, the lech," I said looking at Jo with bemused eyes. "I kept turning my back on him and he kept rotating to try to face me. It looked like we were on one of those dumb carnival rides that twirls you round and round. I put my fingers in my ears to try to stop him. Mercifully, my bus soon arrived.

"For the next few days, however, I couldn't get the incident out of my mind. It was like a film replaying itself over and over, with the shivers it initially evoked, I must confess, still lingering. So a few days later I made my way to the set again, murmuring some cockamamie excuse for being there, glad of the dim light so that he couldn't see my flushed face. When he saw me, he rushed over, "'I borrowed some handcuffs from the prop room so you can secure my hands behind my back. If you spoon-feed me, I'll be glad to take you to dinner, and because of my stupid behavior, I'll even pay for it,'" he said with that stupid monkey grin of his.

"'Your nose is swollen,'" was my icy response.

"'Yeah—clumsy me—I walked into a closed door.'"

"'You bet your goddamn life that damned door was closed!'" I said, hoping my nose wouldn't grow by three inches.

"My second comment was, 'Not on your life.' I tried keeping a stern look on my face, but the sure give-away was that I didn't move.

"'How about coffee, then,'" he said, "'right now at the commissary. Please say yes. That's the only way I can apologize to you for my stupid-ass behavior.'"

Making him suffer was my goal, you understand, so I said, "'A nickel cup of coffee won't do.'"

"'I didn't take you for a gold-digger, Sally. If I buy you a piece of their famous chocolate cake with your coffee, will that do?'"

"'Chocolate cake goes with milk, not coffee.'"

"'Chocolate cake and a glass of milk—a winning combination. I'll have the same. Shall we go?'" he asked with wide eyes and a smile. He came along side me like we were ready to walk, and made certain not to grab any part of me.

"I couldn't resist, nor did I want to, so I said, 'sounds like a gamble but you'd better not blow your last chance at redemption. Otherwise it's Dante's Inferno for you.'"

"So, folks," I smiled happily, "that's how Velia ended up in my arms."

Rachel said,"Your kids are going to love hearing that story, omitting some of the details of course, so be prepared for telling it more than once."

While we were hugging our goodbyes, Sinty pouted, "Salty, I didn't realized how much I missed my older sister until just now."

I kissed him on the cheek and said,"Look at how much we'll be missing by not living around the block from one another."

He kissed me back and asked,"Is it better to have had a brief moment of joy, or, to avoid this deep pang of nostalgia I'm feeling, is it better not to have had it at all?

"Parting, contrary to what the master thinks, is not sweet sorrow. Au revoir, my dears," he said as I noticed a shimmering in both his and Rachel's eyes.

"Until the next time. You know, the four of us could be friends—by choice rather than by genes. Adieu, mes freres—et—mes amis."

PART II

To the Hollywood Titans who
refused to compromise with the truth.

CHAPTER 23

I was deeply concerned with our health, Velia's and mine, so upon our return to Los Angeles, I immediately made a bunch of appointments with doctors—hematologists, nephrologists, ophthalmologists, pulmonologists, and God knows how many other specialists, visits that involved puncturing veins, bad enough for me, but difficult to find on tiny Velia. Whenever we approached medical buildings, she started screaming, always making me cringe. She must have thought me a monster as I struggled mightily to comfort her. Who knows what enduring memories she'll have of her mother and men in white coats.

Though it took several weeks, the doctors knew what they were doing. My blood chemistry, though more complicated than Velia's, had improved greatly, and finally Velia was asymptomatic. My painful engorgement had subsided but once I was pronounced ready, I wanted to make milk again. Could I restart the process? I took some pills that started me swelling again and that made me very happy.

Except for my right eye that blurred intermittently, the doctor said it would get better or not—hardly reassuring, but with baby at breast now, and loving every minute of the warm, moist suckling sensation that bonded me with her, as with all women, in a continuum, primitive, earthy and enormously satisfying, it made me feel like part of a larger piece.

I continue writing apace, sharing my thoughts with her, speaking aloud so she can learn the musicality of English, its pauses, its flow, the occasional foul language I apologize for, all serving a purpose in teaching language to infants. With winter flowers blooming, liquidambar trees still aflame with autumn colors, migratory birds visiting again, my mal disappeared. I had finally arrived on solid ground.

Every Wednesday morning, I visited my personal Nympheas of the Musee de L'Orangerie—the Santa Monica Farmer's Market where I could buy fresh, unadulterated fruits and vegetables displayed beautifully on their individual carts. Colors of orange, pink, purple, yellow, brown, green, in myriad shades too numerous to have names—shapes too difficult to classify accurately, oblong, bulbous, round, oval, pear-shaped, flower shaped, those with fronds or stalks, some with roots still attached, tops still attached—Impressionist paintings all. And those fragrances—sweet, earthy, minty, peachy, apricoty, orangey, tomatoey, and yes, fresh, the fragrance of freshness, unmistakable yet impossible to give any other name to it. The Market was my kinship with Monet at Giverny—and, with a hollow in my heart, of an earlier time, of a time when my father sold fruits and vegetables from his pushcart on the streets of Harlem.

One day a strange thing happened as I was getting organic Fuji apples. They were among my favorite apples, sweet/tart and crisp. I extended my bag to the farmer and was about to pay him when I saw an old woman slyly grab two apples and slip them into her sweater and walk away. Her hair was combed, wore a brush of lipstick, seemed presentable and neat, but her shabby sweater was badly frayed at the wrists. Without hesitation, I walked over to her and said, "Ma'am, I have a bag with some apples I haven't paid for yet. Why don't you add those apples to this bag? I'll pay for all of them, and you can have the whole bag for your birthday. How does that sound?" I asked with an innocent smile. Her face flushed, she looked at her feet, paused and said, "It's not my birthday."

"But within a year, I know it will be, so put them in here and you can make an apple pie or apple sauce or whatever."

With downcast eyes, she put her apples in my bag. I paid for them, gave her the bag and walked away quickly without making further eye contact so as not to prolong her embarrassment. I would return later to buy my own.

I went to another farmer's stand and was buying broccoli sprouts, when I felt a tap on my shoulder. I turned around and heard, "Hi, Sally. Remember me? Tynan Danard?"

My eyes traveled seven inches above me and rested on a slender Irish/Scandinavian woman with shoulder length flowing blondish hair gracing a blue-eyed pink face, and a friendly smile.

"Of course I remember you—slugger," I said with a reciprocal smile.

We both laughed. "Sally, I was standing nearby and saw what you did with that woman," and without saying another word, nodded her head up and down. With a non-accusatory look on her face, asked, "What happened to your self-righteousness? Your famous truculence?" and placed her hand affectionately on my shoulder.

Somewhat embarrassed, I answered, "Children have a way of raising our sights, of civilizing us. Or, in an attempt to civilize them, we ourselves become more civilized. Or is it the passage of time, the writers I've read, the people I've encountered, Paris?"

She nodded her head and left her hand on my shoulder, as though she were thinking of something to say. "I heard you lived there for a few months." I nodded.

"Sally, we're having trouble with the final cut of *Garden Land Road*. Would it be impertinent of me to ask you to see it and give me your opinion?"

"Ty, I'm shocked at your request—and honored, but you know I no longer work for Fox."

"Yeah, I heard. But as a favor, a favor I hardly deserve. You are the mother of that script," and rolling her eyes, said, "more or less. I'd like you to have a hand in the final product. What do you think of my outrageous request?"

I looked at her with bemusement, with skepticism, with irony, hesitated for a moment and wrote my phone number down on a piece of paper. "Ty, call me. Tell me when and where."

She broke out in a lovely smile and said, "Sally, it's great seeing you again—this time the whole of you."

The following day, she called to say, Studio C, 10:00am, Thursday. A pass will be at the gate. Okay?

It was weird saying hello to the gatekeeper who recognized me right away, to walk the streets hoping no one would recognize me, start asking questions. I kept my eyes lowered and walked briskly to Studio C.

I reserved judgment until the film was over—an uncharacteristic trait. When the lights went on, she looked at me for reactions. "Ty," I said, "the film is incoherent. That scene at the Culver skating rink jars and distracts. Leave that scene on the cutting room floor.

Write yourself some transitional dialogue and have that character go to Sunset Beach with his surfboard. Have him ride one big wave after another, set after set, as a group of hapless surfers look at him with envy. On the last big one, have him continue to shore and walk triumphantly back to his car without looking back."

"You know, Sally, that might very well work," she said. "Your Paris scene would have been much better, of course, but Adam scotched it because of the budget. I had no choice but to substitute Culver City—that's how I got to this impasse."

"You mean that was Adam's decision, not yours?"

"Yeah, didn't you know?"

"Merde!"

I invited her to Shabbat dinner a week from Friday at my mother's house.

"I assume it'll be okay to bring my husband?"

"Ty, of course. I should have asked."

Friday night arrived and as I was helping my mother prepare the dinner while trying to keep Velia from waking up, the doorbell rang. I opened the door, and saw Ty and her husband who looked familiar. Before being introduced, I looked at her and said, "Oh, I know Kasio!" There stood a tall, thick eye-browed strong face, a man who looked like he could have opened the door without a key. We both smiled and he said, "When Ty told me she met you, I said that I had seen you around the studio—that I was familiar with your work. A pleasant surprise, Sally."

Without serving appetizers since we were starved by this time, I pointed out where they should be sitting. My mother lit the Sabbath candles and said the prayers. Josiah then said the prayers for the wine and bread. I looked around the table as Josiah was passing out pieces of Challa, and said, "For those of us who struggle with *King of the Universe* stuff, these prayers are important reminders not to take anything for granted—ever—the food on the table, our health, our good fortune, family and friends."

I made eye contact with everyone. "Shabbat Shalom. Time to eat."

We dug in and began eating my mother's exotic food—more like a fiesta for the starving. A huge green salad, fava beans, leek kiftikas which, I explained to them, were essentially leek hamburgers, orzo pasta made with chicken fat, roasted chicken, broiled butter fish with a crust, brown and crunchy, Kosher wine—food, that by the looks on our guests' faces was foreign to them. No apology was necessary because it was, as my mother often said, *comida de la casa,* served with a look that said, *'it's-what-you're-getting-I hope-you-like-it-but-if-not-there's-always-Zucky's-delicatessen-near-by.*

With a mouth full of food, I asked, "So, Kasio, I had no idea you were married to this classy lady. You're a writer, right?"

Unlike the rest of us, he swallowed his food before speaking. "Well, a lower tiered writer, specializing in vampires, bats, ghouls, all those delectable characters that scare the life out of youngsters who keep coming back for more because they know they're safe, yet get that vicarious pleasure of being close to danger and surviving. Yup, that's my stupid-ass career!"

We all laughed, and I said, "Listen, I was no better. I wrote trash extracted from trashy novels, but for some unlikely reason, we make a living at it."

"I'm a cut above both of you," Josiah added, "I'm an *assistant director,* helping to direct the crap you guys write."

"Honey," I said, "that makes us equal. We all belong in the trash heap!"

Ty jumped in, "You guys are too hard on yourselves. You have a useful function, you *entertain*, and there *ain't* nothing wrong with that! And look at all the jobs you create."

With the idle banter continuing into my mother's presentation of baklava and coffee, we sat around, relaxed and stuffed, so I turned to Kasio and said, "You're lucky, vampires won't endanger you with HUAC. You'll never get called."

"I'm not so sure, Sally."

"What the hell can you guys be accused of?" Josiah asked.

"We've all been forewarned," Kasio said, "and I got to thinking about a vampire movie I wrote during the thirties. A movie where the people leading the society were totalitarian vampires sucking blood from innocents. Then, a leader emerged amongst those victims, gathered them together in the hopes of overthrowing those blood suckers, but he wanted to have everyone participate, without a supreme leader, you understand, to give each of them a stake in victory and ultimate governance.

"They finally succeeded in overthrowing the regime, but my script called for the ultimate consequences of group control—you know—more totalitarianism—how ultimately one tyranny replaces another. As luck would have it, budget constraints forced the studio to cut the film after they had won control over the vampires."

"I get it, Kas" Josiah said, "communist ideology without its consequences, right?"

"You got it! So for them I may not be an innocent bystander," he said looking deeply into his cup of thick Turkish coffee.

"Listen, Kasio," I jumped in, "you're innocent until proven guilty. Just show them your original script. If there's any suspicion that you were trying to propagandize about the *beauties of communism,* you can show them the stuff you wrote that was never filmed."

Ty said, "I hope it's that simple, Sally."

CHAPTER 24

In the early months of 1951, General Sherman's second march through Georgia was about to be howlingly repeated in Hollywood. For months we had been dreading the arrival of the House Un-American Activities Committee, made all the more dreadful by their delay of six-months, a delay that heightened the irritability quotient amongst those of us threatened. I assured myself, like I tried to assure Kasio, that we had nothing to worry about. Despite my facade of confidence, I was scared to death.

Josiah could see it in my face when I received my sub-poena. He just nodded and hugged me. He knew better than to give assurances.

I told him I knew why they were holding their hearings in Los Angeles. The Great Appalachian Storm in late November 1950, predictions of the freezing cold of January and February in Washington, and in those early days of television, they noticed that crowds at the New Year's Day Rose Parade wore short sleeve shirts—all determining factors. Besides, why not hold the hearings where movies are made?

And, if they were coming for the warm climate, why not at the landmark Beverly Wilshire Hotel in opulent Beverly Hills?

I was sure that to get their sea legs back, I was still using watery metaphors, they were sub-poenaing Lilliputians first—the B movie writers. Was it because they had had it with the heavyweights? Was it because they believed that communist propaganda was being slipped insidiously into B films? Oh, how sly we were.

Most of the seats in the back were vacant. I didn't warrant more than a wooden folding chair, hard and uncomfortable, made less uncomfortable because I was still carrying around my own personal cushion, a part of me since pregnancy.

"Let the record show that at 10:00am, on February 15, 1951, the House Un-American Activities Committee chaired by Congressman Russell P. Heddbone, is brought to order."

There were two reporters, one television cameraman and his unwieldy camera, a rookie sound guy who kept dropping his microphone while trying to get it on the boom, each time with a screeching sound.

There were seven Committee members, male, business suits, busy adjusting their stuffed chairs suitable for napping, talking to colleagues and staff people, organizing papers, grinning before the camera, waving to friends in the audience. It reminded me of what my schoolteacher friends described as an unruly classroom of pre-teens, or worse, teens. I was certain this was going to be a brief hearing, and that lessened my sense of intimidation. Nonetheless, I continued breathing in shallow breaths—rapidly.

The Chairman rapped his gavel, "Please identify yourself to the committee."

"My name is Sally Apple."

Chairman: "Is that your real name?"

Why would he ask that? "No, my birth name is Saltiel Aboulafia."

Chairman: "Then Sally Apple is your stage name?"

"I'm not an actress, sir, it's the name I used when I first came to Los Angeles in 1935."

"Why did you choose to mask your real name?" he asked like a hostile attorney.

'Mask' is a curious choice of a word. I didn't let my face show any reaction. "Since California was not as heterogeneous as New York City, you know, all the ethnic people with funny names," I said, quickly checking the faces of the committee members, "I felt that a name that wouldn't call attention to itself nor arouse latent prejudices, would be safer."

In one of those tiny fractions of time that upon reflection makes me wonder whether it ever happened, I thought I detected a wry grin from one committee member and an almost audible grunt from another.

The chairman continued, "You have no attorney with you. Why did you choose not to be represented by counsel?"

"I can't afford to hire one. I've been out of a job for several months and secondly, I have nothing to hide, so even if I did have the money I didn't think I would need counsel."

"Good to hear that. We've had enough of paranoid witnesses. Before we examine your contributions to the movie industry, Miss Apple, tell us about Adam Lapidus?"

The question surprised me. "Why don't you ask him directly? You have a *direct* line to him. You don't have to use a *party* line."

"What party? The Communist Party?" he asked, confident he had just caught a fish.

"Of course not," I said, embarrassed at my poor choice of words. "You know, 'telephone line—single or party'—for those unlucky ones who can only get a 'party line,' ha, ha," I said with a weak laugh.

"Don't be cute with us!" he admonished. "Tell us if you ever heard him say anything un-American. Did he ever espouse ideas that sounded communistic, socialistic or anarchistic?"

"No, we never talked about politics—it was strictly business. He was my boss and I was in his stable," I said with a smile, hoping to evoke one in return. When none came, I continued, "You know, stable like in horse. Or more like in slave."

Nothing.

I continued, "He never proposed overthrowing our government, if that's what you mean, at least not to me. About being a 'socialist,' we once had a discussion about how enlightened our Social Security Program is and how beneficial it seems for our retiring citizens. Does that qualify as being a 'socialist'?"

"There are some who believe that Roosevelt's New Deal," he harrumphed, "was socialistic, but I'm not here to discuss that with you, AND let me remind you, madam, that YOU are not here to ask questions," he continued, leaving me wonder why his harsh tone was necessary, "we are the ones asking the questions. Did he ever complain or say anything against America?"

"We're Americans, Mr. Congressman, and we sometimes complain about this or that—President Roosevelt's attempt at stacking the Supreme Court—the incarceration of Japanese citizens—the treatment of our Negro citizens—President Truman's nationalization of the railroads and meat packers," I said echoing op-ed writers with whom I agreed. "To complain, to correct, to ameliorate, to improve our country is not un-American. In fact it's exactly the opposite, don't you think?"

"Miss Apple, let us ask the questions please. Now, what other complaints did Mr. Lapidus express?"

With my rage against Adam barely submerged, I wondered whether I should try to get him into trouble by disclosing what he had once told me. Or, whether the more decent thing would be to forget it—or maybe mention it but not justify it. That might diffuse its potential harm, but if I justified it, would I be digging myself a grave?

Damn! I thought this hearing was about me—not about Adam.

Bewildered, unsure of which tack to take, no time to ponder, and under oath, I was falling out of a plane wondering whether my 'chute would open. I decided to barrel on, see where my impulsive behavior would take me. But suddenly, I found Col. Picquart on my shoulder.

"Well," I said, pretending a confidence I didn't possess at the moment, "I do remember one *astute* observation of his that had never occurred to me. And I emphasize the word, *'astute,'* sir. Last spring at the close of a disturbing meeting, he complained about the way Negroes were treated in America, wondered why they had fought in the Second World War, that had he been a Negro, he might not have.' Something like that."

"Why was it a 'disturbing meeting'?" he asked, peering over his reading glasses.

"Because it was a complaint from your predecessor about Fox's film, 'Gentlemen's Agreement.'"

"That issue is scheduled for another time. Did you agree with him?"

"Of course, Mr. Congressman," I said louder than I had expected. "Separate drinking fountains, separate bathrooms, separate schools, fighting in segregated groups. I know they were drafted, but what were they fighting for anyway? Whose freedom were they fighting for? What freedom? To come back to their former servitude?"

"So you agree with him?" he asked.

"Damn right! Don't you?" I asked.

I remembered his admonition and added, "Yes, sir, of course. I'm mad that some of my fellow-Americans are treated unequally, unfairly. It's *un-American!* Do you think that's what Jefferson and Washington had in mind?"

"I'm going to remind you, Miss Apple, not to ask this committee questions, even rhetorical ones. So do you still agree with his statements?"

"Mr. Heddbone, I'm glad Negroes fought against our enemies during the war. We needed all hands on deck, even though theirs were mostly *below* deck! But we should learn from their supererogatory sacrifices, and give them the freedom they deserve as Americans!" I said, finding I was holding my chin up high, right hand pointing.

He softened his tone and asked, "For those who might be unfamiliar with that word, please define it for them," pretending he knew its meaning.

I learned early in life that the use of unfamiliar, polysyllabic words sounded pretentious and show-offy, that it annoyed some, exasperated others, yet impressed still others, so I said, "Beyond the call of duty, sir. Doing more than what is expected. What Americans should do in every aspect of their lives."

"Thank you. So, you are defending Mr. Lapidus's beliefs then?"

"It wasn't a belief, Mr. Congressman. He was only pondering—asking questions of himself like we all do. He did nothing wrong. It's okay in America for us to question policies—that's what our elections are about, right?" I asked with defiance. "No, I have other quarrels with Mr. Lapidus, but that's not one of them."

"To have him say, Miss Apple, that had he been a Negro he would not have fought for us is in fact *subversive*."

"I'll leave the interpretation of *'subversive'* to you, sir, but that doesn't sound *'subversive'* to me. I do, however, want to make something clear. I didn't say he wouldn't fight. I said he questioned why they fought in the first place."

"Don't go nuancing me, Miss Apple—straight talk, please," another one of his admonitions. I was sure that he was soon going to put me on his lap and spank me.

"Mr. Congressman," I said, "if you had to use a 'colored' bathroom or a 'colored' water fountain, a 'colored' dining room, a 'colored' hotel room, if you had to come in through the basement ... "

He interrupted me with a rap of his gavel and scolded, "Don't lecture me, Miss Apple! And don't ask me any more questions, do you hear? We're the only ones asking questions!"

"I'm not lecturing. As a writer I have to put myself in the shoes of my characters, understand their motivations, right and wrong, otherwise I'd be painting in two colors only. Black and white—forgive the pun. I'm telling you that what we have for Negroes in our blessed country is not so blessed for them."

"They have to know their place!" he barked.

"Was not their place on the battlefield intended to make you safe, sir?" trying to control my impatience and anger.

"One more lippy question from you and I'm going to cite you for contempt!"

"Sorry, sir, it's just ... "

"I'm not interested in your 'just' something or other—we need no explanations from you, JUST answers. Is there anything else you remember about him?"

"Nothing else, sir. Nothing else."

"The 'other quarrels' you mentioned. Were they about politics?"

"Absolutely not, only personal, and irrelevant to our discussion."

"I am finished with my questions for the time being, so Mr. Devereaux," he said looking over to his immediate left, "would you proceed with your inquiry, please?"

"Thank you, Mr. Chairman. Miss Aboulafia, I would like to ask you some questions."

"Sir," I said raising my hand for some stupid reason, like I was asking permission, "the name I'm known by, and have been known by for my entire professional career, is 'Sally Apple.' My husband calls me Sally, so I respectfully ask that you call me by that name. Please."

"As you wish, Miss Apple. Now tell us what your profession is."

"I'm a screenwriter. I *was* a screenwriter—from 1936 to the fall of 1950."

"Employed by whom?"

"Twentieth Century Fox."

"Would I recognize any of the films you wrote?"

Only if you were a fan of 'B' movies—if you could tolerate them. I had perfected the well-crafted tale of the easily discarded, the quickly forgotten—horror movies, zany movies, implausible movies about rocket ships going to planets populated by people in funny costumes fighting the same stupid wars we've always fought on earth only with futuristic looking weapons. Movies that stretched one's credulity—mindless—numbing. He-men with Brooklyn accents fighting animals and hostile natives in impenetrable jungles, cowboys with Bronx accents saving innocent damsels from bad guys. Adaptations of exploitation novels—nothing, I'm sorry to say, that will end up in some future anthology of films with literary merit—even as a footnote. Just in a dustbin.

"That said, however, I believe in make-believe and its role in our lives."

"Tell us something about the process and the people you may have dealt with. We then want to ask about one of your films in particular."

"Okay, so that you have a more complete understanding, once I got through with what I felt confident was a 'shooting script,' other people would get involved. People like re-writers who 'polished' the script, which was another way of saying that they were compelled to justify their salaries by deliberately changing this or that, whether it needed it or not. Then executives who had to earn their bread by adding or subtracting, or thrusting the script in other directions. Oftentimes, when my films finally made it to the screen, I wasn't sure whether I had been the original author."

"Miss Apple, as part of our preparation for these hearings, I had a research assistant view most of your films, and I must agree with you," looking at me without apology, "mindless—but audiences expected two movies and the studios accommodated them. In your defense, however, some of the 'A' movies were also mindless."

"But some," I said, "no, not some—*many* were great and deserve their place in some future anthology. And, I might add, some 'B' movies were also great. Regrettably, I don't think any of mine were."

"Without further editorializing, I want to call your attention to one of your space movies, *'Planet Zeno,'* released in 1945.

"Please tell the committee about it."

"It's about a planet in the constellation Orion populated by two major tribes, *Zenophobes* and *Zenophiles*, both of whom, having gone to the brink of extinction by their constant internecine warfare, developed a vaccine to prevent future conflicts. No more Zeno paradoxes, no more Schrodinger's Cats, no more Hegelian dialectics, no more ambiguities, nor contradictions, doubts, dilemmas, or antinomies. In other words, no more conflicting points of views—only planetary certitude."

"Sounds utopian or perhaps *communistic*?" one of the congressional panel members asked, raising his eyebrows while emphasizing the word, *communistic*.

"No, sir, to the contrary. Their certitude was not imposed from above—it was not official dogma like in totalitarian countries. This vaccine altered their attitude and behavior enabling them to survive. It was now who they had become."

"Whether it was decreed from up above or from within, it is the *communist* ideology, isn't it—insistence on uniformity of opinion? Did the studio heads, like Mr. Lapidus, put you up to that?"

"Absolutely not!" I shouted. "The story was from a science fiction pulp novel that I found in the five-cent bin at Salvation Army. It was loaded with intimate stories of nubile girls behaving like earth's jungle bonobos who serve a vital peace-keeping purpose by fornicating with aggressive males on the verge of warfare."

Anybody squirming? No. Okay then, I'll give them something to awaken them, but before I could continue, one of the barely awake members who seemed to be listening with only a small portion of his brain asked, "What are bonobos?"

"Pigmy chimpanzees," I answered, wondering how anyone could possibly be paying attention—eyes at half mast, frequent interruptions by staff members whispering things in their ears, notes constantly being passed. I found it annoying, but managed to restrain myself. The gavel was in their hands.

"Female bonobos—*like females of our own species, homo sapiens*—are more civilized than males of their species," I said, pausing to quickly scan the faces of the panel members for some reaction.

Nothing.

Bloodless.

But the cameraman and the guy with the microphone decided to close in on me—like this was where the action would be coming from.

I continued, "African female bonobos freely give sexual favors to diffuse the war-like impulses of *inferior* males."

Still nothing.

"In the book, the humanoids on Planet Zeno had advanced to the bonobo stage and had stopped warring. Why? Because the females were doing what bonobos do here on earth."

I was anxious to find out whether anyone was paying attention, and hoping to get some blood flowing, I said *very softly*, "In the novel, the motto was: Fuck—Don't Fight!"

The gavel came down so hard it exploded on its wooden plate like a hand-grenade, breaking into hundreds of shards that scattered on the panel members, on their assistants, on the photographer and cameraman, and on my desk and blouse. It stunned everyone in the room—its reverberation hanging in the air.

"What the *HELL* did you say?" the chairman thundered.

I fired back, ***"FUCK—DON'T FIGHT!"***

Flashbulbs blinded me. "I heard what you said the first time, *GODDAMMIT!* Why the hell did you have to repeat it?" he thundered.

Bemused at the sudden sign of life, I said quite innocently, "Because you asked me to, sir."

"It was just a rhetorical question."

"Sorry, Mr. Chairman. Congressman Devereaux asked me to tell you about the story, and I just wanted to state that in the novel, their method of conflict resolution was as simple as that." Despite angry murmurings, I went on. "You need to know some more details and then you'll see how I anesthetized the story for the movie. In the book songwriters picked up the cadence of the phrase to write catchy tunes with catchy beats ... "

"Enough of that, young lady. You have poisoned the decorum of this court by your scatological language and pornographic themes typical of you liberal Hollywood types. I'm tempted to cite you for contempt!" he said, looking around at his fellow panel members, all of whom had shocked looks of insincere moral indignation, as though each of them had been born of an immaculate conception.

"Sir, please don't," I said softly, raising my hand like a stop sign. I was enjoying the episode and hoped my inner smile wasn't showing. In an innocent voice, I added. "You asked me to describe the story so I wanted to point out the differences between the novel and my script, and how I had sanitized it almost beyond recognition. I couldn't have used the method of conflict resolution described in the book, not only because of the Hayes Commission, but because I knew that the puritanical sensibilities of Americans would be offended by such blatant sexual excesses," and, unable to resist a coda, added, "no matter how salubrious."

"Are you mocking us, Miss Apple?" he asked raising his new gavel.

"Absolutely not, Mr. Chairman," I replied, oozing sincerity, nodding my head vigorously from side to side.

"May I ask, Mr. Chairman, that Mr. Devereaux get on with different questions?" asked Congressman Chenyer, one of the committee members who was the most flagrant abuser of passing notes and of conferring with colleagues and assistants. His physical appearance was as unkempt as his behavior. He was having a bad hair day, gray and stringy; his face was ruddy and looked like he had had a bad case of acne; his tie was askew calling attention to the mismatch of colors between his tie, chocolate brown, and his suit, light blue; his collar looked frayed though that wasn't as clear from where I sat as the frayed cuffs on his sleeves; his shirt seemed un-ironed.

I had shocked him into focus.

"Before the next question, Mr. Chairman," raising my hand again, "it's important to mention what else was in the book so that you could see the extent to which I made changes—to the extent to which I had purified the story through a baptismal bath," I said, not wanting to miss the opportunity to stir their souls, and equally as important, to absolve myself of any suspicion. I was mindful of the tightrope I was on—trying my best not to get jailed for contempt.

"I started to say that in the novel there were song writers, like Anita and Mayer Kahn, promoting this enlightened social program with songs like, 'Caress and Detumesce,' the poignant, 'Love me AND Leave me,' the lovely, 'I'm in the Nude for...' the jolly 'Whistle while you F....'"

The new gavel came crashing down. *"Miss Apple, for heaven's sake, spare us those damn details!"*

That convinced me that I had gotten him to a level from which he could not ascend further. I couldn't resist, however, testing those limits. This was so much fun. "Okay, sir, but, please, bear with me because I must tell you one further detail to prove to you how I removed all the prurience from the novel," I said like a child innocently asking permission to play outside.

"To show you the extent to which I had bowdlerized the novel," I hesitated before dropping my bomb, and pleaded, "Please hear me out, gentlemen," certain I was going to get shot the moment I made the next statements. The chairman's head was moving from side to side, gavel poised.

I heard a tapping on the microphone. "Mr. Chairman, may I interrupt please," a congressmen said, a bemused look on his face. "I remember reading that novel and seeing the film. This is an investigatory body so we need to hear everything this young woman has to say, even though," looking at me and at the chairman, "it may be offensive to our sensibilities. Please let her continue, Mr. Chairman."

He seemed aware of my precarious footing, that I was on the verge of getting ejected or worse, cited, and had gallantly come to my defense. Thankful for the reprieve, I nodded to him and went on, "In the book there were hundreds of Emergency Trucks painted candy apple red, like our Fire Trucks, each sporting a logo that had a holographic picture that, as the truck moved, showed two people—a *perfectly normal picture,* mind you, of two people actively fornicating."

A murmuring shock wave permeated the atmosphere—mouths stayed opened, eyes wide, so I rushed on with absolute solemnity, "Please, you need to have a complete picture."

I was certain that one or more of the members was going to pass out, throw up, throw something at me, lunge at me, call the bailiff, rip off their jackets revealing the insignia of *The Avenger,* or raise a sword like Saint George to slay the evil dragon lady before them.

I sat there demurely enjoying the sight of congressmen breathing fire as I prepared myself for what was next. I went on rapidly, "Woven artistically within that logo were the words, '*Fuck Truck*.'

The chairman ignored the gavel in his right hand and slammed the flat of his left hand on the desk and shouted, *"Miss Apple! You've gone far enough!"*

This time I was sure I was going to be sent straight to hell without the possibility of parole. That congressman, Mr. Nancer LeMay, came to my defense again. "Mr. Chairman, please, if we are to remain true to our policy of *'full disclosure'* we must let her continue," he pleaded.

Without waiting for a decision, I continued, "You need to understand the nature of my work and the concept of 'adaptation,' which is in the nature of screenwriting, but insofar as the people on Planet Zeno were concerned, it was *Darwinian adaptation*.

"Anyway, I'm almost finished, sirs, so let me tell you that these emergency *Fuck Trucks* filled with attractive women who, having received advanced training from skilled practitioners in the art of seduction and fornication, went wherever a conflict was arising and proceeded to lay out inflatable mattresses to *defuse the conflict*, and I emphasize the word, *defuse*, gentlemen, by fornicating lustily and heartily!"

They seemed immobilized so I didn't wait for the fragmentation of another gavel. "For those of you who are sport fisherman who engage in *'Catch and Release'* fishing, this was essentially a *'Fuck and Release'* program," I said, hardly able to contain my urge to burst out laughing, "with the *'Release'* of their aggressive tendencies—by doing you know what," deliberately omitting *that* word again, and just kept looking at them like an innocent child repeating a bedtime story.

I was having the time of my life playing chess with these Puritans.

"I don't know what the hell to do with you, Miss Apple! You insult the committee with your scatological language, you offend us with your pornographic story, you act innocently though there are many signs of disrespect throughout your testimony, you ..."

"Mr. Chairman, please," interrupted Mr. Devereaux. He turned to me and asked, "I don't remember your film being salacious, but I didn't see all of it. Was it? And how did the Hayes Committee let you get away with that?"

"As I said, Mr. Congressman," thinking, *you bastard, I knew you weren't listening,* "having seen the film, sir, you know that I did my best to disinfect the picture," using that word to place myself on their side of heaven, "so it was not salacious at all. I knew about our American sensibilities and the Hayes Committee's attempts at keeping us *un-titillated,* so I removed the sexy scenes and had the vaccine replace *their innate belligerence with conformity.*"

I nodded my head from side to side, as though with regret, and continued, "But, there was one major consequence to the vaccine, one adverse side effect ... " leaving the sentence incomplete, hoping to deflect and postpone what I detected was the look of an imminent contempt charge.

The chairman, barely containing his anger, bit, "And what was that?"

"Lassitude, sir.

"Yes, unfortunately—their joi de vivre had disappeared. That was the price they paid for peace and tranquility—for the uniformity of opinion."

I pretended an afterthought, and with a quiver in my voice, I said, "Oh there was one other side effect," letting my voice trail off, "a reduction of libido ... "

Being heaved out of a saloon in a Western flashed across my mind. "You know there's always a price to pay—like the newly developed varieties of roses—great beauty but no fragrance?"

No reaction. I had stunned them into silence. Their undivided attention was mine. I imagined they were recreating the story in their heads to repeat to their staff and wives.

Josiah was surely going to nominate me for an academy award.

I picked up the slack. "Let me continue just briefly, if I may. In my film, Zenophobe and Zenophile comedians, like those on earth, had dominant genes selected for cynicism. They were the last ones to accept things at face value—the last ones to accept norms of behavior—the last ones to accept subterfuge over truth—the *first* ones to lift the veil of obfuscation—to let us know how things really were, so before the last dose of vaccine took its desired effect, they began calling the inhabitants, *Apathanians*."

That went unnoticed. The new name meant nothing? Don't they get it? Has their attention lapsed so soon?

"Was there," Mr. Devereaux asked with a tinge of know-it-all cynicism souring his question, "any pressure on you by the studio bosses to add propaganda like—if you don't contradict me and just obey, there will be peace?"

They are single-minded.

"No sir, no-way. Besides, history has always disproved that thesis. In any event, there were no contradictions, only uniformity of opinion."

Congressman LeMay asked, "Mr. Chairman, before Mr. Devereaux continues, may I ask one question, please? Mr. Devereaux, okay?"

"Sure."

"Miss Apple, in your movie, did the vaccine give a lifetime immunity to conflict?

"No, sir, it did not. After several years it wore off."

"What about booster shots?"

"Those didn't work. Once the immunity wore off ... " I said letting my voice trail off, a rather nice technique, I thought, showing reflectiveness.

"Did your movie go there?"

"No, sir, when there was a growing awareness that the vaccine was losing its potency, I ended it. I wanted to leave the audience wondering whether the lessons learned about *'living-in-peace-with-apathy,'* were sufficiently salutary that they would now make an effort to *'living-in-peace-with polemics.'*"

"No further questions. Thank you, Mr. Chairman." Looking at me, he said, "Thank you, Miss Apple. Thank you."

Strange. All the others seemed so hostile, so ready to pounce.

"Miss Apple," asked the chairman, "are you now or have you ever been a member of the Communist Party?"

"No, never."

"Would you please tell the committee who among your colleagues are or were?"

"Excuse me?"

"It's a simple question. Give us the names of the communists you know."

"I don't know who is a member of the Communist Party. The FBI might know, but I have no idea! Ask them," I said, expecting another reprimand.

"Give us, then, the names of those whose beliefs sounded *communistic*."

"My God, sir, how in the world am I supposed to answer that? During the war when the Soviets were our allies, there were many relief programs collecting clothing and food for the Russians, the Chinese, the Greeks, the British, and lots of others. Did that make us all communists? Did that make our Liberty Ships co-conspirators as communist abettors because they were carrying food, medicine and arms to the Soviets?" I asked.

"You've been asked before to stop your nuancing, Miss Apple, so don't muddy up the waters. Who amongst your friends and colleagues have espoused communist ideology?"

"Did I know of anyone who advocated the overthrow of our government? NO! Did I know of anyone who tried to influence my writing so that I could write about that putative *Communist Paradise?* NO! Did I know anyone who wrote about that? NO!

"You asked Jack Warner why he produced the film "Mission to Moscow" with all that false propaganda about the imagined achievements of the Soviet Union. And he told you that as our allies against a common enemy, we were sending them Liberty ships with food and guns, and that his film was based on our own Ambassador to the Soviet

Union, Joseph E. Davies' skewed book about the Soviets. That film was pure Soviet Propaganda with a capital 'P'!

"Did that make Warner Brothers a communist front? Or communist apologists? NO! You bought his explanation about their having been our allies, that they were our ships escorted by our own navy ships, and that we were all complicit in aiding an ally, so you let him off the hook.

"And you must have been aware that when Hitler asked the major studios to fire their Jewish employees in Germany, Warner Bros. was the only film company that refused to do so. In that most lucrative foreign market of theirs, they chose to close down shop, while all the other studios, to conform to Hitler's wishes, fired their Jewish employees.

"So to answer your question, no one that I knew at Twentieth Century Fox—not my colleagues, friends or bosses tried to influence my writing, nor did I ever know anyone who tried to influence anyone else. But remember please, those writers who made five hundred dollars a week never associated with those of us making two hundred and fifty dollars a week, and those making a thousand dollars a week never associated with those making five hundred a week, and the same through the hierarchy amongst directors and producers. I only knew about my own lowly group. And writing is a solitary endeavor. There's little time for mixing."

"Are all screenwriters as wordy as you, Miss Apple?" the chairman asked. "Please, don't answer the question. Go on, but more succinctly, if that's possible for you."

I was on a roll, wordy or not, "But on occasion when we did get together, most of us were for improved conditions for Negroes, improved rights for labor, for health and safety benefits, and where those beliefs intersected with the communists, we were all on the same side. But as for their other beliefs and those heinous acts being uncovered about their purges, their tyranny against their own people and conquered subjects, absolutely not, and no one I knew, and I emphasize—*no one I knew*—wanted then, nor wants now, our nation to become communistic. So does that answer your question, sir?"

No reply, but Mr. Devereaux held my glaze. He then said, "Mr. Chairman, I'm through. I think we have bigger fish to fry."

I slammed my hand on the desk. "Excuse me, Mr. Devereaux, you may very well be right, but your tone was an insulting one, and said publicly, even more so. Didn't your parents teach you any manners, SIR?"

Startled, he paused for a moment, unwittingly permitting the chairman to interject in his peremptory manner, "You're excused, Miss. Apple. Stay in town while these hearings are going on. You never know when we might want to call back even the 'smaller fish'."

"Would I be held in contempt if I reminded the chair that he too has no manners?"

"If you don't leave this *very* moment, I might *very* well cite you. It's been a temptation all day."

He looked at the other members and said, "Let's break for lunch. Be back at 2:00pm."

I walked to the door to meet Josiah when suddenly I felt a tap on my shoulder. "Miss Apple, I'm Congressman LeMay. Would you care to have lunch with me?"

"Mr. Congressman, is this like jury tampering?"

"You mean witness tampering?" he said. "No, not at all, just something I want to discuss with you. You're through and the likelihood of the Chairman asking you for more testimony—from even 'small fry'," he said sarcastically, "is practically non-existent."

"Well, Josiah and I were going to have lunch," I said just as Josiah grabbed my arm. "Mr. Congressman, my husband, Josiah."

"So nice to meet your husband, Sally," he said shaking Josiah's hand. Why has he started calling me by my first name? "Your wife performed admirably before those *Big Brothers*."

Without missing a beat, Josiah said, "My wife is well known for navigating difficult waters," giving me a sideways glance.

"Josiah," the congressman said, "you're the next witness, so I shouldn't be seen talking to you beforehand, but, Sally, Miss Apple, please have a cup of coffee with me without Josiah around—for just a moment. Josiah, would you mind?"

Puzzled, Josiah quipped, "No, not at all. I'll sit elsewhere and read your lips."

"Coffee is on me, Miss Apple."

"I know all about Congress's largesse. Thank you."

"Sally, may I call you Sally?"

I nodded.

I sat down and soon the waiter brought two cups of coffee. He must have signaled as we came in.

I was starved, but he offered coffee only and I wasn't going to take advantage.

"I've always been a sci-fi fan," he started immediately, "have always been attracted to a world of endless possibilities, but not of the kind we see with Buck Rogers and Flash Gordon—evil empires engaging in constant warfare, just a replay of what we have on earth, only people with funny costumes, as you said up there, and with new-fangled weapons.

"What I respond to is the kind of sci-fi of which dreams are made, of the 'what ifs,' of fulfilled longings and realized aspirations, of a civilization that has solved many of its social problems, one that has allowed for the efflorescence of its arts—sci-fi that leaves me with a—a—nostalgia for that future ... " and stopped, letting that thought hang.

I was puzzled and impressed, but remained quiet.

"All of which is to tell you that although I did read the novel, Planet Zeno, and saw your film, I don't remember the book having much of what you spoke, the trucks, the songs, many of the other details."

"Oh, my god."

"You were making some of that stuff up, weren't you?"

"Am I still under oath?"

"Would it make a difference?"

I didn't answer—just continued smiling for several beats.

"Since you ask, I'll tell you. Sometimes, I annoy myself with my moral rectitude, so when I see it in others I want to fight back. You and the others exuded that rectitude up there, whether you intended to or not, so I decided to play with your Calvinist beliefs, not realizing that one of you would have read that book.

"I couldn't resist being the flint for their gunpowder—and, yes, I did get carried away, but I'll tell you, congressman," I said, breaking out with a smile,"I got a kick out of doing it. I plead guilty. Am I under arrest?"

"Life imprisonment, that's my sentence, but not in this life, the next one—on Planet Zeno."

"I can live with that." We remained silent, smiling at one another.

"Sally, I saw that bemused look on your face and wondered whether you were playing with us."

"Mr. LeMay," I interrupted,"I detected a bemused smile on your face too."

"Well, I want you to know that you hadn't fooled me, that I thought your inventions about the trucks, the songs and everything else should have found a place in the original text. I'm sorry that no film can ever be made of that, but maybe someday on Planet Zeno, that is, when you get out of jail."

This is weird, I told myself.

"I thought that at any moment," he continued with his engaging smile,"you were going to ask the committee for copyright protection. All along though, I thought the chairman was going to throw you out with a contempt citation. His restraint was admirable, so I have renewed respect for him."

"Mr. Congressman, had you been chairman, would you have thrown me out?"

"Yes, indeed—and cited you—more than once."

"I would have thrown me out, too—and cited me as well." We both laughed aloud.

He got up abruptly and said,"Let me get Josiah."

When he walked towards Josiah, I became aware that he looked to be around 45 years old, six feet tall, had a spirited walk, how pleasant his face was. But what color were his eyes?

They came over and he said,"Josiah, sit down and enjoy lunch with your wife. When Josiah sat down, he leaned over us with both hands on the table, and asked,"Do you have children?"

"Yes, one," Josiah answered.

"Girl or boy?"

"Girl," he said.

"Name?"

"Velia," I said.

He rolled his head back slightly and burst out with a laugh. It was then I noticed that his hazel eyes were not a true green or true blue, but azure, and that it picked up a reflection of the satiny blue of his tie.

"That's a golden note of a name," he said. "Listen to me, both of you. Don't take that vaccine and don't do anything to diminish your libido. Have lots of babies—lots. Society needs more people like you."

"I shook his hand and held it, not knowing what to say but wanting him to stay. I finally said, "Mr. Congressman, I'm glad you're in Congress."

"Sally," he said as he was walking away, "I got a kick out of your testimony."

Josiah got up and said, "Mr. Congressman, please, one moment." He turned around and came back. "Yes?"

"Sit for a bit, would you, sir?" He did but on the edge of the chair. Josiah asked, "Mr. LeMay, how come you're part of that witch hunt up there?"

He immediately got up, placed his hands on the table, leaned over and said, "Josiah, two things you should know. Committees are made up of people from many disparate groups in Congress, so I belong there. Secondly, this is not a witch-hunt. There were no witches in Salem then, and none now," he said emphatically. "Superstition at that time prevailed—with unsupported allegations. In these days, however, there is a communist threat—it's real and supportable. It has nothing to do with superstition and certainly nothing to do with witches.

"We know about the Soviet purges, their imprisonment and murder of dissenters, their lack of freedom of thought, restrictions of the press, the starvation and repression of their own people and those of the conquered countries within their sphere, their attempt at fomenting world wide revolution so that they can increase their hegemony over the planet. Their spies within our own country have enabled them to get nuclear weapons more rapidly than they would have gotten otherwise, their spies within our administration influenced our policy, their encouragement to communists within the entertainment industry, to wit, the movie, 'Song of Russia,' to make it seem that communism were preferable to Democracy—our blessed, yet imperfect, Democracy. So you see, Josiah, our suspicions are well grounded, not because we believe in witches, but because we know who the enemy is. They're real, not imagined, and though our committee has gone overboard, undemocratically sometimes, we need to know where the threats lie so we can deal with them.

"That's a long winded statement from a congressman who belongs to an institution well-known for that," he said straightening up, "so I belong up there, Josiah, and my presence keeps the others honest."

Stunned, we said nothing. He walked away, then looked over his shoulder and said, "Don't despair."

CHAPTER 25

With a rap of his gavel, the Chairman announced, "Let the record show that the House Un-American Activities Committee is meeting at 2:00pm for the afternoon session of February 15, 1951."

Funny, for the afternoon session, three additional people appeared—another cameraman, another radioman and someone else with a legal pad. They had doubled the coverage. Was I that provocative? Do they suspect something?

"The Chair now calls Mr. Josiah Kas…till…noro…testo," pronouncing each syllable just short of spelling it out, and he still got it wrong.

"The name, sir, is Cas-tel-nuovo-Te-des-co."

"Are you represented by counsel, Mr. Kas…, sir?"

"No, to your question, and if it'll help, you may call me by my first name."

"That will be easier, Mr. Josiah. Why are you not represented by counsel?"

"My wife, Sally Apple mentioned at the morning's session we cannot afford to, and since there is no pink or red blemish on either one us, we didn't think it was necessary."

Of course he's nervous—I was too—that's why he's swallowing so hard and sounds so defiant.

"Well, we're here to determine the truth of that. So, your wife is Sally Apple?"

"Yes, I'm delighted to so pronounce."

"Why didn't your wife take your family name? What is this abominable trend of women keeping their maiden names when they get married?"

"Well … "

"Don't bother answering that question—it was only rhetorical editorializing. Now, sir, what is your profession?"

"I'm a director—actually an assistant director—formerly that is, when I was employed at Twentieth Century Fox."

"Are you working now?"

"Only as a free-lancer, a euphemism for saying that I'm mostly unemployed."

"How long were you employed at Fox?"

"Steadily for about seven or eight years except for the two and half years I spent in the army."

"During your employ, were you aware of any suggestions to insert a pro-communist agenda in your films?"

"No, absolutely never!"

"Would you have recognized it as such?"

"I'm not a Soviet scholar, but having an interest in political systems, I've read some things about their system—its cant—its duplicity—its purges—its self-serving alliances—its totalitarian hegemony over its own states and those of Eastern Europe—yes, I know a little, as a well informed citizen should, but to argue publicly against a studied polemicist—I'd be insecure."

"Would you have recognized a studio's attempt at inserting Soviet propaganda such as encouraging labor strikes, replacing management by workers, doing away with capital investment, advocating State control of businesses and institutions, or encouraging Negro agitation?"

"Of course, sir. They never made such an attempt."

"What do you think about those issues?"

"Those are meaty questions, Mr. Chairman, but I will try to answer them as best as I can. For one, I don't believe in state ownership of business, but perhaps for public utilities. I believe that workers deserve more attention to their needs, like better hours, safer working conditions, pensions, un-employment insurance—and if they have to strike for those benefits, I'm in favor of it. As for riots in the streets by Negroes or anyone else, if that's what you mean by 'agitation,' absolutely not, but as for vocal, peaceful expressions of their anger, you bet!

"If that coincides with a Soviet agenda, so be it. Not every issue has to be judged by that litmus test. I don't believe our country is opposed to everything the Soviets claim to stand for. Why their Communist Manifesto, I might add, sounds almost Biblical!"

As the words left him, he clutched the sides of his chair.

"You've read the Communist Manifesto?" he asked with a got-cha' look.

"I read it only once—when I was about nine years old," he said and giggled nervously. "Let me explain. The Soviet Consul General in New York was giving away books, and since I had never owned a book of my own, and it was free, I sent them a penny postcard requesting a copy. Lo and behold, one day I received a small gray book announcing itself in bright red letters, *The Communist Manifesto.*"

"I knew we were heading someplace. What did you make of it?"

"At nine years old? Not much, yet the first page of the Manifesto seemed compatible with what I was studying in my Talmudic ethics classes at Hebrew School. But after the first page of the Manifesto, I lost my way and didn't understand a thing they were saying. I could, however, at Hebrew School, so that's where I learned about those thing, you know about taking care of one another."

"Do you still own that book?"

"No, sir, soon after I received it, it disappeared. My parents probably threw it away."

"Have you ever been or are you now a communist, Mr. Josiah?"

"Well, as an American," he paused, took a deep breath, and said politely but firmly, "I don't think I have to answer that—that it's none of your business what I think or believe in, and I say that respectfully, Mr. Chairman. But in the interest of clarity—in the interest of avoiding any hint that silence might be perceived as tacit acknowledgement—in the interest of respect I have for our governmental institutions, the answer is a resounding NO! Did you hear that, sir? NO. NEVER then, and certainly NOT NOW!"

I was in the front row, wide-eyed and proud of his answers, though those last statements sounded a bit like the lady protesting too much, but I kept rooting for him until I gasped at what I heard next.

"Did you ever associate with communists at college?"

"I never went to college."

From my vantage point I could see only half of his face, but the flushed face he had had initially, quickly drained, as though a stopper had been removed. He lowered his head.

"The record shows that you attended New York City College for two years. Surely there couldn't be another person with that most unusual name," the chairman said, smug in his revelation.

After a long pause during which the chairman had to say, "Well," several times, he rapped his gavel like a drum roll, and Josiah finally spoke, almost inaudibly, "Yes, sir, that was me."

"Speak up, please. No one can hear you," he demanded, relishing in Josiah's embarrassed admission.

Josiah cleared his throat and said, "Yes, I did attend City College."

I gasped. He never told me that. He told me he went to work immediately after high school.

Josiah had often said that the best defense was a strong offence, so defiantly, he said, "Yes, I did attend CCNY, the City College of New York, and a fine school it is! And to answer your other question, I never hung out with left-wingers because dogma never appealed to me. They were always absolutely certain about everything. There was never the possibility of the other. They were always preaching. But I did hang out with liberal students who wanted to improve our society by such things as reversing the depression by engineering a full employment program, getting fairer wages, removing restrictions on Negroes. You know, what young idealists want for the benefit of our country," and, ignoring the look of indignant surprise on his inquisitor, continued truculently, "as for your multiple question about communist commentaries concerning the improvement of Negro conditions, abolition of lynchings, yes, I was for that."

Without waiting for a response, he went on, "And if the Soviets wanted the same thing, then good for them, even though later on we suspected their Machiavellian purpose."

"Please refrain from preaching to us, Mr. Josiah—especially one who was expelled from college. You're here, let me remind you, to answer questions honestly. Can you tell us why you were expelled?"

I gasped. Expelled?? What the hell is going on?

"You know the answer, Mr. Chairman. Why don't you tell us what those document in your hand say?"

"This committee would like to hear it directly from you, sir," feigning respect.

After a deep sigh that was audible throughout the room, he said, "There was a dear high school friend of mine who was getting an 'F' in a physics class that just the term before, I had gotten an 'A' in. He needed that class for his requirements and was told that his teacher was going to be away during the final exam, that it was going to be administered by his aide, so he asked me to take the test for him," his face showing that every word was piercing this old wound, opening up a scab that he must have thought had been well healed. He said nothing, just shook his head in disbelief.

I held my breath.

"You can't stop there, Mr. Josiah."

"I wasn't going to stop there, sir. I was just thinking of the consequences. My wife, future employers—but especially my wife." He was now breathing deeply, sighing after each sentence. "Anyway, the surprising part of my stupidity is that I didn't ponder that decision for more than a few minutes. I wanted to help my friend, and some of these classes were so huge and impersonal no one knew whether you belonged there or not, so I decided to take the test for him."

"Were you paid?"

Josiah gasped. "Yes, he gave me a crisp ten dollar bill, the first ten dollar bill I had ever seen in my life. I cringe when I think about it. But to continue, during the test the teacher showed up and Pandora's jar exploded. I was expelled that afternoon, a permanent blemish on my record. I was mortified then as I am now, surprised to discover that the deep anguish I felt in the pit of my stomach at that time, is identical to the one I feel now."

To no one in particular he asked, "Shouldn't there be a statute of limitations on the stupidities of our youth?"

The chairman looked at Josiah with a mix of pity and disgust, and rapiered, "Not 'our' youth, Mr. Josiah—your youth." He turned to Mr. Devereaux and said, "I'm through. Do you have any questions?"

Mr. Devereaux, as I had discovered this morning, was a mole of a man, furtive, suspicious, eyes sure that they were seeing deception everywhere. The way he kept rolling his hands together, like he had just put cream on them—like he was preparing to pounce—made me squirm.

"Yes, just a few. As an assistant director, Mr. Josiah, how did you view your role?"

I could see Josiah trying to regain his composure. After a few moments, he said, "Many roles, sir. The first was to absorb techniques like camera angles and lighting, then to understand the insights, interpretations, and perspectives of the director and writer, while the third, the responsibility to the actors, actresses and stage hands who are frequently abused by the director or producer, to act the role of mediator, father confessor, marriage counselor, tranquilizer, and over all, a teddy bear with a warm, beating heart." I'm certain he was hoping that that would mitigate the hostility emanating from all sides, especially from me.

"In reviewing several of the pictures in which your name appears," Mr. Devereaux continued, "I see no evidence of spin, but considering you were a New York Jew who attended CCNY, are you sure you never even *entertained* the thought of becoming a communist?"

Flashbulbs popped, the radio boom and cameras swung hard around the room.

Before he could answer, the chairman gaveled and barked, "Mr. Devereaux, that was out of line!"

Josiah slammed the flat of his hand on the desk and shouted, "Mr. Chairman, thank you. For a moment I thought Congressman Torquemada," his finger pointing at the congressman, "was taking me back to the Spanish Inquisition from which my ancestors fled five hundred years ago."

"Mr. Josiah, I will thank you for not calling anyone by a name not his own. You will address all members of this committee with due respect!"

Josiah jumped up from his chair, eyes squinting, jaws clenched and shouted, "Certainly. But I demand the same respect from all of you!" pointing his finger in a scanning motion at each of the members. "My religion has nothing to do with this hearing, and it's none of this committee's damn business whether I'm Jewish, Episcopalian or Zoroastrian!" once again slamming the flat of his hand on his desk with a loud pop.

The flash-bulb fireworks illuminated the room.

Without apology, Mr. Devereaux said, "I have no further questions, Mr. Chairman."

"May I ask then, Mr. Chairman," Josiah asked, jaws still clenched, "why was I called here in the first place?"

"Because you were expelled from a very liberal college," he said raising his voice an octave, "with known leftist leanings. And because the reasons were expunged from your record, I wanted to find out whether it was because you were a communist agitator and organizer. Does that answer your question, Mr. Josiah?"

"Yes sir, it does. Thank you." He rose and unexpectedly asked, "Are you now sure?"

The chairman looked puzzled and said, "Now that you ask, maybe I'm not so sure. I think I have a few more questions."

Josiah's heart must have sunk, as did mine. Why the hell did he have to ask that question—with such defiance?

"Fire away," Josiah said, masking his regret with a smile.

"We know there are many communists in France holding positions of power in the government, so amongst the French directors with whom you worked, were there any communists? Were they infecting their films with communist propaganda?" he continued without pause. "Through the power of cinema, were they trying to persuade their audiences to become communists? Were they trying to persuade you to return to the USA and proselytize—to infect your films as well?" he asked as though he knew the answers and just needed Josiah's confirmation.

"Wow! That's zealotry! Just five or six short years ago we were allies, and now we see how the dynamics of world politics have changed! I guess that a certain amount of paranoia is justified considering how the Soviets have forced their hegemony over Eastern Europe, how opposed they are to our Marshall Plan and the policies of the West. Furthermore ... "

The chairman interrupted, "No editorializing, Mr. Josiah, no political speeches. Please answer the questions."

"No."

"You mean you won't answer my questions? Or is that your answer to all my questions?"

"Mr. Chairman, you don't know who I am. I'm a struggling assistant director looking for work. No one has ever thought I was important enough to try to influence me, except my wife, and as she's discovered, I'm a tough sell. Regrettably, I'm not much of a heavyweight in my industry to influence anyone—yet. I strongly believe, however, in our Constitution and Bill of Rights, but I'm not too sure that this committee believes in them as avidly as I do," he said, scanning the panel members.

Before the gavel could come crashing down, he said, "I don't know what bed bugs you're looking for, but you won't find any with me—or my wife. The answer is NO to every one of your questions—those suggestive questions of yours. SIR!"

"We are here, SIR," the chairman said with equal vehemence, "to protect our Constitution and Bill of Rights from those who are determined to substitute a totalitarian ideology for those noble ideas enumerated by our Founding Fathers. If you don't realize that now, you will in the future. The Soviet Union is an enemy of ours, both physically and philosophically, and the sooner you understand that, the better our country will be. There were many who were fooled into believing their claptrap because it sounded so plausible, so Biblical, as you said, especially relevant during our Great Depression. We understand how good, loyal Americans resonated with their themes, how they were open to believing in those seemingly ameliorative, but ultimately specious ideas.

"We in America were in trouble then, yes, but we pulled out of it by retaining our ideals, imperfectly manifested as they were, imperfectly manifested as they still are. We are a decent people, sir. We improve in stages—slowly—but further improvement will follow in its inexorable path in our flawed yet great country. As a society we have worked for the betterment of a large body of our citizens, perhaps the largest body in all of civilization's checkered history, and we continue striving towards the goal that that body will increase in size every year."

"Well, sir, that was a political speech."

"To show you that we do indeed believe in our Constitution." His face was flushed and with the same passion, he continued, "We do have a right, you know, to try to uncover those *bed bugs*, as you called them, that might attempt to undermine our way of life—to corrupt our way of life with a Soviet/Marxist ideology that someday will prove to have been built on a house of defaced cards." After a pause, he added, "Built on a house of *defaced* and *defecated-on* cards!

"So, Mr. Josiah, we're glad to hear your 'No' to the questions I asked. Whether you think so or not, we are on the same wavelength."

The Chairman seemed disgusted at the suggestion and said in a peremptory manner, "You are excused, Mr. Castlenuovo-Tedesco!"

I met him at the door and without holding him in the crook of his arm like I usually do, we walked silently to the car. He said, "You drive honey. My head feels like Jell-O."

"So does mine, Jo. Let's have dinner at the commissary while we try to get through the smoke and ash."

"Let's not. I don't want to see anyone. I don't want to talk to anyone. I don't want to review anything with anybody. I need to get into the shower—to wash everything away."

"I'll stop at Zucky's and pick up a couple of pastrami sandwiches to eat at home."

"Good idea. I need a mood elevator."

I tried not to look at him as I drove but couldn't resist furtive glances. "I know you don't feel like talking, Jo, but we agreed not to have any secrets from one another. You never told me about CCNY."

"Not now, Sally. I'm all washed out."

I was undeterred. "Not only was taking that test a stupid thing to do, but challenging the chairman at the end was another stupid risk you took. Why the hell did you do that?" I asked, unable to contain myself. "And why the hell didn't you ever tell me about this?"

He looked over at me with an appearance of disgust, "Listen, I asked you to give it a rest. Please pay attention to my needs. All afternoon, I was standing over the trap door of the gallows waiting for it to spring open—and it did. I need to rest my brain."

"But I'm your wife. And, you'll remember that all morning I was over that trap door too, waiting for someone to pull the latch. You can't leave me wondering what the hell happened to you before, and what the hell happened to you today."

He swallowed hard and said, "Were you a model of restraint today, Miss Apple? Were you not inviting a citation for contempt? Were you not playing cute with those high-powered guys? Congressman LeMay was wise to you. Where the hell was your supposed level head during all of the proceedings?"

"Well, it was screwed on better than yours! You stupid ass! And as if that weren't enough," I continued, "omitting something is the same as lying. You made up that garbage about those two years after high school. You lied to me, you schmuck! Why didn't you tell me you went to college and that you got expelled, you stupid shit-head? You fucking shit-head liar! You belong to a new species. Homo Stupidus!"

"Why don't you go screw yourself!" he shouted back. "Let me off at the corner. I'll go to the movies at the Aero Theater. Forget the sandwich. You've ruined my appetite, not to mention what was left of my disposition! And don't forget, my dear—go screw yourself!"

Quick to anger, quick to reconsider, I began to regret my outburst—a throwback to my early years. His look of despair was painful to see, so I forced a slight smile and said, "But the baby will want to see you."

"Kiss her for me. Tell her her mother is a shit, with a shitty sense of shitty timing," he yelled slamming the car door. Through the open window, he added, "and tell her that her shitty mother doesn't deserve her!"

I roared off, hoping he heard my Parthian shot, "Nor is her lying fucking father worthy of her either!"

CHAPTER 26

"OH, hi, Josiah, your two babies are so glad to have you home! She just finished feeding at the trough and whispered that she was dying to give you a hug. Here, see?" placing her gently on his chest. "Tell daddy how glad you are to see him, go ahead."

He ignored me, took her in his arms and pressed his face against her warm, peachy plump sleepy face, remained there for a few moments while he patted her gently on her back and continued to breath in his daughter's ineffable fragrance. Burping deliciously, he said, "Oh, Velia, my dear, that was such a great welcome."

"Let me put her in her crib," I said reaching over to her with a smile in my voice, "then we can sit and talk."

"No, leave her with me for awhile—she feels so toasty—this way we can talk without shouting at one another."

"I'm not going to shout anymore."

"Yeah, I can bet on that, can't I?"

"Absolutely," I lied, still smiling.

"You know, Sally, while I was sitting through the movie, I couldn't decide which of these two words would better describe you. Virago or harridan. Which one would you choose?"

"That bad, huh?"

"Worse. Because of your usual lousy timing and lack of diplomatic skills, you can be a real shit sometimes, and that always makes matters worse."

"That's exactly what I thought. What movie did you see at the Aero?" hoping it was a comedy.

"I don't even remember. All I could think about were the today's hearings and your voice yelling at me. It was all a mud pie—and still is."

"Shitty wife, huh?"

"Yeah—occasionally—actually—often."

"Well, maybe I'll learn from Velia how to give innocent, undemanding, and unconditional love. Please, Josiah, don't take offense at that. There was no sarcasm intended. I'm speaking only to myself, but aloud. There's a balance out there, I know. It's just that I haven't gotten the correct triangulation as yet. Put her to bed, please," I asked softly. "I need to be the one cuddling up with you right now."

Before he could respond, she suddenly threw up all over him. "Oh, my poor baby," he said. I jumped up and grabbed her. "Please clean her up while I jump in the shower. Feel her head—see if she's running a fever."

I pressed my cheek against her forehead,"She seems cool. I wonder why that happened-t seemed everything was okay just a moment ago." I undressed her, cleaned her and rocked her until she stopped crying and fell asleep. I had always wondered whether it was better to feed her again since she now had an empty stomach, or whether it was better to let her stomach relax. From the looks of her you knew that she had never missed a meal, so I decided against another feeding.

I laid her in the crib and with my fingers brushed the fine hair away from her forehead. When I passed the bathroom door and saw him drying himself, I heard him whisper, "That must be some sort of record."

"What record?" I asked.

He looked surprised that he had said that aloud and said, "Getting vomited on three times in one day!"

It broke my heart to see the drowning look on his face so I picked up my towel and began drying his back. I hugged him, hoping he wouldn't push me away. "Stay nude, Josiah, please. Come to bed, let's just hug one another. Can you tolerate that right now from a horrible and remorseful wife who should have known that you must have been enormously hard on yourself when it first happened, and today in the retelling. Where was your supportive wife?"

He pressed my arms closer to his body for a few moments, then turned and said, "These are tough times for us, Sally, what with a new baby, neither one of us earning any money, living on your family's modest real estate income—and these damn hearings. What we have to do is to protect one another—take care of one another—defend one another, refrain from jumping on one another—respect one another—to pause—to let our frontal cortex quiet our angry hearts—and—quiet our angry tongues."

Tears began to well in my eyes and I said, "Yes, my darling, that's something to strive for."

"Problem is," he continued, "our brain waves travel at lightening speed, but yours seem to bypass the censoring region of your brain, so when something happens, *whammo,*" he whispered a shout and clapped his hands like a cymbal, "you're off galloping towards the stars *at the speed of light*, so slow down, okay? It'll be much healthier for the three of us."

My tears began to fall as I rested my head on his shoulder. I slowly unzipped my skirt and let it slip to the ground. I hung up my towel then left him to go into the bedroom to remove the rest of my clothing. I tossed the blanket off and, without a hint of seductiveness, said, "Come to bed, my dear, dear Josiah. I need to hug you, very tightly."

He came to bed, placed the blanket over us and hugged me tightly, and after a few moments, whispered, "That does feel good, Sally. Quiet, without passion, just the kind of warmth I need on this very cold day."

"Yes," I whispered, hugging him even tighter, letting our bodies speak their secret language of comfort and understanding.

After awhile, Jo said, "Honey, I hated you for what you said on the way home today, but I want you to know how proud I was of you when you told the truth about Adam, without rancor or vindictiveness. You rose above it all. He may never find out, but I think that son-of-a-bitch would have been pleased."

"I think getting us to Europe and giving me an impossible task was part of his plan to get me out of his life, but it backfired on him. Ultimately, I had to do what was right today, which I must tell you I wasn't going to do when I first started. I really wanted to stick it to him—but someone got in my way."

"Col. Picquart?"

"Yeah, he kept shouting in my ear."

"But who knows, it might have been, as the cliché goes, a blessing in disguise. You may very well sell your novel. Which reminds me—with all these subpoenas and hearings, and Velia, have you managed to get any more writing done?"

"Well, I'm very close to finishing, so I sent a query/cum synopsis letter to six literary agents."

He sat up startled, and asked, "You did? You never said anything."

"I didn't say anything because I wanted to surprise you."

"So, have you heard anything?"

"Yes," I smiled, "I received responses from all of them—by return mail—six pre-printed postal cards," I paused to increase the suspense, and added, "with very well written rejections."

"Damn."

"Maybe you'll help me re-write the synopsis."

"I can only do that when you let me read what you wrote."

"Oh, that," I said, rolling my eyes. "Yeah. Soon."

"Can't wait."

"I know we're still in today, but do you have any appointments at the studios for tomorrow?"

"No, I've almost given up. They're running scared because of television and its effect on the movie audience. New movies are drying up and people are getting laid off."

"You're not thinking of changing industries, are you?"

"No. Television studios are cropping up, some as offshoots of the movie industry, some by actors who can't find work and are setting up production companies to make television programs, some by directors and producers. The industry is changing and I've been remiss in sticking with movies. Tomorrow I'm going to be looking for a director's job filming episodic programs for TV. Yeah, I think that's where my focus is going to be from now on," he said as much to me as to himself.

"You think movies are dead?"

"Not dead—metamorphosing into a new reality. You know, in nature or industry, the pattern is Darwinism. Adaptation or die."

"Hug me some more, Sally, tightly," he said with a slight shiver, not from cold but from somewhere deep inside, from a secret undisclosed place. I saw in his eyes and heard in his tone, not a hopeful anticipation, but a fearful one, almost a foreboding. It made me gasp, I hoped, imperceptibly.

"Go for it, Josiah," I said, "not as an assistant anything, but as a full blown something. It's a new industry and all the crapshooters will be coming out to play. Go for it, baby!"

I hugged him tightly, for both of us.

Soon I asked, "What's that emerging between your legs?"

The following morning I awoke realizing that I shouldn't expect Josiah's oboe d'amour to be always in perfect tune, nor my counterpoint to be always in perfect harmony.

Josiah was eager to start his day so right after breakfast, he shaved and showered and got dressed in his best suit—double breasted, forest green with pin stripes of a darker green, leather buttons, a pale green silk handkerchief in his breast pocket quietly announcing its presence, and a matching silk tie with white stripes, set off elegantly by a starched white shirt. His olive complexion was compatible with every color he wore.

Just then, Velia woke up and I started feeding her, and as usual, loved the suckling sensation. He came over and kissed her forehead, lingering, breathing her in an out, and said, "Honey, I'm going to check out some television studios, so I'll see you later. Wish me luck."

"You bet!" Before he could open the door, I said, "Jo, I heard that Adam is going to testify in a few days, and I'm tempted to attend. I'm curious to find out what he's going to say."

"Don't go there, honey. To hell with him. You'll just get agitated again. Stay home and take care of Velia, and continue writing."

"Yeah, I guess you're right."

CHAPTER 27

"What's that Sally?"

"It's a wire recorder. One of our tenants slipped out without paying his rent and left this behind. My mom thought that I could use it to record ideas when I'm not near pencil and paper. Last summer Popular Science Magazine described it an article."

"A little thing like that can record stuff? Most of those devices need a mule to haul them."

"Yeah, it's a Minifone Portable Wire Recorder with batteries that last over two and a half hours, and is small enough to fit in my purse."

"What's the wrist watch for?"

"It has a built in microphone."

"What? Have you joined the F.B.I.?"

"No," I giggled, "but it's a fun little device."

"Well, I gotta' go. My second interview with a bunch of people at a fledgling television studio. See you later."

"Honey, you look confident and resolute. Bon chance!"

I wore my mother's rakish black hat that covered part of my face, a gray scarf that covered my neck, and sat in the third row, in the corner, within earshot, not easily noticed. My watch faced the panel and with a twist of the wrist, the witness chair.

"Let the record show that this meeting of The House Un-American Activities Committee is convening on February 19, 1951," Mr. Heddbone presiding.

"The Chair calls its next witness, Mr. Adam Lapidus."

Even at a distance, walking briskly down the aisle, the panel members could see the dominant feature of his face—his attention arresting green eyes that, as he approached, seemed to glow from within, and the closer he got, the greater the intensity. No one paid attention to what he was wearing or even how tall he was, though he was properly attired in a well-tailored, high fashion suit that the chairman, as I later wrote when I chronicled the events of this day, must have thought, 'Hollywood types could well afford. For them, appearances are all that count, anyway.'

The woman walking down the aisle behind him had long brown/ blondish hair, and from afar looked resplendent in a blue serge business suit that couldn't quite mask a bosom larger than one might have expected on so small a frame, no more than five foot one, that she had a tight, well proportioned body, that she had a blue-green silk scarf hanging around her neck and shoulder, a scarf that shimmered in the bright lights of the room like water in a lagoon. When she got closer, they saw a pair of shapely legs on fashionable high heels, and with her erect posture and thrust out chin, she exuded confidence, and because there are such things, visual pheromones.

She introduced herself with a smile that unveiled a cascade of beguiling surprises, perfectly arranged and proportioned teeth, bright white, a small heart shaped mouth framed like parenthesis by two shallow dimples, and with the slight crinkle around her eyes and brows, her face exuded an unthreatening warmth. She was, as even the Calvinists among the congressman must be thinking—very pleasing to the eye.

It was clear from her face she understood the role that beauty played in the calculus of human transactions, and that beyond that, her substance would soon emerge, and so, with her queenly demeanor, she acted, ever so subtly, on the knowledge that substance, enhanced by beauty and style, is accepted more amiably.

With all eyes fixed upon her, she laid her hands flat across her files so everyone would notice that she wore no wedding ring. Hard to believe she wasn't married. Made me think she removed it whenever going to court, aware that, especially in this particular case, some congressmen, who were not unknown to engage in extra-judicial activities, might be more amenable to her arguments knowing that there was the possibility, and always the hope, that after hours she might succumb to the aphrodisiacal pull of power.

Every chair was filled. There were three television cameras, three sets of microphones, six reporters with legal pads, and an equal number of photographers with trigger-happy flash bulbs.

After an embarrassing delay, the chairman looked at Adam and said in an authoritative voice, "Please tell us your name."

Adam sported a warm smile hoping to convey the image of being one of the *friendly witnesses*. "Yes, sir," he said boldly, "my name is Adam Lapidus."

"Are you represented by counsel, Mr. Lapidus?"

"Yes, I am, sir. Her name is..."

"Let her identify herself, please."

She rose from her chair and said, "My name is Jessica Agoura."

"And you are licensed to practice law in the State of California?

"I am, sir. I have a JD and my attorney number is, 26,360," then sat down.

"Thank you," he said, taking his time before moving his eyes away from her. He then turned to Adam and asked, "Mr. Lapidus, do you have a statement you'd like to read?"

"No sir, I have none, but I'm prepared to answer any question—every question—that is, all questions."

Mrs. Agoura rose once again and asked, "May I ask a question of the committee first?"

"Certainly," he smiled.

"I've read the previous testimonies, and there is some confusion amongst a few of those witnesses about a concept whose veracity I would like for you to confirm or deny, please," she said politely.

"If we can, yes, of course," the chairman said, welcoming the opportunity to continue his gaze.

"The concept," she continued, "is the '*diminished Fifth*.' That is, if, during the testimony, my client admits membership in any group—and I want to strongly urge you *not* to infer anything from my question—that should he do so, he is *not* obligated to tell you the names of other people with whom he was involved within said organization?"

Adam turned to her with a look that shouted, *Jesus Christ, why the hell did you ask that question for?*

"That's a mistaken notion, Miss Agoura. If your client hides under the cloak of the Fifth Amendment and refuses to tell us what groups he was a member of, then he doesn't have to answer any questions about others within that group. But, if he tells us without invoking the Fifth, that he is or was a member of any group, he is obligated to tell us who else was in that group. If he chooses not to, then he is subject to a contempt citation that may lead to a prison term. Is that clear?"

"Thank you, Mr. Chairman, that answers my question," she said as she sat down. "But, sir, a clarification, please. The Fifth was a great leap forward for our mutual protection. It shouldn't be construed as 'hiding or cloaking' but more like..."

"We know all about our Founding Fathers and our constitutional protections and none of us needs to attend a *continuing education* seminar this afternoon, so don't remind us of the obvious."

"I hope I won't have to, sir."

He looked at her askance and proceeded with his questioning. "Mr. Lapidus, are you now, or have you ever been a member of the Communist Party, or a member of any of its front groups?"

Before Adam could answer, she rose again and said, "Mr. Chairman, my client will answer all your questions, but, sir, I respectfully remind you that our Bill of Rights, yours and mine, is one of the greatest documents ever conceived, upon which you and your colleagues have sworn allegiance, and our First and Fourth Amendments unequivocally state that he and you and the rest of us have freedom of speech and that involves freedom of thought, and that the Fourth insists on the right of people to be secure in their persons against unreasonable searches and that includes their minds ... "

He struck his gavel with a sharp rap, raised his voice and hissed, "Again I tell you, Miss Agoura, don't ever remind us of our oaths to the Constitution! We've studied it far more carefully than you or any other two-bit attorney has. And we know all about the Bill of Rights! So save the preaching for your pulpit!"

Rising from her seat again, she shouted, "Excuse me, *SIR! That* is a contemptuous remark! I *demand* your apology, Mr. Chairman!"

Adam rose and turning from one to the other implored, "Please, both of you, calm down," and placed a strong hand on her shoulder forcing her to sit down. Still standing he said very quietly, hoping that his hushed tone would lower the energy level that had developed. "I don't want us to have a shouting match before we even get to the substance of this hearing. Sir, I know you recognize that ad hominem attacks are uncalled for. Mrs. Agoura doesn't deserve that kind of insult. You wouldn't appreciate that kind of accusation against you, so please, sir, I beg you, I beg all of you, let's all calm down and proceed more civilly okay?" he said in a disarming way, his eyes shining their green light.

"O.K., Miss Agoura," the chairman said flatly, looking at her so coldly that it cast doubt on his sincerity, "I shouldn't have called you that. The chair apologizes."

"That works fine for the chair," she said in a voice dripping with acid, "but how about for the person sitting in it?"

"Don't be cute with me, counselor, otherwise you'll find yourself where you don't want to be."

With chin raised, she said, "Where I want to be, *SIR,* is under the protective umbrella of our Constitution and its *implicit and explicit* demand for mutual respect."

He ignored her and turned to Adam, "Let's move on. Mr. Lapidus, you have the floor."

"Thank you, Mr. Chairman," Adam began, the thought flashing across my mind about the transient nature of first appearances, "but before you ask any more questions, I want you to understand that notwithstanding my attorney's opinions, I do not intend to hide behind any Constitutional Amendment," he said, "which, because of such short notice, we never had time to discuss, and though I don't think this committee, as Mrs. Agoura started to say, has a right to invade my privacy," he slipped in, "I will answer all your questions without fudging or evading, so fire away." I wondered how he got that all in without taking a breath.

Mrs. Agoura rose and with her hand on Adam's shoulder, chin thrust forward, said, "A point of information, please, Mr. Chairman," and without waiting for permission, said, "our Constitutional Amendments, indeed all the articles in our Constitution, were not meant as a place to *HIDE,* as my client mistakenly said, but to *PROTECT.*"

Her brief lecture over, she sat down and raised her hand to abort another reprimand.

He rolled his eyes and said, "I asked whether you are now or were ever a member of the Communist Party?"

She rose again and said, "Mr. Chairman, please, before my client answers, may I speak for just another moment?"

"Miss Agoura, we need to get on with these hearings. I'm going to permit you one more interruption, then you'll have to remain quiet. *What is it now?"*

"With due respect for your committee and with due recognition of the press in our midst, asking my client the question about whether he was, or is, a member of the Communist Party would be tantamount to my asking you, 'whether your wife was, or is, a prostitute'?"

Flashbulbs exploded, cameras swiveled from her to the panel and back, loud gasps were heard. Everyone was stunned. The gavel came crashing down with such a sharp bang that everyone jumped, momentarily deafened. The chairman rose so abruptly it looked like he was heading straight for the ceiling. With an incendiary look on his face, he roared, "What the hell kind of question is that, *Goddamnit!?"*

"Sir, please don't look so hatefully at me. Please. I ask that question because our press," quickly scanning the reporters, "would have a headline in tomorrow's paper with some variation of: *"'Chairman of HUAC Denies His Wife Was Prostitute!'"*

The gavel came crashing down once again. Again, everyone jumped. Flashbulbs continued popping.

"That's outrageous!" spittle flying over his desk.

"Exactly!" she said slapping her hand on the desk so hard that the sting must have lasted well into the session.

The chairman looked at his committee members hoping for a sign, but none came. He remained standing, the lion breathing fire, poised to pounce. "Bailiffs," he spit-hissed, "escort *that woman* out of these chambers immediately, and if she shows the slightest resistance, grab her by the hair and drag *that thing* out of here!"

She looked at the chairman, herself a viper ready to strike, her upper lip quivered with scorn, rose, put her hand on Adam's shoulder, squeezed and turned around, a bailiff on either side, and walked out slowly, shoulders back, spine ramrod stiff, face tilted upward, and heard over her shoulder, "You have insulted the dignity of this court—Madame Bovary!"

Before slamming the door behind her, she shouted, "*Et tu, Brute!*"

The chairman paused for a moment and tried to regain his composure. "We'll take a ten minute break," he said.

With everyone back and seated, the chairman said, "Mr. Lapidus, we are mindful you're no longer represented by counsel but I do want to resume the questions. Are you okay with that? Answering questions without counsel?"

"Yes, I am."

"Please state your occupation."

"I've been for many years a line producer at Twentieth Century Fox Studios."

"Let me repeat my earlier question. Have you ever been or are you now a communist?"

Adam paused and asked, "The Communist Party is still legal in this country, is it not?"

"Yes, it is."

"No, sir. I have never been, nor am I now, a communist," he said and turned his head when he heard the audience murmur.

"Have you ever belonged to a Communist Front Organization?"

"I don't know what such an organization looks like or what it's name would be, or how I would be able to tell in the first place, so the answer is, I think not."

"If I were to name some Front Organizations, would you tell me if you were a member?"

"Don't bother, Mr. Chairman. I'm not a joiner. I don't like paying dues. I don't like meetings outside the studio. I don't like *hail-fellow-well-met* situations with their forced gaiety. I don't play poker—I hate the smell of cigars—I hate scotch—and, like Greta Garbo, I want to be left alone. Frankly, I *prefer* to be left alone, and once I get home, there's no prying me away."

"You've worked on many films, correct?"

"Yes, sir."

"Have you ever worked with communists and have they ever tried to influence the outcome of a story?"

"As to your first question, I've been criticized as being *all business*, one who rarely makes friends with colleagues, so I would have to answer your first question with, *how the hell would I know?*" he asked, smiling to ease the impact.

"You will refrain from using disrespectful phrases at this hearing. Do you understand that, Mr. Lapidus? Our government institutions must be respected, *Sir!*"

"Forgive me, Mr. Chairman, even though I agreed to disclose everything I know, I guess I'm still seething that as an American I have to be subjected to such probing," he said, and before there could be a response, continued, "now let me answer your second question. There are only two things that influence a movie—does it have a compelling story that entertains, and what is its moneymaking potential? And, if it has some artistic merit, or asks the audience to reconsider some of their pre-conceived notions, all the better.

"You're asking, of course, whether someone tried to influence me or the writer or the hundreds of other hands in the process, to insert propaganda like, *their system is better than ours,* and *that we should consider replacing our government with one better attuned to the principle 'of the people, by the people, and for the people,'* the answer is *NO*.

"To our shame, however, we still have Negro stereotypes like Stepin' Fetchit, portrayals of bumbling Negro janitors and housemaids, depicted as feckless, lazy, stupid, crap-shooting, watermelon-eating fools. I must tell you that as an American, I'm mortified at that insulting portrayal of our fellow Americans."

"You've given me a perfect segue to my next question. Our records show that you once said, that had you been a Negro, you would not have fought for America during the Second World War. Is that true, Mr. Lapidus?"

The surprised look on his face remained for a moment, but quickly replaced by his response, "*Damn right!*"

"One more infraction like that, and you can count on a contempt citation! Is there any part of that statement you don't understand?"

"Sorry, sir. I got carried away. Let me clarify something. I never said that I would *not* have fought. What I said was, I *might never have fought.* There is a difference.

"Now, let me go on with a less passionate voice. Stepin' Fetchit, whose real name was, Lincoln Perry, was an intelligent, complex individual, with feelings no different from yours or mine," scanning all the panel members, "and with no less a penetrating mind than all of us in this room. In the early 1940's, with the help of the NAACP, he tried to get billing *and pay* equal to white performers, but was rebuked by the very studio for which I've worked all these years.

"I'm ashamed of that, sir! I'm ashamed of lynching! I'm ashamed of separate toilets! I'm ashamed of separate drinking fountains! I'm ashamed of separate entrances to public venues! I'm ashamed of their inability to dine with us! I'm ashamed of their inability to stay at the same hotels as we do! I'm ashamed at our American apartheid system!"

He raised his voice higher, "I know they were drafted, but I don't know why they fought. They could have gone to Central or South America. What the *hell—heck* were they fighting for anyway? To help us become victorious so that when they returned, they could still be treated like *three fifths white—three fifths human*? Why, they weren't even treated as *three fifths anything*. They were treated like scum! No, sir, had I been a Negro, I would have thought twice about putting my life on the line to help win the war for those who treated me so abominably! And neither would any one of you on this panel!"

Congressman Al Rosenmyra tapped his microphone. "Mr. Chairman, may I make a comment on what he is so passionately describing?"

"Yes, by all means," the chairman said, glad for the respite.

"Mr. Lapidus, may I remind you, sir, that our Founding Fathers were acutely aware that, *the perfect is enemy of the good.* Had they sought total abolition of slavery, had they sought total equality for the Negro, had they sought institutionalized equality, they might not have been able to coalesce us into a unified whole. *That would have been perfect,* but in so doing we may very well never had had a United States, but a chain of vulnerable weak links, and that was untenable. So they swallowed hard and compromised, and allowed some states to live *free* and others *slave*.

"And, like yourself, Mr. Lapidus, I share your disgust about conditions. Had it been up to me, I would have chosen *'free.'* My forebears, fortunately, made that choice for me. You should know that many of us in Congress are trying to change these horrid things.

"That's all I want to say, Mr. Chairman. I relinquish the floor."

"So, am I hearing you correctly," the chairman asked, "you would not have fought for America?"

"Sir, I can only have vicarious feelings about the torment of being a Negro, but I do know that I'm no jingoist, so as best as I can project myself into their daily humiliations, I must honestly state that I probably would not have fought. But that they did, does them honor—that they did shows that they wanted to prove their equality with whites—that they did shows their rebellion against subordination.

"They are human beings, sir, with the same spectrum of abilities, emotions, desires, aspirations, failures, and demons as you and I." His shoulders slumped like he was spent, and his face, had a look begging to be dismissed. Then he added, "And—a deep-seated need for respect!"

"Mr. Lapidus," the chairman went on as though whatever had been said had no merit, "if it was good enough for our Founding Fathers to regard the Negro *as three fifths that of a white man,* it is good enough for me."

"So," Adam asked, "in the chair's wisdom, Abraham Lincoln doesn't deserve a place as one of our *Continuing Founding Fathers*? Nor President Truman for desegregating the armed forces?"

"President Lincoln," the chairman said smugly, "you'll remember, did not go to war to free the slaves, but to preserve the Union, so I'm not sure which side of this room he would have felt more comfortable in."

"I can answer that ... " Adam said.

"Don't bother, please. I've heard enough preaching for today."

"Mr. Chairman," Congressman George J.B. Krieger interrupted, tapping on his microphone, "may I have the floor for a few moments, please. I would like to ask a question or two."

"Yes, JB, but remember we're not through, not by a long shot, so make your questions brief."

Adam's shoulders remained slumped.

"Mr. Lapidus, so that we might have a clear picture of who you are and understand more fully the values that guide you, I want to take your remarks and elaborate on them for a moment. Negroes have a long and honored tradition of hope, so can you imagine yourself a Negro—can you immerse yourself into the Negro's psyche, and decide that *I'm going to show those bastards—all of us white folk—that I'm as good as they are. I'm as smart as they are—I can learn skills as well as they can—and if I prove those things to be true in combat, I can become a fellow American—that I can be represented fully by the concepts of the Declaration of Independence and the Constitution. And that this would be a way to transform whitey my tormentor, into an equal?* Can you project yourself in that manner, and perhaps then decide to fight along with us?"

After a long pause, Adam said, "Perhaps. Ideally. But what happened? They did all those things, Mr. Congressman, but the reality of the situation was, and with very few exceptions, still is, that I'd probably end up cleaning pots and pans—and toilets.

"And to prove my point, you all know the Dave Brubeck jazz group, right? To his credit, he had a mixed race band during the Second World War and entertained our troops all over the European theatre. They got caught in the Ardennes Forest during the famous Battle of the Bulge, and leaving their instruments, they picked up rifles and fought courageously to help blunt the German attack, barely escaping with their lives. Six or eight months later, when the war was over and they were discharged, they disembarked in the south. On their very first day back, while still in uniform, they went to a restaurant. To their amazement, the proprietor refused to serve the black players in Brubeck's group.

"Can you on the panel imagine yourself at that moment, and, as the congressman just asked, can you transform yourself into a Negro and acknowledge your outrage at this poisoned irony?

"And for those of you bemused by such irony, you've chosen this hotel, gentlemen, The Beverly Wilshire Hotel in Beverly Hills, this iconic symbol of affluent white America, as a place to hold your hearings. Are you aware of how disgraceful your choice is??

"Dr. Ralph Bunche, grandson of slaves, summa cum laude graduate of U.C.L.A., PhD from Harvard, the State Department's first Negro delegate to the General Assembly of the UN, *Nobel Laureate,"* he began shouting, "was asked to give the Commencement Speech at U.C.L.A. in June of 1950, just last summer. And—he was refused lodging *at this very hotel.* Why?

"No matter his towering intellect nor his achievements—no—his color was the determinant!

"How does that make all of you *Americans* up there feel?

"Frankly, it makes me want to puke!

"One other thing—remember the Tuskegee Airmen? After the war, they returned to South Carolina and discovered that the German and Italian prisoners of war being held there, were able to go to the theater, the movies and restaurants that Negroes themselves could not attend. How does that grab you?" he asked looking like he really was going to puke.

Congressman Kris Hanks, shaking his head from side to side, interrupted, "Did you ever express similar feelings about the Japanese?"

"And as for the Japanese, no, I don't think I ever did publicly, but I thought about it, and I must say, that they too took heroic actions by fighting to protect and preserve the freedom of a country which denied them such freedom. That is ironic as well, and for me, unsupportable."

"Mr. Chairman. I relinquish the floor."

With a tap on the microphone, Congresswoman Arlen Chammers asked, "Mr. Chairman, may I have the floor, please?"

"Yes, indeed."

"Mr. Lapidus, did you ever instruct Stepin' Fetchit not to serve in the military?"

"I never produced one of his films and I did not know him well, just a nodding acquaintance. Besides, he was too old for the military. So to answer your question directly, no."

"Did you ever instruct any other Negro or Japanese not to serve in the military?"

"The answer, ma'am, is *never*, but I want to make the record clear. You said, "...instruct any *other* Negro or Japanese." Your use of the word, '*other*,' implies that I may have instructed someone else. You have to understand that I instructed *NO ONE* not to serve. Let there be no doubt about that with any of the committee members," he said, scanning all their faces.

"But now that the war is over, the Japanese are ending up like before—gardeners. And, if they ever get their farms back, growing strawberries.

"You are indeed a pessimist, Mr. Lapidus," the congresswoman said.

"Yes—events never seem to disappoint us."

"I relinquish the floor, Mr. Chairman."

"May I remind you once again, Mr. Lapidus," the chairman said, "that you are under oath. If it turns out that our investigation shows that you did, you will have perjured yourself. And further, that would have been subversion—what got you here in the first place. Now I'll ask you once again, did you ever urge anyone, white, black, yellow, not to serve in the military?"

"Mr. Chairman," came a strong voice from the rear of the room. Everyone turned around to see his attorney standing at the doorway with a raised hand say, "I would like to take my place again. I will confer with my client quietly without disrupting your proceedings. I need to speak to him before he answers any further questions." She assumed that her peremptory manner would get her a reprieve and began walking briskly towards the witness bench.

The chairman looked at the committee members for a sign of disapproval, and finding none, was about to say 'no,' when he found her, with her long strides, already besides Adam. He looked at her and murmured to one of his assistants about how some women have lost their place in society. "Just don't take too long. We have other witnesses who await their turn. *And*—no outlandish questions."

In a stage whisper she asked, "Adam, you've got to tell them the truth, otherwise you're going to be in trouble."

"Jessica, I have nothing to hide. I'm telling the truth and I don't care about their insinuations."

"It's easy for you to say that, but they have the power of the government behind them, and right now, we're going through a dark period in our history with unproved allegations and insinuations, so we have to make sure we rise above it, as we will some day. Figure this stage as our 'terrible twos.' Did you ever urge anyone to dodge the draft?"

Adam turned away from her without answering, rose and said, "Mr. Chairman, every question implies a suggestion, so I want to make it absolutely clear to all of you, for the tenth time. I never asked anyone to run away from a draft notice, nor did I ever ask anyone to reconsider fighting for a country that denies him true citizenship. I thought about the rationale behind their actions—we are, after all, Americans, but I *never*, and I emphasize the word, *never* discussed my inner thoughts with anyone except Sally Apple, who probably was the one who told you about my concerns in the first place, right?" he asked, hoping that that would be the end of it and hoping to confirm his suspicion.

I gasped aloud.

"It's none of your business where we get our information!"

"Am I not entitled to know who my accuser is?" he asked.

"She did not accuse you of anything, Mr. Lapidus!" he said. "And this committee will determine the truth of your statements. Are there any further questions from the committee?" Seeing no one raise his hand, he said, "In that case, you are excused, but stay close to home since we reserve the right to call you back for further questions."

"One other thought, sir." Adam said.

"A brief one, I hope."

"In my reading of the First Amendment, Mr. Chairman, and I say this respectfully, our government cannot abridge our freedom of speech, and certainly not *of thought*, and ... " Jessica squeezed his knee.

The chairman rapped his gavel lightly and said, "Let me interrupt you for a moment, not of thought until that thought is expressed, but once expressed, you are not entitled to that freedom of speech if you used *fighting words*, and in your case, it's up to us to determine whether you expressed '*don't fight—ing words*.' And that might be a subversive act not protected by the First Amendment! You are excused. Please leave."

Adam turned to Jessica and said, "Jesus Christ! Does he have me there?"

"He's got to prove it first."

"Whether he does or not, and he never will, I'm sullied by this interrogation."

"Don't be so sure, Adam. It may be a matter of shooting for headlines—to put their names before a public who might elevate them to higher office."

"In the meantime, with all those insinuations, what happens to my career?"

"Nothing—so far. Let's get out of here."

He grabbed her arm and walked down the aisle together. "I'm surprised that the members asked questions—the way they were passing notes and speaking to their staff," he said, "I was sure no one was paying attention—nor did they seem to care."

"Adam, they hear what they want to hear—they come in with pre-conceptions and then look for denial or agreement. That's how it works. Let's go for a cup of coffee."

When they got to the door, they heard a sharp rap of the gavel. "Oh, Mr. Lapidus, I failed to ask you one more question. And one of my colleagues would like to ask you a few questions as well. Would you please take your seat again? We won't be long. Members, please be seated. I apologize for my omission."

Adam turned to Jessica and said, "What the hell?"

"Let's show some confidence, Adam. Walk tall!"

Even before they took their seats the chairman asked, "Mr. Lapidus, as I was gathering up my papers, I realized I had forgotten to ask you a simple question," looking as though he were asking the time of day, "Did you ever know anyone who fought as a member of the American Lincoln Brigade during the Spanish civil war of 1936-1939?"

"Oh, shit!" he said swallowing hard. "Not that I can think of."

"May I remind you that you're still under oath and that if we show a contradiction, you may be indicted."

I saw Jessica give him a sharp kick. He gasped. "Well, sir, now that I think about it, I did know someone who fought in that war, but I don't know any of the details."

"Who was it?"

He heaved an audible sigh, paused and said very slowly, "My boss—Peter Nathan."

At that news, the audience murmured loudly, photographers went to work and I gagged. Then total silence.

"Please tell us more."

"No, I can't, sir. It was a long time ago, and, as I said, I don't know the details."

"How did you hear about it? Did someone tell you? Did you hear it directly from Mr. Nathan?"

He squirmed and said, "From Mr. Nathan."

"What did he say?"

"I can't. I didn't pay attention. I know Ernest Hemingway and Arthur Koestler were there, but I know few details. I'm afraid my memory would be an untrustworthy guide. Ask him yourself."

"You know that once you name names, you are required to answer all further questions."

"Not if I can't remember. Are you going to give me a truth serum that will uncover a deteriorating memory? Absent that, you don't want me to invent some, do you?"

"Don't be smart or impatient with us, Mr. Lapidus. Answer the question."

"Other than what I told you, I don't remember anything else, and as a matter of fact, I scarcely remembered that. I'm not being evasive, Mr. Chairman, I know nothing beyond what I told you. I can give you nothing else. May we go now?"

The chairman looked directly at him for a long time. Adam never flinched.

"You are excused."

"This is the last time, right? At least for today?"

"*Mr. Lapidus!* he heard as the gavel rapped.

"Thank you, sir."

"Oh, I forgot. Congresswoman Quanil Rosenson wanted to ask you some questions."

"Oh, Christ!"

The congresswoman, preempting a gavel rap, quickly asked, "Did you, Mr. Lapidus, ever subscribe to the Daily Worker?"

"What?"

"Simple question. Did you or did you not subscribe to the American Communist Party's official organ, the Daily Worker?"

"No, of course not."

"Why do you say, *of course not?*"

"Because I told you several times, I'm not a communist."

"Did you ever read it?"

"Sometimes. Yes."

"If you're not a communist, why?"

He sighed heavily and fired off, "What the *hell* is it your business what the *hell* I read?"

"Don't be disrespectful, Mr. Lapidus! Try to keep your tongue clean. We're trying to put together information you may not be sharing—your associations, your propensities, winking at certain ideologies, your inclinations and leanings. You know, what you may have been *leaning* towards."

"This is outrageous, ma'am! I'm free to think about anything I *damn* want to, and read whatever I *damn* well want to, and you're free to question me only on my *actions*, not on my *beliefs*."

"I'll ask whatever I damn well please. Why did you sometimes read the Daily Worker?"

They stared at each other for an electric minute. "Because I'm a sports nut. It had a fine sports page and I'm interested in different views from different sources."

"So what did you think of Lester Rodney?"

"*What?*"

"Great sports writer, wasn't he?"

"You read him, too? Does that make *you* a communist?

"I'll ask the questions, Mr. Lapidus. When you become a congresswoman, you can ask the questions."

Everyone smiled except Adam.

"I should have taken the Fifth. Your questions are *absolutely un-American!* How dare you?"

"Don't let me ask the chairman to cite you for contempt. I'm driving at something, something important for the record. Please cooperate with me. And be patient, okay?" she asked with a friendly smile that surprised us considering the line of questioning.

He continued staring at her.

"What would you say was his great contribution, Mr. Lapidus?"

There was a long pause. No papers were ruffled. No one said anything, just waited. Adam looked puzzled, wondered whether the congresswoman was friend or adversary. Then he said quietly, "Mr. Rodney joined the American Communist Party when he was hired by the Daily Worker, about 1936, I believe, and almost from the beginning he wrote about how *un-American* it was that baseball, our national pastime, didn't permit Negro players to play. How aghast he was at that. How it was imperative that, as *Americans*, we allow them to play."

"Did you know him personally?"

"Never met him, but I loved him for that!"

"How about other newspapers? Did they complain as well?"

"Silence, ma'am—pure silence. When Joe DiMaggio was asked who had been the best pitcher he had ever faced, without missing a beat he said, 'Satchel Paige." Nobody else in the media reported it. Nobody except Rodney."

"If Negroes weren't allowed to play, how come DiMaggio faced him?"

"In post-season exhibition games. When Rodney asked Dodger manager, Leo Durocher, about hiring Negro players, Durocher said, " ... in a minute, if I got permission from the big shots.'

"Rodney had a social conscious, I tell you, and for about ten years, it was he and the communists who kept exerting pressure to integrate Negroes into baseball."

"Did you support that endeavor?"

"You betcha!

"Hundreds of gifted Negroes were disenfranchised because of our apartheid system. That you fail to see that is disgraceful!"

She ignored his pointed finger, and asked, "What did *you* do about it?"

"Nothing, sorry to say, except express my outrage to all who would listen."

"So if you favored abolishing the ban, why didn't you join the Communist Party?"

"Listen, everybody. I detest the whole architecture of communist ideology and governance. I believe in personal initiative, in *competition—in democracy.* Stop thinking about this whole scheme of things as *all or nothing.* Just because you like one aspect of a political system doesn't mean you have to embrace the entire system. I ask you to try to understand the nuances of what I'm saying. Please!"

"Don't patronize us, Mr. Lapidus. We are a sophisticated group. We don't need you to remind us of nuances."

"Well, then, if I tell you I like bacon, it doesn't mean that I like the rest of the hog, okay?"

"I'm asking you for the second time—don't be impatient with us. Pay attention to *our* nuances. When we ask you what may appear as a simplistic question, we have in mind more complex themes. Now, let me ask you if you know who Kenesaw Mountain Landis was?"

"Yes. He was Baseball Commissioner."

"And?"

"You know this already, so I'll tell you what you already know. Much to his credit, Lester Rodney was actively petitioning him, and the baseball owners, to integrate baseball. He even organized picket lines at ballparks. He was an unsung hero, folks, communist or not, and I'm proud to say, I supported that. *And That Doesn't Make Me A Communist! That Makes Me A Good American!*"

"Support how? Did you ever join those picket lines, Mr. Lapidus? Did you ever write to your congressman—your senators—your president? What did *you* do to reverse that despicable policy?"

Chastened, we heard, "Nothing, ma'am, nothing—except to complain to people who agreed with me."

"Well, sir, you *damn well* should have done something better than that! Anyway, it's a moot point since Branch Rickey of The Dodgers hired Jackie Robinson who was the first Negro to play in the majors in this century, April 16, 1947. And, to his credit, he had the guts *NOT* to fight the taunts, epithets, watermelon slices, Sambo dolls and all the other disgraceful acts of his fellow Americans. Dan Bankhead followed him and hit a homer on his first at-bat in the majors. Then Larry Doby who was the first Negro to hit a homer in The World Series."

"Well, you too are a baseball—nut."

"Yup! But to go on, when this hotel refused to accept Dr. Bunche, you should have organized a picket line in front of this hotel! *Protesting! Loudly!*"

All eyes were focused on Adam. When he raised his head, his green eyes had lost their luster. Ever so slightly, his head bobbed.

"No further questions, Mr. Chairman. I wanted this on the record—to let everyone know that words are not enough!"

"You are excused, Mr. Lapidus."

Jessica and Adam walked arm in arm towards the door, and I heard her say, "We still on for coffee?"

"I've had enough stimulation for today. How does a martini sound?"

"Like you hate scotch, I hate martinis, but some Cream Sherry sounds good to me. Besides, I need to get more information from you before we do battle again."

I went to the bathroom and waited until they were seated in the bar. I was hoping to get a seat close enough so I could hear everything, yet remain incognito. Fortunately, the price of drinks in bars is inversely proportional to the amount of light. I found a spot within earshot, kept my hat on and ordered a large pot of tea.

"You know, Jessica," Adam said twirling his olive, "I feel like a vampire has just made a meal of my vital fluids. Does it matter anymore if something is true or not? Innuendos, insinuations, hints, associations, why they're all damning and can be perceived as true even when they're not. How the hell do you counter that? Have we become a nation of paranoids? Is this what communism has done to us? Do I sound desperate and exasperated?"

"Have another martini. It's a short-term memory eraser as well as mood elevator. How does Sally Apple fit into this scheme of things?"

"You're wrong about the martini. It's making me remember—something unpleasant. A long time ago, I rescued her from the secretarial pool when she deceived her way into writing a screenplay. It's a long story. Don't ask. Nonetheless she's been a dependable writer for many years."

"Yeah, so?"

"I'm getting there. One day Peter Nathan announced the re-emergence of the hearings, and that specifically, they were after our film, *Gentlemen's Agreement.* In a vulnerable moment, I blabbered to Sally about how films portrayed Negroes and Asians in demeaning roles. It was then that I foolishly expressed my private thoughts about Negroes, their many contributions to the culture of America, our apartheid society, the Tuskegee airmen, the segregation in the army, my surprise that they ever fought for our country, and President Truman's blessed desegregation after the war.

"So, she remembered and told the committee? Why would she do that? After all, you rescued her so she would have been grateful. Was she trying to get even about something? Did you make her angry enough to torpedo you?

"Oh, waiter," she asked, "more ice for my drink."

Adam stared at her and said, "I can't believe what I did, Jessica. It wasn't one of my *finest hours*. Does my attorney have to know everything? Are you in the confessional box? Am I? Are you Catholic?" he asked, the gin beginning to take over.

"Doesn't matter, but if I'm going to help you, you need to tell me all you know, except," she said, "if you murdered anyone."

"Okay. I'll try not to slur my words—to finish before it becomes necessary to drive me home." He turned to her and said, "You know, Jessica, you don't need to know everything about me, Goddammnit. You're not my therapist, you're not Jesus, though your name was derived from his," he continued with a glazed look, trying to keep his eyelids from going half mast, "you're not Mother Theresa, nor my mother, and certainly not my wife, so this is the end of the line. The subway has just left Confessional Park, so stop with your inquisition. That's a run-on sentence, isn't it? Am I maundering?"

"Yes, but I don't get it."

"It's okay to leave a puzzle unfinished, Jessica. The important thing is that she's back home, writing a novel about what I assume is her Machiavellian boss and about all the other detritus she picked up during her research in Paris. My shenanigans were for naught, and that Sally Apa—la—chia betrayed me—that's not her name. It's similar—that fink—she exposed me—after all I've done for her—that snitch. How dare she? She's the only one I ever told. I never encouraged anyone not to fight. We are, warts and all, a blessed nation, and though I told them something different, I do believe in our resiliency and decency. We'll get religion soon. Dr. Bunche achieved a lot and that's promising, but in the meantime, they're going to kick me in the ass, aren't they?"

"You are maundering, Adam, but it's not as bad as you think. You acquitted yourself quite well up there. You told them what your values are, and what you think America should be striving for. I was proud of what you said, but that congresswoman was right, you know. You should have taken action. It's an important reminder.

"But if they call you back, I'll go to bat for you. If there's anything else that's relevant you gotta' tell me."

"But they weren't proud of what I said—and you're not the judge or the jury. How about joining their committee?"

"Adam, by the dim look in your eyes and your slurred speech, three martinis are all you can handle. I'm taking you home."

"Actually, Jessica, one martini is all I can handle. I gotta' go to the toilet. Don't wait up for me."

"Waiter, we need something to eat and some strong coffee, please."

While he was gone, she peered over at me for a terrifying few moments. I poured cream in my tea. When she got up and headed in my direction, my tea became creamed with dread. At that moment, mercifully, he left the bathroom so she returned to her table. Even in the dim light, his face was pallid. Way off-color.

She must have understood the effect of sound on an inebriated brain and whispered, "How do you feel?"

"Real empty."

"How does some chicken soup sound?"

"In this place?"

"Bars always have soup on hand. If not home-made, they open up a can of Campbell's and pretend." She motioned for the waiter. "Have any soup?"

"Sure do. What kind?"

"Chicken noodle?"

"For two?"

"Yes. Bring lots of crackers and coffee."

The waiter looked at Adam and said, "That's the right thing to order right now. It's good and it's homemade."

"Yeah, I'll bet," he slurred.

"No, really. The owner used to work at MGM's commissary and learned how to make Louis B. Meyer's famous chicken soup. It's almost as good as theirs!" he said putting his hand on Adam's shoulder, "it'll make you feel right at home, sir."

With a vacant look, Adam said, "I don't work there."

"So, Adam," Jessica asked, "since you're not telling me much about Sally, how much did you leave out when you mentioned your boss?" She looked at his sick face and added, "Are you well enough to talk about it?"

"Wait 'till the soup comes."

"Let me remind you that we're covered by attorney/client privilege. No one can force me to betray that trust."

"Why should I tell you anything more? It's between him and me and it's none of your damn business or HUAC's. If you want to know more, ask him yourself."

"Listen, buster, so long as I'm your attorney, I need to know whatever might compel them to call you back so I can prepare a strategy. If you think the truth is all the strategy you need, you're Goddamn mistaken. There are appearances that have nothing to do with reality. To get roasted, you don't have to be *IN* the fire—just at the same barbecue. So get off your high horse, and give it to me straight. *GOT IT?*"

The waiter brought coffee and two bowls of soup whose wispy fragrance wafted in front of them. Adam didn't respond to the reprimand. "Even the smell is making me feel better."

"Good," she said.

"I just burned my tongue."

"Yousureashelldid!"

With a hint of a smile, he said, "I'm sorry—I'm still reeling from the interrogation. That's the Goddamn nature of these hearings and the Goddamn zeitgeist of our times! They're all out of context! But the zeitgeist of the thirties was different. We lived through a terrible depression that made us question the viability of our economic system. Twenty-five percent of our people were unemployed. We had the 'worst of times' while the Soviets had, we were told by their believers, 'the best of times.'

"Adam, I lived through all of that. I know the story. Don't repeat it. Get on with yours."

He ignored her and went on, "The largest ethnic group in our country is German, and they couldn't believe that Nazism, with its growing repressive measures, was an 'ism' that had to be stopped. After all, how could Charles Lindberg, that iconic American, be wrong about his support for Nazi Germany? During the Spanish Civil War, General Franco, supported by Fascist Germany and Fascist Italy, waged a brutal war against Spain's legally elected democratic government. And the communists were among the few voices in our country speaking out *against* the Fascists."

About to continue his monologue when Jessica interrupted, "Stop, already! You're not on trial here and I'm not the judge. Stop rationalizing your behavior. Did you lie on the stand when you said you were not a communist?"

"Hell No! We need to understand why others might have joined." He paused and continued, "It was the communists in our country that rallied for racial equality and improvements for labor. So what was wrong with many of us allying ourselves with them?"

"*Us?* Did you or didn't you? Were you or weren't you?"

"I told you. *No!* I've said that a hundred times today!" he said wiping the spittle from his mouth.

"So, why didn't you?"

"During the Depression, yes, I resonated with some of their themes even though far removed from our Founding principles. But I couldn't because I have a visceral hatred for empire. Inherent in empire is subjugation, yet we only heard glowing reports from the Soviet empire. Perfection is unattainable—yet the communists in our midst told us what they had achieved—full employment—full bellies, abundance of everything, and then came the cotton-candy implausibility of Joseph E. Davies' book, *Mission to Moscow.* The whole construct seemed unconvincingly Utopian.

"What about those persistent rumors of the millions who starved during Stalin's forced collectivization in the Ukraine, of Stalin killing thousands of his former colleagues, of the enslavement of his subjects. I believed those people like Ayn Rand, who spoke of the degradation and impoverishment of the Soviet people and their loss of freedom. I reeled from the shock of the Ribbentrop/Molotov pact that destroyed Poland. No, ma'am, I wasn't buying all that slop—all that dreck."

"O.K., stop. The soup is working fine. So you didn't join. You're sure? Are they going to nail you for lying?"

"How many times do I have to tell you? Besides, I'm not a joiner."

He kept slurping his soup and continued with his rant,"Did you read the Dewey Commission Report about all those frame-ups, those repressive ... "

"Stop already, so what does this all have to do with my original question?"

"What question?"

"The question I asked before your first bowl of soup."

"I'm going to order another. Louis B. Meyer has a magic touch, both in and off the screen. Want another, Jessica?"

"Yes, since that's gonna' be my dinner. After today, we need to settle our stomachs."

"The question was?"

"Peter Nathan."

"Oh, yeah. To get it right, call him."

"I'm not his attorney, but I hear he's gotten a gunslinger."

"Oh? He didn't tell me, nor that he was subpoenaed."

"You report to him, don't you?"

"Yes, but since I returned, we're had little contact. He's been busy in administration, and I plunged into three projects simultaneously. He's going to need a gunslinger when going before those Neanderthals."

"They're not Neanderthals, Adam. Consider them pastors trying to keep their flock from evil. And if the evil has already infected us, they're trying to excise it."

"More like an exorcism."

He dove into his second bowl and said, "Jessica, I don't want a preacher to tell me what orthodoxy I should believe in. Our country is built on an idea. *A noble and elegant one.* And I bought into it. That's the only orthodoxy I need. So the committee can shove their pious certitude up, as that apt expression says, *where the sun don't shine.*"

"Adam, the committee is right, you know. The films, *Mission to Moscow* and *Song of Russia* were science fiction garbage—all those falsehoods about full pantries, everyone healthy and happy, untrue, yet insidiously seductive."

"Yeah, so how does that differ from what I was saying?"

"Well, you're angry with the committee but maybe it just wants us to face reality, not falsehoods, so as not to fall into the trap that has befallen the downtrodden people of the Soviet Empire and its satellites. Is that not plausible, Adam? Despite our having fallen short of the ideals of our Founding Fathers, we do have more freedom here than in any other place in the world. So, isn't their duty to awaken us to the seductive power of false illusion?"

He stared at her left hand. "Are you having trouble at home, Jessica?"

"What?"

"I noticed up there you weren't wearing your wedding ring. Does that mean trouble at home?"

"No, Adam—besides client/attorney privilege goes one way only. Since you ask, before I entered the chambers, I went to the ladies room, washed my hands, and forgot to put my wedding band back on. That's all," she said in such a way that I doubted its veracity, but Adam's mind was too clouded to really know. She reached into her purse and put it on.

She kept looking at his head as it was bobbing up and down and asked again, "I'd like an answer to my question. Remember—my question of a few minutes ago? Peter Nathan?"

"O.K. what little I remember. After several tennis matches one day, thirst encouraged us to have more drinks than we should have. The television was showing past newsreels of the Spanish Civil War when Pete pointed to a huge boulder on the screen. Said that he had been with several American Lincoln Brigade volunteers shooting from behind it—that it was in the Jarama Valley, an important supply route between Valencia and Madrid, one that the Loyalists were desperate to keep open. That's all he said. That's all I know."

"Forgive me, but since attorneys are required to take classes in Paranoia 101 and Cynicism 102, can you tell me whether it was more than a coincidence that you sent Sally to Europe at the same time that Peter sent you there?"

"I learned a lot there."

"I didn't ask that. How come you and Sally were there at the same time?"

"Leave me alone will you," he said as he raised his hands in a throw away motion. "I'm exhausted and need to go home.

"One other thing, Jessica, if you ever get a chance to speak to Pete, ask him to tell you about Mississippi—the lynching he once witnessed."

CHAPTER 28

When the door opened, I looked for that rare smile, and asked, "Glad to see you home, Jo. How did it go today?"

"I could almost taste it, honey. I think I may be the one directing a pilot on television," he said coming towards me.

"Great!" I rose and kissed him with a tight hug. He needs this badly. "Velia is asleep so we have a few minutes before her next feeding. Tell me everything."

"I read the script and told them how I would shoot it, and they seemed to agree with my vision. They were interested in filming it like a big movie, but I told them that their project wouldn't translate into miniaturizing it for television—that we must consider this new medium as a new species, not as a homunculus. And then I told them some details of what I would do with the actors, with the scenes, with the long shots, etc.

"For the first time since I've been interviewing, everything seemed to fall into place," he said with a hopeful look. "Hope I'm not kidding myself."

"You're not, Josiah. You'll make a terrific director. Let your imagination run wild, and even if you have to pretend, exude lots of confidence. That's usually reciprocated."

"Confidence? Well, yes, I guess I did today. Or maybe the prospect looks so promising because my fee is lower than others."

"That's the way it is in the beginning. When will you hear from them?"

"They're anxious to get started. They said next couple of days."

"I'll stay off the phone—make sure it's not off the hook."

He smiled and asked, "So what are you doing with that machine near your typewriter?"

"Just transcribing some stuff."

"With you there's no such thing as *just some stuff.* What are you up to?"

"Well," I paused, wondering what his reactions might be, "I attended the hearings today."

"Adam's hearings?"

"Don't get so excited, honey. I was curious about what was going to happen, especially as it might have affected me."

"Good Lord, Sally, you haven't dug up your old habits—habits I thought you buried in France?"

I paused, twitched my lips and nose, swallowed a couple of times, and said, "I recorded the entire session. It's quite innocent, Jo. Nothing to do with us—just with my need to know everything about everything—especially—that it did not affect me."

"Did it?"

"He suspected it was I who told of his opinion about Negroes fighting, but the chairman said it was none of his business."

"And, in a couple of days, they're calling Peter Nathan."

"I was right all along," he said with a resigned smile, "no female ever has a Jr. or Sr. behind her name, or Roman numeral I, II, or III. I'm going to start a trend that can be used by other wayward females. Your name will now be, Sally Apple, Whacko!"

I smiled, happy he wasn't angry with me, and said, "Okay, I'll abbreviate it to WK so that people will think it's a specialty like, MD or DDS or PhD."

"You are a lost cause, my dear. Let's see if I can find you under the covers before she wakes up."

"The chair of The House of Un-American Activities Committee calls the next witness on this 22nd day of February, 1951. Please be seated."

We saw two gentlemen approach the witness chairs, confident, heads held up high, shoulders back, no hint of condescending smiles nor apprehension, both with salt and pepper hair, each with bright brown eyes. One wore a lightweight gray suit with a crease sure to give a paper cut, a pale pink shirt with a perfectly starched collar that had no appearance of having a choke hold on the wearer, framing a burgundy silk tie perfectly knotted, fitting precisely in the center of the angles of his collar.

The other man was wearing a midnight blue suit, almost black, a white shirt with subtle maroon stripes, a starched collar and an azure blue tie also fitting precisely within its angles.

As they got closer to the witness chairs, with their erect posture and tailored clothes, they appeared to grow in stature, and the long aisle became a Brooks Brothers runway.

I had my place again, out of the sightline.

With the media attention given the hearings, all the seats in the gallery were filled. Three television cameras began to whir at the figures, radio mikes were swinging towards the witness chairs, reporters began scribbling on their pads, and a casual glance at the committee members watching the two of them approach could have detected the slightest of smiles.

The chairman, without any hint of making his welcome a warm one, said before they got comfortable in their seats, "Please identify yourselves."

The blue suit got up and said, "My name is Peter J. Nathan."

"Are you represented by counsel, Mr. Nathan?"

"Yes, sir," turned to his left, nodded, and sat down.

The chairman said, "Please identify yourself."

"My name is Aurelius T. Carter, attorney at law. #26010," said the gray suit, standing erect. He then sat down, still erect.

"Duly noted."

"My client has a prepared statement to read. May he proceed?" Mr. Carter asked.

"No, Mr. Carter. Perhaps at the end of the testimony."

"Why is that?"

"Your client was a member of the American Lincoln Brigade and as such, we have chosen to allow him to read it at the end, or, we may elect not to have him read it at all," he said.

Mr. Carter got up and said, "Excuse me, Mr. Chairman, but you've allowed others to read statements before their testimony. I don't understand the nature of your discrimination."

"It's not discriminatory—it's elective—our discretion—not yours. We'll proceed with our questions. Please sit down."

He remained standing and spoke at a higher pitch, "I object strenuously, Mr. Heddbone, all discrimination is elective and discretionary. You're treating my client based on pre-conceived assumptions and possible misinformation, not on his testimony. Is this not a hearing to determine the truth, sir?"

"Absolutely, and it's the *truth* that we intend to get at, so stop stalling and let's proceed with the questioning. And once again, I ask you to sit."

He started to then rose, "The gavel is in your hand, Mr. Chairman, but as graduates of Johns Hopkins University, I want to tell you what their motto is so that you'll understand how unimpeachable Mr. Nathan's testimony will be." Before he could be gaveled into silence, he said,

Veritas Vos Liberabit

"Do you know what that means, sir?" Mr. Carter asked, and without waiting, haughtily went on with the translation.

The Truth Will Liberate You

The chairman turned to the members and with sarcasm dripping from his words, said, "Well, it's curious to note, my fellow congressmen, that all of our witnesses, *and their counsel,* are members of the clergy who can never resist the temptation to preach to the heathens before them."

Mr. Carter said, "Your sarcasm is palpable. Do you know the derivation of the word, sir?" Without waiting for an answer, he continued, "It's Greek and it means to cut flesh, but you have *not* succeeded, *sir*!"

"Another outburst from you, Mr. Carter, and you will be expelled! That is not sarcastic, *sir*! It's a declarative statement, so sit down and let us *proceed*! And stop showing off your erudition. We're all well educated here. Despite your high-falutin' motto, Mr. Nathan is under oath, so he'd better observe the requirement of telling the truth. And that truth might not liberate him, *but* enlighten us. Now let us *proceed, sir*! And Goddamn it—sit down!" he said watching Mr. Carter sit down with clenched jaws.

There was a tap into the microphone and one of the congressman, Maximilian Jerez, said, "Mr. Chairman, this committee cannot best serve its mandate by continuing in the tense atmosphere that's been generated here." With a winning smile that must have helped get him elected, he scanned the witnesses and the panel members, and said, "Through no fault of any of the participants, sometimes things get off on the wrong foot—quite inexplicably," he continued, dripping maple syrup. "So since it was my research assistant who did the preliminary investigation, and I have studied those reports," he looked at the chair and asked, "may I proceed with the questioning?" The chairman took a deep breath and said, "Yes," relieved that someone else would begin the kick-off.

Cong. Jerez looked directly at the attorney and said, "You quoted a Latin proverb, Mr. Carter. I will quote a French one—one that I hope will set a less contentious stage in these proceedings,

Verite Sans Peur

"Do you know what that means, Mr. Carter?"

"I certainly do," and without attempting to translate it, seething still, said, "I certainly do."

"Would you tell us, please, what it means?"

He stood up and said, "*The Truth without Fear.*"

"Exactly! And that's the atmosphere I want to establish for the next few moments. You can sit down again, thank you, Mr. Carter." He turned to Peter Nathan, and went on without any hint of suspicion or anger, "As the chairman said, you are under oath, Mr. Nathan, so I urge you to tell the truth. Not so much because you're under oath, but because it's the right thing to do, and, as Mr. Carter reminds us, we hope that it *will set us free, and without fear.*"

With his engaging smile still in place, he looked from one to the other and asked, "Are we on the same wave length, gentlemen?"

They answered, "Yes, sir."

"Good. Just so that you know, I have no pre-conceived notions about who you are, what you did, what you do, your values, your politics—nothing. This is a hearing about discovery. We learned some things about you that may or may not be true so I hope that you'll help us discover what is, and what is not. Okay?"

Peter Nathan answered, "Congressman Jerez, *Verite Sans Peur.*"

He nodded, stopped smiling, and said, "Now, information in our possession has it that you fought with the Abraham Lincoln Brigade in Spain during that devastating civil war from 1936 through 1939 during which a tyrannical Fascist regime replaced a Democratic one. Is that true, sir?"

The gavel came crashing down. Everyone jumped. The chair yelled, "Mr. Jerez, we're gathered here to discover what this witness has done. We're not here to hear about your interpretation of history. Just ask the questions in a straight forward manner and avoid inserting your political leanings."

"Indeed, Mr. Chairman, but it's a matter of historical fact that a Fascist regime replaced the Loyalists who had been elected democratically five years earlier. These are facts, sir, and as you know, all facts are true—by definition—and not open to interpretation."

The gavel came down again. Reporters scribbled at a frantic pace. With a look that conveyed impatience and irritation, the chairman said, "Why in the world can't we get a through line in these interrogations? Listen, congressman, there's no such thing as historical truth! The Peloponnesian War in 431 BC is still being argued about, as are the three Punic Wars, the last of which resulted in that still much-discussed Carthaginian peace. And all the other Goddamn wars and Goddamn political events throughout history, they're all open to interpretation. Only the laws of gravity and the speed of light are not open for interpretation, so lay off your editorializing or I'll take over." He paused and asked, "Do you want to resume your questions or not?"

He spoke with such anger, that his neck swelled causing the clips on his factory-tied bow tie to loosen their hold. The tie popped on his desk, followed a moment later by the top button of his shirt. He glanced at them, shrugged his shoulders and unbuttoned several more buttons on his shirt revealing thick tufts of Cro-Magnon hair. He set the tie aside and heaved a sigh of relief.

"The witness must be surprised," Congressman Jerez said, "to find dissension in our midst, that congressman, even those on this committee, are not always in agreement." He turned to the chairman and said, "I've been requested to proceed. Shall I repeat my question, Mr. Nathan?"

"Not necessary. Let me answer your question about the Brigade," he said. "Your information is correct," causing a stir amongst the congressmen and audience. Flash bulbs blinded him temporarily. Reporters wrote furiously.

When Mr.Carter kicked him, he turned and saw him scowl.

"May I confer with my client, please?" Mr. Carter asked, barely masking his anger.

"You may—for just a moment."

He leaned close to Peter's ear and said between clenched teeth, "Goddamn it, Pete, this isn't what we discussed. You were to plead the Fifth. Now you're going to have to tell everything. What the hell went through your brain just then, you stupid SHITASS! Too late to rewind this movie now!"

"Aurelio," he replied, "I don't know what came over me. I'll explain later—as soon as I sort it out. I started something and have to finish it. Stay with me, please."

"I have no choice since you just torpedoed our ship. You're going to have to drift alone because I don't have a life preserver to throw you. And even if I did, I wouldn't give it to you, you schmuck!" He pushed him hard on his shoulder and said, "Let's see how buoyant you are, wise guy!"

Mr. Nathan looked at the chairman and noticed he had gotten the attention of all the congressmen. He took a deep breath, let it out slowly and began, "In my prepared statement I was going to tell you that as an American, my actions here or abroad, unless they were, or are, a threat to our country's security, are none of this committee's business, and I say that as one who respects our institutions and of the elected positions you've earned, that amongst our inalienable rights, gentlemen, is the privacy of my non-threatening activities, but since I was prevented from reading it earlier … "

"Please speak up. We can hardly hear you."

Surprised, he asked, "Did you hear what I just said?"

"Yes, we heard everything," the chairman said, "just make it louder. Go on, and speak directly into the microphone."

Certain that they hadn't heard a thing, he asked, "You mean you heard me say that the question is none of this committee's business?"

"Like hell it isn't, Mr. Nathan. We're the ones to determine whether your past or present activities were, or are, a threat to our country's security, so get on with your story. And don't give us the business with the First, Fourth or Fifth. We're heard all of that from unfriendly witnesses whom we've cited for contempt. Are you prepared to join that club?"

Without waiting for a response, he added, "And while you're thinking about that, you should know that this committee has an abhorrence towards those who fought with the Brigades—all those communists who wanted to turn *their* countries *and ours* into Soviet satellites. So give us all the details to the best you can recall, sparing us nothing. The entire truth."

"I just did!" Mr. Nathan said and nodded his head from side to side in resignation. He realized that his reversal of strategy wasn't going to have the impact he had hoped, so he increased his volume and continued, "Mr. Jerez asked the question which I answered truthfully. I didn't fudge. So please accept that what I'm about to tell you continues to be the truth, Mr. Chairman, "*not*," he said, looking at him with a piercing gaze," '*to the best I can recall*,' but because there's no need to search my memory banks All I have to do is close my eyes. It's always there, right behind my eyelids, leaving me with little peace.

"So let me tell you the genesis of joining the Brigade, so that you'll understand that not all of us who fought were communists, but, we were all anti-fascists." With a louder voice that raised his confidence as well, he added, "*so that you won't be taken in by appearances only, gentlemen.*

"During the thirties, before I joined the studios, I was a roving reporter for the Tribune charged with covering the changing political climate of Europe. On April 26, 1937 I arrived in Guernica, Spain, the very day that Gen. Franco, with the help of the Nazis and Il Duce's Italians, decided to transform that thriving city into *fire and ash, rubble and body parts.*"

He paused for a moment, swallowed, then looked at Cong. Jerez and said, "The Condor Legion of the Luftwaffe led the attack with their Heinkels and Dorniers, followed by the Italian SM79s. Wave after wave, like obedient soldiers, they took turns bombing and strafing huge columns of families with children in tow, who were trying to make their way towards the center of town where larger buildings might give them better protection. They looked like a horribly injured giant worm—a worm that was being dismembered piece-by-piece.

"When I saw the indiscriminate murder of these women, children and men, non combatants all of them—flesh aflame … . Have you ever smelled burning flesh, gentlemen?" he asked, scanning the panel, hoping no one would have encountered that repulsive smell. "I saw charred bodies with limbs blown off, randomly scattered pieces of bloody human flesh, and suddenly, a mother carrying a bleeding child on one arm and in her other hand—a leg."

He took another deep breath, and continued, "That made me puke. Literally." He looked like he was about to do the same on his desk. "You never forget the look of terror on little kids—their faces opened wide—eyes, brows, nostrils, mouth, the look of innocence destroyed, of disbelief—of horror. Nor on their parents. It's branded on your retina with a hot iron," he said swallowing hard, again and again. He paused between each word and said, "You—never—forget—their—screams. Never. It's enough to break your heart—irreparably!

"As Virgil once said, *There are tears in things.* That day Guernica was in tears!

"You never forget the high-pitched, piercing whistle of bombs dropped by dive-bombers," he choked out moving his head from side to side.

We knew by looking at him and listening to his doleful tale, he regretted being an eyewitness. He then said in a cracking voice, "It was the stuff of lifelong nightmares, only nightmares that persist throughout the day. It's a curse, I tell you—this eidetic ability of mine. I wish—I wish that there were some switch in the brain that could permanently erase those images, those smells, those sounds … "

Cong. Jerez seized that pause to relieve him of his anguish, to regain his composure, and asked, "Mr. Nathan, do you know why Guernica was chosen?"

"May I have a glass of water, please?" The chairman nodded to one of his staff. He drank the entire glass and asked for another. That gave everyone a momentary pause from the gruesome tale.

"Guernica, known, by the way, in the Basque language as Gernika, was chosen because it was part of the autonomous region of the Basques and of great significance. Franco's intention was to destroy the loyalists in Guernica—to break their spirit. But the city also represented a strategic point on the way to Bilbao. By destroying Guernica, his forces could take Bilbao, and with that, end the war in Northern Spain. Franco knew that Monday was their market day and that most of the people would be out shopping, so he chose Monday to maximize the slaughter. And that he did.

"At first I was immobilized by what I saw, but then I realized I had to escape those bombs and strafing myself, so I started to join the crowds heading towards the center of town, when I saw something strange. Running in the opposite direction—fighting the crowds, there was a man carrying an accordion. I couldn't imagine where he was going, so I decided to follow him. He soon stopped beneath a huge oak tree that I later discovered was called, Gernikako Arbola, a tree that had symbolic meaning for the Basques. Underneath the broad reaches of its strong limbs the Biscayne Assembly held their meetings. For them the tree represented their history—their—identity. It was their tree of life!"

The chairman, in a quiet voice, asked, "Mr. Nathan, this is an interesting story, but where are you taking us? We don't have time to listen to personal anecdotes."

"It's taking us to the catalyst, Mr. Chairman, to the very reason I joined the Brigade, so bear with me for a few more moments, please."

The chairman looked around at the members of his committee and saw that he had to let him continue.

"With the accordion on his chest, ignoring the exploding bombs, the shrapnel, the acrid smell, the burning market stalls, the unmistakable stench of burning flesh that had collected under the tree, and unconcerned with his own safety, he started playing. He sneered at the wave of planes going about their grisly business when suddenly I realized he was playing Bach's *Toccata and Fugue!* On his accordion! I couldn't believe it.

"I was close enough to see his eyes. Never before had I seen *death* in a person's eyes, a piercing furious, angry *death wish* for the bombers. I could see the muscles of his jaws rippling, his nostrils flaring, and to my surprise, he was singing note for note along with the music. No, not singing—more like shouting. It was an act of defiance unlike anything I have ever witnessed!

"He was playing so furiously that I thought his accordion would explode. With his eyes focused on the bombers, I realized what he was doing. *He was spitting in their eyes!*

"As he played, tears were streaming down his face, and at that moment, my own tears began to form. I suddenly realized that he was fighting back—eloquently—with the only weapon at his disposal!

CIVILIZATION'S WEAPON
BACH'S MUSIC!

"It was a scene, I must tell you, gentlemen, that remains as vivid today as it was then. I still shudder as I relive it—even after all these years, I shudder still." He gained his composure and continued, "I stayed until he finished—the episode could have lasted—I don't know—five minutes, ten, twenty. How long does that piece take anyway?

"At the end of the piece, he removed his accordion, stuck his chin up, and clutching his precious weapon with both hands, shook it up at the skies, muttering some Basque words that were probably as bad as existed in any language. That choked me up. The indomitable spirit always does that to me anyway," he said, his voice tapering off, breathing deeply.

With tears on the edge, he changed the subject, and said. "For all of those bemused by trivia, when I returned to the Unites States, I discovered that the Nazi President of the Reichsmusikkammer, the highest institution controlling music in The Third Reich, prohibited regional accordion bands from playing classical music in Germany and in all their conquered territories, because, they claimed, it was a *"nigger jazz instrument, and therefore, an abuse of the music of our great masters."*

"Anyway, I followed that heroic accordionist as he walked rapidly in the direction of the crowds—to look for friends, relatives—who knows? Suddenly I saw him stop to pick up the remains of a young girl, five or six, blackened by fire, missing one of her legs, the other blown off below the knee, and he lost it. I put my hand on his shoulder and wept along with him.

"The very next day I quit the Tribune and joined the American Lincoln Brigade."

Before anyone else could make a comment, Cong. Jerez said, "Why did you join? By writing about your experiences, you could have had a profound effect. You could have wielded your pen like a thousand rifles! Or is that too much of a cliché for you?"

"All clichés are true, Mr. Congressman. Of course, you're right, but in my case the horrors I witnessed, the heroics and eloquence of that accordion player's response made me want to pick up a rifle—to take some direct action myself. I had to *physically* take sides. There was no choice for me. It was an instantaneous decision. I didn't struggle with my conscience nor did I waiver for a moment. I had to do something beyond writing. *Right away.* I could no longer remain a chronicler of those hideous events. I had to take up arms against Franco and his cohorts in crime."

"Mr. Nathan," Cong. Jerez said, "spare us the details of the savagery and barbarity you subsequently witnessed, but ... "

The chairman rapped his gavel and said, "Congressman Jerez, please, let him tell his story without your editorializing. We're getting the picture without your continued politicizing."

Cong. Jerez ignored the caustic comment and asked, "Mr. Nathan, so how did you locate the Brigade? Did you know at the time that the Brigade was made up of communists, at least most of them? And did you fight with them for the duration of the war?"

"As a reporter, I had sources who put me in touch with them near the Catalan region. So after I left Guernica, I joined the 450 men trying to keep the important supply road between Valencia and Madrid open for the Loyalists. That battle in the Jarama Valley continued until June 1937. By that time, more than half the volunteers for the American Lincoln Brigade had been killed or wounded.

"I had a couple of bad scrapes, but nothing punctured or broken. I didn't even know how to fire a rifle—no training whatsoever—other than point and shoot."

"You're lucky to have survived," the congressman said.

"You're absolutely right. Luck had *everything* to do with it."

"How long did you fight for?"

"Not long—just through the middle of June. During that time, however, I found that the Soviet Comintern had organized all the front groups fighting alongside the Loyalists. They wanted to crystallize the conflict so that it became an either-or proposition, the Fascists against the anti-Fascists, but it was far more complicated than that. The Comintern rallied us behind the slogan: *Spain—the tomb of Fascism.*

"I made an effort to speak to the volunteers, one from France, a young student, in his mid-twenties, who said matter-of-factly, *After we turn Spain communist, next my country.* Wait a second, I thought, this war was about returning the democratically elected Loyalists to power. I wanted to determine whether that was the hope of the others, so during another break in the fighting, I asked a teacher from Belgium who said, *First Spain communist, then Belgium—just wait.*' I was astonished to hear the same from a Hungarian, a Chilean, a Greek, and then when I heard it slip from our commander, Boris something-or-other, it became clear to me that the Soviets had an over-arching agenda—not of supporting the Loyalist Government of Spain as many of us had supposed, but of *replacing* it with a *communist government.*

"Remember that many of these volunteers came from repressive countries, so I had assumed that fighting the Fascists meant that when they got back home, they would try to replace their governments with democracies. But these guys wanted to replace them with a communist government. You realize we're talking about a hodge-podge of people from all walks of life—seamen, lumberjacks, students, teachers, writers, dancers, artists, union organizers, miners, actors, athletes, adventurers. Albanians, Canadians, Poles, Americans, Germans, Chinese, Finnish—people from more than fifty two countries, all struggling with the economic problems of the twenties and thirties, disillusioned, the whole lot of them, but ever hopeful of what could be. Yes, more than 50% had been members of the Young Communist League in the United States, but the rest of us who were not communists had also supported equal rights for Negroes, better working conditions, etc. We were idealists struggling mightily against the Fascist specter, seeking answers for the failure of our capitalist system. We were searching—longing for something better.

"Another chink in my armor occurred while we were being besieged by Italian troops. A group of Loyalist troops came to our assistance, but when they called for communist reinforcements they knew were near by, the communists stalled until we were terribly bloodied. When it looked like the fascists might win the day, they appeared, but by that time it was too late. We were on the run, disappearing into a forest of cork trees. We regrouped and while licking our wounds, I spoke to our sub-commander, a supporter of the Loyalists, who had barely survived himself, and he whispered to me, quite cynically, that this is what's it's turning out to be.

"I made a serious effort to talk to many of the Brigaders," he continued, "after all, I had started as a reporter. These guys knew nothing about the profound difficulties in the Soviet Union. They just believed in that propaganda crap about the Soviet *heaven on earth.*

"The capitalist system was bankrupt, and they believed the communist system was the correct one—the one to be emulated everywhere. And why not? From what they were told the Soviet Union had full employment, no starvation, factories going full blast, free health care, free education—you know all the stuff we heard about in the thirties from the true believers. It was, they claimed, a utopian dream that had been realized. Many of those volunteers were persuaded, as they tried to persuade me, that their system must indeed be superior."

Cong. Panther interrupted and said with obvious cynicism shaping his words, "I remember that Eugene Debs in his early days, said that 'Socialism was Christianity in Action.'" He let that idea float for a moment.

"That was before," he continued, "he went to jail for questioning America's entry into World War I. Congress, with the Espionage Act of 1918, had made it illegal. And for those of our members who haven't followed his career, let me state that in the early twenties, after his release from jail, he became increasingly disillusioned with Lenin's repressive methods and communism in general, so he broke with his old Bolshevik friends and became a Democrat," looking around at his colleagues with a grin, "but it made little difference. People still called him a *commie*. Once stigmatized, you're stained forever."

He leaned forward on his desk and asked, "Tell us, Mr. Nathan, were you sympathetic to the views you spoke about—about the bankruptcy of capitalism?"

"I had been an early cynic of the Soviet system because I had delved into the archives of the Tribune where several of us checked the rumors about their repressive measures, and double checked them by speaking to those who had escaped or defected. I didn't buy that much proclaimed myth of theirs. Besides, I had an unrequited love affair with Frances Perkins," he quipped with the hint of a smile, his first.

"But I want to add as well, that it was okay not to be a jingoist about our country. It was okay to question the system that had led to such dire consequences—to try replacing or improving it." With a firm voice, he said, "I made a conscious decision to improve it, the Perkins Way."

"Mr. Nathan, please allow me to interrupt you for another moment. We, on the panel know all about Secretary Perkins, but I ask the chair's permission," turning to the chairman, "to ask Mr. Nathan's interpretation of the Secretary's beliefs so that it can be entered into our official record. Okay with you, Mr. Chairman?" He received a reluctant nod. "So tell us, Mr. Nathan, leaving out the intimate details of your amorous relationship with Secretary Perkins, what appealed to you about her views?"

"All of you know this better than I, of course, but in 1933, soon after FDR appointed Frances Perkins as the first woman Secretary of Labor, she announced a sweeping proposal to restructure our social system. Federal unemployment relief, minimum wages, a lid on maximum hours worked, compensation for workers injured on the job, workplace safety regulations, a national pension system, a ban on child labor, workers' rights to organize, all under our democratic umbrella. I bought into that and knew that in time, we would get those good things. I couldn't understand why American communists were willing to support the *unsupportable* beliefs that those benefits were already present in the Soviet Union. Why take a chance on a *questionable* system when we were already heading on the right path?"

The Chairman rapped the gavel lightly to ensure that he would be the next one asking questions. "So, Mr. Nathan, before you continue with your war-time experiences, are you telling us what you think this committee wants to hear, or are you telling us what your true political philosophy was—and—is."

"Mr. Chairman, for heaven's sake, please, what you're hearing is the *truth*. Despite my years on this earth, I am a romantic. Without sounding preachy, I believe, like Secretary Perkins, change can be made *within* our system and not by its replacement. I believe in the truth of Aristotle's statement, *that when everyone is responsible, no one is responsible*. I believe that our individual entrepreneurial spirit is superior to any collective. I believe that after the calamity of the great depression, to prove the strength of our core beliefs, we could and would make corrections—that our democratic institutions would ultimately ensure, as though our Founding Fathers had built in some social teleology, an improving beneficial equilibrium.

"To go on, I was in the lion's den over there—completely unsuccessful in deflating the hopeful aspirations of the communist optimists in our midst. But I must say, I didn't try very hard. After all, we were fighting for a common cause, we needed each other, and, I didn't want to get shot from behind.

"Besides, a Cassandra is universally hated.

"You know what our American policy was. Why some of you may have had a hand in fashioning it. Western governments signed a non-intervention pact preventing aid or arms from going to the Loyalist Government, but the Soviet Union and Mexico were not signatories and sold them arms. So by doing nothing, the West was helping Franco."

"Let me remind you," said Cong. Jerez, "during that time some were protesting."

"Yes, some prominent ones, Albert Einstein, Dorothy Parker, Gene Kelly, Paul Robeson, Helen Keller, Gypsy Rose Lee, a few writers, Ernest Hemingway and Lillian Hellman, all of whom helped to strengthen anti-fascism in the United States. Those were the vocal anti-Fascist Americans who were opposed to Hitler, Mussolini and Franco.

"Robeson, Hellman and her lover, Dashiell Hammett, were at the forefront of efforts to stop Germany's rearmament, of boycotting them, of supporting the Soviets as the bulwark against Fascism. But many others, not communists, supported the actions against Germany.

"And the irony—the duplicity of those true believers, was that as soon as the Hitler-Stalin pact was signed, Hammett and Hellman stopped their attacks on Germany. The American Communist Party, reversing itself, was now urging us to stop agitating against Germany—to stay out of war with them. Both Hammett and Hellman were in the League of American Writers and served on its *Keep America Out Of War Committee*. The others, however, kept up their attacks."

"Go on with your experiences in Spain, please," the chairman said.

"Despite the Comintern's attempt to unify all the anti-Fascist forces, we were attacked by *anti-Fascist* factions and other factions each trying to emerge topside. With the realization that those *for Franco and those against* were slaughtering us, I recognized the futility of what I was doing. Internecine warfare can be the worst kind of warfare. It wasn't just us against them—it was some of us against some of them—and some of us against some of our own 'us's', and all of us against some who were against all of us, but not really, only partially, and who exactly were 'the them' and who exactly were 'the us?' It was a maze of conflicting forces, impossible to navigate—the slaughter ghastly!

"I couldn't hold my food down or my spirits up." He took several deep breaths. "Do you need to hear more, gentlemen?" No one answered. With a distant look that suggested he was remembering but wishing he could forget, it appeared he couldn't stop anyway—like he had crossed his personal Rubicon.

"Some of us found ourselves on the wrong side of history. Going from one city to another, it was the same, fighting ineffectually—no plan, no strategy, just shooting at anyone in uniform only to find that those in uniform were sometimes Loyalists. The stench of the battlefield never left me. It's inextricable, buried in my pores, submerged within layers of skin so that when the outer layer sloughs off, the inner layer comes up stinking. It's always there, the putrid smell of decomposing blood and flesh, the toxic odor of explosives, the sweat of my own unwashed body. Even now, when I'm about to smell something, a flash of apprehension overwhelms me and I pause. It's hard to enjoy the fragrance of a rose without anticipating that, like my skin, it might exude the smell of putrefaction."

With head bowed, it looked like tears were falling. He changed course with his lugubrious story and said, "On a different note, we had some Italian volunteers, mostly communists, who encountered scouting parties of Fascist Italian soldiers. During such encounters, the Fascists periodically gave them important information.

"Once we got a machine gun—jammed."

The chairman asked, "Instead of joining the Lincoln Brigade, why didn't you join the Eugene Debs Group, socialists, not communists?"

"I heard that such a group existed, but no one seemed to know where they were. The only anti-Fascist group I could locate was the Lincoln Brigade, so that's the one I joined. Please understand that I was thinking *anti-Fascist* only—not communist, socialist or anything else. May I go on? Though I relive parts of this story almost every day, I need to finish this publicly—once and for all. Okay?"

Without waiting for a reply, he continued, "I was so distraught at the carnage in Guernica, that I rationalized that when a house is burning, you don't care who helps you put out the fire. War makes for strange bedfellows—look at our alliance with the Soviets against the Nazis."

The next question came from a voice on the panel, but couldn't tell from whom. "How long were you fighting?"

"Not long—six weeks or so. I know because within three or four weeks after I got to the front, many of my colleagues had been killed or maimed, and the remaining dozen or so of us were instructed to join another group north of us. I did, fought for awhile, then abandoned the group."

"You abandoned your friends—*your mission*?" the chairman asked. "So much for the depth of your *commitment*!"

We were puzzled. Why would such a rabid anti-communist ask that? Was he trying to embarrass him, rattle him, weaken anything else he might say? Bastard!

The chairman asked, "Would you please tell this committee why?"

"Does the name General W.G. Krivitsky sound familiar?"

The first to speak was Congressman J. Quinlan Panther. "Chief of Soviet Military Intelligence?"

"Yes, right. He told me that before the war, Stalin had sent him to Spain."

"He told *YOU*? So you *were a communist*!" the chairman asked as though he knew it all along. "Are you still one?"

Mr. Carter jumped in, "Mr. Chairman, sir, the First Amendment allows us freedom of speech and thought, and … "

"I know all about the First Amendment, counsel, but I'm asking it anyway." He stared at Mr. Nathan, "Well?"

"Interrupt me as much as you want, Mr. Chairman, but my client doesn't … "

Mr. Nathan put his hand on his arm and said, "Aurelius, stop please. Thank you for coming to my defense. I know I promised you something else, but I've changed my mind."

He turned to the panel members, "I value the protections afforded me by our Constitution but I don't want to call on those protections right now. I intend to tell the whole truth, not only because I have nothing to hide, but because if anyone believes deeply in something, he or she should not fear full disclosure. *The Hollywood Ten* should have had the courage of their convictions. I know they told the committee that you had no business asking them about their political beliefs—*and they were right*. But if they truly believed that communism was the preferred *socio-political construct*, one superior to our own, they should have come out and flatly said so. They should have had the courage to support their beliefs in your presence. There was no reason to have used the First or Fifth—or to obfuscate with their convoluted replies.

"After all, we know the political affiliation of each of you on the panel, and though we know there is wide disagreement amongst you, we don't question your patriotism … "

"There is a profound difference between patriotism and encouraging overthrow of our government. Continue with your response but stop taking such lengthy steps to explain everything," said the chairman.

"Sir, I'm not a poet. I'm incapable of distilling complex thoughts into twenty-five words or less. If you'll allow me, I want to explain that I am not now, nor have I ever been, a communist. On the other hand, the communists in this country, before the Hitler/Stalin pact, were among the most vocal anti-fascists. Why should they be ashamed of that? Like many of them, I was opposed to Franco and Hitler. What was wrong with my saying so and putting my money where my mouth was? There were about 2,800 American volunteers fighting fascists in Spain and I wanted to join them. I wanted to kill!"

"Vengeance?" Cong. Jerez asked.

"Yes. Guernica-induced vengeance!"

"I want to get on with this hearing," the chairman said, "but it seems we're getting another history lesson wrapped up in autobiography. Mr. Jerez, focus your questions and get to the point quickly."

"MR. CHAIRMAN," the congressman responded, "this is a man who fought against fascism *before* the Second World War. He was a *volunteer,* not a *draftee*. The least we can do is try to understand what happened to a *non-communist*, why he fought, and why he didn't fight for the duration of that *bloody* war. So please, sir, this is an opportunity for us to learn additional details about our recent history."

"Congressman Jerez, I know my history. That's how I knew when those Greek and Roman wars were fought, so don't lecture me, I'm not an uneducated philistine!" Sighing audibly, he continued, "And for the record, the comment should be amended to say 'happened to an *alleged non-communist*, etc.' Just make it brief. We don't have all day."

Cong. Jerez looked at Mr. Nathan and said, "Forgive this impolite interruption, sir. "Mr. Chairman, point of clarification. Mr. Nathan is not an *alleged non-communist*. Our presumption of being innocent until proven otherwise prevails, so it's best to leave the word *alleged* out of our conversations."

He didn't wait for a response, but turned to the witness again. "Tell us what happened with the General and all those *communists*." looking out of the corner of his eye at the chairman.

"Sir, I ask all of you respectfully, please, to pay attention to the details as well as to the over-arching issues. As I said earlier, those fighting, whether they were members of the American Lincoln Brigade, the George Washington Battalion, the John Brown Battalion, or the Debs' Group were profoundly affected by the international turmoil, economic and political, of the 1930s—our Great Depression, Japan's invasion of Manchuria in 1931, Hitler's ascendancy in 1933, its suspension of civil rights, its persecution of Jews, Mussolini's assault on Ethiopia in 1934. And then on July 19, 1936, Spanish generals, with support from Germany and Italy, attacked Spain's freely elected democratic/socialistic government.

"You've got to give these volunteers some slack—idealists with the best of intentions need to be given slack—always—even when their actions go awry.

"By your yawn Mr. Chairman, I see that you're either bored or impatient with my testimony. I'm leading up to what you're looking for. It's just that context is important," and with a smile in his eyes and voice, hoping to appeal to the chairman's background in history, continued, "just think, if you will, of Herodotus and Thucydides."

"Give me a break, Mr. Nathan. No one deserves to be in that constellation," he barked, "just don't make your context 1000 pages long!"

"I was referring, sir, to the need for context, not to equivalence. Those volunteers were people who hoped that their presence would stop the continuing rise of international fascism. When the Brigade was first organized in early 1937 there were about 450 engaged in a losing battle to keep that supply road open between Valencia and Madrid. By the time I got there at the end of April or early May, half the volunteers, the first racially integrated military unit in US history led by Oliver Law, their Negro commander, had been killed, including Law. Seven or eight weeks later, about the time I left, more than 300 had been killed or wounded," he said shuddering. "At one point, in the lull of a furious battle, we heard soldiers approaching us from the woods singing *The Communist Internationale*. Delighted to hear that song, about twenty-five of the communists from our group, thinking they were reinforcements from comrades in arms, greeted them enthusiastically. We watched in horror as those singers opened fire on our men, shredding them with meat-grinder machine guns." Tears welled in his eyes. He took a deep breath and looked forlornly at each of the panel members.

With his voice cracking, he continued, "Imagine—pieces of you—plowed under in some distant land. For those of you who've been in combat, you know about the rain and mud, the freezing cold of a late spring, the lack of food, lousy sanitation, loss of personal hygiene, the artillery explosions with its unforgettable acrid smell and promise of impending death, the staccato chatter of machine guns spitting their lethal charges towards unwilling victims, the blood, the death of your friends—you know it all—you know it all," he said, his voice tapering off.

"It's a wonder," as tears wet his cheeks, voice cracking, "that those of us who survive, can ever sanction war again."

After several deep breaths to control his tears, thankful that there were no calls for abbreviating his tale, he continued, "I referred to General Krivitsky before, so let me tell you what, in addition to the killing, was devastating to me. After another furious battle, 10 or 12 of us survivors, deafened by the noise, blinded with ghost images of the flash of explosives, caked with the splattered blood of our comrades, regrouped in a cave, heaving a sigh of relief for its brief and temporary respite.

"We sat in that moldy-damp, fecal-smelling dark cave feeling like abandoned rats. No one said anything. We didn't have to. We shared an unspoken bond—palpable, resonant—drawing us together.

"I passed some weak coffee around and introduced myself to the person on my right. He introduced himself as casually as if he had been a waiter, 'I'm General Krivitsky, Chief of Soviet Military Intelligence.'

"It took a moment to register, and then I asked myself—had I heard right? Waking from my stupor, I asked, "*YOU WHAT? YOU ARE?* What in the world are *YOU* doing here?'

"He was moving his eyes wildly, like a compass gone berserk, looking everywhere as though he were wary of bats preparing to pluck his eyes out. His body twitched like he had St. Vitus's dance. In fragmented English, he told me he had decided to defect to the West. Immediately I thought I was being set up—a trap that might cost me my life. War has a way of turning every sense into radar. I became very suspicious.

"In a meandering way he explained, *'I had been in frequent touch with the Republican Spanish Ambassador to France, Luis Araquistain, who was aware of my activities to replace the current Prime Minister, Senor Largo Caballero, with a Stalin approved communist puppet, something I succeeded in doing—albeit with much effort. But in so doing I had to fight the*

POUM, an anti-Stalinist Marxist party made up of Republican opponents of the communists—and against the anarchists—against the liberals—against the socialists and Trotskyists, all of whom were fighting the fascists while at the same time fighting each of the others who in turn were fighting everybody else.'

"Forgive this amount of detail, gentlemen," he said looking at each congressman, "but you need to know what happened and why. My fatigue disappeared immediately, and I listened with rapt attention, noticing that he never stopped rubbing his forefinger back and forth against his nostrils. It was like seeing a rabbit going into anaphylactic shock.

"The General growled on, *'I had been sent to meet the leaders of POUM to persuade them to join the Communist Party so that together we would have a better chance of defeating the rebels. I thought success was within my reach, when suddenly members of the Communist Military Unit attacked them—against my orders! They knew I was there and what I was doing, but they wanted to become chiefs! More importantly, I knew where many of Stalin's bodies were buried, about the purges that were taking the lives of many of the original revolutionaries, when suddenly I had an epiphany. This was Stalin's way of eliminating me—not by firing squad like he did with my colleagues, but by betraying me in a battle that would surely lead to my death. Of course, Stalin could then send my family a telegram—how their husband and father had died fighting for a just cause, heroically—for the people's cause.'"*

Mr. Nathan continued, "Looking at me for the first time, but furtively, the General said in disbelief, *'I barely escaped with my life, came further south looking for my other units who might not have been told of their attempt to murder me, who regarded me still as their leader, but then I ran into you stragglers fighting your bloody hearts out.*

"'What general do you know,' he asked rhetorically, *'enters battle voluntarily? Being older and wiser, he leaves that to others, but I had no choice, I picked up a rifle to protect myself, to survive! And as you can see,'* he *continued with an unfriendly look, 'my hand is always on my rifle.'*

"In so many words, that's what he told me. That war, like others, was chaotic. It's been neatly mythologized, but it was much more than the simplistic description of the war as being between Republicans and Fascists. He confirmed to me what I had learned from others, that the C.N.T., the U.G.T., the F.A.I., the P.S.U.C.—so many groups with acronyms standing for what, I no longer remember, fighting against one another and against the Anarcho-Syndicalists and the Left-Wing Socialists, all of whom were being attacked by the Communist Party members, all of whom were fighting the falangists, the fascists in the Spanish government and their allies, the Nazis and Italians! It was a nightmare—a Spanish Labyrinth with multiple layers, multiple parties, each with its own agenda, but with the over-arching determination of Stalin to turn Spain into his westernmost colony and impose his version of totalitarianism.

"To deal with the war's complexities, I had to invent an entirely new vocabulary for myself. *The war had lost its Manichean clarity.*

"Internecine warfare," he continued with a pained look on his face, "is the worst kind of warfare. I said that before, didn't I?"

"The communist appetite for power was insatiable, and during critical battles they frequently withheld arms from Caballero and his government because credit for its success would have gone to the Republicans rather than to them. The Soviets, as one of the two suppliers of arms, the major one at that, often controlled the outcome of these battles.

"The depth of that Sisyphean imbroglio took my breath away," he said, and in the telling, he was no longer in the witness box, no longer on stage, but telling his personal story, exposing his anguish—as though to a psychoanalyst who had unleashed his demons. It was as intimate a moment as he may have ever gotten with strangers.

"And as I tell you about my experiences my stomach churns. I hope my story tells you why I hate the Soviets. They had gotten control of all the important Spanish ministries, including the Chief of the Cipher Bureau. All secret communications received by the Republic from abroad were known to the Russian embassy *before* the Spanish government received them. The ambassador and the General knew that Stalin was not interested in preserving a democratic government, but in imposing a communistic one, and that he was not interested in helping win the war except on his terms, that he was more interested in tying the hands of Hitler and Mussolini in Spain. After all, Italy had more than 70,000 troops fighting there, while Germany about 20,000, plus three squadrons of Junkers, three of Heinkels, 51s, 99s and 70s, and floatplanes.

"Stalin wanted them bogged down there so they couldn't carry out their policy of aggression in Eastern Europe and the Baltic states, and, ultimately against the Soviet Union. Adding to my disillusionment, the General told me that most of the gold reserves of the Bank of Spain had been transferred to Moscow, ostensibly to pay for the weapons they were sending. An amount he estimated to be about 574 million dollars.

"After he gave me his blow-by-blow, I got up and walked around the cave trying to control the wave of rage coursing through my trembling body realizing that I was living through a nightmare. I picked up my rifle and was about to smash it until I realized it was the only way I had to protect myself.

"I looked the General squarely in the eye, and asked, '*Are you really going to defect?*' He bobbed his head and said, '*Yes—yes.*'

"Disgusted, I yelled at everyone, '*What the hell am I fighting for? A pox on all their houses!*'

"I decided that my life was more important than those fighting in this muddled, muddied mess, that I would have to escape this seething cauldron. Even as a student I never bought into communist philosophy that 'the ends justify the means.' It was now clear what their ends were—and I could tolerate neither their ends nor their means.

"If the means are corrupt, how can the ends remain uncorrupted?

"As if to place a seal on my decision, the General told me he was trying to get to the USA because he had learned that Neville Chamberlain, the Prime Minister of Great Britain, saw '*nothing threatening by a German and Italian victory in Spain.*'

"And defect the General did. He got to the United States before the Second World War started.

"So here I am, gentlemen," gazing around the room, spent, sweating, holding tightly onto the sides of the desk, his chin quivering uncontrollably, eyes half-open, jaws clenching and unclenching, a face inscribed with revulsion, with contempt. "I have nothing to redeem for, nothing to apologize for. I never was, nor am I now a communist."

After a pause, Congressman Jerez said, "Mr. Chairman, *he* told the story but *I'm* the one that feels washed out. No further questions."

The chairman asked, almost apologetically, "Mr. Nathan, thank you. Nothing much has changed with the Soviets. Please understand that this committee might go overboard sometimes, but the threat is real, our mandate clear. You must be tired, but I want to ask you a question. Do you know of any communists currently working at the studio?"

"None, sir, but I don't ask to see their wallets. I'm still on the same page as those who want to see complete rights for the Negro, better working conditions for the working man, and all the things you've heard dozens of times. If that should sometimes coincide with communist ideology, good for them, but I submit it's a disingenuous belief, intended to ensnare and seduce.

"Ring Lardner Jr. who was a communist and who shared an Academy Award for the screenplay, *Woman of the Year,* which, I might add, had no communist commentary, was fired by Twentieth Century. Other than him, I know of no others.

"And sir, reliving that nightmare has left me exhausted. Are we through?"

"One other question before we button up. I ask for your patience for another moment. Did Twentieth Century Fox ever make a movie extolling the virtues of that supposed *Communist Paradise in the Soviet Union?"*

"Not on my watch, Mr. Chairman. We never produced, like MGM, as false a film as *Song of Russia.*"

"But you made the film, *Gentlemen's Agreement* which, you claimed, would address the alleged anti-Semitism in this country."

"It wasn't our thesis, sir, but Laura Hobson's well-documented description of the subtle, and not so subtle, anti-Jewish prejudice in our society."

"Did you believe it?"

"We wouldn't have made the film if we hadn't. It was the right thing to do—to let thoughtful people examine their pre-conceived notions AND their behavior. Yes, sir, it was one of our finest hours."

"We'll come back to that film at another time. Thank you, from all of us. You are dismissed."

"One moment, please, Mr. Chairman," Congressman Rosenmyra interjected. "I would like to put some closure to these proceedings. May I ask Mr. Nathan a question?"

"A brief one, please."

"Mr. Nathan, you mentioned the film, *Song of Russia.* Do you know who wrote the film?"

"Yes. Paul Jarrico and Richard Collins."

"That's correct—both communists. Do you know them?"

"Never met them."

"You live in Bel Air, don't you?"

"Yes."

"You live on Linda Flora Drive, right?

"Yes."

"Do you know that Paul Jarrico lives at 727 Linda Flora Drive?"

"No."

"You sure you don't know Jarrico?"

"Mr. Congressman, you never have to ask me whether 'I'm sure' about what I've said. Don't ask me that again. It's insulting. If I'm unsure of something, I'll state that upfront. I don't know Paul Jarrico!"

"Still, you're in the same neighborhood and yet you haven't met … "

"Sir, we live in the hills of Bel Air. The only way in and out is by car. I get into my garage, start the engine and off I go without meeting neighbors."

"So on weekends, there's no opportunity for social contact with neighbors?"

"My job, sir, knows nothing of weekends—or nights. We know nothing of the 9 to 5 world, and Mr. Jarrico, as a writer, confines himself to his office either at home or at the studio, probably day and night, and since I don't have a dog that needs walking, I hardly know the neighbors on either side of me."

"Please don't get impatient with me. I'm driving at something."

The chairman asked, "And where is that, for heaven's sake?"

"The F.B.I. just released a document describing a recent interview with Richard Collins in which he stated that he had once been a communist, but was no longer, and that prior to his appearance before this committee, he had had a conversation with Jarrico. Mr. Collins said that Mr. Jarrico asked for Mr. Collins's assurance that he would not name any names before this committee. Mr. Collins said, that yes he would agree to that, if Mr. Jarrico would give him his personal assurance that in the event of a war between the United States and the Soviet Union, Mr. Jarrico would do nothing to help the Soviet Union.

"Mr. Jarrico refused."

"Wow!" Pete said.

"Thank you, Mr. Nathan. Mr. Chairman, he's yours."

"Wait!" Mr. Jerez shouted. "One other question, please. Mr. Nathan, the motto, the one from Johns Hopkins University, '*the truth liberating us*,' do you feel liberated now?"

"Sir, psychoanalysts will confirm that exposing secrets from the deep recesses of the mind, can indeed be liberating, but at this point I'm too washed out to know for sure, so to answer your question, I'm glad this ordeal is over with everything coming to light, but I'll need time to determine if these disclosures will liberate me or condemn me."

"You are excused, Mr. Nathan."

"The question is, Mr. Chairman, has my testimony liberated this committee?"

There was only a light rap of the gavel.

Aurelius T. Carter gathered his papers, but Pete just sat there, breathing deeply, letting it out slowly, then rose. Both were silent as they got into the lobby. I followed, hat tucked rakishly. Pete turned to him and said, "I'm not sorry about what I did. I know I promised that you would direct all questions to the First and Fifth, but I just couldn't do it. I had to talk. Maybe those pithy sayings were the catalysts that enabled what had been percolating inside of me, to geyser out. I don't know, but I had to explain the antecedents going into my decisions. They had to know. To have done otherwise felt like it would have been cowardly, dishonest. You understand?" he asked.

"How naive you are, my *former* friend. Don't you think they know? Do you think they're stupid? They have an agenda and they seduce you into saying what fits into their preconceptions. To hell with the truth.

"It's all *a-priori*!

"It's all *le droit de roi!*

"You were the king's fool in there. I hate when clients disobey me! I can't believe it—after all our strategy sessions. What the hell was that all for?"

"Aurelio, a drink would do us good, in quiet, dark privacy. I need to unwind, to tell you why, maybe even more. Meet me at my house. Whadya' say, old friend?"

"What for? So we can plan another strategy that you'll flush down the toilet? You betrayed me in there, you shit head! Go screw yourself!" and started to walk away.

Pete grabbed him by the arm and pleaded, "C'mon, just to talk. Our strategy sessions are over. Meet me at my house."

"Don't be so sure, Pete. Besides, I don't want to set foot in your house again."

"Last request—let's go to The Cellar. It's dark, quiet, and they serve food which will enable us to drink more than we would on an empty stomach."

"See you soon, okay?"

I stayed behind, out of their immediate concern.

They soon walked into a darkened room. I heard Aurelius say, "Can't they afford to pay their electric bills in this place? You are Peter Nathan, aren't you?"

As soon as they were seated, I found a suitable table and turned my recorder on. Aurelius said, "Didn't your momma ever tell you that you've gotta' listen to your lawyers and doctors? That they're omniscient? Was that expensive education wasted on you, you numbskull? Why the hell didn't you listen to Mr. Know-it-all here?"

Peter smiled, "Listen, Aurelio, my dear friend, I don't want you to put me on the defensive. I'm pretty much drained, but let me remind you about your eponymous self, *Marcus Aurelius,* the famous follower of Epictetus, the Stoic. When I was sitting in that electric chair up there, I had a strong urge to disabuse them of all of their pre-conceived, unwarranted value judgments about those of us who fought the good fight—to fight fascism, and in the very process, resisted becoming communists, and still worked for social justice.

"My goodness, I got that all out in one breath. Had I remained silent, left all those things unsaid, I would have betrayed the man you were named after, you understand? Please, say you do."

"You trying to impress me, you son-of-a-bitch, about how much you remember from school—tearing at my heart through my brain? You're rotten to the core, you know. So you bought into that motto at Johns Hopkins—that bullshit about *The Truth Will Liberate You*? The truth finally does come out—beneath that carapace of yours, you're made of oatmeal.

"No wonder we're friends!" Aurelius continued, "that's gonna' cost you this round of drinks."

"You pay for dinner, then."

"Like hell I will. We'll split it."

"You fool—in this cellar, you would have gotten away cheap."

"Remember it's the Beverly Wilshire Hotel."

They looked at the menu, and as I predicted, ordered two bowls of soup and a round of drinks. When the waiter left, Aurelius asked, "Since you showed off by mentioning the Stoics, I'm entitled to do the same thing just so that you're not the only smug pedant here. Remember Dr. Jaqueline Painter's class we took, *From Kant to Wittgenstein?*"

"Sure do, the prof who never put me to sleep—besides, she looked like Venus."

"Remember her description of *verism?*" Without waiting for an answer, he said, "You did it up there, Pete. You did it. Though it's perverse of me, I'm proud of you!"

"What? I thought you called me your 'former friend.'"

He ignored Pete and continued, "You fulfilled its requirement of a rigid representation of truth and reality—without omitting its ugliness, its vulgarity. You did the right thing up there, Mr. Nathan. The right thing! And for us blacks as well—your support and understanding—every bit helps."

They drank their first bowl in silence. When they ordered their second and another round of drinks, Pete asked, "Aurelio, did I ever tell you about the time I was a cub reporter in Mississippi—my first job?"

"Don't know."

"About the lynching."

"What? You actually saw one? No, you never told me!"

"Yeah, in the twenties—small city—a crowd had gathered around a tree in the center of town—the town tree—majestic—venerated—planted by the first settlers. For years it had been their meeting place. They were whooping it up like they were having a carnival. When a man tightened the rope around the neck of a young black kid and let him go, the crowd roared and cheered. I vomited right on the backs of the people in front of me. At first they didn't realize what had happened, but as they turned around, I covered my mouth and got the hell out of there. Never apologized, either.

"After I regained my composure, I rushed to the office and started banging out my column. With tears falling over my typewriter keys, I started,

"'Name? Abraham Jefferson Adams.

"'Born in this town here of 'Nowhere Special' 'bout seventeen years ago—not sure 'xatley, cuz my family, we keep no close records of those things—too busy workin' to buy grits and stuff. Knew most near everybody in town, worked here and there, tryin' to learn diffr'nt thing—till I meet Cassey—white skin like Momma's nice cup—thin—so thin you could see almost clear through it—lots of pretty flowers we don't see 'round here 'tall. Mindin' my own bizness, workin' real hard diggin' up her flower bed, then sudden like, she leans over, kisses me on back of my neck. Next thing I know, arms and legs are broke and find myself with rope around my neck—sure of dying from fear even 'fore they drop me …'

"Something like that, Aurelio, and like we remember most everything that happened during a traumatic event—like it's branded on our memory with a hot iron—I remember it still. While I was pretending to be that hapless kid, writing it from his point of view, trying to bring some humanity into play for all those barbarians in town, I hadn't realized that the publisher was looking over my shoulder. He suddenly pulled the paper right out of my typewriter and I jumped. Eyes ablaze, he tore it up right in front of me."

"'Pete, two things,'" he said loudly enough for everyone to hear above the presses, "'One, our Founding Fathers called *darkies* three-fifths humans, so don't ever try to make them what they're not. Two, if I published that, I'd lose my advertisers and go out of business, and probably be run out of town by my townsfolk.

"'Oh, yeah—third thing—you're fired.'"

"Startled, I said, 'Your *townsfolk* murdered that poor kid—*boss-man—without a trial.* Do you see any irony between that boy's name and what your *fellow citizens* did to him?'

"So my unfinished story cost me my job. That night, I took out a map of the USA, measured the distance to the farthest point away from this town, and left the following morning. Haven't been in the south since—even for movie premiers—I let others go in my stead."

"Pete, heroes who struggle and lose are still heroes."

"I ain't no hero, my friend—not by a long shot."

"You are to me, my old college friend."

"You won't think so when I tell you the rest of my checkered autobiography—the dark side."

"Do you think I work for one of those movie-confession or ecclesiastical magazines? *My mind is made up about you. You don't have to disabuse me of my pre-conceived notions,"* he said, gently mocking their previous comments.

"Actually I need to get something off my chest, something that's been haunting me for awhile. Since you're handy, literally and figuratively, let me tell you, then I can be done with it."

"Ah, the attorney as pastor, priest, or rabbi. What are you anyway?"

"How do you think the committee would have reacted to that question?"

"I would have demanded a retraction before you answered!"

"Or, if I tried, given me a black-and-blue—like this morning."

"Stop whining. Get on with your tell-all."

"I'm stalling because I don't know where to start," he said looking at his empty bowl. Aurelio looked at him—silent. After a few moments he asked, "So?"

"You know what, on second thought, it's none of your cluttered mind's business. It's between Adam and me, and three's a crowd, a stupid cliché I'm using anyway. Forget it."

"I see a web of deceit and guile. Let's play that game of getting warmer and warmer. Am I hot or cold?"

"Forget it—you ain't close."

"Whatever it is, I'll appeal to Him personally—you won't go to Hell. You're going to miss the place, however, because all the interesting people are there."

"Stop smiling. I feel terrible about what I did—all my machinations."

"You're obviously talking about what you're not talking about, but if you are talking about your talk this morning, that talk had nothing to do with machinations. Follow?"

"Cluttered and convoluted."

"Okay, silent Sam, whatever those machinations were, that's what being human is about. We are known to scheme at times, but I have a direct line to you know where, so I'll intervene."

"Thanks, Gabriel, but I'm still worried about this morning. Problem is, I don't know how this is going to play out—with the committee—the studio bosses. Transparency is not always good. Being called before the committee is damaging enough without the revelations I made. The studio bosses are running so scared that they'll fire anyone with the slightest hint of heresy."

"Let's not anticipate. It'll blow over soon."

"Not before it cripples more people, many of whom are innocent, I'm afraid."

"Despite my years of practice of seeing deep into the rectum of people seeking their version of *justice,* I haven't lost my belief in that Latin expression, *Vincit Omnia Veritas.* Remember it, Pete?"

"What gives with you today? You're going to make me puke."

He nudged Pete and said, "That seems to come easily to you."

"I gotta' tell you. When I had that epiphany on the witness stand, I thought of that expression. Let me show off, too, *Truth conquers all things.*"

"Do you believe it, Pete?"

"You seem to."

"That's always my assumption, but sometimes the truth does more harm than good."

"Well, maybe we'll both go to Hell."

"With conversations fiery and nonstop."

"You stole that. 'Fess up."

"Stole what?"

"The stuff about the most interesting people being down there."

"True, but I can't remember from whom. Do you?"

"Samuel Johnson?"

"Sounds like something he might have said."

"So,Aurelius, my friend, how do you manage to maintain your joi de vivre as a proctologist?"

CHAPTER 29

I heard someone bounding up the stairs—two at a time. The door swung open and Josiah greeted me doing a soft-shoe dance while singing, "Sally, Sally, my salubrious Sally, your sassy swain s'finally swayed 'em!"

I jumped up and gave him a prolonged hug. "They don't know how lucky they are to have you. You're gonna' wow 'em. You must be so relieved—I'm so happy for you—for us. Wait 'till Velia hears about it."

I took out the only two crystal wine glasses we owned, opened up a bottle of cheap California champagne, one I had put in the refrigerator in anticipation of news worth celebrating, and with a hunk of Kasera cheese, what my father used to call, Kashkaval, and some crackers, we sat around the cocktail table while he told me about the job.

"It's a half hour comedy, more like a play than a film. About an elderly couple pretending a divorce so that they could get their four children to cancel their golf dates, tennis dates, bridge dates, dinner dates, concert dates, theater dates, shopping dates, their *'isn't-a-phone-call-every-now-and-then-sufficient?'* reluctance to visit—to get them all together, finally, for dinner.

"I know exactly how to shoot it and what I expect from the actors. It should be a lot of fun."

All I could do, as we finished the champagne and cheese, was look at him with loving eyes and a loving smile.

"The casting director wants me to review some of his choices, so I'm meeting him tomorrow at 7:30am in Burbank. You don't know how excited I am."

"I sure do, Jo."

He went to see our sleeping treasure, hovering over her for a few minutes. We did that often, watching her sleep, breathing in and out, and every now and then stealing a soft kiss on whatever part of her was exposed.

When he came out of her room, I told him the news. "Guess what? Got a call from a staff member of the committee's chairman."

"What the hell do they want now?" he said more loudly than he should have.

I put my finger to my lips and said in a loud whisper, "Shhh. They asked me to appear, voluntarily this time, to answer more questions. Strange, isn't it? Me and my salacious stories."

"Maybe they want to hear more details about the other pornographic movies you scripted."

"Oh, yeah."

The doorbell rang and Josiah got up. I heard him say, "Yes, I'm Josiah Castelnuovo-Tedesco." Some indistinct comments then the door closed. Josiah came in with a puzzled and frightened look.

"It's a sub-poena from HUAC. I'm being called back too," he said slumping on the couch.

"What the hell?" I said. "Why should you get a sub-poena and I a simple request?" He didn't respond but his chin sunk to his chest.

His face turned sallow from sanguine, so I went to his side and put my arm around him. "Tell me, is there something I should know, something you're not telling me—like before?"

With a wan smile, he said, "Not a thing, Sally, not a thing."

The way he said it made me worry even more.

"You sure?" I asked, snuggling even closer.

"Not to worry—not to worry. Let's see what other stupid questions they can ask," he said with a broader smile, hoping to prevent me from going all insomniac.

"I'm going to ask them for a two week postponement. I'll be damned if they're going to cost me this job!"

For the next ten days he was so focused on the details of each scene, so focused on drawing out the strength of each of the actors, on getting them to metamorphose from the screen and stage to the close-ups needed for the television screen, that we talked about the hearings just once—the night before.

This time I sat in the audience section without trying to hide my face, my wire recorder remained in my purse while my watch was pointed to wherever the action was.

"Let the record show that on March 1, 1951, the House un-American Activities Committee is convened at 10:00am. The Chair calls the next witness to the stand, Mr. Castelnuovo-Tedesco."

So as not to project diffidence, I suppose, I saw Josiah taking long forceful strides down the aisle. Velia is with my mother so I'll stay as long as this crap goes on. Why is my heart beating so fast?

Fewer than half the seats in the gallery are occupied. There are two television cameras, one radio station, one reporter with a camera—seems benign. When I looked at the chairman's face, it scared the life out of me because as he sat there all imperious like, he looked ready to raise his sword and smite Jo dead.

"Mr. Josiah—that's okay again, isn't it, to call you by your first name?" he asked innocently, belying the look on his face.

"Yes, of course." "You're not being represented by counsel again?"

"No, I can't afford one. Besides, I have nothing to hide, so fire away."

"In your previous testimony on February15th, you said that at City College you never hung out with left-wingers, that you suspected something Machiavellian about, to quote you, *'those noble communist aspirations for health and workers' benefits, improvement in our treatment of Negroes, etc.,'*" he said somewhat higher than his normal speech, "and that you never entertained becoming a communist, so … " pausing as he leaned forward on his elbows, staring at him fiercely, "I'm going to ask you a simple question. While you were a student at CCNY—that is before you were expelled … " letting that sink in while he took his time looking at the reporters, then at the audience, "did you ever travel abroad? Let's say, for example—to Moscow?"

I saw Josiah's head slump. My heart sank. I felt like he was in a chess game, and that within these first few moves, the chairman was about to steal his queen.

"Mr. Josiah, I asked you a simple question that needs no reflection. Your answer should be a simple yes or no."

Jo put his hands on his cheeks and leaned forward on both elbows.

Oh, my God—this is going to hurt.

"Mr. Josiah? Shall I have the question printed out for you," the chairman persisted, "or did you hear me the first time?"

Josiah finally raised his head, and resigned to the inevitable, leaned back on his chair, put his hands behind his neck and looked like he was at the beach on a reclining chair facing the sun, and said, "Well, Mr. Chairman, I thought I had double-locked that door, but it seems you found the key. For the second time in my life I understand what it must feel like for an animal to be skewered before being barbecued. Only when that happens, the animal is dead first. But I'm still very much alive."

"Reserve your similes, if you will, for *your own* time," he pounced. "For *our* time together, just give us the facts without embellishment."

Damn! Where is this going?

"The answer is, yes."

I gasped aloud as my hand rushed to cover my mouth. That lying son-of-a-bitch! That's twice. How can I ever trust him again?

The audience gasped aloud as well, cameras swiveled, flashbulbs popped, and as the radio boom was swirling around it knocked the reporter's camera to the ground leading to a lot of name calling. Then there was total silence, all eyes riveted on Josiah while I was sick to my stomach, trying to figure out why his face had suddenly hardened—why he looked tough enough to enter the ring.

"Let's not play the hunted and hunter. You're under oath and it will help you enormously if you told us the truth about everything—without prompting—without sparring. Now start from the beginning without any of your self-serving omissions, and we'll try to reconcile your testimony with our records."

Josiah looked disgusted. "I guess I could ask you for a recess so I can hire an attorney to defend my rights, but then we'd really be in the jungle, wouldn't we? And I'd go broke in the process."

With continued strength in his voice and demeanor, he continued, "So I'm going to take a chance on the decency of this committee and in what I believe is our American sense of fairness," slowly looking at each of the committee members and at the reporters, as though challenging them to rise to a higher standard, "and tell you exactly what happened, and the rationale behind what I did." With chin thrust forward, he asked, "You're okay with that, right, Mr. Chairman?"

With the slightest smile, the chairman said, "Mr. Josiah, one of our nation's mottos is: 'In God We Trust.' I propose an additional one: 'In Truth We Trust.' Are *you* okay with that?"

"As they say in Hollywood, sir, *we're on the same page*."

It didn't seem to lower the charge in the air, but it added an air of civility. I hope.

"So proceed, please."

"In 1933, my first year at CCNY, Hitler had been elected Chancellor and that alarmed many of the academics at school which, of course, ignited passions amongst the poly-sci majors like me. We were frightened, especially the Jews on campus, but the only people protesting were the communists, so I was attracted to them. I went to meetings but I couldn't afford dues. I barely had enough money to buy essentials, and at that time I was still stuffing cardboard in my shoes.

"Towards the end of May or early June of my first year, as the semester was drawing to a close, I received a letter from the Soviet Consul General in New York stating that some of their friends had spoken highly of me, and went on to ask if I were the same person whose letter-to-the-editor had appeared recently in the NY Times, and coincidentally, the one who had requested a copy of the Communist Manifesto eight or nine years earlier, and if so, to visit them. With a name like mine no one could mistake me for anyone else. I was impressed by the attention—eager to learn why they wanted to speak to me, so I went.

"I had never been outside The Bronx or Manhattan, not even to Queens or Brooklyn, so when they offered me free transportation and lodging to attend a Writers' Congress that summer in Moscow, I jumped at the chance."

"A writers' congress? Why you?" the chairman asked.

"I had written a couple of essays for the campus paper, one of which mentioned my fear about Hitler, drawing a parallel between his threat and that of the Spanish Inquisition which resulted in the murder of Jews and the expulsion of my ancestors. That history was very much alive in our family and remains a part of me. Jews always look forward, of course, but we constantly remind ourselves of our susceptibility and vulnerability, the pogroms, wanton killings, forced ghettoization, forced baptisms, quota systems, and all the other horrors.

"The past, for us Jews, is always present!

"Another essay I wrote was about the poverty I saw during the Great Depression, the abuse of Negroes, the lack of public social services, why it was imperative to revisit our social structures, and the importance of paying close attention to the proposals of FDR's new Secretary of Labor, Frances Perkins. When I re-read those essays years later, I was embarrassed at how pompous and pedantic they were, but elementally they were true.

"The letter that got published in the NY times was about the latter. The Soviet Consul General must have thought I was a writer—a big mouth—a know-it-all—unafraid to voice strong opinions, but also young enough to be persuaded that communism, not FDR and Perkins, was the way to go."

"So you went to the Writers' Congress in Moscow?"

"Yes. Of course you know that."

"Don't assume anything. Just give us the details."

I can't believe what I just heard. That lying shit!! If Velia were in my womb, I'd be giving birth right now. I was breathing in gulps. He went to Moscow? Why the hell didn't he tell me that? What other secrets is he harboring?

Josiah took a deep breath and said, "I hope you have reserved a lot of time, gentlemen, because it's a long story about idealism and disillusion."

"And deception, Mr. Josiah," he sneered, "don't forget *deception*!"

"There was no intention to deceive, sir, and I didn't perjure myself. You never asked me whether I had traveled abroad."

"No, but we did ask you about your affiliations and you denied having gravitated towards the communists, and you gave us that spurious rationalization garbage."

"Mr. Chairman, it was not spurious. Let me explain—there was no sharp division on campus between the communists and the liberals. We seemed to want the same things," and with a sweeping gesture and an angry voice matching the chairman's, he said, "this is what's wrong with these hearings—there's no context. We have to understand the zeitgeist of the thirties! We were going through a terrible depression with twenty five percent of our work force unemployed, yet we were told that in the Soviet Union there was full employment, workers enjoying full benefits from the state, sick pay, reasonable hours, safe working conditions, and equal rights for minorities. God, you must have heard that a thousand times already! For some of us in college who were so inclined, especially the poly-sci majors, we checked that crap out and found it to be a fiction, *real garbage*. Nonetheless, out of desperation, others fell for it, thinking it was time to question the viability of our economic system. So you've got to forgive us, okay?"

"Preaching should be done by someone better qualified, Mr. Josiah, not a hypocrite like you who deceives by omission," came the chairman's unsympathetic response.

"You realize, Mr. Chairman, my wife is in the audience and knows nothing about this," he said turning around to look at me. "I'm surprised she hasn't thrown up, or worse, fainted. Don't be surprised to hear that after this hearing, she files divorce proceedings."

"Please keep your personal problems, personal. Get on with the details, but you're confusing everyone. You said that you discovered that that '*workers' paradise*' was a fiction, yet you jumped at the chance to go to Moscow. You are contradicting yourself in a big way, sir!"

"You were once seventeen, sir, but I don't know whether you were ever poor or had traveled far from your birthplace. I was all three, seventeen, poor, and un-traveled. And, it was a FREE TRIP. And, the next semester, I could write a smashing paper contrasting academic reports with personal experience. And, it was an unprecedented ADVENTURE for me! You bet I jumped at the chance!"

"Okay, okay, lower your voice and continue with your story which I hope is not going to take us into breakfast."

Josiah said, "Okay, I'll telegraph the rest to you," and seeing the astonished look on the chairman's face, gavel poised ready to come crashing down, he quickly added, "Please don't get upset. I don't mean that literally."

"You just saved yourself a reprimand, sir."

"Sorry. That was a figure of speech. What I meant by *'telegraph'* was a truncated version. When we got to Moscow, we were put up in a cockroach-infested hostel, only cold water coming out of the tap, an outhouse, miserable food, all of which baffled me since they wanted to impress us with their glorious achievements, but I rationalized it by thinking that we were just lowly students unaccustomed to anything better. We were also told to speak to no one on the streets, like I would have understood Russian anyway. And that at the meetings there would be a translator, but that we were asked not to speak, just to listen and learn. I was thrilled at the experience so had no difficulty following orders.

"Was there any attempt at indoctrination?" asked one of the congressmen.

"You bet! Every day before lunch and dinner, we had to attend a meeting in a cold, windowless room that made us feel like we were in solitary. The leader must have been American because in perfect English he harangued us with dogma and conformity, of the need, like the early Christians, to spread the word when we got home about the Soviet utopia, about this great experiment that will bring heaven down to earth. You know, The Second Coming!

"They showed us film after film of thriving collective farms, dozens of tractors, and brightly dressed farmers singing with joy at their abundant harvests. Films of factories with modern equipment producing farm equipment, consumer goods, clothing, furniture, appliances—films of bustling cities filled with well-clothed pedestrians, smiling and chatting in restaurants brimming with food, lots of automobiles—films of building projects with huge cranes above them. It was a beautiful and impressive sight.

"Our leader told us, *'When you return to your bankrupt society, you must speak to everyone about the purity and benevolence of communism, that that it is the only way to salvation.'* They must have thought we would resonate with Christian themes, and they continued with, '*...the guiding policy is each according to his means and each according to his needs—-that everyone is responsible because everything belongs to the state which, in our system, belongs to all the people, and people are sovereign.*'

"We were influenced, I must admit, by his convincing rhetoric, yet intimidated by his authoritarian delivery. We were beholden to the Soviets for this extraordinary opportunity, and several times when we mentioned to him, rather diffidently, that we saw little evidence around us of what was in the films, his response, which sounded rehearsed, was that Rome was not built in a day, that all those things we saw were happening in other parts of the Soviet Union, and that most parts of Moscow were undergoing these great changes, but we had to be patient because Rome, blah, blah, blah ...

"With the dry prose of Marx and Hegel and Lenin, by the time we left those sessions our eyes were glazed, our bodies felt like someone had struck the funny bone of our entire being.

"At the Writers' Congress, we were told, the speakers were famous people, most of whom I had never heard of at the time, but whose work I later read. The novelist, Isaac Babel, told us about how relieved he was at the new freedom of expression, about how during the previous four years he and other writers were forced to write about the success of the five-year plans. One theme they had to abide by was, *'All novels must make workers feel happier under the five-year plan.'* If the book suggested it was only 99% true, he said, there was a good chance it would not get published. If it were only 50% true, there was a good chance the writer would never be seen again, he said as his eyes quickly scanned the auditorium.

"Then Boris Pasternak spoke, then Bukharin and Maxim Gorky, about how optimistic they were about the new leniency and that finally they were going to be able to express themselves freely. Their frightening disclosures and the word, *finally,* registered with me. The implication, of course, was that heretofore, they had nothing of the sort!

"Then someone got on the podium, and to my surprise, began speaking in English. He identified himself as a junior at Dartmouth."

"Do you remember his name?"

"Yes. Budd Schulberg."

"Did you ever talk to him?"

"Not really. Even though we were all students, for some reason the students from each campus were discouraged from intermingling with students from other schools, so the three of us from CCNY stayed pretty much to ourselves. During the sessions we were told, '*we were there to listen,*' and with few exceptions, we were not to engage with anyone. At the end of one long day, however, I bumped into Mr. Schulberg in the restroom so I introduced myself, told him I was anxious to talk to him, but he was rushing off somewhere, didn't have time to talk. I'm disappointed because I later became an avid fan."

Someone from the panel was going to interrupt, but Josiah was on a role and barreled on. I was riveted but nauseous, trying to contain my fury. That lying bastard leaving out a whole part of his life—a goddamn important part. I had told him everything about my life and he told me everything about his, supposedly, but left out all this stuff. If there's no trust in a marriage, there ain't nothing! It's the *sine qua non* of a life together. That prick!

"You know the rest," he said. "By 1938 every one of those writers had either been shot or silenced. Some committed suicide—presumably. Others disappeared. Maxim Gorky was poisoned in 1936. Bukharin, editor-in-chief of Izvestia, one of the Soviet-controlled newspapers, was dismissed and arrested in 1937 and shot in 1938. Boris Pasternak saw what happened to his contemporaries, stopped writing original work, and focused on translations only," Jo continued, each word blackened by gloom and disgust.

"Those reports drifted to the USA much later, '*unsubstantiated rumors,*' the apologists argued. When I was there it was a heady time, and I must tell you that hearing all those intellectuals with their air of hopefulness, and the indoctrination lectures were convincing, yet confusing. It sounded like *The Lady doth protest too much.*

"Despite the spirit at the Congress, there was a grayness—a pall over the attendees. One evening we slipped away from the restrictions of the hostel and found a dispirited look on people walking the streets—a fearful look—wary. It seemed a joyless society.

'We went to a coffee shop that refused to take our rubles, insisting instead on dollars. I had a few American coins they wouldn't accept, but one of my fellow students from CCNY, a Russian major, had some paper dollars they gladly accepted. When she asked for a dish of what looked like a sweet role, with three forks, they looked at her, then at us, like we were spies. We returned the look as though they were spies. It was creepy,"

"That was hardly a truncated version, Mr. Josiah. Give us the names of those in your group, like the Russian major, and others who came from other universities," he asked, looking for a mother load.

"The Russian major was Berty O'Riley, pretty and perky—going into her senior year, majoring in Russian studies. Originally she was enthusiastic about our trip and told us she wanted to confirm or deny the reports from our library and teachers. Speaking Russian fairly well, she managed to slip by some of the restrictions and got a little personal time with the speakers and the attendees. At first, she refused to give us her impressions, but at the close of the Congress … "

"Sir? The Congress went on for how long?"

"Five days. When it ended on Friday, we expected a farewell dinner with all the participants, but that didn't happen, so the three of us dined alone at the hostel. Dining was a misnomer. It was salami, fatty and moldy, sauerkraut, a pickled something, but a great dark bread with something to spread on it, something with a taste we couldn't pinpoint. It was then that Berty said that she thought the writers were feigning enthusiasm about the future—that their optimism was more like wishful thinking—that they were gathered together to try to bolster their spirits—that it was all pretense. It was disappointing to realize that their exalted dreams were illusory.

"Nonetheless, when we returned to CCNY and I wrote my reports for class, I tried to act in a scholarly, disinterested way so I balanced my personal experience with the hopefulness and assurances from the speakers that improvements would be coming. I didn't have the certainty Berty did, so I rationalized their difficulties as growing pains of an experimental society."

"What happened to Berty?"

"She's a professor at a college in the mid-west, and, like Ayn Rand, a vocal anti-Communist."

"And your other friend?"

"Idealist, great spirit—killed by a car—outside CCNY."

"So, Mr. Josiah, you've had an interesting student life, including how you exited CCNY. You were expelled the following year, right?"

"Yes, sir. It's public."

"Upon your return from Moscow, did you join the Communist Party—at least for a brief period?"

"After what I just said, do you have to ask that question?"

"Well, your 'balancing act' implied doubts."

"No, sir, but I tried keeping an open mind."

"After what you saw and heard, why wasn't your mind closed?"

"Mr. Congressman, weren't you taught in college to always keep an open mind?"

"Do you have an open mind about Fascism?"

"No, I do not."

"Why not?"

"I know about Fascism, there's nothing to consider."

"So there's something to "consider' about communism?"

"You're making me feel young and stupid again. I was confused."

"By doubts and ambivalence?"

"Confusion would be more like it. Before I left for Moscow, they seemed to want the same things as I did, so I didn't see them as a threat. I didn't have the certitude then that I have now, so when I returned, I thought it would be better to try Mrs. Perkins's way, improve things within our system rather than to try something radically different, something fishy, spurious.

"And when I began working I discovered I liked owning things—things that money can buy, like my own house. I like entrepreneurship—things that spur personal initiative to bring out the best in us. I like capitalism, warts and all. Also, I'm a hard worker. I shouldn't get paid the same amount as someone who isn't—or isn't as smart. Nor for that matter, should I be paid the same as someone who's smarter than I."

The look on the chairman changed from skepticism to moderate doubt. He asked, "So tell us about Spain."

Spain? There's more? When I heard that I doubled over and went into false labor. I started to dry-heave. Why, I married a secret operative, a spy, a serial liar, a dishonest son-of-a-bitch husband! How can I ever trust him again? And that bastard spent a lot of time *under my bedcovers*! He betrayed me! I'll never speak to that prick again! Now I know why the word, 'prick' became a pejorative. I've been *raped*!

He took several deep breaths, slow and hard. He glanced at me and saw daggers of death in my eyes.

"Okay, sir, briefly," Jo began, speaking fast, "I want to get this repressed tumor out of my life—to once again breathe without dread. I was so concerned with the rising tide of aggression under Hitler and Fascism, I decided once again to take advantage of the Communist Party's largesse and went to Spain. Mind you, not as a Communist Party member, but as an anti-Fascist warrior!" he said leaving no room for doubt.

"You say that, Mr. Josiah," the chairman said in a prickly tone, "but your behavior speaks a different story,"

"Well, sir, I can't seem to change your mind about my metamorphosis and ... "

"And cadging," the chairman quickly interjected.

"Mr. Chairman, you're right about that. I never had any intention of reimbursing them for either trip. They were freebies and I took full advantage of them."

"*Them*,'" came the response dripping with contempt, "being both the trips and the communists, right?"

Josiah didn't respond. When I saw his head drop and how he slumped in his chair, I knew he was a defeated man.

I felt nothing for him except, like the chairman, contempt. Screw him! When he comes home he'll find his clothes on the street.

"Let me go on, sir, and show you how really contemptible I am."

The audience murmured, flash bulbs popped and paused, waiting for another surprise.

"I knew that American socialists under Eugene Debs had formed, 'The Debs Column for Spain,' and I wanted to join his forces ... "

"And desert the people who brought you over in the first place?" one of the congressman asked.

With those questions, I wondered whose side these congressmen were on.

"You got it!" was Jo's quick response. "With those persistent *rumors* and my personal experience, any sympathetic understanding I had for the communists was rapidly dwindling.

"The communists gave me a rifle and some cursory training in preparation for joining the American Lincoln Brigade down south. On the way, we entered Guernica the very day of that hideous bombing. I had never seen or imagined anything like that. Nor have I ever read anything that accurately described the kind of mayhem I witnessed." He shivered when he said, "Seeing it first hand was a life altering experience.

"Despite my efforts to repress what I observed, sometimes in the quiet of the night I wake up and see flashes of the mayhem. Sometimes I shiver uncontrollably and go to the bathroom to heave. But the visions of that day never end up in the toilet—they just hover, never far—waiting to pounce at an unexpected time. It's a newsreel that never seems to end.

"The movies lie, gentlemen. When people are shot in the movies, you never see brains splatter everywhere, or guts spilling out—or an arm blown off—or blood gushing from a burst heart—or the look of horror on a victim who realizes that at that moment his life has come to an end. You just hear 'bang-bang' and see someone drop. In real life, it's not like that at all."

No one interrupted this time. He swallowed hard, trying to compose himself, and then revealed, to my astonishment, other shocking events. "I heard there was an American journalist in Guernica and I made an effort to meet him, but with all the chaos, it was futile."

"Do you remember the journalist's name?"

The chairman said, "Don't waiver now, Mr. Josiah, you are still under oath.

Everyone heard his sigh, "Yes. Peter Nathan."

Ohhhhh. My God! What the fuck is happening? I began shivering uncontrollably.

I never met him, but as we left that devastated city, my commander said he had heard that the journalist was searching for the

Lincoln Brigade, to join them. Since I was going to slip away to find the Debs group, I figured I'd never hook up with him. But then something devastating happened.

"Before I could slip away, my group met up with an anti-Fascist Spanish platoon, Marxist but anti-Stalinist. My commander, a communist and Stalinist, got into a loud squabble with their commander. I didn't speak Spanish well enough to understand colloquial Spanish spoken rapidly, so I didn't understand what was going on, except that it was explosive. No matter how bad it was, I couldn't have anticipated fighting *against* them, only *with* them. After all, we were all anti-Fascists. I saw my commander whisper something in his ear motioning him to walk to a more secluded spot. I had been riveted to the argument so my commander beckoned me. I couldn't imagine why. Suddenly, *my* commander ordered me to shoot *their* commander. I was stunned! I couldn't believe what he had asked."

Josiah looked shocked, like he was reenacting the scene. "I balked and said '*no*.' He removed his pistol and pointed it at my head. I hesitated for a moment, not knowing what to do. He took a step closer, cocked his pistol and shouted, 'Shoot him or I will shoot you!' I was terrified!

"Without thinking, I turned my rifle on my commander and fired. I don't know how I beat him in shooting first. Maybe he had no intention of pulling the trigger. Maybe he never thought that that would be my reaction. Who knows?" He kept breathing hard. "Why I didn't shoot the other guy, I have no idea, nor have I ever been able to figure that out," he said, shaking his head in disbelief from side to side.

"I've never killed anyone before. *My God, oh my God,"* he said with head bowed, tears overflowing, choking out, "You know what it's like? Point-blank that way? To this day, I can see his eyes roll back, blood gushing out of his mouth like a geyser, spurting all over my face—his skull exploding in pieces spilling brains all over me." He sobbed out, "*Oh, my God,* I had never killed anyone before—you understand?? I love life! But that was nightmare stuff—and continues to be so. He let his head bang on the desk, and said something unintelligible, choking out the words, asthmatically, in loud sucking sounds.

Without thinking, I rushed over and pulled him out of his chair, hugged him tightly, sobbing myself. "Josiah, you'll be okay. You are okay.

Don't cry. You're home, you're with someone who loves you, with a baby who loves you. We'll take care of you, always, don't worry—you're with family," I said choking out the words.

Whether flashbulbs popped or not, we couldn't tell—whether cameras whirred, we couldn't tell—whether microphones whistled, we couldn't tell—whether the gavel came crashing down, we couldn't tell—whether the chairman shouted, we couldn't tell. It was the two of us only—alone together—transported into a transmundane sphere—metamorphosing into the soaring sounds of a celestial symphony—into Barber's Adagio for Strings, Debussy's Claire de Lune—Mahler's Eighth—Holst's Jupiter—Bach's Toccata in Fugue, Beethoven's Ode to Joy. Into a shimmering aurora borealis—-into the dazzling diamonds of the Milky Way—into a coruscating Haley's comet, tail ablaze—into an exploding super-nova—into the brilliant birth of a new galaxy.

It was the end of Time. It was the beginning of Time.

Esse quam videri.

At that moment, I became Josiah.

At that moment, I understood everything.

When we arose out of our transcendence, we could hear the chairman quietly ask, "Please, folks, be seated."

I sat down in the chair alongside Josiah, holding his hand tightly with one hand, and with my other hand caressing it with loving warmth, all the while I kept my eyes on his troubled face, understanding his anguish of living through this nightmare silently, and now aloud, for all the world to hear.

"Mr. Josiah, we now know who you are. Thank you. We ask your patience in answering two minor questions. You had just shot your commander. How did the men in the other group react—and the men in your group?"

I gave him a tissue to dry his face, he drank some water, found his place again, and said, "As for the other group, since our commander had taken their commander away for what seemed a private conversation, none of their group was around, and isolated shots were often heard. As for our group, we were a-rag-a-tag gaggle, sir. They were as astonished and bewildered as I was. I looked at them briefly and ran away fast. It wasn't until I was over a ridge that I realized any one of them could have shot me in the back."

"Final question, Josiah. Did you ever meet up with the Debs Brigade, or for that matter, The Lincoln Brigade?"

"Mr. Chairman, at that moment, I was through—emotionally and physically. When an anti-Fascist Stalinist wants to kill an anti-Fascist non-Stalinist, I realized this was not a war I wanted to die in. I got the hell out by working my way back to the Pyrenees. We had come that way in the first place because the State Department prohibited Americans from entering Spain through normal channels. It's the way I came and the way I escaped.

"From the moment I got back to the United States, gentlemen, I never took for granted where I belonged—in this blessed country of ours." He then turned to me and, with chin quivering, said, "Or my place besides my wife."

"Thank you, Mr. Castelnuovo-Tedesco. You are excused."

CHAPTER 30

We never spoke of it again.

The next day, I took him and Velia to a house in Brentwood Park, between San Vicente and Sunset Boulevards, to breathe in the fragrance from the blossoms of the eighteen pittosporum trees the family had lovingly planted many years ago. Earlier, on four or five occasions, I brought Velia here by myself to introduce her to this, my favorite fragrance, lingering under the branches that embraced us with its generous offerings, hoping that it would be indelibly imprinted on her olfactory nerves, that it would remind her someday of the insouciance of her childhood—that it would give her the heightened sensory appreciation for those things in life that often go unnoticed.

Josiah had been too busy looking for work, so this was the first time for him. He inhaled deeply, breathing in that sensuous, intoxicating fragrance. We stayed for as long as we could before the owners could get suspicious, and call the police to arrest the loiterers outside their home.

"This sub-committee is in session on March 3, 1951. Will the next witness come forward and take your place in the witness box?" Chairman Heddbone said.

"For the record, please identify yourself."

"Sally Apple."

"Let the record show that you were *not* subpoenaed to appear before this committee, that you were asked to appear not before the entire committee, but before a sub-committee, a more intimate one, one to which you came voluntarily to help us understand more fully the dynamics of the movie industry and the influence others have on screenwriters."

With mock indignation, I asked, "How intimate?"

"Miss Apple, no quips please."

Jerk! That was in poor taste.

"I'm not certain I can help, gentlemen. I played in the little leagues, but I'm no longer employed by Twentieth Century Fox. I did, however, spend fifteen years there, so I'll tell you what I think, but you'll get a more accurate, more over-arching point of view by questioning the major players."

"We've had a spotty record on that account from both friendly and hostile witnesses, but a perceptive minor player is able sometimes to give a viewpoint unencumbered by the larger issues. That's why you're here, Miss Apple, and try, if you will, to keep your scatological," he paused, "your colorful words in check,"

"I'll be the model of decorum, Mr. Chairman."

Without a subpoena, how relaxed I am.

"I'll start off by asking you a fundamental question. In 1947, when this committee was chaired by someone else, Jack Warner of Warner Bros. said, that when he made the film, *Mission to Moscow,* an adaptation of a book written by Mr. Joseph E. Davies, our Ambassador to the Soviet Union from 1936-1938, a book glorifying Stalin and the Soviet Union, their abundance of food and machinery, rationalizing the purges that had killed thousands of their citizens, rationalizing the Hitler/Stalin pact, Mr. Warner said that he didn't know how a film like that could influence anyone.

"And when Louis B. Mayer of MGM was asked about, *Song of Russia,* he said that it was little more than a pleasant musical romance about a boy and a girl, that except for the music of Tchaikovsky, it could have taken place in Switzerland.

"Do you believe that films in general, and these specifically, have little or no influence on audiences?"

Without missing a beat, I responded, "My husband accuses me of shooting from the hip without regard to consequences, so, I'm gonna' shoot from the hip, but I can predict the consequences this time. This shot will boomerang, and I'll never again be able to work for any studio—ever.

"I'm not under oath, but it makes no difference." I slowly scanned the panel, and continued. "I've seen those films and both of their statements are disingenuous. They knew better, but were trying to persuade you of their innocence by assuming a sanctimonious posture. In reality, they were saving their as—their necks. Frightened as they were, the studio heads had instituted the famous *'blacklist'* of communists, fellow travelers and *innocent liberal non-communists.*

"To those two films, I want to add another, *North Star,* circa 1943, written by Lillian Hellman with a score, to add greater gravitas to the film, by Aaron Copeland. Let me give you some context. Though she herself was not a communist—presumably—her lover, Dashiell Hammett was. The *de facto rulers of the American Communist Party were the Soviets,* and *they dictated policy.* After Hitler assumed power, the communists urged action against Germany. To Hellman's credit, she was one of 38 authors petitioning Roosevelt to boycott German goods.

"When Hitler and Stalin signed their pact on August 24, 1939, Stalin told the American communists *to stop agitating against Hitler.* She joined the *Keep America Out Of War Committee,* and all further actions by communists against Hitler stopped.

"As to that film, *North Star,* her screenplay takes place on a thriving collective farm with Ukrainian peasants dancing happily with abundant food, new machinery. A workers' paradise. Workers' paradise, indeed! No indication that upwards of four million people starved to death during Stalin's forced collectivization program. What we saw, however, was an alternative economic system that, in light of our recent experience in the Great Depression, was superior to our own. *Did that have an effect, you ask?*

"As the film progresses, those happy peasants are murdered by Nazis. Remember, it's 1943—we were allies against a barbaric enemy, and our administration was mobilizing support for aid to the Soviets. The film urges us to join forces with this enlightened nation to subdue the Nazis—*so that they can then return to their enviable situation, and we can return to our own economic difficulties.*

"Of course we had to help them, but did it not suggest that we did not have the better form of government? *Did that have an effect on us?"* I asked scanning the congressman with raised eyebrows.

"Before the war, Miss Hellman signed on to petitions like one called, *An Open Letter to American Liberals* applauding the verdicts of the Soviet show trials in which *all the old leaders* of the communist revolution confessed to their crimes of undermining the Soviet Government. Imagine," I said, feigning innocence, "to a person, they all confessed. By the time the third trial of theirs finished, almost every important Bolshevik from the Revolution had been executed! And several thousand Red Army officers had been shot. You know all of that, of course.

"Like Hellman, Ambassador Joseph Davies wrote that he too believed they were guilty, that they all deserved to die.

"When John Dewey was asked to form a committee seeking to establish the truth, Miss Hellman urged people *not* to cooperate with him.

"And when the Soviets instructed the American Communist Party to oppose granting asylum to Trotsky, she too opposed it. She did, however, support Roosevelt when he ran a fourth time.

"What does this tell us about her?"

Congresswoman Marika interrupted, "You seem to be on an unstoppable roll, Miss Apple. It's hard to interrupt you so I waited until you took a breath. Several questions. The first, do you know if Hellman supported the Abraham Lincoln Brigade?"

"In 1938, your records must show that she was one of the speakers at a rally supporting them—urging them on—eloquently."

"We wondered whether you knew that," she said, "and that leads me to my second question, an epistemological one. How do you know what you know?" she asked eyeing me with suspicion.

"Fair question. You don't know me, but candor is one of my characteristics, often a relationship-destroying one—as you can now tell by how I'm destroying my future as a screenwriter. Another thing you don't know about me is that my fiction is saved for my profession—that it *never* appears in my private life. I *never* make things up to suit a discussion.

"So how do I know what I know? Before I was sent to France on an aborted mission to write a screenplay for Fox, I was itching to do an original piece of work to elevate myself above my usual adaptations of second-rate novels. I have a tendency to immerse myself in projects as though writing a dissertation. I focused on writing something nuanced about the love affair some of our loyal and decent Americans had had with communism, to try understanding the 'whys' of that romance, the underpinnings of how they came to believe that replacing our form of government with a Soviet-style one was better than trying to improve our own from within, ala Frances Perkins, and how some, but not all, became spies for the Soviets, people like Harry Dexter White and a bunch of others, and of course, Alger Hiss who just last year was convicted for perjury.

"Commonalities existed between non-communists and communists in their opposition to segregation, improvement of workers' rights, tenant rights, the whole basket of human rights and social ills. You didn't have to become a communist to work towards achieving those goals. Yet despite the revelations about the totalitarian abuse of their citizens by the Soviets, some became and remained communists, continuing to be apologists for them. I wanted to understand how many became disillusioned, why they informed on their colleagues, their rationale. That's not a brief answer, is it?" I asked with a smile. Before she answered, I continued, "You noticed also my propensity for run-on-sentences."

She smiled and said, "Thanks for resting your vocal chords. So your testimony is from research for a movie?"

"Yes. Problem is, Hollywood is now frightened by the committees' accusations, innuendos, associative guilt—indeed their *inquisition.* We're intimidated—and though many are innocent, they're being blacklisted by virtue of their very presence before you. Your committee and Senator Joe McCarthy are turning this era into an American version of *La Helle Epoque!"*

The chairman bellowed, "I beg your pardon!!" and banged his gavel. "I speak for all the members of this committee. This is *NOT* an inquisition! Nor are we trying to create *Hell* for people! It's a fact-finding committee to determine the extent of communist influence in films *intended* to influence public opinion. You have said as much! When you tell us more about the film, *Song of Russia,* I believe you will confirm what many on this committee already know. We'll try not interrupting."

"Before I go on, let me tell you that many of the current films are about the evils of totalitarianism persisting in the Soviet Union and throughout the world. The possibility of writing such a screenplay is on a distant horizon, somewhere between nursing my baby and writing a novel. And since my daughter needs her next breast-feeding soon, I will *briefly* give you my take on that film and others.

"*Mission to Moscow* and *Song of Russia* were produced during our alliance with the Soviets. From a distance, they seem propagandistic. At that time, however, our government sought ways to establish good will towards them, so the studios had their cooperation and support in making such films. We mustn't dismiss that factor in evaluating *effects*. Were many Americans becoming more sympathetic to the Soviets during the war? Of course! *Mission to Moscow*, with Ambassador Davies' imprimatur, was the kind of film expected to help cement good will between us. Was it a true reflection of conditions there? Davies had been brain washed, gentlemen. Leaving his skepticism behind, he bought into the Soviet rationale for everything they did, saw little that displeased him. His book tried to persuade Americans that his view was correct, that anything to the contrary was pernicious rumor.

"*Song of Russia,* was written by two communists, Paul Jarrico and Richard Collins. Interestingly, one of the advisors on the film, Anna Louise Strong, had lived in the USSR for many years, and was, in the 1940s, the chief propagandist in our country for the Soviet Union. Imagine what counsel she gave.

"To summarize, we find the protagonist, Robert Taylor, a conductor on tour in the Soviet Union, sees peasants wearing beautiful blouses and shoes working on their bountiful collective farms, new machinery for harvesting and tilling the soil, each family with its own radio, full larder, full stomachs—everyone smiling. Then those same peasants visit Moscow, which, to those who knew, was forbidden without special permission, eating at five-star restaurants with abundant food. It was a most egregious misrepresentation of reality. Pure Soviet-influenced propaganda by American writers who had an agenda and that was to have us reconsider our allegiance to our American system!

"During the HUAC meetings in 1947, your predecessors heard testimony from Ayn Rand, the Russian émigré philosopher/novelist/essayist, testifying about the falsehoods in the film—the provocative opening scene showing Robert Taylor conducting his symphony orchestra playing our *national anthem that gradually dissolves into the Soviet national anthem*. What conclusions would you draw from that outrageous scene?" I went silent, letting that float for awhile.

"We had good reason to justify our commitment to help them against the Nazis, but in the process, we didn't have to deceive Americans. True, Louis B. Meyer tried, he said, *to cut propaganda out*, but the end result was pure deception, so you can imagine what the original screenplay must have been like. And when he said that crap about *except for the music of Tchaikovsky, 'Song of Russia,' could have been about Switzerland*, he was right. It was more like Switzerland than Russia. So why the hell didn't he name it, *Song of Switzerland?*" I shouted, slapping my hand on the desk. I let that percolate for a few moments as well.

"I assure you that the Swiss would not have been unfamiliar with Tchaikovsky's music, listening with full stomachs, enjoying democracy—untouched by repression."

I was unstoppable.

"Those studio heads seduced your committee with their testimony, but it was dishonest. As for Jack Warner and Louis B. Meyer's spurious comments about the effects of films on audiences, the answer seems obvious.

"Unless you have move questions, I rest my case. May I go now?"

"I know you want to go home," the chairman said, "but, your indulgence for another moment, please. Can you give an example of a film made by Fox intended to influence the American public?"

"I need to go, sir, but the most important one that comes to mind is *Gentlemen's Agreement*, a film adapted from Laura Z. Hobson's book about pervasive anti-Semitism in the USA, hidden and overt. If art serves any purpose, besides pure entertainment of course, it should challenge pre-conceived notions—evoke questions about past behavior that should be reconsidered and changed. It does that by personalizing conflict, thrusting the audience into the protagonist's life, so that they views events as though happening to them. And that film did it to me, and I hope to you. In some overt and subliminal way, that film may have brought some people to realize that Jews were discriminated against, that as humans, Jews had a right to be treated as Jesus recommended in his Golden Rule. And not because he was Jewish."

The gasps came from panel members and the audience. When the murmurs subsided, the chairman said, "I can't believe that much of what I saw in the film exists in these United States."

"Then, Mr. Chairman, as an experiment, pretend you're Jewish. Assume the name Cohen, go to your country club, a good hotel, apply for a job at a major corporation—see for yourself how far you get."

"Miss Apple, you may go now," he sneered. "Thank you for your insights," he said as though he didn't mean it. I got up, nodded, walked to the door, but as I reached it, I paused for a moment, said, "Mr. Chairman," and returned to my chair.

"One other thing. It bothers me when someone says one thing but actions show the opposite. Should Jack Warner testify again, ask him why he said that films have little influence, when during the thirties his studio produced films of social realism, gritty dramatizations of labor unrest like the 1935 film, *Black Fury;* or *I am a Fugitive from a Chain Gang,* a pessimistic view of America during the Depression; or the 1933 film, *Wild Boys of the Road,* about young people turning into tramps because they find no work—and quite a few more indicating his social awareness that belies his statement that films have no influence.

"*Heroes for Sale,* in 1933; *Massacre,* in1934; *Black Legion; Meet John Doe.* The film, *They Won't Forget,* excoriating lynchings in the south; *Death in the Deep South* about Leo Frank, a Jew in Georgia falsely accused of murdering a 13 year old, being lynched by a mob. I won't go on, but to their credit, Warner Bros. exposed social ills within our country, the little guy fighting against corrupt big wigs, against prejudice. Realistic populism, invariably hopeful, always with a promise that things were going to get better. And, of course, their chest-thumping, proudly American, *Yankee Doodle Dandy,* in 1942."

Before I could sum up, Cong. LeMay interrupted. "Miss Apple, you *are* a film buff, aren't you?"

"It's both my profession and passion, sir. My husband compares me to baseball nuts who can quote every statistic. There are nuts in every segment of society, aren't there?" hoping they would miss the mockery.

Bemused, the chairman said, "You belong to an admirable profession, warts and all."

I was shocked and said, "Like our Congress, right sir?" Before he could comment, I added, "You're right! During the height of the Depression, studios were latter-day Medicis, encouraging the arts, employing thousands of artisans—craftsmen like carpenters, electricians, plumbers, set designers, costume designers, composers, musicians, writers, dancers, choreographers, acrobats, performers of all kinds. They employed hundreds of directors, producers, actors, *and thousands* of extras, an astonishing feat that created a new industry with a culture all its own. Despite occasional blunders, to the credit of studio heads and their benighted value system, they helped Americans define who they were, who they could aspire to become. They gave us hope—they gave us a love of decency—a sense of American fairness, and we brought that to an eager and admiring world. I'm finished, Mr. Chairman. When I get to the door, I'll go through it. Thank you for inviting me back.

As the door swung open, I heard, "Oh, Miss Apple. Miss Apple?"

"Now what? I've gotta' get home. Yes?" I asked in an unmistakably rebarbative tone.

"What recommendations would you make to us?"

"Go home," I shouted louder than I should have.

"You mean back to Washington?"

"Yes. Right away."

The chairman said, "Please understand that we have a responsibility to protect our country from people who are trying to overthrow us, or at least persuade us to change our form of government. To quote you, *to have our national anthem segue into the Russian national anthem,* so how can we go home?"

"Because in America, we have thoughtful and decent people on all sides of the political spectrum, as you saw in Fox's, *Gentlemen's Agreement,* and other films that Warner Bros. made in the thirties. There's a counter-force at work, a dialectic that will ensure that we'll eventually do the right thing in protecting our form of government.

"Wasn't it Churchill who said, '...that the world can rely on America to do the right thing—after it exhausts all other alternatives?'"

"As you can see, Miss Apple," he said, "our nation is under threat, and we shouldn't continue policies that could be tantamount to committing suicide, so we can't go home until we expose them."

"At what price, Mr. Chairman? You're stifling dissent in the process. You're intimidating us. In the process of exposing the guilty, you have destroyed the lives of the innocent, many of whom believe that you're conducting *constitutionally unauthorized* hearings. Certainly, if you have evidence of criminal wrongdoing, prosecute. Absent that, let us work out our problems without fear, AND," raising my voice with my hand on the door knob, "since you're involved in ridding our country of threats, then after you leave us, work on de-segregating our country, racially and religiously—in both the south and the north. Until we solve those problems, we can never measure up to the *noble idea of America*."

One of the southern congressmen, said, "Mr. Chairman, let this opinionated woman go—*once and for all*."

In a Parthian shot, I added, "Like prosecuting the lynchers, those who burn Negro churches, insist on separate water fountains, *etc., etc., etc.*! Goodbye, everyone."

When I slammed the door behind me, I thought I heard Congressman Panther shout, "So what can we do to prevent future, *Songs of Russia?*"

CHAPTER 31

Josiah was going on many interviews, had gotten five directorial jobs, none episodic, and with one questionable exception, had received favorable notices. We hoped his career was launched. I kept writing apace, enjoying my narcissistic journey of discovery and creation. Velia was showing an easy smile, deep dimples, large dark eyes like a seal pup, just as fat, and non-stop blabbering.

Toward the end of July, the phone rang. Jo answered.

"Hi, Josiah. It's Pete Nathan. I thought you were still in Paris, but then I heard that you and Sally had testified. When did you guys get back?"

"In December."

"You've had your baby then?"

"Yes—a treasure."

"They all are. Is she home?"

"Velia or Sally?"

"Velia?" he chuckled. "You are romantics, aren't you?"

Matching the chuckle, Jo said, "The goose-bump kind."

"When it comes to certain music and babies, I too am the 'chills-up-and-down-my-spine' kind—but not like the Johnny Mercer song."

"Just a second, she's through nursing, but she's burping her. Let's see if we can trade.

"Honey, it's Peter Nathan."

"Mr. Nathan," I asked, "hi, how are you?"

"Good—did you get my letter?"

"Yes."

"Weren't you interested?"

"After my blow up with Adam I had no future at Fox, so I didn't bother writing. Why are you calling, Mr. Nathan?"

Josiah winced so I apologized, "I could have said that better. Sorry."

Gentleman always, he ignored my comment. "Can you come to the studio at 11:00am tomorrow—for a friendly chat. Bring Velia so I can meet the newest Apple from your orchard. Think you can make it?"

I paused, glanced at Josiah and said, "See you tomorrow at 11:00. Just the two of us, right?"

"You mean the three of us?"

"Yes, of course. Tomorrow, then."

I let my hand rest on the cradled phone, turned to Josiah, and asked, "*What?*"

"Don't anticipate. You've nothing to lose, and possibly something to gain. Don't start your crazy process of imagining all the permutations. Think of it as a free lunch," he said in his assuring way that invariably failed to reassure.

"My testimony hasn't been published, otherwise I wouldn't have gotten an invitation, but a summons to report to the gallows," I said.

Josiah grinned and said, "With all that's happened, I never imagined an invitation from him."

"Jo, maple syrup dripped over every word. At Fox, he had the reputation of being the head viper—with velvet fangs."

"Yup. Once after seeing dailies he told a director to control a Shakespearean actor's mugging and reshoot the scene. The following day dailies showed no improvement so he fired them both. Once is all you get with him."

"Right now," I said, "I can't be fired from unemployment."

Never successful in turning off the spigot, I had a sleepless night--scanning the horizon of possibilities, feeding and changing Velia, but when I arrived, I was energized.

His secretary asked me to sit, but as soon as I did, she said, "Mr. Nathan will see you now." When I walked in, I noticed two large mahogany bookcases filled with books placed horizontally and vertically, many with bookmarks suggesting frequent use, an oriental carpet with an intricate red and blue floral design, contemporary Danish walnut furniture, and an accent piece, a French Empire chest housing several pieces of ancient Roman/Persian perfume flasks. The walls were covered with mahogany paneling speaking of old world elegance, a place where cigars were smoked, sherry consumed, and inhibitions became uninhibited.

"You're observant, Sally," he said. "I saw you scan my office. Like what you see?"

"Not as intimidating as I imagined someone in your position would have."

He smiled, walked towards me and said, "So this is your Velia."

He tucked her under the chin and she began to cry. I said, "Sorry, Mr. Nathan, I need your bathroom—diaper change."

When I returned, he asked, "May I try again?"

"Sure," and I placed her in his arms.

"Ah, that's better. She's even giving me a wary smile. I'll settle for that." He then asked her, "Where did you get those big black eyes from?"

"The Mediterranean," I said with a baby voice.

He chuckled. "Until she begins to fret, may I hold her? It's been many years. You know, memories. Longing—regrets—we won't go there."

He pointed to the leather sofa. When I sat down, I found it lower than his chair. The leather, fit for royalty, was so smooth I kept running my hand over the length of the arm until I realized I had to stop. "May I call you Peter?"

"Yes, certainly." Without missing a beat, he said, "I fired Adam this morning."

"*What?* He was so good at what he did! After all those years?"

"After what he did to you, your response surprises me."

"What he did to me was despicable, nonetheless, the studio lost a good man. Why?"

"You."

"Meeee?"

"Yes. The studio doesn't want anyone '*subversive*' around—someone who might not have fought during the war. He testified as much—after you blew the whistle on him."

"Hold on. I came to his defense. If he's guilty, so am I!"

"Adam's an employee, you're not. Because of our nemesis—TV—movie attendance is down, banks are more discriminating about lending money, especially to any studio which had employees testifying before HUAC. Even though innocent, having made an appearance can be enough to bury you.

"The forests are burning hot. People want only pristine snow," he said, his face tinged with disgust.

"You testified, didn't you?"

"How did you know?"

"Easy to guess."

"Yes, a grueling few hours, as it must have been for you," expecting details about what I had said.

I didn't bite. "Are you safe?"

Just then we heard a knock. His secretary opened the door and said, "Mr. Lapidus is here. Shall I ask him to wait?"

I blanched. "Sally, it's Adam's last day and Velia's sound asleep. If I let him in, she'll keep us all quiet. It wouldn't hurt for you two to remember how you used to be."

"Neither of us is how we used to be. What's the purpose? See how I handle hand-to-hand combat?"

A thin smile emerged. I continued, "We'll recognize each other. It was less than a year ago, but as to who we are today, that's another story. We may be intellectually and emotionally unrecognizable to one another. Yeah, invite him in. Let's get it over with, whatever *it* is."

He nodded to his secretary.

When Adam walked through the door and saw me, he froze in place and jerked his head between Peter and me. "Adam," he said, "I know you remember Sally, but you've never met Velia. Come say hello to Velia Apple," hoping that an infant's presence might disarm.

He walked over to her, scarcely glanced at her then looked at his shoes. He walked over to me and spewing hot lava, asked, "You know what they call people like you, don't you?" I could see his jaw muscles rippling.

"Sure—finks—rat finks—stool pigeons—stoolies—snitches—squealers—informers—tattle-talers—whistle blowers," I responded without raising my voice. "There are other pejoratives—to rat on—to rat out? Or, how about, to sell out—sell down the river—finger? Do I qualify for all of them, Adam," I sneered, "or do you have a favorite?"

"You had to tell, didn't you?" he asked between clenched teeth, hovering over me.

Peter cradled his warm, contented friend and remained silent. I hoped Velia would not awaken and cry, ruin this scene. If anything went awry, there would be no second takes. I wanted to see how this would play out, especially since Adam and Josiah had informed on Peter—a word I chose out of all the options because of its intellectual honesty.

He sat down and remained silent. I hated silence so I said, "Actually, in our society, our literature, our media—being an informer has gotten a bum rap. There's nothing wrong with informing a store manager that you've seen someone steal a sweater, or your superiors that in their midst might be an embezzler, or on the misdeeds of executives or co-workers, or on those in public trust who have abused that trust. What's wrong with exposing treachery—or bad behavior? Or, in your case, Adam, your Janus-faced behavior, lousy towards me, noble towards society?

"In other words, Adam, there's nothing wrong with telling the truth. Why, do you suppose, are there so many expressions meaning the very same thing—for one action? Those terms should be trashed! We've got to disabuse people from thinking that *to inform is to destroy*. If someone is guilty, so be it! Let it be known! Edmund Burke said that the idea behind Democracy is to behave properly *even when no one is looking*.

"So, Adam, there's always danger of disclosure, or what you would call, betrayal, but what I would call—indeed what we should all call, *doing the right thing, Adam. Doing the right thing*!" I said in a subdued shout.

"What Kant referred to in his Categorical Imperative."

I leaned forward, and with pointed finger continued, "I told something about you that made me proud of you. I thought the committee would be proud too, but we're not living in a Period of Enlightenment—yet. But believe me please, I never thought it would cost you your job, only raise your professional stature.

"Someday," I said, "if you read my testimony, perhaps you won't hate me so much. Your thoughts about war and Negroes weren't subversive to me at all—quite the contrary. They were the thoughtful concerns of an idealistic American, and *I told them as much.*

"What you did to *me*, however," I said quietly, mindful of Velia's presence, "was *subversive*, and for that I may never forgive you! So," I said through clenched teeth, "you can shove your self-righteous rectitude up your rectum!"

"Rectitude, Sally, is a rare commodity," he sneered. "Being sent on an assignment and doing something else doesn't qualify you for sainthood. Turns out the studio paid you for writing a novel. How does that square with your Parisian quest for honor and integrity?"

I put my head down for I don't know how long. When I finally looked at Adam, I found Col. Picquart still on my shoulder. "*You're right.* It wasn't my original intent to deceive—I had intended to fulfill my part of the bargain—but it got away from me. The end result is always what counts, so I essentially betrayed you and the studio and took money under false pretenses. So, who am I to pass judgment?"

His unwavering stare bore right through me.

"But, Adam, what you did to me was *intentional*. It was subversive and Machiavellian. I was so loyal to you and Fox, worked so hard to do a good job, but you betrayed me, you son-of-a-bitch. At least I started off trying to do the right thing."

"Your betrayal, my betrayal—is there a difference, Sally?"

There was a brief moment of silence, then Peter said, "Adam, you're the one who *finked* on me about the Lincoln Brigade, weren't you?" ignoring my word, *'informed.'*

Adam reacted with an astonished look while I just pretended one. He took a deep breath and said, "With one sentence only, Pete. I was under oath, said that was all I knew, that the details would have to come from you."

"So, Adam," Peter said, "When I pointed out that rock behind which I was shooting, I mentioned Scylla and Charybdis—I was right, wasn't I?"

Adam replied, "Pete, I don't remember either one of us saying that aloud, but we both thought about it."

"So in Sally's list of pejoratives, would yours qualify?" Peter pursued.

"No, it qualifies under her definition about never being wrong when telling the truth. Funny, I told the truth about our treatment of Negroes, and it cost me my job—a few years from retirement." I shifted positions. "Pete—you think you're next? After all, mine was only talk—you took action."

I didn't let on that I knew. I wondered if Peter's heart was racing because nothing showed. Quite matter-of-factly, he said, "Who knows? Right now, the whole industry is scared and insecure. And, I think that sometimes, telling the truth can be wrong."

Velia, still asleep, was submerging the loud expression of sour tempers, but the seething volcano within us was palpable.

"Well, Sally," Adam said, "it wasn't my finest hour."

That shocked me. "I guess it wasn't mine either."

With a slight smile, he said, "When your novel gets published, put me down for 50 copies—for friends and relatives."

"Sight unseen?"

"Sight imagined—imagination run wild, backed by carloads of research."

"That depends on *if* it gets published."

Because Josiah's testimony was still fresh, I said, "Peter, even if Adam hadn't said anything, they would have found out about you and the Brigade—you couldn't hide that."

He nodded and said, "Paranoia is pandemic."

"Speaking of paranoia," Adam said, "did you see the New York Times yesterday, July 29, 1951?"

Peter said, "No. It's here waiting for a free moment."

Adam got up, searched the paper and said, "Here—a statement by President Truman.

"'This malicious propaganda has gone so far that on the Fourth of July in Madison, Wisconsin, people were afraid to say they believed in the

Declaration of Independence. A hundred and twelve people were asked to sign a petition that contained quotations from the Declaration of Independence and the Bill of Rights. Yet, one hundred and eleven of these people refused to sign that paper—many of them because they were afraid that it was some kind of subversive document and that they would lose their jobs or be called communists."

We shook our heads in disbelief.

"Paranoia is one thing, reality quite another," Peter said, "after we saw the Soviet conquest of Eastern Europe, I don't blame Truman for alerting us to the *Red Scare* and the threat of worldwide revolution. I saw what happened in Spain—whether from the right or the left—totalitarian is totalitarian."

"Despite Lillian Hellman's denial," I said.

Velia was beginning to stir but Peter continued, "Though it didn't surprise me, I was shocked when in the late forties, Communist Party members in the arts, trade unions, and everywhere, were saying we were on the verge of plunging into Fascism, masterminded by whom? *President Truman!"*

"Didn't the studios hire Eric Johnston just a few years ago," I asked, "as their chief lobbyist in Washington to support Truman's policy of countering Soviet expansion by showing them that Hollywood was interested in curbing, not abetting communism?" surprised to note my confidence and non-deferential conversation with two former bosses, as though I belonged in high-level discussions.

Peter nodded.

Later, I discovered that Peter had engineered this discussion—to see if my fires were still stoked enough to belt Adam—and to see if I had a broad view of things.

He turned to Adam and asked, "You still friends with Meta Reis Rosenberg?"

"Yeah, she's rising so fast I rarely see her."

"You know Meta, Sally?"

"No."

"She started off as a secretary, became a script reader, then an agent, and is now a producer. I met her when she married Irving Reis. After divorcing him she married George Rosenberg. During her early days, she had supported the Communist Party, got disillusioned and dropped out. When questioned, she denounced her political past, and along with Richard Collins—of *Song of Russia fame*—gave the committee names of communists they knew."

"That goes back to the original point, doesn't it?" asked Adam.

Peter ignored the question, looked at me and said, "You have one remarkably quiet baby here, Sally."

"Only," I smiled, "because she's in the primo capo's hands. Were she in mine, she'd be wailing by now."

Adam, looking at both of us, said, "Baby and all, this seems like a dysfunctional family gathering, with my accusing you, Sally, you accusing me, Pete accusing me, and now as the circle closes, and I'm no longer in your employ, Pete, I feel free to tell you, that what you did to me was *subversive*. You wanted me out of the way last summer for what we expected were the resumption of the hearings, and sent me to Italy—just like I sent Sally to France. So, Pete, J'Accuse!" he said without rancor, looking at me when he said, 'J'Accuse,' then, moving his glance to Pete.

My chin dropped and I thought, Velia, my dear, remain quiet a bit longer, please.

Still whispering, Peter said, "Adam, my action was manipulative, not subversive. You learned a lot, right? There were benefits."

"Had Sally not mentioned that Negro-in-the-Army thing I might still be employed by Fox, right?"

"Adam," Peter replied, "you think you told only Sally, but I had heard it from others as well."

"You know what?" Adam said, "I'm glad I did! Those bastards should know what's it's like to be black in this country. I did my duty as an American! Screw 'em!"

"Yet, Adam, I never told anyone about me—except you." And, echoing Adam's comment, "But you know what? I'm glad I told them everything. They heard my condemnation of the communists—first hand experience—and if that doesn't help me, then screw 'em, too!"

A cold shiver ran through me when I realized that even if Adam had not mentioned it, Josiah had in his testimony. I kept shivering until Peter asked, "Are you okay, Sally?"

"Just got a little chill. I'll be okay soon." If Josiah's testimony is made public, we're screwed. I breathed deeply, and hoped Velia would cry so we could stop this conversation.

I quipped, "We're not being recorded for a confessional movie magazine, are we?"

They smiled and I changed the focus, "Funny thing is that in the USA the Communist Party thought of themselves as being like any other part—like the Democratic Party or Republican Party, never acknowledging that neither Party was part of a world-wide conspiracy being directed by Moscow!"

I turned to Adam and said, "In Paris my research led me to issues of dishonesty, disloyalty, betrayal, honor, duty, responsibility. I see similarities between what happened in fin-de-siécle France and the HUAC hearings, the Hollywood Ten and Joe McCarthy. The French would say, *'plus ca change, plus c'est la meme chose.'"*

Adam got up and said, "I packed all my things, Pete, and now begins the job search. The three of you spared me from giving a one-hanky farewell speech—or a Philippic. For some reason, I feel better."

He walked over to me, took my reluctant hand, and said, "I may very well have done you a favor—keep the jury sequestered for a bit—we'll soon hear the verdict."

He walked to Pete, gazed at him, nodded and left.

We remained quiet until the door closed. With a distant look, Peter said, "I wonder how in the future, our dimming memories will remember what happened here today—three different recollections, I suspect ... " letting his voice trail off.

"She's getting restless, Sally, so before she gets your undivided attention, let me tell you why I invited you."

"I suspected Adam's *popping in* was no accident."

"Adam was just one of the reasons."

"You've been known as feisty and blunt, and in the process you've managed to irritate quite a few people. Your candor, however, has made those you offended, return to you for an honest answer. Sylvestra Gindling, for one, the director of the film, *Never Trust The Weatherman—Unless She's a Woman,* someone whom you ticked off because of your public criticism for using a regular weather balloon instead of one you wanted, an Albuquerque colorful cartoon-balloon."

He was speaking with such a straight face that I wondered whether he was going to fine me for past misbehaviors. He continued, "But for the final cut she sought your advice."

Where the hell is this going?

"Oscar Marya—same thing. On the set of, *Pelican Beach,* he had to throw you out because you had antagonized him with your criticism about the beach scenes and phony whales. Before the background music was recorded, however, he invited you to see the final edit—to get your truthful comments."

He paused and asked, "Think you'd like to work in my new section that will explore the possibility of making movies—not for the big screen, but for that *Giant Midget, TV*? I was too dumbstruck to respond immediately, but he spared me by adding, "Remember that cliché? Something about recognizing profound changes, and rather than fighting, joining?"

My first question was stupid, "What about my book?"

"How close are you to finishing?"

"Maybe another chapter—maybe two."

"How long?"

"Three weeks."

"Can you start then?"

"Before I decide, " ... work in my new section" is vague. I'd want to be in charge," I blurted out in my uncensored way, hoping my scarf hid my quick swallow.

"It's what I had in mind."

Velia began fussing.

"What a dreamboat she's been with you, her surrogate father. I'll take her now." "You can't have her—her fist is wound around my finger. Like she's saying, *Keep in touch.*"

We languished over that thought. I gradually peeled Velia's finger away and said, "What a day. What a day. Oh, salary?"

"Not sure yet. You're a beginner, yet a pro. We'll make sure you can support her growing appetite for essentials—and an Ivy-League education—like Barnard?"

There I was—the Cheshire cat.

While I breathed her in, he said, "When I see someone like Velia, I realize how a sleeping child acts like a moderator, a crisis manager, a calming influence. When a harsh thing is spoken quietly, it doesn't stir the blood like it ordinarily might, often leading to a reciprocal response.

"During today's contentious discussion, subdued because of your treasure on my lap, the softness it brings on, it occurs to me that congressional meetings, and meetings among warring countries, should have infants in their midst—to quiet passions—as reminders of the consequences of war."

"You are a dreamer."

"Call me next week."

On the way home, I wondered when more testimonies would be made public—Pete's and Josiah's.

Oh, Velia, will you have such dilemmas? Despite Kant's imperative to tell the truth, some things are better left unspoken. Josiah's silence.

A week later I met Pete and was heartened to hear him say, "Sally, glad you're here. Got details about your salary, benefits, etc. Let's go to your new office. Where's Velia?"

"With Josiah. She sends her love."

"Send her kisses in return."

"I finished my novel last week."

"You did? Can you start Monday?"

"Can hardly wait."

The cottage had two offices and a lobby. "This is it, Sally. Your office is here," he pointed, "your secretary there. On your desk there's an outline of targets, expectations, people to see, that sort of thing. You can get it next week."

"May I have it now? For some preliminary thinking?"

"Sure."

The following week, I met my secretary, and, well prepared with notes proceeded to take charge. It was furiously busy—I interviewed someone from a network, a writer/producer with a pitch that sounded puerile, but with my input, could become a lively project. I contacted some of my former associates—costumes, make-up, sets, editing, etc., and was so energized I never had lunch.

I missed Velia terribly. She was with my mother who acted like she was her mother, so that was good.

The following Monday, I arrived at my office, and called Pete. He was in a meeting. I left word.

CHAPTER 32

"Pete?" the hardened voice asked.

"Yeah—Darren?"

"Can you come to my office right away? It's important."

"Can it wait about twenty minutes? I need to finish this report."

"No, can't wait. The report can. Come."

With feigned cheerfulness, he said, "On my way."

He laid the phone back. A chill came over him, as though he were about to be thrown into a cold, dark cellar.

CHAPTER 33

"Rachel, hi, it's Sally. How're you doing?"

"What a pleasant surprise. Great. How's our family song bird, Velia?" she asked.

"She took her first wary steps a few days ago, not bad for a chubby thirteen-month old—has three teeth.

"Her health's been restored? Yours?"

"We're going to live to be a hundred."

"Good, we'll help you celebrate. When are we going to get together?"

"Turns out, real soon. My novel has been published and the publisher has arranged a number of book signings, the first one of which will be in New York next month. How you like *them apples*?" I quipped. "I've taken a leave of absence for a couple of months."

"That's terrific news! Wait 'till I tell Sinty. He's going to burst with joy that his sister got her first novel published!" she said with undisguised glee.

"I'm excited too Rachel. I can hardly wait to see the corrupting effects fame and fortune will have on me—if I'm lucky."

"I'm glad we'll see you before the inevitable happens," she laughed. "You never told us what it's about. What's the name?"

"Actually, it was Josiah's suggestion." I paused a moment and said,

THE FABULOUS LIVES OF SALLY APPLE

THE END

ABOUT THE AUTHOR:

Jack Salem, a New York native, moved to California as a teenager, received his bachelor's degree from UCLA and studied marketing and advertising at the University of Southern California and Columbia University. He later spent a glorious summer studying philosophy at Oxford University.

When his children were 9 and 10, he and his wife spent their life savings on a year-long grand tour of Europe.

His first novel, "Heirs to the Pushcart Fortune," was published in 2007.

Made in the USA
Charleston, SC
27 April 2011